THE ART OF THE LAW

A NOVEL

Scott Douglas Gerber

ANAPHORA LITERARY PRESS

QUANAH, TEXAS

ANAPHORA LITERARY PRESS
1108 W 3rd Street
Quanah, TX 79252
https://anaphoraliterary.com

Book design by Anna Faktorovich, Ph.D.

Published in 2018 by Anaphora Literary Press

The Art of the Law: A Novel
Scott Douglas Gerber—1st edition.

Library of Congress Control Number: 2018907299

Library Cataloging Information
Gerber, Scott Douglas, 1961-, author.
    The art of the law : A novel / Scott Douglas Gerber
    276 p. ; 9 in.
    ISBN 978-1-68114-448-1 (softcover : alk. paper)
    ISBN 978-1-68114-449-8 (hardcover : alk. paper)
    ISBN 978-1-68114-450-4 (e-book)
1. Fiction—Thrillers—Legal.
2. Fiction—Mystery & Detective—International Mystery & Crime.
3. Fiction—Thrillers—Psychological.
PN3311-3503: Literature: Prose fiction
813: American fiction in English

THE ART OF THE LAW

A NOVEL

SCOTT DOUGLAS GERBER

For My Grandparents

"Art is never chaste. It ought to be forbidden to ignorant innocents, never allowed into contact with those not sufficiently prepared. Yes, art is dangerous. Where it is chaste, it is not art."
—Pablo Picasso

PART I

The Artist's Model

"I often get asked what makes a good artist's model and the answer isn't necessarily classical beauty. The best models are comfortable within themselves and are skillful at promoting their spirit, irrespective of size or looks. That's what helps to make a memorable painting."

—Rembrandt van Rijn

CHAPTER 1

Blue and red splotches rummaged through his brain like squirrels trapped in an attic. He rubbed his eyes with the heels of his hands to make the splotches disappear. They didn't. They almost never went away. He shot up from the bed and pushed the blanket to the floor. Sweat drenched his body like a roiling current over smoothed stones.

Nevin Montgomery was having a flashback. He had lots of those. They were the price he paid for an adolescence spent roaming the streets of Dorchester, Massachusetts in search of a poor kid's most affordable high: a huff of aerosol propellant gas from a plastic bag or a solvent-soaked rag.

Nevin stubbed his toe when he staggered to his feet. "Shit!" he said. The bed wasn't his, and he didn't know where the obstacles were. He flipped on the floor lamp and tried again to shake the splotches from his head. They weren't part of a flashback after all. They were real, and they were coming from outside the bedroom window of the guest cottage to which he had been assigned. He yanked open the curtains with a quick tug on the drawstring. A full moon shone against the black sky like a spotlight on a Broadway stage. Nevin lowered his gaze and identified the source of his distress: an ambulance parked in Andrew Windsor's driveway. The driveway—as long as a city block and as rugged as a country road—was a good five hundred yards from Nevin's window, but the ambulance's beacon was bright enough to guide a ship through a nor'easter.

Nevin scrambled for his pants, shirt, and shoes. He rushed out the door and sprinted across the manicured lawn that separated the guest houses from the main house. He arrived in time to witness two paramedics exit the main house pushing a gurney. Lauren Windsor was following closely behind them. Nevin recognized her from a photograph he was shown prior to his arrival.

Lauren Windsor was Andrew Windsor's wife. Andrew Windsor was the most celebrated American painter of the day. His seascapes hung in every major gallery in the world. Private collectors were known to pay seven figures for a single piece. Bill Gates owned two of Windsor's paintings. Jeff Bezos owned three. *Forbes* magazine estimated Windsor's net worth at seventy-five million dollars.

"What happened?" Nevin asked, when he caught Mrs. Windsor's eye. He finished buttoning his shirt and combing his hair with his hands. He looked as if he had lost a bar fight.

"Hannah's dead," Mrs. Windsor answered. She secured the belt on her bathrobe, a silk kimono adorned with chrysanthemums, streams, and kanji. Even at four in the morning she was perfectly attired.

"Who's Hannah?" Nevin asked next. He had been briefed by one of the senior partners at Palmer & Lodge about the various Windsors who lived at the family compound on the shores of Cape Cod. Hannah's name had never come up.

Mrs. Windsor hesitated… seemingly unsure about how much to reveal. She primped her hair with her fingers. She said, eyes dancing with distrust, "Hannah was one of my husband's models. She had been posing for him for years."

It took the paramedics less than five minutes to load Hannah Burgoff's lifeless body into the back of the ambulance. They exchanged the sort of superficial pleasantries that people frequently exchanged at the expense of the more appropriate alternative—respectful silence—while they waited for law enforcement to arrive. The circle of onlookers grew to a baker's dozen as family, friends, and staff became aware that something was awry. Bad news traveled fast in paradise too.

Black-capped chickadees, buff-breasted sandpipers, and gray-cheeked thrushes began to announce the coming morn when the small crowd's attention was suddenly drawn to the siren song of the county sheriff's squad car speeding through the daybreak. The deputy in charge spoke privately to the paramedics for a few moments, and then sent the ambulance on its way to the coroner's office with three quick taps on the vehicle's roof.

"Where's Mr. Windsor?" the deputy sheriff said, approaching the ever-expanding circle of budding conspiracy theorists. His name tag read JOHN STEELE and he looked the part. His hair was cropped short, his chest was bursting through his uniform, and his hands looked strong enough to crack walnuts. Mickey Spillane would have been proud.

"My husband's in bed," Mrs. Windsor said, distrustfully still. "He's not well. He hasn't been well for months. And he certainly isn't well enough to murder someone, if that's what you're implying."

Deputy Steele said, "I'm not implying anything, ma'am. But somebody's dead and I need to find out why." He retrieved a small notepad from his shirt pocket. "Anybody?"

Silence.

Deputy Steele's eyes searched the crowd. "Did anybody see anything unusual? Did anybody hear anything?"

More silence.

The slowly rising sun painted a tapestry of yellow and orange swatches above the deserted beach behind the expansive oceanfront compound. Many a similar vista had inspired Andrew Windsor's most famous seascapes.

Then: "I might've heard something."

"*Might* have?" Steele said. "And who might you be, sir?" The deputy's attention was quickly focused on the tall young man in the front of the crowd. The deputy made a note on his pad: *white male, tall, about twenty-five, brown hair, brown eyes, athletic build, disheveled appearance.*

The young man said, "My name's Nevin Montgomery. I'm an attorney with the law firm of Palmer & Lodge. I arrived yesterday afternoon from Boston to help Mr. Windsor update his testamentary documents."

Steele said, "Update Mr. Windsor's what?"

"His testamentary documents. You know, his will and trust." Nevin tucked his shirt tail into his pants. He was in lawyer's mode now and lawyers were supposed to look spit-shine perfect. At least that was what Bartholomew Lodge had told Nevin two years earlier when Nevin had showed up for his job interview in khakis and a blazer rather than a suit. Nevin continued: "I haven't met with him yet, though. Like Mrs. Windsor said, he's not feeling well."

Steele wrote down what Nevin had said, and then asked, "Where are you staying?"

Nevin pointed to the guest cottage next to a towering oak about five hundred yards from where they were standing. "Over there."

There were four guest cottages on Andrew Windsor's magnificent property. Nevin had been assigned to the most modest of the four: a one-bedroom bungalow that dated from the 1920s. The other three could have passed for single family residences. Nevin didn't know who was staying in those, but he assumed the occupants were somewhere in the crowd.

Deputy Steele continued with his questions. "You said you might have heard something. What do you think you heard?"

"Someone walking around outside my bedroom window. I could've been dreaming, but I'm a fairly light sleeper. I'm pretty sure I heard it." Nevin left out the part about a possible drug flashback in his answer to Deputy Steele's question.

"Did you get up to check it out?"

Nevin shook his head no.

"Why not?"

"Because I didn't think it was any of my business. I'm a guest here. Just because I thought I heard something doesn't mean that someone was doing something they shouldn't be doing. It might seem that way now—what with someone getting killed and all—but it didn't seem that way then."

Deputy Steele flipped to a clean page on his notepad. His eyes returned to Nevin's. Neither person had blinked in what seemed like a full ten minutes. "Like I said to Mrs. Windsor, who said anything about someone getting killed?"

Nevin reddened. "Nobody. I just assumed that's what you think happened. Otherwise, why would you be interrogating me like the Spanish Inquisition?"

Deputy Steele questioned several more people before allowing everyone to go back to their rooms. He asked that nobody leave the property before he had a chance to interview the rest of them later in the day. He assured them that there was nothing to be nervous about—that it was routine procedure—but nobody believed him. After all, a woman was dead… a woman that apparently only Mrs. Windsor had known anything about. Nevin Montgomery certainly didn't know anything about the woman.

But how could the rest of Mr. Windsor's family and staff not know anything about Hannah Burgoff?

CHAPTER 2

Nevin Montgomery returned to his guest cottage at a much slower pace than he had exited it. His mind turned somersaults as he tried to process what had just transpired. He was an estate planning lawyer with a major Boston law firm—a lowly junior associate to boot—and yet he appeared to have found himself smack-dab in the middle of a homicide investigation. Deputy Steele had gone out of his way to not call it that, but it was pretty clear to everyone at the scene that was what it was.

Nevin's breathing began to quicken and his mouth became dry. He was getting nauseous again. He had decided to specialize in estate planning—the law's most sedate area of practice—to avoid the chaos and stress that had dominated his youth and driven him to drugs. He was eight years sober and he had no interest in revisiting the dark side of his personality. His dark side had led him to OD twice in his teens—the second time he had been pronounced dead by the EMTs only to reawaken in an almost supernatural trance—and he lived in silent fear that the third time wouldn't be a charm. He had managed to kick drugs—inhalants, speed, crack, heroin: name it and Nevin had ingested it—thanks to a high school English teacher who had been astonished by how smart Nevin was and who had refused to let his young charge throw away his God-given gifts. The teacher's name was Daniel Harrington, and Nevin owed him everything. Nevin had felt so indebted to his former teacher that he had invited him to his graduation ceremonies from both Harvard College and Harvard Law School.... *Harvard*—who could have imagined such a thing? Mr. Harrington, that was who.

Nevin's high school friends had been surprised when they learned that he was going to college. They were stunned when he told them that he had been accepted at Harvard College and then, four years later, at Harvard Law School. They knew that Nevin was "wicked smart"—it was Nevin who had always managed to figure out how they could cobble together enough money for their next fix—but they didn't know that he was borderline genius. Even street punks from Dorchester understood how prestigious Harvard was. Ben Affleck and

Matt Damon had documented it in *Good Will Hunting*, their Oscar-winning saga about a group of young men like Nevin and his friends.

Nevin had decided during law school that estate planning would be his best bet for staying on the straight and narrow. Litigation was too stressful: arguing motions before a judge, cross-examining witnesses in front of a jury, delivering a make-or-break closing statement at the end of a trial, etc. Corporate law was likewise too tension inducing. Nevin hadn't realized that at first, but a summer spent interning at Palmer & Lodge had showed him the light. Nevin had assisted a myriad of lawyers during the course of that summer who had worked several days in a row without sleep in order to close a multi-billion dollar business deal on the best possible terms for their client. The lawyer leading the transaction team had boasted to Nevin over dinner shortly after the deal was done that corporate lawyers worked harder than litigators. "TV shows always focus on courtroom lawyers—*Law and Order*, *The Good Wife*, *Harry's Law*, and the like—but that's bullshit," the team leader had said after several glasses of single malt Scotch. He went on to trumpet that the adrenalin rush of transactional law was what had drawn him to the field. Nevin had had the opposite reaction, and he desperately searched for a different specialty. During the last several weeks of his summer internship he had stumbled upon one: wills and trusts law.

Estate planning was the formal appellation of the type of law that Nevin practiced. A *will* was the foundational document of an estate plan. It enumerated how a person wanted his or her assets disposed of when he or she died. A *trust* was the most important component of an estate plan. It was the document that described how the decedent's property should be managed by a fiduciary for the well-being of the beneficiary. Although lawyers who billed by the hour almost always proclaimed otherwise, only a small percentage of people actually needed a will, let alone a full-blown estate plan. Most people weren't rich enough to justify opting out of the state's intestacy rules, a formal body of legislative statutes and court decisions that specified who was entitled to the property of a person who died without a will. Nevin's parents certainly didn't need an estate plan. But Andrew Windsor did, which explained why Nevin had been instructed by Bartholomew Lodge to take a drive to the Cape.

Bartholomew Lodge was one of the founding partners of the Boston law firm of Palmer & Lodge. The other, Anderson Winston

Palmer III, died five years ago, which meant that Lodge alone called the shots. The six members of the firm's executive committee were technically in charge, but everyone who walked the marble hallways of Boston's most profitable law firm knew otherwise. Lodge and Palmer had taken a huge risk three decades earlier when they left their equity partnerships at the mega-firm of DeMoura, Thoma, & Alders to start their own shop, and Lodge wasn't about to relinquish control of the firm that bore his name and into which he had poured so much of his time and energy. Lodge was both highly respected and well-liked by almost everyone at the firm, and only one person seemed to mind that he ran the show. That person, though, was Joshua Jones... the lawyer who was trying to fill the void left by Anderson Palmer's death.

Joshua Jones was one of the primary reasons that Palmer & Lodge was the most profitable law firm in Boston. With his Ivy League resume, his family connections, and his willingness to outwork and outwit everyone in his path, Jones had become the youngest partner in the history of the firm. He had leapfrogged several more experienced lawyers in the process, but Anderson Palmer had championed the promotion as a signal to the firm's two hundred other lawyers that results were what counted at Palmer & Lodge. Jones, however, wasn't satisfied. Although he was proud of his unprecedented professional accomplishment, he valued power more than respect. He wanted more. He wanted Bartholomew Lodge's position: managing partner... deal broker... king maker.

Of course, Lodge knew that. Jones might have been an extremely talented lawyer, but subtle he wasn't. For example, nary a week would pass without Jones asking Lodge when Lodge was going to take his "well-deserved retirement" to fine-tune his golf game, sail his yacht, and play with his grandchildren. Lodge would ignore the question, mention that he was late for a meeting, and leave his ambitious young partner stewing about how he could move the old man out.

Nevin Montgomery glanced down at his feet and noticed that his shoes were wet. The dew had begun to gather on the grass as the sun started to rise above the shoreline surrounded by a collage of blues, reds, and yellows that were vivid enough for an artist's palette. He paused to enjoy the view, and to allow his heart rate to return to normal. Nobody liked being interrogated by the police, least of all recovering substance abusers who had spent much of their adolescence running from their sirens. He placed his index and middle fingers to the side of his Adam's apple and pressed firmly to locate his pulse. He kept count for thirty seconds and multiplied by two. Ninety beats per minute, he said to himself. A bit on the high side, but still in the normal range for an adult male in the prime of life.

Nevin resumed walking. The wind rustled the pitch pines scattered along the dunes, further contributing to their stunted growth and sporadic needling. On the Windsor compound itself, a bay-leafed willow bowed to the emerging sunlight that welcomed the new day. Dorchester it definitely was not: there wasn't a broken streetlight, an overturned dumpster, or a stray hubcap anywhere to be seen. There was no cacophony of car alarms either, and certainly no random gunshots sounding in the distance. Nevin now knew how the other half lived, or at least he thought he did. He had been at the Windsor compound for all of twelve hours. Hannah Burgoff's mysterious death proved that there was more to living the high life than breathtaking sunrises and five-star accommodations.

Nevin was determined to try his best to refocus his attention on the task he had been assigned: finalizing Andrew Windsor's testamentary documents. Bartholomew Lodge had initially told Nevin that it was a routine matter that he had decided to assign to Nevin as a reward for a first year with Palmer & Lodge of excellent work. "Three days in paradise with no heavy lifting," was how Lodge had characterized it at the time. But then Lodge had mentioned that Mr. Windsor had intimated during a recent telephone call that he might want to make some changes to his will. Lodge hadn't told Nevin what those changes might be—Lodge insisted that Windsor hadn't specified what they were—but Nevin was smart enough to know that when a mercurial artist dropped a hint like that it would probably lead to trouble.

Could that trouble be murder?

Nevin hoped not. He couldn't handle the stress.

A large flock of Canada geese squawked overhead. Nevin gazed in wonderment at the military precision of their V-shaped formation. He had never seen that awesome display in Dorchester. Pigeons and an occasional lost seagull, yes. Wild geese, no. He stumbled over a felled tree branch from the distraction. He hit the ground awkwardly, like a running back tripped up by a linebacker at the forty yard line. He laughed, brushed the dirt from his pants, and then had his attention distracted yet again. This time, his attention wasn't distracted by beautiful migratory birds. This time, it was distracted by a beautiful woman silhouetted by cottony clouds and a majestic seascape standing quietly in front of one of the larger guest cottages on the property.

She looked to be about twenty-one. She was slender and stood approximately 5'2". Her hair was long and black... like that of a wild mustang. Her skin was the color of a copper penny. She was either Italian, Hispanic, or Portuguese. Nevin was too far away to know for sure. What he *did* know, however, was that she hadn't been in the circle of onlookers when Deputy Steele had arrived to inquire about Hannah Burgoff's death. Nevin would have noticed someone that breathtakingly gorgeous. She didn't seem to notice him, though. Instead, she knocked quickly on the cottage's door and disappeared inside.

CHAPTER 3

Catina Cruz entered the house as silently as she could. It was early in the morning and she didn't want to disturb anyone. She removed her shoes and tip-toed across the hardwood floor. She switched on a table lamp and maneuvered her way around a maze of furniture to the broom closet. The closet was dark, but she knew its contents by heart. She reached for the *Swiffer* and began to sweep the living room. The *Swiffer* picked up dirt better than a broom, and it was also a lot quieter, which was its most compelling virtue as far as Catina was concerned. Catina knew how much Meredith Adams Windsor hated noise. How could Catina not know? Mrs. Windsor had once screamed at Catina to stop using that "goddamn broom" because the sound of the straw bristles scratching across the hardwood floor reminded her of "fingernails across a chalkboard.... It makes my skin crawl just thinking about it." But Mrs. Windsor also hated interacting with Catina under any circumstances—broom or no broom—which explained why Catina was cleaning the house at 5:30 a.m.

Meredith Adams Windsor, wife of James Windsor—Andrew Windsor's son—had hired Catina two years earlier after noticing her photograph in the local newspaper. Catina had won the Massachusetts state horse jumping competition in the fourteen-to-sixteen years-old age group and Mrs. Windsor had been struck by how beautiful the young woman—a girl at the time—was. Mrs. Windsor had tracked down Catina in New Bedford, where Catina lived, and had convinced Catina's mother that a world of opportunities would open to Catina if Catina would come to work and live at the Windsor compound on Cape Cod. After much soul searching Catina's mother had agreed, and Catina had been working and living at the Windsor compound ever since.

Catina finished sweeping the living room and started to dust it with a soft cotton rag. She always got nervous when she dusted the room because many of the furnishings were antiques. She trembled every time she recalled the first time she had dusted it: a rainy April morning on which she had accidently knocked an expensive *Fabergé* egg to the floor and broken it into a dozen pieces. When Mrs. Windsor had been alerted to the mishap, she had let loose with a barrage of profanity that would have made a drunken sailor blush. Catina had run from the room in tears and telephoned her mother in New Bedford begging to come home. But sixteen-year-old Catina had been met with surprising indifference by her mother, whom Catina later learned was dusting a painting given to her by James Windsor at the precise moment of Catina's call.

Catina had been left with no choice. She had dropped out of high school at her mother's insistence to move to the Windsor compound, and although she had earned her GED several months into her time with the Windsors, she had no real marketable skills. She certainly couldn't make any money jumping horses. In fact, she didn't own a horse. She couldn't afford it. She had to borrow one of the Windsors' horses if she wanted to ride, and they didn't always grant permission. Frankly, she was lucky she was pretty. But for that, she would have never been hired as the Windsors' gal Friday.

Catina finished the living room and moved to the kitchen. Her mother had worked two jobs when Catina was a kid and Catina had been forced to learn how to cook at least a few basic dishes. It was either that, or go without eating. A Portuguese breakfast was a simple affair: typically, bread with butter, ham, cheese, or fruit preserves and milk and coffee. Lunch was usually a traditional soup. Of all its cuisine, it was in the soups that Portugal's history was most evident: its occupation by the Romans, then the Moors, and its legendary exploits in seafaring and trade. Indeed, Portugal's national dish was a soup: Caldo Verde, a delightful mixture of potatoes, onions, and kale— often accompanied by slices of chourico or linguica, or broa cornbread for dipping. Dinner was eaten late in the evening and consisted of freshly caught fish broiled with delicate spices. Meat and poultry were generally served only by families with money, which certainly didn't include Catina and her mother. A Pastel de nata, a Portguese egg tart pastry, was a rare Sunday treat.

Catina reached into her pocket and retrieved her iPod. Andrew Windsor had given it to her for Christmas. She had been surprised when he did, both because she didn't think that Mr. Windsor knew who she was and because an iPod was the epitome of modern technology, which Mr. Windsor famously detested. She placed the buds into her ears, switched on the candy bar sized device, and navigated to a favorite song: Adele's *Someone Like You*. Catina admired the power and feeling of Adele's voice and she also was inspired that someone so young could accomplish so much. Adele was twenty-one when she wrote that song, which was only four years older than Catina. Adele was winning Grammy awards and performing in sold-out arenas. Catina was scraping by on minimum wage and cleaning rich people's houses.

Catina turned up the volume on her iPod and reached for the dish soap. The Windsors were apparently so spoiled and lazy that they didn't bother to put their soiled plates, glasses, and cutlery into the dishwasher. How difficult was that to do? But now the previous evening's meal was caked onto the dinnerware and Catina had no choice other than to roll up her sleeves and scrub it off. If she didn't, she would never hear the end of it, and she certainly didn't have the stomach for yet another of Mrs. Windsor's screaming fits.

Catina's iPod shuffled its way through the two dozen songs that she had loaded onto the device. At $1.29 per song Catina had to be selective about what she purchased from the iTunes store. Moreover, she didn't have a computer of her own and she was forced to ask permission to use the computer in the kitchen of the main house when she wanted to buy new music. The senior Mrs. Windsor—Lauren Windsor, Andrew's wife—was always nice about it, but Catina didn't want to abuse the privilege and she therefore asked infrequently. But it had been about six months since Catina had purchased any new music and one of the other members of the Windsors' staff had mentioned that Cee Lo Green had released a new album and it was great. Catina had become a fan of the effervescent R&B singer during season one of *The Voice* and she decided that now would be a good time to ask the senior Mrs. Windsor if it was okay to use the computer again. Her foot started tapping at the thought of downloading Cee Lo's #1 smash *Forget You* and putting it on repeat for a week.

Catina grabbed the *Swiffer*, a fresh dust rag, a can of *Lemon Pledge*, and a bottle of *Windex*. She froze in her tracks as she prepared to enter James Windsor's studio at the south end of the so-called guest cottage in which he had lived for more than two decades. Her foot stopped tapping and her heart started racing. She began to tremble and sweat. She threw up in her mouth. She wiped her face clean with the dust rag. She took a deep breath, inched towards the door, and slowly turned the knob. It was an old house, and most of the doors creaked. This one was no exception. She pushed it open a crack and glanced inside. Much to her relief, the studio was empty. She stepped over the threshold. The early morning sun shone through the window and lit the room in soft reds and yellows. A similar sight was the subject of James Windsor's most famous painting, *Morning in the Artist's Studio*.

Catina cleaned James's studio once a week like clockwork. She had seen the painting many times before. She loved it. She wasn't dumb. She had heard the staff talk: James wasn't nearly the painter that his father was. That was true. No American painter currently living was as talented as Andrew Windsor. But that didn't mean that James wasn't talented too, or that he owed his success, modest though it was when compared to Andrew's, to his father's name. That was Catina's assessment at any rate. The rest of the staff felt otherwise. The rest of the staff considered James to be a spoiled, womanizing hack who would be lucky to teach art at the local community college if his surname wasn't Windsor. Instead, he got to sleep until ten and have his meals cooked for him and his house cleaned for him while the rest of the world had to work for a living. Most of the staff couldn't hide their resentment of James. Catina couldn't hide her trepidation.

Catina began to dust the windowsills and workstations. It was an old house and no matter how many times she cleaned it there was always dirt that was difficult to remove. James's studio was usually the dirtiest room in the house. Painting was a messy business, and James was messier than most, at least according to his mother. Lauren Windsor had mentioned that fact to Catina early in Catina's tenure with the Windsors when the senior Mrs. Windsor had discovered Catina on all fours, elbows deep in soap and water. Mrs. Windsor had wandered over from the main house in search of her son. He was nowhere to be found, but Catina, whom Mrs. Windsor had never met prior to the encounter, was impossible to miss. Mrs. Windsor was both married to an artist and the mother of an artist, and she was used to being surrounded by beautiful women. But the petite young woman with the raven hair and doe eyes that Mrs. Windsor had stumbled across that day was the most beautiful thing Mrs. Windsor had ever seen. She could certainly understand what all the buzz had been about among the staff.

"Did you see the girl that Ms. Meredith hired, Ms. Lauren?" the senior Mrs. Windsor's longtime housekeeper had said on Catina's first day at the compound. "She's prettier than one of Mr. Andrew's seascapes.... And that's saying something."

The cook, an elderly gentleman everyone called "Chef" who had worked for the Windsors for more than forty years, had simply mentioned to the senior Mrs. Windsor that "This is gonna be trouble."

Mrs. Windsor knew perfectly well what Chef had meant: her son would have a difficult time keeping his hands to himself... no matter how young the new employee happened to be. All he needed to know—all he needed to *see*—was how beautiful she was.

Catina had spent two hours cleaning James's studio. It was immaculate. The windows were now so clear that it didn't seem like they were paned with glass. The original luster had returned to the hardwood floor. The workstations, previously stained with so much stray paint that they resembled a Jackson Pollock painting, were clean enough to host a Sunday dinner.

It was menial labor, and Catina disliked it, but she nevertheless smiled at a job well done. She wiped her face with a clean paper towel and reached for her water bottle. She took a long drink. She collected her cleaning supplies and thought about which room she should turn to next. She decided on the Windsors' bedroom. She had received a text message ninety minutes earlier from Meredith Adams Windsor advising Catina that she and her husband had gone to Maine for a couple of days of rest and relaxation. Catina knocked on their bedroom door to be sure. There was no response. She knocked again. Still nothing. She pushed open the door and found James Windsor lying on the bed with a glazed look in his eyes. "Good morning, Catina," he said. "Come in and close the door."

CHAPTER 4

The law firm of Palmer & Lodge, P.C. was housed on the 30th, 31st, and 32nd floors of 100 Federal Street in the financial district of Boston, Massachusetts in a skyscraper commonly known as the "milk bottle" because of its unusual shape: a bulge of several stories near its base that gave pedestrians a wider survey of the street but at the same time provided the building with more floor space at higher levels. Palmer & Lodge was composed of two hundred lawyers, forty paralegals, fifty administrative assistants, five investigators, and two dozen miscellaneous mail room clerks, copy room technicians, and similar support staff. The views of the city were spectacular—Boston Harbor to the east, Faneuil Hall to the north, Chinatown to the south, and the Suffolk County Courthouse to the west—which was why Anderson Winston Palmer III and Bartholomew Lodge had selected the office space three decades earlier after they had decided to break away from DeMoura, Thoma, & Alders to start their own shop. Of course, Boston had grown a lot in those three decades, but both Palmer and Lodge had enough friends in City Hall to fend off potential obstructions to the breathtaking vistas of their chosen location.

Palmer & Lodge was more than a lovely office space. It was the most prestigious law firm in a city filled with blue blood partnerships and professional corporations. Hale & Dorr and Ropes & Gray used to be the top dogs in town, but Palmer & Lodge had been ranked above them for the past five consecutive years in the annual survey of the best law firms conducted by the *Massachusetts Lawyers Weekly*, the state's leading legal periodical. The assessed criteria included billable hours, capitalization of recurring clients, percentage of lawyers who made partner, academic pedigree of the lawyers at the firm, and staff morale. Joshua Jones contributed well to four of the five categories: He billed an astonishing three thousand hours per year, half of his clients were Fortune 500 companies, he made partner two years ahead of schedule, and his law degree was from Harvard. But for the overwhelming strength of his performance in these four areas, his deficiency in the fifth—his corrosive effect on staff morale—would surely have led to his early exit from the firm.

Indeed, there had been some concern expressed by the firm's executive committee prior to the vote on whether to make Jones a partner about Jones's negative impact on the staff. One member of the committee had reminded his colleagues that several of Jones's secretaries had quit during Jones's five years at the firm. Another had mentioned that most of the paralegals refused to work on Jones's cases. A third had discussed complaints he had received about Jones's poor treatment of the custodial crew. But in law, as in business, the almighty dollar trumped everything and Joshua Jones was without question the top earner at Palmer & Lodge. As a result, at the unprecedented age of thirty-two, he was elected partner. It wasn't unanimous, though. Bartholomew Lodge had voted no. As a founding partner, Lodge possessed enough power to kill Jones's future at the firm, but he was too genteel to do it. He was content with a symbolic gesture, which a no vote on partnership certainly was.

At the moment, Lodge was elbows deep in deposition transcripts. New England Bank & Trust Company was caught up in a nationwide mortgage scandal and it was Lodge's job to minimize the damage. New England Bank was the largest financial institution in Boston and Palmer & Lodge's most lucrative client. During the past five years alone, the firm had billed almost eight million dollars to that account. Lodge couldn't afford to let the golden goose die. The firm needed a steady stream of its golden eggs. In fact, it was Lodge's personal involvement in the New England Bank mortgage matter that had convinced him to transfer principal responsibility for redrafting Andrew Windsor's testamentary documents to Nevin Montgomery. Windsor was one of Lodge's favorite clients—Lodge was an art aficionado and he got a kick out of interacting with America's most famous living artist—but all of his time was being taken up with New England Bank and he had a lot of confidence in Nevin.

Joshua Jones didn't share that confidence, however. Jones's office was on a different floor than Lodge's, but that didn't stop Jones from confronting Lodge on more than one occasion about the inappropriateness of Lodge's decision to permit Nevin to handle the Windsor matter with only token oversight from the partnership. Jones was presently on his way to confront Lodge again about the matter. The corridor full of junior lawyers and support staff parted like the red sea when Jones exited the elevator and made a left turn towards Lodge's corner office. They had seen this movie before and they didn't want to become collateral damage.

The instant Jones reached Lodge's threshold, he said: "If you're too busy to finish the Windsor matter let me do it. I've got time, and I'm certainly a lot more experienced than Nevin is."

"Good morning to you too, Joshua." Lodge pushed aside the deposition transcript he was reading and lifted his eyes to Jones's. "Would you like a cup of coffee or a muffin? Or perhaps both? The muffins are from *Tony's* in the North End. They're fabulous. The coffee is from *Caffee Vittoria*. I splurged this morning."

Jones said, "Nothing for me, Bart. But thanks for asking."

Lodge poured himself a second cup of coffee and broke the end off of a blueberry muffin. "To what do I owe the pleasure of your visit?" Lodge smiled.

Jones smiled too.

However, both men knew that their interactions were almost never much of a "pleasure."

Jones said, "I need to talk to you about Nevin."

The smile disappeared from Lodge's face. He tossed the chunk of muffin back onto the plate and wiped crumbs from his fingers with a linen napkin. "For Pete's sake, Joshua, can't you give that subject a rest? Believe me, I'm well aware of how you feel about Nevin. The executive committee is also aware.... You asked us to terminate the poor kid after he had that slip up at *McFadden's* a few months back."

Jones hadn't blinked since Lodge had started talking. "It wasn't a 'slip up', Bart. He was stumbling drunk and the police had to be called. And I shouldn't need to remind you that *McFadden's* is right around the corner from the office. Staff were present. *Clients* were present." Jones extended his arms from his sides, with his palms facing the sky, in the universal sign of *what-the-fuck*.

"I'm not condoning Nevin's behavior, Joshua. But he was drunk, not high. Our zero tolerance policy with him is about drugs, not alcohol."

"That's the sort of distinction that a good lawyer would try to make, Bart."

"Thanks for the compliment."

"I didn't mean it as a compliment."

"I know you didn't. Thanks anyway. Is there anything else I can do for you? In case you haven't noticed, I'm in the middle of reviewing deposition transcripts. I've got a trial next week, and it's not an insignificant one."

"New England Bank?" Jones studied the stack of transcripts on Lodge's desk.

"New England Bank. The Feds are hot and heavy this time. Apparently, the president needs to try and control the political damage before the election. The mortgage crisis is killing him in the polls. I'm a lifelong Democrat—I'm from Massachusetts, like you—but that seems like an inappropriate reason for utilizing the criminal justice system."

Jones smiled. "Everything's always about politics, Bart. You know that."

"But it shouldn't be." Lodge thought again about Nevin Montgomery. Unlike Jones, Lodge wasn't smiling. What Nevin was battling struck close to home.

Lodge watched Jones exit his office. When Jones was gone, Lodge stared at the photograph of his son on the corner of his desk and began to weep.

CHAPTER 5

Nevin Montgomery retrieved his briefcase from the closet and placed it on the desk in the den of the small guest cottage to which he had been assigned. He snatched a *Coke Zero* from the refrigerator and the bag of *Cape Cod Potato Chips* that the Windsors' staff had kindly left for him. He tore a couple of paper towels from the dispenser above the sink and returned to the den to begin preparing for his meeting with Andrew Windsor. After the previous night's shocking development—the mysterious death of Hannah Burgoff—Nevin had no idea when that meeting would occur.

Nevin snapped open his briefcase. An unexpected smile crossed his cleanly shaven face as he thought about how much grief his high school buddies would have given him if they could have seen him now: a highly paid attorney with a major Boston law firm visiting the magnificent Cape Cod compound of the most famous artist in America in order to revise that artist's testamentary documents. Nevin needed to give the guys a call. It had been too long. They had shared too much.... He had always resented people who left old friends behind, but he had become one of those people. He didn't like it and he was determined to make amends.

Nevin devoured a handful of potato chips, took a swig of soda, and wiped his hands clean with a paper towel. He reached inside his briefcase and removed the accordion file that contained Andrew Windsor's will.

The will was five pages long. A will's length was dependent upon the testator's objectives. Some testators had elaborate plans as to how to distribute their wealth that necessitated many pages to express. Others had straightforward ideas for their assets that required only a few pages to spell out. Five pages was about average, even though Andrew Windsor's estate was far from average. In fact, Mr. Windsor's estate was the most complicated estate on which Nevin had worked in his young career.

Wills had always been subject to what the law termed "formalities." In the Middle Ages the ecclesiastical courts permitted oral wills of personal property and courts of equity enforced oral devises of uses.

The Statute of Wills of 1540 required that wills of real property (i.e., land) be in writing. The Statute of Frauds of 1677 included additional requirements: devises of land had to be signed by the testator and subscribed by witnesses, and wills of personal property from thenceforth were required to be in writing. The Wills Act of 1837 unified all of the rules for real and personal property, and added the requirements that the testator's signature must be at the end of the will and that the witnesses to the will must be present at the same time.

The central function of these formalities was evidentiary. If a will wasn't in writing, the argument went, witnesses might either "misremember" or deliberately lie about the alleged statements of intention by the testator and the testator, by definition deceased, would be unavailable to clarify the record. The ceremony surrounding the execution of the will caused the testator to appreciate the seriousness of the event, which helped to confirm the testator's intent.

Many modern scholars believed that the traditional requirements for wills were too strict and they had managed to persuade most state legislatures and courts to modify them. The Uniform Probate Code, for example, eliminated the requirements that witnesses sign in the testator's presence and that the testator sign the will at the end.

But big firm lawyers tended to be conservative and Bartholomew Lodge was more conservative than most. Nevin had learned that Lodge had gone so far as to write a letter to Professor John Langbein of Yale Law School—the most prominent scholar behind the liberalizing trend—to raise concerns about the professor's proposed rule of "substantial compliance," by which a noncomplying will that sufficiently approximated the prescribed formalities to fulfill their underlying evidentiary purposes would be admitted to probate. Lodge, in contrast, had pursued the traditional route when drafting Andrew Windsor's will: he had asked the witnesses to sign together in Windsor's presence and Windsor himself to sign at the bottom of the will. Lodge also included an attestation clause that recited that all of the formalities were duly performed so as to avoid the rare but not unheard of circumstance of the witnesses testifying in probate court that the will was not duly executed. The attestation clause read:

*On June 15, 2005, Andrew Meyers Windsor declared to
us that the foregoing instrument, consisting of five pages
including this one, was his will and he requested us to act
as witnesses to it. He then signed the will in our presence,
all of us being present at the same time. We now subscribe
our names as witnesses in his presence and in the presence
of each other.*

    Michael Kinstler
    William Morrone

Nevin was impressed with the care by which Lodge had drafted
Windsor's will. Nevin had taken four courses at Harvard Law School
on the subject—Wills and Trusts I, Wills and Trusts II, Estate and Gift
Taxation, and Estate Planning—and he knew the blackletter law inside
and out. But the will that Lodge had prepared for Mr. Windsor was the
first real will that Nevin had ever read. Nevin himself was too young
to feel the need for a will, and his parents were not wealthy enough to
justify the expense of having one prepared for them and Nevin couldn't
draft one for them because of the legal ethics rule against conflicts of
interest.

The biggest lesson that Nevin had learned in his estate planning
courses at Harvard was that the testator should treat everyone on
the same line of succession equally. That wasn't a lesson about law. It
was lesson about life. But his professor, a septuagenarian whose thick
southern accent masked a mensa-level intellect, cared more about life
than about law. Nevin could still hear his professor imploring the class:
"Even if Junior is lazier than a three-toed sloth and sneakier than a
South Carolina rattlesnake, give him the same share as his brothers and
sisters."

Apparently, Bartholomew Lodge had imparted this same lesson
upon Andrew Windsor. All three of Andrew Windsor's children were
awarded a one-third share of Mr. Windsor's estate upon the death of
their mother, Lauren Windsor, including the "three-toed sloth" and
"rattlesnake" of a son, James. Nevin had never met James Windsor, but
Lodge had briefed Nevin on the Windsor family secrets shortly before
dispatching his young charge to the Cape.

Frankly, when it came to James, there weren't many family secrets left. A quick *Google* search had led Nevin to an avalanche of tabloid stories—from *People* magazine to the *Boston Globe*, and every sort of publication in between—about James's wandering eye and mediocre talent. **James Windsor, son of America's greatest living artist, seen cavorting on Nantucket beach with stunning brunette**, one headline had proclaimed. **Painter's son spotted at Boston hotspot with buxom blonde**, read another.

When Nevin had asked Lodge about James, Lodge had simply said, "He's a cliché." Then Lodge had added, "And I think that's one reason Andrew wants to revisit his testamentary documents."

Nevin had asked next, "What's the other?"

"His concern for the Cape's environs. Almost nobody knows it, but Andrew Windsor is one of the most committed environmentalists in New England, and it troubles him deeply to see his beloved Cape Cod being turned into an amusement park."

Nevin's parents had somehow scrapped together enough money one summer when Nevin was in middle school for the family to spend a week at the Cape. Nevin, now a well-paid lawyer, had spent two weeks at the Cape earlier in the summer and he had noticed that the Cape was much more of a tourist trap now than when he was a kid. He could understand Mr. Windsor's concern about the environment, and he admired him for wanting to do something about it. If, that was, Lodge's supposition was correct.

Nevin decided that it was time to ask Mr. Windsor himself what his intentions were.

CHAPTER 6

The sky was blue and the ocean was calm. Birds chirped from the treetops. Dogs frolicked on the grass.... These were nature's juxtaposition to the misdeeds of man.

Two groundskeepers were trimming the hedges. Sweat poured from their foreheads as they did their best to make the compound's landscape as pristine as one of Andrew Windsor's famous paintings. They clearly knew that was impossible, but Nevin admired how arduously they were trying. Nevin's parents had labored for a living and he had profound respect for everyone who put in a hard day's work.

Nevin rang the buzzer at the main house. A distinguished-looking butler who resembled Mr. Carson from *Downton Abbey* greeted the young man as if he were a visiting dignitary. "Good afternoon, Mr. Montgomery. Are you finding your accommodations acceptable?"

Nevin said, "They're fantastic. Thank you."

The butler said, "I'm delighted you are enjoying them. Please let me know if there's anything you need. The Windsors want all of their guests to have a pleasant stay."

Nevin thanked the butler again, and then asked, "Speaking of the Windsors, is Mr. Windsor available?"

The butler smiled and said, "I'll be happy to check for you, sir. In the meantime, please make yourself comfortable in the drawing room." The butler escorted Nevin to an elegant room in the middle of the large house. Nevin had never before been escorted to a "drawing room." His family and friends were lucky if they had a living room. But his family and friends weren't rich New England WASPs.

Not surprisingly, Andrew Windsor's paintings dominated the room. A lovely seascape that was almost certainly painted from the beach that adjoined the compound hung on the south wall. An exquisite painting of a full moon glistening above the ocean adorned the west wall. The north and east walls contained, respectively, portraits of Lauren Windsor and someone whom Nevin suspected was Hannah Burgoff. Hannah had been concealed in a body bag by the paramedics, and Nevin had no idea what she actually looked like. But the painting had been recently hung—a stepladder rested conspicuously nearby—

and Nevin had a gut feeling it was of Hannah.

The furnishings appeared to be antique and expensive. At Nevin's parents' house they were old and cheap. The Windsors probably shopped at *Sotheby's*. Nevin's parents scavenged at yard sales. As Nevin sat patiently waiting for the butler to return, he couldn't help but wonder what it would have been like to have grown up amidst such plenty. What would it have been like to never want for anything? to live in the lap of luxury? to have servants attend to your every need? to be able to go to college without working at night to pay for it? Nevin couldn't understand why—according to Bartholomew Lodge— James Windsor had turned out to be such a jerk. At least Nevin had an excuse, or that was what he told himself when he thought about all the bad things he had done in his younger years.

But those days were behind him now. He had kicked drugs. He had earned two degrees from Harvard. He worked as an attorney with a prestigious Boston law firm, and he got paid handsomely for it. He was sitting in the "drawing room" of the most famous artist in America.

Nevin retrieved a coffee table book from the table in front of him and began to leaf through it. The book, also not surprisingly, was about Andrew Windsor's paintings. High quality photographs were accompanied by glowing descriptions of the paintings in question. "*Sun Above the Shoreline* revealed Windsor's kinship with Cape Cod," one of the entries read. "It's as if Windsor and the Cape were one." Another entry described the painting being assessed—that of a tall oak tree that Nevin recognized as providing shade for the guest cottage to which he had been assigned—as "one that only Andrew Windsor could have painted." Nevin had to admit that the painting was superb, but he wasn't sure why "only" Windsor could have painted it. Nevin wasn't an art expert, but he had been dragged to enough galleries by girlfriends over the years to know that *many* artists had painted similar pictures. Perhaps not as well, but they were lovely nonetheless.

Experts frequently debated how a great artist was formed. In sports, it was usually size and speed that determined success: great athletes were stronger and faster than their peers. In politics, effective leaders had the natural ability to inspire and to instill confidence in their judgment. In science, breakthroughs were typically made by men and women who were both brilliant and passionate about a specific task or project.

But in art, whence did greatness spring? Renowned artists came in all shapes and sizes: Toulouse-Lautrec stood barely five feet tall;

Gilbert Stuart was six-three, a giant in the late-seventeenth and early-eighteenth centuries. Andy Warhol was rail-thin, apparently preferring pharmaceuticals to three square meals a day. Claude Monet seemingly never passed a café he didn't like. Great artists also were raised in different circumstances: Pablo Picasso was born into comfortable middle-class surroundings in Málaga, Spain. J. M. W. Turner was raised in less affluent environs in England. The one common characteristic shared by all great artists? An innate appreciation of beauty. Most people, including most mediocre artists, knew whether something was "pretty" or not. But only a handful could appreciate—and replicate—*beauty*.

Nevin heard someone approaching. He lifted his eyes from the coffee table book. The young woman he had seen entering one of the other cottages on the Windsor compound moments after Deputy Steele had finished interrogating the crowd that assembled on the night Hannah Burgoff had been discovered dead swept into the drawing room like an ocean breeze through the window of a musty house. She was the personification of the beauty that Andrew Windsor had dedicated his life to re-creating.

She said, "I'm s–sorry, sir. I didn't realize the Windsors had guests."

Nevin said, "There's no need to apologize. I'm Mr. Windsor's lawyer. I hardly qualify as a 'guest.'"

Nevin's self-deprecating remark drew a shy smile from the young woman.

She was the most beautiful woman Nevin had ever seen. Her long black hair glistened even more up close than when he had seen her from a distance and her copper skin was more luminous. Nevin also could see that she was Portuguese rather than Italian or Hispanic.

But before Nevin could say anything else to her, and before he could ask for her name, the butler who had greeted him at the front door reappeared and said, "I'm sorry, Mr. Montgomery, but Mrs. Windsor says that Mr. Windsor is too tired to meet with you today. She passes along his regrets. She also wants me to let you know that she's certain that her husband would understand if you returned to Boston this afternoon. He knows you're a busy man."

Nevin had been concentrating on the butler's remarks like all good lawyers were trained to do. When the butler had finished speaking, Nevin noticed that the beautiful young woman had disappeared from the room as unexpectedly as she had entered it.

CHAPTER 7

Deputy Sheriff John Steele quickly opened the coroner's report that the coroner himself had hand-delivered moments earlier.

The coroner, a heavyset man named Steve Murdoch, said, "Remember it's only a preliminary report, John." The coroner stuffed the uneaten half of a glazed donut into his mouth. He reached into his shirt pocket and retrieved a cigarette.

The irony that the coroner—the county's medical doctor charged with determining the cause of death—was both overweight and a heavy smoker wasn't lost on Deputy Steele. "This is a no smoking building, Steve. You know that."

"Sorry. I forgot." The coroner returned the cigarette to his shirt pocket.

Steele shook his head. "When are you of all people going to stop eating that junk and smoking those cancer sticks?"

The coroner blushed. "My wife asks me that same question every day, and I'll answer you the same way I answer her: I'm trying. I'm really trying. But old habits are difficult to break. Believe me, I kick myself every time I reach for a smoke and every time I eat something I know I shouldn't."

Steele, who had never smoked and whose most egregious dietary indulgences were an occasional scoop of Chappaquiddick Chocolate Chip ice cream from the *Cape Cod Creamy* and a lunch portion of clam strips at *Flo's Clam Shack* on payday, said, "I'm glad you're trying, Steve. I bet your wife is glad too."

"She is. But she thinks I'm not trying hard enough." The coroner tossed the third of the three donuts he had brought with him—the one he hadn't consumed yet—into the wastebasket next to Steele's desk. "She's right." It took him a bit longer to discard his cigarettes, but he did that too. "Goodbye old friends," he said with a wistful smile.

Steele said, "Good job, Steve. I'm proud of you, and I bet your wife will be as well."

"Thanks, but let's see how long I can abstain. You don't get a body like this by exercising a lot of will power." He spun around like a plus-sized fashion model.

Steele laughed, and then became serious. "Hannah Burgoff was strangled?"

The coroner's report stated that she died of asphyxiation, which *Taber's Medical Dictionary* defined as "the condition of being deprived of oxygen." But Steele was a cop, not a doctor. Besides, the dictionary went on to state that "asphyxiation is sometimes used as a form of torture," which meant that Steele's interpretation of the word was at least within the realm of possibilities.

The coroner wouldn't commit to it yet, though. He said, "It's too early to say. As I said, this is a preliminary report."

Steele motioned for the coroner to take a seat, which the coroner did. "But what about what the report says about 'scratches' on the neck and 'contusions'?"

The coroner ran a hand across his balding pate. "You're putting me in a tough spot, John. By law, I can't state publicly the cause of death until after I complete the final report, which won't be for several weeks because of the forensics involved. But as an overweight chain-smoker with a receding hairline who attends the same church with you every Sunday, I might be able to say something off the record."

Steele nodded. "We're off the record."

The coroner said, "She was strangled."

John Steele tossed the coroner's preliminary report onto his desk and rubbed his eyes with his fingers. He had read the preliminary report five times, including four times after the coroner had left to do more work on the final report. The coroner had reiterated that the final report wouldn't be ready for several weeks. Steele had said that he couldn't wait that long, but he knew he had no choice. However, Steele also knew that he didn't need to wait for the final report before he could do some additional poking around on his own. He decided that now was the time to do some poking.

He began by trying to talk with the sheriff himself.

In Massachusetts, as in many states in America, the county sheriff was elected by the voters. And while most sheriffs tended to have substantial law enforcement experience, not all did. Some were elected to office for the same reasons that many other government officials were: because of a charismatic personality and friends in all the right places. Sheriff Philip W. Joyce certainly was. Sheriff Joyce was only thirty years old and he had worked in law enforcement for less than five years. But the cameras loved him, and the voters did too. That was why the previous sheriff—a gruff old coot straight from central casting for a Sergio Leone spaghetti western starring Clint Eastwood—hadn't stood a chance in the previous year's election. As political scientists had documented many times, modern elections were about flash and sparkle. The previous sheriff of Barnstable County was about substance and results. The voters of Barnstable County preferred the former by a two-to-one margin.

Sheriff Joyce's office door was closed.

Deputy Sheriff Steele knocked on it.

Joyce said, "Come in."

Steele pushed open the door and entered Joyce's expansive office. The young sheriff was staring intensely at his computer screen. Steele said, "Is this a bad time?"

Joyce smiled, and said, "No. It's the perfect time." He swiveled his chair away from his computer. "I'm studying our budget numbers."

"How do they look?"

"Terrible, of course. We're no different than every other government department in the county… shoot, in the state. We've got no money."

"I guess that means we can't hire a replacement for Tom."

Tom Watkins had retired earlier in the year after forty years as a deputy sheriff for Barnstable County. He had said that he was too old to do the job right, but Steele knew the real reason: Watkins, a big supporter of the man Joyce had defeated in November, thought that Joyce was too young to be sheriff.

Joyce said, "Unfortunately, that's correct." He glanced over at his computer screen. "I've been crunching the numbers backwards and forwards but I just can't make it work."

"Why can't we just use Tom's salary to pay a new guy? Tom's off the payroll now."

Joyce smiled. "But he's not."

Steele's brows furrowed and his eyes narrowed. "What do you mean?"

"Under the terms of the agreement the county made with county employees ten years ago, when a county employee retires after twenty-plus years of service, he receives one hundred percent of his salary during his first year of retirement."

Steele smiled sheepishly. "Oh. Yeah. I remember now." Steele was impressed that Joyce knew that information. After all, Joyce wasn't working for the county at the time. Steele had to give Joyce credit: the new sheriff had done his homework. "What are we gonna do?"

"Handle more cases with fewer people. That's all we can do. I know it sucks." Joyce leaned forward in his chair. "Speaking of cases, wasn't that Steve Murdoch I saw leaving the building?" Joyce's office had a large window that faced the parking lot.

"Yeah. He was delivering the preliminary report in the Hannah Burgoff case." Steele handed Joyce the report.

The new sheriff read it. He lifted his eyes from the closing page. "She was murdered, wasn't she?"

Steele nodded. "Steve said he won't know for sure until he finishes the final report, but he told me off the record that, yes, she was murdered."

"Given where she was killed, I suspect it won't be long before the national media pays Barnstable a visit. The media lives for scandals involving the rich and famous."

Steele nodded again. "I know. That sucks too."

But Steele couldn't tell how the new sheriff actually felt about the looming publicity.

CHAPTER 8

Deputy Steele returned to his office and opened a bottle of *Vitamin Water*. It was lemon, his favorite. His kids had called it his "lemonade" when they were little and his two oldest had been known to hawk it at their sidewalk stand when the *Minute Maid* mix their mom had prepared had all been purchased by thirsty passers-by on any number of sweltering Cape Cod summer days. Steele had admired his children's get-up-and-go. Not many five- and seven-year olds could identify a problem—insufficient inventory—let alone solve it by raiding their dad's stash of *Vitamin Water* to re-stock their stand. His only regret had been that a bottle of *Vitamin Water* cost a lot more than the twenty-five cents his kids had charged for it. But he had never said anything about it. He loved them too much to care.

Steele finished his drink and decided to check in with a few colleagues in the Sheriff's Office to see if they had any ideas about the Hannah Burgoff case. The sheriff hadn't been much help. Perhaps some of the other deputies might have some useful opinions on the matter.

Steele began with Jack Peterson, a no-nonsense cop who had been a deputy sheriff in Barnstable County for almost as long as Tom Watkins. Unlike Watkins, however, Peterson had decided not to retire when Philip Joyce was elected sheriff. Peterson was born to be a cop, and Steele always knew that Peterson would die a cop. There were no golden years of golf and shuffleboard in his future.

Peterson's door was open.

Steele said, "Gotta minute?"

Peterson glanced up from the report he was reading. "Sure. What's up?"

"I was hoping to pick your brain for a few minutes about the Hannah Burgoff case."

Peterson smiled. There was nothing Peterson liked better than brainstorming with a colleague about a tough case, and Steele knew that. Peterson said, "Grab a seat."

Steele moved a small stack of accordion files from the only other chair in Peterson's tiny office. He placed the small stack on top of a larger stack on Peterson's desk and then sat in the now empty chair.

Both men smiled. They had been through this dance many times before. Jack Peterson was a packrat and nothing was ever going to change that.

Peterson said, "What's the latest?" He tossed the report he had been reading on top of the large stack that Steele had rearranged on his desk.

Steele said, "Steve Murdoch said she was murdered."

"You mean he said that off the record?"

"Yeah. Off the record."

Peterson knew how Murdoch operated: that Murdoch was loath to go on the record unless he absolutely had to, such as when he was testifying in court. Peterson also knew that "off the record" didn't mean that one cop couldn't share what Murdoch had said with another cop. This wasn't a high school gossip circle about who liked whom. This was a homicide investigation. Death isn't a game.

"What's your gut telling you?" Peterson rocked back in his chair. "We both know that ninety percent of this job is listening to our guts."

Steele nodded. He hadn't been a cop for as long as Peterson, but he had been one long enough to know that Peterson was right: the best cops had the best instincts. And Peterson's instincts were usually dead on. Steele said, "I was hoping that you would tell me."

Peterson laughed, which he rarely did. He opened the jar of jelly beans that was lodged between two of piles of paperwork on the corner of his desk. He popped a handful into his mouth and then passed the jar to Steele. Steele was health conscious, but he didn't want to be rude. He shoveled a handful of the candy into his mouth. Peterson said, "If jelly beans were good enough for Ronald Reagan, they're good enough for me." He finished chewing. He never finished thinking.... He was always thinking. He was a terrific cop. "What do you know about that young lawyer who's staying at the Windsor compound?"

Steele finished chewing too. "How do you know about him?" Steele had a good idea about how Peterson knew, but he wanted Peterson to confirm his supposition.

"Because news travels fast around here, John." Peterson reached for another handful of jelly beans. He jiggled them in his hand and then tossed them into his mouth. "The citizens of Barnstable are like the little old ladies down at *Rosie's Beauty Salon*: always gossiping about what's going on in town. They're usually right, and it usually saves me hours of investigation time."

Steele chuckled. Then, he turned serious. "The lawyer's name is Nevin Montgomery. I don't know much about him beyond that. He showed up at the crime scene when the paramedics were there, but so did a lot of people. I don't think he had anything to do with Hannah Burgoff's death, though."

"How do you know that he didn't? Have you interviewed him?"

"Not yet. I was waiting for the coroner's report. But he's on the top of my list of people to talk to."

"Good." Peterson reached again for the jar of jelly beans. Each handful was larger than the last. "Tell me this, John: why would such a young lawyer be asked to write Andrew Windsor's will?" Peterson smiled again. "And, yes, the ladies down at *Rosie's* told me about that too."

"I think he's revising it, not writing it. I think Mr. Windsor already has a will."

"That makes my question even more important because, by definition, Windsor plans to make some changes to his will. And there's a lot of money involved. At least most people think there is."

"Why do you think Mr. Windsor would want to do that? Make changes, I mean." Steele was the one who reached for the jelly beans this time. He figured that he had cheated on his diet once already today and a second time wouldn't make matters much worse.

Peterson rocked back in his chair and glanced up at the ceiling. Silence filled his office for the first time all day. The air conditioner hummed softly in the background like a film score in a Saturday matinee. He finally said, "Who knows why any of the Windsors do anything they do. It's a soap opera over there. They're like most rich people.... They're nuts."

Steele had been watching Peterson contemplate his question. He agreed with Peterson's answer. "I know. When I was a kid my dad used to tell us stories about what he had seen and heard about the Windsors. That Senator Kearney was hanging around at their compound.... That Jessica Lange was playing tennis with Mrs. Windsor.... That Morgan Freeman was stumbling drunk at one of their parties.... My sister and I thought he was making it up to entertain us while we were doing our chores."

John Steele's father had been a deputy sheriff in Barnstable County also. He had been stabbed to death trying to break up a barroom brawl when John was fifteen. His sister was eleven at the time, and she had never fully recovered from losing their father so young. And that was why the son had followed in the father's footsteps and become a cop. Steele loved his father, and he loved his sister. He owed it to both of them to be a cop, and to be a damn good cop.

Peterson said, "Truth is stranger than fiction, as the saying goes. You've heard the real story behind the Hannah Burgoff paintings haven't you?"

Steele shook his head. "No. What is it?"

"That they're part of an elaborate hoax. The most important part."

Steele's brows furrowed. He rubbed his hand across his face. "What do you mean?"

"That Andrew Windsor's popularity has declined in recent years.... That his art is considered too old-fashioned for our high-tech age.... That he doesn't have as much money left in the bank as people think.... That his wife is freaking out about that and that *she* came up with the plan to unleash the 'secret' Hannah paintings on the world as a way to rekindle interest in her husband's art and, hence, replenish their dwindling bank account."

Steele couldn't believe what he was hearing. He said, "How do you know all that?"

Peterson smiled at his favorite colleague. He reached for a fourth time for the jar of jelly beans. "Because the lovely ladies at *Rosie's* said so."

CHAPTER 9

Nevin Montgomery changed into the same suit he had worn the first time he tried to meet with Andrew Windsor. Nevin owned multiple suits at this point in his legal career but he had brought only one with him. He had never expected to remain at the Windsor compound for more than a night. It had now been three. He grabbed his briefcase from the kitchen table in the cottage to which he had been assigned and hoped that Mr. Windsor was finally well enough to speak with him. Bartholomew Lodge was a patient man. Joshua Jones was not. Nevin was working for Lodge on the Windsor matter. However, Nevin knew that Jones was none too happy that he was.

Nevin rang the doorbell at the main house. The butler who had greeted him the first time—the one who resembled Mr. Carson on *Downton Abbey*—answered the door this time also.

The butler said, "Good morning, Mr. Montgomery. I trust you've come to see Mr. Windsor?"

Nevin nodded. "That's correct. Is he available?"

"I'd be happy to check for you."

The butler escorted Nevin to the drawing room and then excused himself for a minute to inquire about Mr. Windsor's availability.

Nevin sat on the same sofa on which he had sat the first time he was in the Windsors' house. This time, though, the beautiful young housekeeper was nowhere to be found. Nevin was disappointed. It was difficult to blame him: he was a guy and she was a beautiful woman. It was no more complicated than that... at least not yet.

Nevin admired the spectacular view of the ocean through the large picture window that was the signature architectural feature of the room. White-capped waves crashed against jagged rocks and sprayed mist high into the air. Seagulls soared across the crystal blue sky, rapturous in flight. The sun reflected against the roiling sea like a dancer across a stage.

Nevin sunk back into the couch and smiled. Only a few years removed from the hardscrabble streets of Dorchester, he had to pinch himself to believe that his life had taken the positive turn that it had. He had battled his demons—his addiction to drugs—and come out on top. He made a mental note to call Mr. Harrington to say hello and to tell his favorite high school teacher that he was still clean and sober.

The butler returned with the news that Nevin was hoping to hear: "I'm pleased to report that Mr. Windsor is available to meet with you now. Please follow me, Mr. Montgomery."

The butler led Nevin through a labyrinth of hallways and up several flights of stairs. One of Andrew Windsor's paintings hung on every wall. Each was seemingly more beautiful than the last.

Nevin said, "It's like a museum in here."

The butler said, "Indeed it is, sir. Mr. Windsor has been touched by the hand of God himself, if I may be so bold. It's a privilege to work for him."

"How long have you worked for him?"

They passed yet another beautiful painting.

The butler said, "I've been in service for forty years. The last thirty have been with the Windsors. I've enjoyed every minute of it."

Nevin couldn't help but think of Anthony Hopkins's character in *The Remains of the Day*. "For whom did you work before the Windsors?"

"For Senator Kearney's family." The butler stopped. "We're here." He knocked gently on Andrew Windsor's bedroom door and led Nevin inside. "Mr. Montgomery is here to see you, sir."

Andrew Windsor sat up in his bed. "Thank you. That will be all for now."

The butler left Windsor alone with the young attorney.

Nevin noticed that Mr. Windsor looked a lot older than he had in the photographs that Bartholomew Lodge had shown him in Boston. His hair was completely white rather than salt and pepper, and his skin was gray rather than tan. His eyes were watery, and he appeared to have a difficult time focusing them. In short, he looked as if he was dying, which was why Nevin had been sent to his home in the first place.

Windsor coughed, and then coughed again. "Please. Have a seat, Mr. Montgomery."

Nevin spotted a wooden chair to the left of Mr. Windsor's bed and sat in it. "Please call me Nevin."

"Only if you call me Andrew." Windsor coughed again.

"Do you need anything? Water, perhaps?"

"That would be good. Thank you."

Nevin stood from his seat and reached for the pitcher of water on Mr. Windsor's bedside table. He poured him a glass.

Windsor took a long drink. "Thank you, Nevin."

"You're welcome." Nevin smiled. "I'm glad you're well enough to see me today."

Windsor took another drink. "I'm not, really. But I'm smart enough to know that I needed to."

Silence filled the room. A light breeze scented the air with the smells of the ocean: a potpourri of salt, seaweed, and sand. The open window made the room a bit cooler than Windsor's doctor preferred, but Windsor insisted on having at least one window ajar. "I'm not dead yet," he had said when his doctor had recommended closing the window. "Without the sea, I might as well be." The doctor acquiesced. He had known Andrew Windsor for too long to believe that America's greatest living artist was speaking metaphorically.

Nevin finally said, "Before we turn to the business at hand, I just wanted to say how much I admire your work. I don't know how you do it. Paint such beautiful pictures, I mean."

Windsor proceeded to tell Nevin how. "I learned how to paint by watching my father. He was an artist too. Much better than me, really. I know the so-called experts maintain otherwise, but most art critics don't know what they're talking about. They're usually frustrated artists themselves, and they take their frustrations out on other people... people like my father."

Nevin asked, "Who was your father?"

"C. S. Windsor. I'm surprised Bart Lodge didn't tell you that."

Nevin reddened. "He probably did. I'm not very good with names."

"Not too worry. You're young, and you're a lawyer. Don't feel guilty about not knowing about my father. But you need to know now. You need to know for the work you've been asked to do for me." Windsor took another drink of water. "My father was the finest illustrator of children's books in American history. Even his critics concede that much. They simply insist that what he did wasn't, quote, 'art,' in the grand sense of the word. But they're wrong. The children's books he illustrated would be just words on paper without my father's illustrations. But with my father's illustrations children were transported to magical worlds of make believe where life's lessons were taught and learned. I'm sure your parents read many of those books to you when you were a child: *The Rabbit and the Grasshopper*, *Ted E. Bear Finds a Home*, *The Boy Who Learned to Laugh*, to mention three of my personal favorites."

Nevin nodded. "You're right. My parents read all of those books to me. I loved them, especially the illustrations. And I agree with you: the books wouldn't be nearly as meaningful without the illustrations."

"Thank you for saying that, Nevin. It means a lot to me, even to this day—which very well might be my final day." Windsor started to cough again.

"Have some more water." Nevin filled Mr. Windsor's glass and held it to his client's mouth. "Are you OK?"

The water had done the trick: Windsor had stopped coughing. "I'm fine, all things considered."

"Do you want me to come back tomorrow?"

"No."

But at that very moment Lauren Windsor appeared in the doorway and said, "Yes. Yes, Mr. Montgomery. Come back tomorrow."

Andrew Windsor smiled. "I suppose you should, then."

Nevin agreed and exited the room.

CHAPTER 10

Lauren Windsor threw the morning's edition of the *New York Times* into the wastebasket with a force that belied her petite one-hundred-pound frame. "God dammit!" she screamed.

One of the servants came rushing into the study. "Are—Are you OK, ma'am?"

Mrs. Windsor turned on her heel and said, "Yes. Now please leave me in peace."

The servant did as she was instructed.

Mrs. Windsor retrieved the newspaper from the wastebasket and re-read the article that was printed on page 1 of the Arts section. The headline blared: **HANNAH PAINTINGS A HOAX, EXPERTS CONCLUDE**. The article was written by the *Times*'s chief art critic and included quotes from three of the nation's foremost art experts: a professor of art history from the Rhode Island School of Design, the curator of the Chicago Art Institute, and the proprietor of the largest private art gallery in New York City.

The art history professor described how it was a surprisingly common practice that dated back hundreds of years for artists to paint a series of "secret" paintings that they would one day unveil upon the world to revive interest in their work. "Even Da Vinci did it," the professor explained. The curator of the Chicago Art Institute reported that demand for exhibits of Andrew Windsor's work had fallen off dramatically over the last decade or so, while the proprietor of the private art gallery stated that he didn't stock any of Windsor's paintings for sale anymore because "almost nobody wanted to buy them."

Mrs. Windsor closed her eyes in disbelief after she finished read-ing the article about her husband's work for a second time. This time, she didn't toss the newspaper into the wastebasket and emit a guttural scream. This time, she folded it into a neat rectangle and placed it in a file in her desk marked ANDREW'S PRESS CLIPPINGS. She had accumulated many such clippings during their fifty-plus years of marriage. Several in the early years had been mildly critical of her husband's work—"Andrew Windsor's art is amateurish and better suited as illustrations for children's books" was one assessment that had been particularly hurtful and that had managed to simultaneously insult Andrew and his father—but as the years passed and Andrew's paintings began to suggest that he was an artist with a unique vision of nature who possessed the self-confidence to reveal that vision on canvas, the reviews had become nearly reverential in their praise. *Life* magazine had proclaimed in a cover story that Mrs. Windsor had framed and hung above her desk, for example, that her husband was **AMERICA'S GREATEST ARTIST**. Sadly, with the article in the morning's *New York Times* that reverence was gone. More importantly as far as Mrs. Windsor was concerned, the article was accurate.

How did she know the article was accurate? Because she had managed her husband's business affairs during all of their many years together. Andrew Windsor might have been uniquely talented when he was working with oil and canvas, but he had little interest in, and less patience for, the financial side of his chosen profession. Indeed, he recoiled every time someone referred to what he did as a *profession*. He would always say, "Law is a profession. Teaching is a profession. Medicine is a profession. But art... art is *life*."

However, Lauren Windsor knew that *life* cost money, especially when they had started to have children.

Andrew and Lauren Windsor had raised three children together: two daughters and a son. The girls had never been any trouble. Sara, the oldest, had always done wonderfully in school. She was valedictorian of her high school class and went on to earn a B.A. in English from Princeton University. She had taught that subject at Northfield Mount Hermon in western Massachusetts, one of the finest prep schools in the nation, before dying tragically in a car accident several years earlier. Amanda—Mandy, to her family and friends—had earned her undergraduate degree from Williams College, where she had met and subsequently married her husband of fifteen years, a terrific guy named Allen. Mandy and Allen lived in New York City with their two young children. Allen worked as an investment banker with Goldman Sachs. Mandy stayed home with the kids, doing what most stay-at-home moms did: chauffeur her children from one activity to the next.

James, on the other hand, had been the proverbial problem child. He was habitually truant when he was young, he would get into fights when he did manage to make it to school, and he spent more time at the Sheriff's Office trying to talk his way out of shoplifting and vandalism charges than he did doing his homework. In fact, the only thing that had kept him out of the juvenile detention center in Weymouth was his father's fame and fortune. As James well knew, being the son of Andrew Windsor was a virtual get-out-of-jail-free card in southern New England, especially when the son showed flashes of artistic talent in his own right, albeit not nearly of the level of his father or grandfather.

Lauren Windsor tolerated most of James's imperfections, as most mothers would. But one that she had a difficult time overlooking was how he treated women. She had two daughters of her own and it cut her to the core to hear the stories that circulated around town about how James had been overly aggressive with many of his girlfriends. At first, she didn't believe the stories. After the tenth or eleventh report, she couldn't deny them, even to herself. She had spent many a sleepless night trying to understand why James was mistreating women like he was, and she had pleaded with Andrew on more occasions than she could count to talk to James about it.

"Please, Andrew," Lauren would say. "You're his father. He respects you. Talk to James and get him some help, if that what it takes. *Please.*"

Andrew would always promise his wife that he would talk to James, but he never did it. He also never explained why he never talked to him. When Lauren would ask her husband why he hadn't talked to their son yet, he would simply state that he had been busy working on a new painting and that he "would get to it later."

Later never came.

Lauren Windsor retrieved her day planner from the middle drawer of her desk and studied the schedule of events at the compound. Their property was large, and her husband was famous, so there were always a lot of activities for her to manage. Tommy Kearney, the senior U.S. senator from Massachusetts, was slated to have dinner with her and Andrew later in the week. Tommy was the scion of the Kearney family, the so-called royal family of America. His friendship with Andrew dated all the way back to their prep school days together at Phillips Academy Andover. Even then, Andrew was the sensitive artist who preferred spending time alone in the great outdoors with his paints and canvases, while Tommy was the gregarious friend to everyone and destined for a career in politics. Somehow, though, the two became great pals, perhaps because of a shared but unspoken interest in beauty… an interest that Andrew revealed in his art and that Tommy demonstrated by his endless pursuit of young women. Lauren had never said anything about it, but she had long suspected that her son's inappropriate behavior towards women could be traced to his years of watching how Tommy Kearney treated them. James, she knew, admired Tommy more than he admired his own father.

But that was a battle to be fought on another day. Today, Lauren had to figure out what to do about Nevin Montgomery. She had never liked lawyers—who did?—and she especially disliked those who posed a threat to her financial well-being. She didn't actually know why Montgomery was meeting with Andrew, but she had managed her husband's business affairs long enough to realize that any time a lawyer was involved it wasn't good. Lawyers were paid to either cause problems or to solve problems, and it was usually the former—even when the objective was the latter. The fact that Andrew hadn't told her why he was meeting with Montgomery only made her feel worse about the young lawyer's presence at the compound. She needed to figure out some way to convince him to leave.

The sooner the better.

CHAPTER 11

Apparently, Nevin Montgomery still had time on his hands. Lauren Windsor had made certain of that when she ordered him out of her ailing husband's bedroom. Nevin had telephoned Bart Lodge to see if Palmer & Lodge wanted him to stop trying to meet with Mr. Windsor, but Lodge instructed Nevin to try at least once more. That certainly wouldn't be today. In fact, Lodge had told Nevin to take the rest of the day off. Of course, Nevin was supposed to bill that time to the Windsor account. Billing… for lawyers, it was always about billing.

Nevin decided to explore the Town of Barnstable for a few hours. Barnstable was the largest town on Cape Cod. It was named after Barnstable, England. Barnstable, Massachusetts was settled in 1638. Agriculture, fishing, and salt works quickly became its major industries. By the last part of the nineteenth century there were some eight hundred ships harbored in the town. This came to an end with the rise of the railroad, which had arrived in 1854, and of steamships. However, by the late-nineteenth century Barnstable also was becoming world-renowned as a tourist destination. It remained so to this day, in large part because it had long been home to the Kearney family, including, at present, U.S. Senator Thomas Kearney. Barnstable was especially popular with tourists during the summer months when the town's many beaches were packed with sun worshipers of every age, size, shape, and color.

Barnstable was likewise famous for its many quaint shops, and it was in the main shopping district on Coastline Avenue that Nevin currently found himself. He ducked into a tee shirt shop and rummaged through the sale rack. The clerk asked Nevin if he was looking for anything in particular. Nevin answered that he was just browsing. He spotted a tie-died long-sleeved tee shirt with BARNSTABLE, MASSACHUSETTS embossed across the chest, brought it to the register, and gave the clerk a twenty. The clerk placed the shirt into a white plastic bag with the shop's name etched on the side—CAPE COD TEES—handed Nevin the bag and $1.27 in change, and thanked Nevin for the business. Nevin said "you're welcome" and ducked into another shop. This one was a candy shop that specialized in salt water taffy. Nevin watched a guy prepare a fresh batch. When the guy had finished, he asked Nevin whether Nevin would like a sample. Nevin answered in the affirmative and the guy offered him a small chunk of vanilla. Nevin mentioned how much he enjoyed it and purchased a small bag.

Taffy, though, was hardly a meal. It was lunchtime. Nevin surveyed the shopping district's directory to see what his dining options were. He hadn't eaten seafood for a while, and what better place to redress that craving than Cape Cod? He noticed several choices. He settled on *The Lobster Roll* for the commonsensical reason that he loved lobster rolls. They were expensive, and he had never tried one until he started making a nice salary at Palmer & Lodge, but now he could afford to splurge. Besides, he said to himself as he headed towards the oceanfront establishment, he would be billing his lunch to the Windsor account.

The Lobster Roll was located half a block from the end of the main drag of the shopping district. The building that housed the restaurant resembled most of the structures in the district: wooden, weathered, and cozy. The waitress who seated Nevin provided him with a prime lunch spot: a corner booth with a view of both the ocean and the main street.

The waitress smiled and handed Nevin a menu. "I'm Ruthie. I'll be your server today. The lunch special is a lobster roll with a side of slaw and fries for $18.95. It comes with a soft drink." She smiled again. "Our lobster rolls are out of this world."

Nevin returned the waitress's smile. "Sold. But hold the coleslaw, please. Do you have lobster bisque?"

"Absolutely."

"Then I'll start with a cup of that, please. And a *Coke* to drink."

"Great choices. I'll be right back with your soda and soup." The waitress headed towards the kitchen.

Nevin wondered what the waitress's backstory was? He always wondered what the backstories were of the people he met. Mr. Harrington, the high school English teacher who had changed Nevin's life, used to emphasize the backstories of the characters in the novels they read in English Lit. Today's popular fiction was more concerned with plot twists and action scenes, but the novels that Mr. Harrington had assigned were character driven. Nevin had been interested in people's backstories ever since.

The waitress returned with Nevin's *Coke* and lobster bisque. She also brought a glass of ice water with lemon. She deposited all of it on the place mat in front of her handsome customer. She smiled and said, "I'll be back in a few minutes with your lobster roll. Enjoy the bisque!"

"Thanks. It looks great." Nevin watched while the waitress left to check on another of her tables. He tasted the bisque. It was fantastic: creamy, and the perfect mix of broth and mild seasonings. It contained several chunks of lobster, which, perhaps surprisingly, was a rare ingredient for most lobster bisques that weren't prepared in high-end restaurants. He savored a second spoonful as he surveyed the other customers lunching at *The Lobster Roll*. Most of them appeared to be families on holiday. A few were local businesspeople eating with colleagues. He was the only one flying solo. He flew solo a lot. He dated occasionally—mostly women he met while running errands on the weekends or exercising—but the partners at Palmer & Lodge kept him too busy to have much of a social life. He wasn't complaining, though. His assignments were almost always interesting, the pay was very good and, most important of all, working hard took his mind off the cravings—the *hunger*—that recovering drug addicts constantly fought. As Nevin knew all too well, medical experts now considered the disease of addiction to be chronic. It required long-term effort to recover, and relapse was common. Medically, addiction was more like hypertension—which required daily treatment with medication and lifestyle changes, and which often recurred—than a broken bone, which was set, healed, and was largely forgotten.

Nevin hated the thought of battling a drug addiction for the rest of his life. But he had no one to blame except himself. He, like everyone else, possessed free will. He, like everyone else, could have said "no." Unfortunately, he had said "yes" too many times. He was lucky he wasn't dead.

Then, he saw her. Then, he spied her out of the corner of his eye. She was walking down the street with a shopping bag in her hand. This vision. This angel. The young woman he hadn't gotten off his mind since he first encountered her in the drawing room of Andrew Windsor's magnificent home. He dropped his soup spoon and raced for the door.

The waitress who was serving him asked from an adjacent table, "Is everything OK?"

Nevin answered, "Yeah. I'll be right back." He yanked open the door, turned to his right, and spotted her about to cross a connecting street. He called out, "Hi! Remember me?!"

The young woman stopped and spun around. She clearly wasn't used to people beckoning her on the street. She made eye contact with Nevin and appeared to recognize him. She waited while he caught up to her. Finally, she said, "You're Mr. Windsor's lawyer, correct?"

"Correct." Nevin glanced down at the bag she was carrying. "Doing some shopping, huh?" It was a stupid question, but at least it kept the conversation going.

"Yes. I've got the afternoon off and I needed a few things."

Awkward silence filled the summer air. Tourists passed on the left and the right. A local police officer smiled and tipped his cap. Seagulls dive bombed a slice of pizza that someone had dropped on the sidewalk across the street. A shopkeeper tried to shoo the birds away.

"Do you have time for lunch? I'm eating at this really nice seafood restaurant down the block." Nevin pointed to *The Lobster Roll.*

"That's too expensive for me. Most of the restaurants in this part of town are."

"Don't worry about that. It's my treat. Besides, I'll bill it to the Windsor account."

That brought a smile to the young woman's face.

Nevin had never seen such a beautiful sight.

He held the door for her and led her to the table at which his lobster bisque had grown cold. He signaled for the waitress.

The waitress hurried over. She brought a second menu and handed it to the lovely young woman who had joined her handsome customer. The waitress said to the young woman, "Would you like a cup of lobster bisque too?"

The young woman said, "Yes, please." She had never tried lobster bisque, but she had overheard the Windsors say how wonderful it was. She looked over at Nevin.

Nevin was already looking at her. In fact, he hadn't taken his eyes off her since he spotted her on the street. He said, "I still don't know your name."

She blushed. "Catina... Catina Cruz."

Nevin extended his hand to make her formal introduction.

Catina placed her hand in Nevin's.

Her hand was soft and warm. A tingled raced through Nevin's

body. He forgot what he was going to say next. He settled for, "I'm Nevin Montgomery. It's nice to meet you, Catina."

It was more than nice.

She said, "You, too."

"Is 'Cruz' Hispanic?"

"Portuguese. I'm from New Bedford—the whaling capital of New England."

"I went on a whale watch there last summer. It was great."

"It's OK. A lot of people are out of work, though. More than in the rest of the country, I think."

The waitress appeared with Catina's lobster bisque. She also brought Nevin a fresh bowl. She removed the cold bowl and said, "Bisque tastes terrible when it's cold."

Nevin said, "Thanks."

The waitress said, "You two certainly would make beautiful babies."

Catina blushed again.

Nevin smiled and considered the possibility. He was coming to an age where settling down and raising a family were not unreasonable expectations. His mother certainly had those expectations of him. But he also knew that he had learned Catina's name only a few moments earlier. Lust was not a strong foundation on which to start a family, and at this point that was all Nevin could honestly say he felt for Catina. He decided it would be best to change the subject. "How long have you been working for the Windsors?"

"About two years."

"What were you doing before that?"

"Going to high school."

Nevin straightened in his chair. "High school?… How old are you?"

"Tw—Twenty." Catina didn't bother to tell Nevin that she had dropped out of high school. She also didn't tell him her real age. "How about you? How old are you? Where are you from?"

"I'm twenty-seven. I grew up in Dorchester."

"Dorchester?… Dorchester makes New Bedford look like Paris."

They both laughed.

Neither had been to Paris.

Nevin asked, "Do you like working for the Windsors?"

Catina answered, "Sometimes. The compound is beautiful and there are usually lots of interesting people around, but I just do grunt work for them. You know, cleaning, running errands. Stuff like that."

She left out the part about sleeping with James Windsor.

Nevin said, "As my parents always told me when I was a kid, there's pride in a hard day's work."

"Do they still say that now that you're a lawyer?"

Nevin shook his head and smiled. "How original: a lawyer joke." He finished his bisque. "How did you land a job working for the Windsors when you were living in New Bedford?"

"Mrs. Windsor—Andrew Windsor's daughter-in-law, not his wife—saw my picture in the newspaper."

"Why was your picture in the paper?"

"I won an equestrian competition here on the Cape."

"Why would that make the Windsors want to hire you?"

Catina grew quiet. She stirred her bisque. She took a sip of water. She finally said, "I don't know. You'll have to ask them that question. All I know is that my mom thought it would be a good opportunity for me. You know, it would get me out of New Bedford and I'd be working for someone really famous who had really famous friends. Frankly, we were shocked when they called."

"I, for one, am glad they did."

"Why's that?"

"Because I wouldn't have met you otherwise."

CHAPTER 12

The evening sky was aglow with ribbons of white light set against a new moon. The ocean that bordered the Windsor compound had become a reflecting pool of dancing colors. Claps and crashes of waves echoed in the distance. Wolves issued warning cries to the creatures of the night.

A nor'easter was on its way.

Nevin Montgomery closed the curtains and returned to his books and papers. He had been instructed to help Andrew Windsor redraft his testamentary documents and he was bound and determined to do precisely that. Of course, he would need to meet with Mr. Windsor for more than ten minutes to accomplish his task. But, he knew, eventually he would be allowed to see Mr. Windsor for a sustained period of time. Nevin also knew that he needed to be fully prepared when he did because his next meeting with his client would likely be his last.

Nevin had drafted wills before, but never a trust. There were a number of different types of trusts. But all types were required to contain four basic components: (1) someone must create the trust; (2) some other person or entity must agree to hold money and/or property for the benefit of someone else; (3) some money and/or property must be held by the trustee for the benefit of someone else; and (4) someone else must benefit from the trust.

Because all types of trusts had the same four basic components, the only distinguishing features were the manner in which they were created and the purpose for which they were created. It was these distinguishing features that allowed lawyers to differentiate the various types of trusts that existed. With respect to Andrew Windsor's existing trust, that was created by his Last Will and Testament, which meant that it could become effective only at his death. He was free to amend it until he died, and Bart Lodge had informed Nevin that was what Mr. Windsor intended to do.

A quick perusal of Windsor's trust document revealed that he had created what was called a "Dynasty Trust," which was designed to last beyond the time permitted by the Rule against Perpetuities (generally, the lifetime of any beneficiary living at the time of the creation of the trust, plus twenty-one years). Dynasty Trusts were often designed to last forever, with generation after generation receiving distributions from the trust. That, for example, explained why Tommy Kearney could live like a king on a U.S. senator's salary: his great-grandfather, Carrick Kearney, had established a Dynasty Trust after making a fortune importing Irish whiskey from County Louth in the northeastern corner of the Emerald Isle.

Mr. Windsor's existing trust contained an additional provision that directed a portion of his assets—twenty percent of his wealth, to be precise—into a "Marital Trust" for his wife's benefit. His children and grandchildren were happy about the Dynasty Trust provision, and his wife was happy about the Marital Trust provision, although she undoubtedly would have preferred that one hundred percent of her husband's wealth be bequeathed to her.

Nevin heard his smartphone ring. He pushed aside newspapers, clothing, and other clutter in a frantic quest to locate the device. It was underneath the Sports section of the morning's *Boston Globe*. He answered it in the middle of the third chorus of his ring tone, a tinny recording of Aerosmith's classic rendition of the Tiny Bradshaw song *Train Kept A-Rollin'*. Seemingly every son of Boston, no matter what age or ethnicity, was an Aerosmith fan.

"Hello," Nevin said.

"Nevin?"

"Yes."

"This is Joshua Jones."

Nevin's head started to throb. Shit, he said to himself. Not that asshole. Aloud to Jones: "Good evening, Joshua. Is everything OK at the office?"

"Everything's fine here. I'm calling to see how things are going there."

Nevin hesitated. He didn't know how to respond. He didn't trust Jones. Besides, Jones wasn't the partner in charge of the Windsor file. Bart Lodge was.

Jones said, "Nevin? Can you hear me?" Jones sounded like an old *Verizon Wireless* commercial featuring that regular joe in the black horn-rimmed glasses.

"Yes, I can hear you. I'm just wondering why Bart didn't call me. Isn't Andrew Windsor his client?"

"Mr. Windsor is *the firm's* client. Bart is technically the partner in charge of the file, but every partner at the firm is responsible for every client in the firm. Didn't we teach you that during orientation?"

Jones's crack about "orientation" was a predictable attempt by a petty partner to remind a young associate who was whom in the pecking order at Palmer & Lodge.

But Nevin resisted the urge to reply in kind. Instead, he said, "All things considered, things are going well."

"'All things considered'? What does that mean?"

"That Mr. Windsor is ill and I haven't been able to meet with him yet."

"You've been there for several days now. What on earth have you been doing?"

"I've been doing what Bart told me to do: wait patiently and prepare." Nevin paused, and then added, "I'm still billing, though."

Jones apparently didn't get the joke. He said, "How much longer do you plan to wait?"

"Not much longer. In fact, I was re-reading Mr. Windsor's trust document when you called. I hope to discuss it with him first thing in the morning."

Silence from Jones's end of the line.

Jones finally said, "Let me know how it goes. It goes without saying that we can't afford to screw up Mr. Windsor's testamentary documents."

It goes without saying? Nevin said to himself. Why did you say it then? Aloud to Jones: "OK." He counted to ten. "Is there anything else? If not, I need to get back to reviewing Mr. Windsor's documents."

"Just keep me posted, is all. And feel free to give me a call if anything comes up that you don't feel prepared to handle."

"Will do. Bye." Nevin tossed his smartphone onto the table. He picked it up again and tapped the OFFICE icon in his contacts list.

"Good evening, Palmer & Lodge," a cheerful voice said.

"Hi, Jill. It's Nevin Montgomery. Can you put me through to Mr. Lodge, please?"

Jill was the after-hours receptionist.

"Hi, Nevin. I hope you're having fun on the Cape. I'll buzz Peggy."

Peggy was Lodge's administrative assistant.

"Bartholomew Lodge's office. This is Peggy. May I help you?"

"Hi, Peggy. This is Nevin. Is the boss in?"

"Hi, Nevin. Yes, he's in, although I think he's on his way out to meet his wife for a late supper in the North End. I'll put you right through."

Nevin listened to thirty seconds of Muzak. Then he heard: "Hello, Nevin. How are things going with Andrew Windsor?"

Nevin said, "I'm going to try to meet with him again in the morning. I'm calling because I just got off the phone with Joshua Jones."

"Oh. About what?"

"About Andrew Windsor."

Lodge chuckled.

Nevin couldn't tell whether Lodge was amused or exasperated.

Lodge said, "I'm disappointed but not surprised. Joshua has been trying to convince me for months to let him take over as lead partner on the Windsor file. He likes to make it sound like he would be doing me a favor because of how busy I am, but it's a transparently opportunistic move on his part. Andrew Windsor is rich and famous. Joshua is ambitious. One plus one has always equaled three for Joshua, and he is invariably the three."

"I'm sorry to hear that. What do you want me to do?"

"Keep doing what you're doing. You're doing a fine job."

"But I haven't spent more than ten minutes with Mr. Windsor, and there's no guarantee that I'll get to spend time with him in the morning either. That seems far from 'fine' to me."

Lodge chuckled again.

This time Nevin could tell it was a good sign.

"I've known Andrew Windsor for thirty years, Nevin. More importantly, I've known Lauren Windsor for thirty years. I know how protective she is of him. I also know how protective she is of their money. Eventually, you'll get the time you need with him to update his testamentary documents. As you know, I drafted his existing documents. What you're describing in terms of barriers to access is no different than what I faced thirty years ago. Hang in there, and keep trying. That's what I did. And that's all the partners can expect you to do."

"Including Joshua Jones?"

"Well, maybe not Joshua. But let me worry about him. I've been doing that for years."

CHAPTER 13

Bartholomew Lodge had informed Nevin Montgomery that most artists were nocturnal animals and that Andrew Windsor was no exception. Consequently, Nevin thought it best to wait until after lunch to try to meet with Mr. Windsor. In the meantime, he decided to visit the Barnstable Point Museum, which was home to three generations of art by the Windsor family. Andrew, being the most successful artist in the family, was the featured attraction.

The Barnstable Point Museum was located in a converted nineteenth century boathouse. The glass-walled lobby overlooked Cape Cod Bay and the rolling countryside that inspired many of Andrew Windsor's best-known paintings. The museum was surrounded by beautifully maintained wildflower and native plant gardens. A groundskeeper smiled as Nevin strode up the rocky steps to the entrance. "Enjoy your visit," the groundskeeper said, waving a soiled glove.

Nevin said that he would and entered the building.

He was greeted by a docent, who cheerfully informed the young visitor that admission was free on Wednesdays. The docent was attired in a blue blazer and tan khaki pants. He had a full head of white hair and a pencil thin mustache. His skin was bronzed by the summer sun. He appeared to be in his late-sixties.

Nevin asked, "Is today Wednesday?"

The docent chuckled and answered, "Yes."

"Then it's my lucky day."

"Would you care for a guided tour? Those are free on Wednesdays also."

"Absolutely."

The docent smiled. "Follow me." His arm swept through the expansive corridor that led to the exhibition rooms. "How much do you know about art?"

"I know that Leonardo Da Vinci painted the Mona Lisa and that Michelangelo painted the Sistine Chapel. That's about it, though."

"So you don't know much about American art?"

"I know that Andrew Windsor is a famous American artist, but I only know that because of work."

"What kind of work do you do?"

"I'm a lawyer. I'm in town to go over some documents with Mr. Windsor."

"Don't tell me: you're killing time because Mrs. Windsor is making it difficult for you to see Mr. Windsor, right?"

"Right. How did you know?"

"Because I know Mrs. Windsor." The docent motioned to a couple of other museum staff members within earshot. "We all know Mrs. Windsor."

The other staff members nodded and smiled.

Nevin returned their smiles. "At least I'll learn something while I wait. Lead the way."

The docent said, "Let's start with his seascapes. That's what Mr. Windsor is most famous for." He led Nevin into a large room in which a dozen of Andrew Windsor's seascapes hung. "A number of his best were purchased by other museums or private collectors."

Nevin surveyed the room. "Yours are beautiful too.... All of them. I especially like the one in the corner. I love how dramatic it is."

"You have fine taste, young man. That's my favorite too. It's called *A Storm in March*. Mr. Windsor painted it about ten years ago. He's had many offers for it, but he says this one isn't for sale."

"Well, I'm sure I couldn't afford it anyway."

Nevin and the docent laughed.

Nevin moved from one painting to the next. *Ocean at Morning, Waves and Rocks, Seagulls on the Horizon…* Nevin now understood why Joshua Jones, as ambitious and calculating as he obviously was, had called for an update: an artist such as Andrew Windsor came along only once in a lifetime and Palmer & Lodge couldn't afford to screw up his estate plan.

Nevin asked, "Are these oil paintings?"

The docent answered, "Yes. But Mr. Windsor is even more renowned for his tempera."

"His what?"

"His tempera paintings."

"What are those?"

"Tempera paintings are when the artist mixes color pigment with egg yolk. Egg tempera was a primary method of painting until after 1500 when it was superseded by the invention of oil painting. Mr. Windsor prefers tempera, though. It lasts a long time—examples from the first century A.D. still exist—and it allows for great precision when used with traditional approaches that require the application of numerous small brush strokes applied in a cross-hatching technique. When it's dry, it produces a smooth matte finish. Tempera colors don't change over time, whereas oil paints darken, yellow, and become transparent with age. On the downside, because tempera cannot be applied in thick layers like oil paints can, tempera paintings rarely have the deep color saturation that oil paintings can achieve. The colors of an unvarnished tempera painting resemble a pastel, although the color deepens if a varnish is applied."

"Can we see a few?"

"Absolutely."

The docent was clearly delighted by Nevin's interest in Andrew Windsor's art. He led Nevin into a room in which several of Windsor's most recent temperas hung.

The docent continued, "We're now in Exhibition Room 3. The first painting on the right is called *The Old Barn*."

Nevin said, "I passed it on the walk over." He studied the painting. "It's wonderful. I can actually see the grain in the wood."

"That's because of the tempera, and because of Mr. Windsor's attention to detail."

Nevin examined each of Windsor's recent tempera paintings. When he reached the sixth one he said, "Is this Hannah Burgoff?"

"Yes."

"She's not that pretty. It's a great painting, but Gisele Bündchen she ain't."

"She didn't need to be. As Rembrandt famously said, a great model isn't always beautiful in the classic sense of that word. Instead, she's comfortable with herself and capable of promoting her spirit. Mr. Windsor obviously felt that Hannah fit the bill."

Nevin concentrated on the painting for several minutes. Hannah was sitting on a plain wooden stool in the old barn that was featured in the previous paintings. "Mr. Windsor was right. It's difficult to take my eyes off her."

"It's too bad she passed away."

Nevin and the docent grew quiet as they considered the paintings of the recently deceased model and wondered how she had died.

Nevin thanked the docent for the tour, deposited a ten dollar bill into the museum's donations jar, and exited the building. He had received his culture fix for the year. The only other museum that Nevin could remember visiting was the Museum of Fine Arts in Boston, and that had been as part of a high school field trip. At least he *thought* he had visited it: he and his buddies had sniffed enough glue on the bus ride into the city that he didn't remember whether they had ditched the class at the entrance to make some mischief on their own. But like so many things Nevin had missed out on in his youth, he now planned on going to museums more often. He was surprised by how much he enjoyed the Barnstable Point Museum.

"Mr. Montgomery?"

Nevin stopped and turned around. Deputy Sheriff John Steele was exiting his squad car in a rush. Nevin waited for him. "Good afternoon, Deputy Steele."

"Good afternoon. Do you have a few minutes?"

"Sure. Any news on who might've killed Hannah Burgoff?"

Steele shook his head. "Not really. But like I said a few nights ago, we haven't ruled it a homicide yet, although I do agree that's probably what it was."

"What can I do for you?"

"Probably nothing. As you may recall, I had mentioned to everyone the night of the incident that I might have some more questions for folks and I've been meeting with people ever since." Steele gestured towards the museum. "I saw you leaving the museum so I thought now might be a good time to talk to you. Is now OK?"

"Now's fine."

Steele retrieved an iPad-mini from the passenger's seat of his squad car. "I uploaded my notes onto this." He showed it to Nevin. "The department just got about five or six of these fancy things. The new sheriff thinks they'll make us more efficient. Personally, I prefer pen and paper."

Nevin said, "Me, too. Even though it's a mini, it's not small enough to fit in your pocket."

Steele read aloud what Nevin had reported the night of the incident: that Nevin had heard some noise while he was sleeping and that he had been awoken by the flashing lights of the ambulance.

Steele then said, "Anything else?"

Nevin searched his memory. "No—other than that Mrs. Windsor is making it very difficult for me to meet with her husband about his testamentary documents."

Steele made a note of that in his iPad. "She wasn't too happy about my wanting to meet with him either. But I'm willing to give her the benefit of the doubt at the moment because Mr. Windsor isn't well. Perhaps you should do the same."

"I am. That's why I toured the museum today: to give Mr. Windsor time to regain his strength. I'm going to try again in a few minutes, though."

"Then I'll wait until tomorrow. I was on my way to try to see him when I spotted you. I think one visitor for the day is plenty. And I suspect you need to return to Boston at some point in the near future. Besides, I still have a couple other folks to interview in the meantime."

CHAPTER 14

James Windsor was painting angrily. He was known for that—for what critics sometimes referred to as the "ferocity of his brush strokes." But today he was angrier than usual. He had just returned from a board meeting at the Barnstable Point Museum during which he had noticed that none of his work was on display. When he had inquired about it, the director had said that it was "only temporary" and that the museum needed the space to showcase James's father's Hannah paintings. "The phone has been ringing off the hook about Hannah," the director had said. "As you probably know, the *Boston Globe* published a long article on the front page of the Arts section yesterday about the paintings and we've been receiving one call after another about them ever since. I'm getting calls on my cell phone about them, for gosh sake." The director had paused, and then added, "The museum is proud of your work, James, and it will be on display again soon. I promise."

The director's last remark hadn't satisfied James. He had stormed out of the board meeting vowing to "reconsider his affiliation with Barnstable Point." The problem for James, however, was that it had been more than twenty years since any museum in the country had been willing to exhibit his work by itself. It was always required to be part of a Windsor family exhibit, with James's father's work receiving pride of place.

Indeed, art critics were almost uniformly caustic in their evaluations of James's work. The *New York Times* had referred to his debut show twenty-five years ago as "pedestrian" and "derivative of his father's, but without his father's sensitivity and subtlety." The *Boston Globe* had said that the only reason that James Windsor's art received any attention at all was because of "who his father and grandfather were: icons of American art. But they deserved the attention they received. They had talent."

Although James had never said so publicly, the harsh criticism of his work had led him to many unhealthy habits, not the least of which were that he drank too much and that he fooled around with too many young women. His mother was broken hearted about it, but all she had been able to do was watch the train fall off the tracks.

"Hold still," James said, returning his attention to the task at hand. "The painting won't work if you keep moving around. I've told you that before."

Catina Cruz apologized and promised to do better. She needed to scratch an itch but was too afraid to do so.

James dipped his brush into his well-worn palette—a gift from his grandfather—and finished painting Catina's hair. Her hair was as black as a crow's feathers and he had no trouble finding a color to match. The tricky part was to portray the silky texture and thickness in a natural fashion. His father was a master at that. The son always struggled with it, although he never admitted it. Next, he painted her face. The key here was to suggest how clear and soft her skin was. As James aged, he had come to realize that what made younger people so attractive was the suppleness and freshness of their skin. When he was in his teens and twenties, this had never occurred to him because he was surrounded by people of his own age every day at school. But now that his encounters with youth were limited almost exclusively to those who modeled for him, he realized it. And as an artist, he was obsessed with it.

James said, "Remember that no one knows I'm painting you, and I want to keep it that way for a while." He paused for a moment and glanced over at Catina.

She said, "I remember."

Catina might have been young, but she wasn't stupid. She knew why James wanted to keep the paintings quiet for the time being: because he was hoping to make a splash with them like his father had done with the Hannah paintings. Art collectors ate up "secret" paintings, and they tended to pay a premium for them.

"Good." James returned his attention to the canvas. He began to paint Catina's cheekbones. They were high… like those of Keira Knightley, the beautiful and talented English actress.

Catina sneezed. "Sorry."

James threw down his brush. "Dammit, Catina. See what you made me do?"

Catina examined the work-in-progress.

A tan streak from the paint that James had been using for Catina's face had blotched the black paint he had used for her hair.

"Sorry," she said again. "I couldn't keep it in."

"You should've tried harder. It's gonna take me hours to correct the damage." James studied his watch. "My wife will be home in about ninety minutes. We don't have much time."

Catina knew that James wasn't talking about the "time" he needed to finish the painting. "I—I don't feel well. Can I head back to my room now?"

James wiped his hands on the towel on his workbench. He walked the four short steps to where Catina was sitting. He said, "No."

***

Catina Cruz gathered her clothes from the floor of James Windsor's studio, dressed in a rush, and sprinted from the room. She didn't bother to say goodbye to James, but he didn't seem to mind. He had gotten what he wanted. He always did.

Catina squinted from the sun when she made it outdoors. James illuminated his studio by candlelight alone, and it took Catina's eyes a few moments to adjust to the daylight. One of the groundskeepers waved at her and asked how she was doing. She knew that he was merely being polite. All she said was, "Fine."

She wasn't "fine," though. She hadn't been "fine" in a while. She couldn't remember the last time she was actually "fine." She headed for her bedroom in the back of Andrew Windsor's house so that she could try to make herself feel better, at least temporarily.

Her room was small, but neat. If working as a housekeeper for the past two years had taught her anything, it was how to make a room neat. Her bed—one half of a twin set—would have passed inspection at the Naval Academy and the small desk in front of the one window in the room didn't have a pen or piece of paper out of place. She had a small bouquet of wildflowers that she had picked on an early morning walk displayed in a glass vase on the nightstand next to her bed. A poster of a New Bedford whale watching expedition hung above the headboard, and another poster—this one of Robert Pattinson, her celebrity crush—was displayed next to the door.

Catina sat on her bed and stared out the window. She felt nauseous, as she usually did after having sex with James. When was it going to stop? she said to herself. He was getting more demanding each time… making her do things she didn't know how to do.

She considered calling her mother. She decided against it because she knew that her mother either wouldn't believe that James Windsor had been taking advantage of her or wouldn't care if she did believe it. Sadly, Catina's mother was a testament to the adage that just because someone was physically capable of bearing children didn't mean they should. Jerry Springer and Maury Povich had enjoyed lengthy television careers as a result of this cultural phenomenon.

Catina thought about who else she might call. She couldn't think of anybody, which made her more sad than she already was. It was lonely not having any friends—she couldn't remember the last time she had a *real* friend—and it was also unhealthy. No woman was an island, as the saying went.

So, she sought comfort where she too often did: in bath salts.

But these weren't the bath salts that wealthy women sprinkled into a warm tub to relax after a hard day of shopping or lunch engagements. Rather, they were the synthetic drug that Catina removed from her tee shirt drawer that contained substituted cathinones, which had effects similar to amphetamines and cocaine. They resembled bathing products such as Epsom salts, which explained the street name. And they were inexpensive—about twenty-five dollars per fifty milligram packet—which was how Catina could afford to purchase them.

Bath salts were swallowed, snorted, smoked, or injected. The typical dose was between five and twenty milligrams. The use of bath salts in the United States had increased dramatically in recent years, in large part because of their widespread availability, cheap price, and sensationalist media coverage. Catina had been introduced to them at a New Bedford nightclub when she had gone home for Thanksgiving. She had ended up having sex with the guy who had given them to her, and he had also told her where she could buy them when she returned to the Cape. She was grateful that she had purchased a bag at the local tattoo parlor the previous week. She needed something to take the edge off… something to help her forget what James Windsor had made her do.

The most intense high was experienced when the bath salts were injected, but Catina was afraid of needles. She didn't like the taste when she swallowed bath salts, and she didn't like the attention that smoking them generated. She preferred to snort them. She poured about ten milligrams onto the back of the *People* magazine she had bought at the grocery store and rolled a dollar bill into a tight tube. She arranged the powder into three symmetrical lines and inhaled each in rapid succession. She sat back on her bed. She began to feel strong—one hundred

Scott Douglas Gerber

and eighty degrees the opposite of how James always made her feel—and she also started tearing off her clothes and pulling on her hair.

At that precise moment, her smartphone rang.

PART II

The Artist's Palette

"Art is made to disturb. Science reassures. There is only one thing valuable in art: the thing you cannot explain."
—Georges Braque

CHAPTER 15

Deputy Sheriff John Steele maneuvered his squad car down the gravel road that led to Andrew Windsor's magnificent compound on the northern tip of Barnstable Harbor. A soft breeze scented the air with a mélange of salt, sand, and sea. Gray and white gulls glided through the wind, their black-tipped wings changing their flight path like a sailboat's rudder across an ocean current. The gulls' harsh wails sounded in the sky and signaled to the flock that it was time to feed. One particularly enthusiastic gull took that as a cue to nosedive to the ground about ten yards in front of Steele's car to intercept and consume a field mouse who was too startled and slow to avoid the inevitable.

As a lifelong resident of Cape Cod, John Steele had witnessed all of this before. His boyhood summers were spent at the beach where gulls frequently outnumbered people and where he was taught at an early age how to shield food and drink from the kleptoparasitic scavengers. Steele had killed his fair share of gulls in rock throwing competitions with his childhood buddies. He wasn't proud of that fact. As a father to three kids of his own, he counseled his children against it and punished them when they disobeyed.

Steele parked in the circular driveway in front of Andrew Windsor's house. He was greeted at the door by the same butler who used to greet his father when his father was a deputy sheriff.

The butler said, "Good afternoon, Deputy. How's your father enjoying his retirement?"

Steele smiled. "He says he's bored and that he'd like to return to work. But my mom says she's never seen him happier or more relaxed. His golf game certainly has improved. He spanked me by ten strokes the last time we played."

The butler chuckled. "I'm glad to hear it. Please give him my best." He stepped to the side so that Deputy Steele could enter the house. "I'll let Mr. Windsor know that you're here."

"Thank you. But before I speak with Mr. Windsor, may I see his studio? You mentioned when we spoke on the telephone earlier that Mr. Windsor said that would be OK."

"Certainly. Please follow me."

The sheriff's department's forensics unit had thoroughly examined Andrew Windsor's studio the morning after Hannah Burgoff had been discovered dead. However, John Steele wanted to get a sense of the room for himself. Steele was impressed by the scientific advances that had been achieved in law enforcement in recent years, but he was old enough to trust his instincts as well. Police work was like golf in this respect: some players were successful because they had wonderful technique, while others flourished as "feel" players. Steele was a feel player.

The butler said, "Take as much time as you need."

Steele said, "Thanks."

The butler exited.

Steele began to explore the studio. He was certainly no art expert, but he had lived in Barnstable County all of his life and he knew that he was standing in the present day's most distinguished artist's studio. The first thing he noticed was how messy it was. Dried out brushes, soiled rags, and broken canvases were strewn all around the room. The next thing he noticed was that there were no finished paintings hanging on the walls. He wasn't sure why that was. He knew that most artists were egomaniacs and tended to surround themselves with their own self-proclaimed "masterpieces." He also had passed about a dozen pieces of Andrew Windsor's art hanging on the walls throughout the rest of the house. Perhaps Mr. Windsor had been incapacitated for longer than Steele was aware? Steele made a mental note to inquire about it. If Windsor had been seriously ill for an extended period of time that would have made it highly unlikely that he could have killed Hannah Burgoff. Good detective work was largely about *eliminating* potential suspects. Agatha Christie had made a fortune as a result of that thesis. John Steele had made a career out of implementing it.

Steele strode around the room not knowing what he might find or what he was looking for. In addition to eliminating possibilities, good detective work also involved being open to *un-imagined* possibilities. He had solved many a previous case by uncovering evidence that had never occurred to him until he stumbled upon it. For example, he had caught the killer of a college co-ed five years earlier by discovering a used condom stuffed into a discarded *Coke* can that was tossed into a dumpster near the parking lot at Hyannis Beach, and he had been able to locate a missing child after spotting a book of matches from a Provincetown motel on the ground of the Osterville playground from which the child had been abducted.

Steele studied every square inch of the room, which had remained closed to everyone not involved with the police investigation from the moment that Steele had first arrived at the scene four days earlier. Nothing seemed unusual or out of place, with the notable exception of the bright yellow police tape fastened across the entrance to the room. Paint cans, both opened and unopened: check... par for the course in an artist's studio. Old bed sheets splotched with a rainbow of colors from a flurry of brush strokes: ditto. Empty coffee cups and soda bottles piled into a wastebasket next to an easel: nothing unusual about that. Working artists needed to quench their thirst too.

But then Steele noticed something he hadn't anticipated: Every one of the broken canvases that littered Andrew Windsor's studio—Steele counted ten of them, which seemed like a lot—were, what appeared to Steele at least, *completed* portraits of Hannah Burgoff. Steele was realistic enough to understand that artists, with their tendencies towards perfectionism and childish temper tantrums, might occasionally destroy a particular work-in-progress in a fit of pique. However, these didn't seem like works-in-progress: they were, as far as Steele could tell, finished and wonderful. Mr. Windsor might have been seriously ill, but Steele had received no report from any credible source—from any source at all—that he was also mentally unhinged. And only someone who was emotionally unstable would destroy ten beautiful works of art that were probably worth a million dollars each.

Steele slipped on a pair of rubber gloves to protect the integrity of the crime scene. He bent down to more closely examine the mangled paintings. The first was a traditional portrait of a younger Hannah Burgoff, which confirmed to Steele's otherwise untrained eye for art that the decimated paintings were *completed* works. He estimated that the painting had been done about twenty years earlier. Hannah was seated on a tall wooden stool near the window at the north end of Windsor's studio: the window that overlooked Cape Cod Bay. The painting was as much about the harsh beauty of the Cape—white-capped waves crashing against jagged rocks served as the backdrop to the portrait itself—as it was about the then thirty-ish year old model. The younger Hannah was interesting looking, but certainly not beautiful in the classic sense of the word. Her face was softened by the twenty or so extra pounds she apparently weighed at the time and her bosom—highlighted by the artist via the simple technique of unfastening several buttons more than social convention would deem appropriate if this had been anything other than a portrait—was more voluptuous as a result. Her wistful smile and vacant eyes suggested a distance between artist and model that added to the mystery of the work, and that made the work nothing short of magnificent.

In the next portrait, Hannah was standing on the beach in the winter. A decade appeared to have elapsed: Hannah's skin had lost some of the elasticity of youth and her features weren't as sharp as they were in the first portrait. But the distance between artist and model remained. In fact, distance—remoteness, distrust—permeated all of the paintings that had somehow been vandalized by an as-yet-unidentified person or persons.

Steele stood to his feet and walked to the window. He scratched an itch on his nose. A fading sun hung low on the horizon and teamed with a series of gray clouds to announce the coming of an afternoon storm. Pitch pines rustled in a gusting wind, while the gaggle of gulls that had welcomed Steele to the Windsor compound continued to circle high above in search of prey.

It was a scene that only Andrew Windsor could have done justice.

CHAPTER 16

The butler was waiting for Steele when Steele exited Andrew Windsor's studio. The butler asked, "Did you find what you need?"

Steele answered, "I'm not sure, to be honest about it. But thanks for letting me look around. Is it still OK if I talk to Mr. Windsor?"

"Absolutely. He's expecting you."

The butler knocked on Andrew Windsor's bedroom door and announced that Deputy Sheriff John Steele had arrived to ask him a few questions.

Windsor sat up in his bed and waved Steele into the room.

The butler left the two men to speak in private.

Steele said, "Thank you for agreeing to meet with me, Mr. Windsor. I appreciate it. This shouldn't take long. I know you need your rest."

Windsor said, "Take as long as you need. I'm torn up about Hannah's death. I'll help in any way I can."

"Thank you." Steele typed a quick note on his iPad about how softly Andrew Windsor was speaking and about how frail he looked. "Are you feeling any better?"

"A bit, I suppose. But let me give you a piece of advice, Deputy Steele: Never get old. It's no fun. You always feel like garbage and you can't do what you used to do."

"Including paint?"

Windsor gazed out the window for a long moment. The nor'easter that had been brewing all morning had finally arrived in all its glory. "Yes," he finally said. "When I was young like you, and a storm like this hit, I would place my easel next to the window and paint until my fingers blistered." The great artist paused and shook his head. "Now my fingers are too crippled with arthritis to hold a brush for more than a few minutes at a time. As I said before, Deputy: Don't get old."

Steele flashed a sympathetic smile. "I'll make a note of it. I say the same thing to my kids when my back stiffens up after chasing them around the yard playing soccer."

Steele did make another note, but it wasn't about Mr. Windsor's advice not to grow old. It was that Windsor couldn't possibly have killed Hannah Burgoff. He was too sick and weak to have done so.

Lauren Windsor entered the room. Her hair was pulled into a top-knot, her clothes were straight from the pages of *Vogue* magazine, and her perfume smelled as sweet as spring flowers. In short, unlike her husband, she was the epitome of vibrancy.

She walked to the bed, bent at the waist, and kissed her husband on the cheek. She combed his thinning white hair with her fingers. "How are things going in here? Do you boys need anything?"

Andrew Windsor said, "I'm fine, Lauren. But perhaps Deputy Steele would like a cup of coffee or a glass of water or cola."

Mrs. Windsor turned to Steele. "Would you like something to drink?"

"No thank you, ma'am. I'm fine. Besides, I don't want to overstay my welcome. Mr. Windsor was kind enough to give me a few minutes and I should repay that courtesy by letting him get some rest."

Mrs. Windsor said, "I appreciate that, Deputy. I really do. I'll show you out."

Steele thanked Andrew Windsor for his time and followed Lauren Windsor out of the bedroom.

Steele said, "I have to admit I was a little star struck in there."

Mrs. Windsor said, "You had never met Andrew before? I thought you were Ronnie Steele's son?"

Steele made a note—only a mental note for the moment—that Mrs. Windsor obviously had inquired about his background before he met with her husband. Aloud to Mrs. Windsor: "I am. My dad mentioned that he had met Mr. Windsor at a couple of local fundraisers when he was a deputy sheriff, but I never had. I remember seeing him from a distance once, but I wasn't brave enough to introduce myself to him. I figured that he got more than his share of interruptions as it was and that I didn't need to add to it." Steele held the door for Mrs. Windsor when they reached the point in the large house where the private living quarters ended and the more communal spaces began. "I don't know anything about art, but even I know how famous Mr. Windsor is. How could I not? As you mentioned, I grew up around here."

"If you think my husband has charisma now—and he does—you should've seen him when he was at the height of his creative powers."

"What was he like?"

Lauren Windsor paused, clearly trying to come up with a word or a phrase that would do her husband justice. She chose: "Beautiful.... At its core, art is about beauty. My husband was beautiful. I don't mean beautiful in the physical sense of the word. He wasn't Warren Beatty, who was the Ryan Gosling of our day. He wasn't pretty. But he was a force of nature. He was a force of nature like his paintings are forces of nature. Many of my husband's most beautiful paintings, as I assume you've noticed, are about the harsh beauty of the natural world: waves crashing against rocks; rainstorms ravishing trees; snow coating fields; hawks feeding on mice. Andrew was a lot like that when we were younger."

Steele nodded. "I can still see some of it now."

"'Some,' maybe. But only *some.* It's been a long time since I've seen the man I married."

Steele made another quick note—formal, this time—about how much Mrs. Windsor was reporting that Mr. Windsor had deteriorated over the years. "How long is a 'long time'?"

Lauren Windsor straightened one of her husband's paintings that had been hanging crookedly on the wall in the hallway. "It's difficult to say. It's been a gradual process."

"Approximately. I don't need an exact date."

"About five years, give or take."

"Did anything trigger it? Or was it simply part of the aging process that we all eventually experience?"

"A bit of both, I suppose. Believe me, I've lost a step or two as well." Mrs. Windsor's eyes met those of John Steele.

Steele could only imagine how beautiful—how *pretty*—Lauren Windsor must have been when she had first met Andrew Windsor more than fifty years prior. She remained beautiful to this day.

Mrs. Windsor continued, "But I really started to notice a change in Andrew when Sara died."

Steele nodded to signal his condolences. He was a father himself and could only imagine the grief that Mr. and Mrs. Windsor must have felt when their daughter had been killed in a car accident.

Mrs. Windsor adjusted another painting. "Losing Sara would have been difficult for Andrew under any circumstances, obviously. It's been difficult for me too... again, obviously. But he blames himself for her death."

Steele looked puzzled. "Why on earth would he blame himself? I thought she was killed by a drunk driver on the Mass Pike?"

"She was. But she was on her way to visit us. We hadn't seen her for a while because she was busy with work—she taught middle school math at Northfield—and Andrew begged her to come home for the long Labor Day weekend. Sara was always Daddy's little girl, so she came.... She wouldn't have come if I had asked."

Steele didn't know what to make of Mrs. Windsor's final remark. He made a note to try to learn more about Mrs. Windsor's relationship with her children and why it was apparently less than ideal.

CHAPTER 17

It was three o'clock in the afternoon by the time John Steele had finished at the home of Andrew and Lauren Windsor. He was famished. He decided to grab a quick bite at *Flo's Clam Shack*. His wife had been on a Vegan kick in recent months and Steele needed to satisfy a craving for a main course that had a parent. Of course, he wasn't planning to tell his wife about it.

Flo's Clam Shack was named that for a reason: it was a shack originally owned by a woman named Flo who specialized in fried clams. It was a favorite among locals and tourists alike. Guy Fieri had filmed a segment there two years earlier for his hit Food Network show *Diners, Drive-ins, and Dives*. Guy had been particularly impressed with the clam strips and hushpuppies. Those were Steele's favorites too.

The lunchtime rush had ended and Steele managed to find a seat without having to wait.

A middle-aged woman with a welcoming smile approached Steele's table. She said, "Look what the cat dragged in…. Does Becca know you're here?"

Becca was Steele's wife.

Steele chuckled. "Of course not. And I'd like to keep it that way."

"We'll have to see what kind of tip I get. I'm sure you know that PTA is Thursday night. Becca and I are on the fundraising committee together."

Steele sunk back into his chair. "You do know that extortion is a crime, don't you Julie? What's the owner doing waiting tables anyway?"

"One of the girls called in sick. Besides, Grandma Flo always taught me to keep my finger on the pulse of every part of the restaurant. One of the most important parts is the wait-staff."

"Sounds like good advice. How are the clam strips today?"

"Terrific, as usual."

"I'd like the lunch portion, then, please. And a cup of chowder and a *Diet Coke*."

The lunch portion was heavy enough to anchor a boat, and the cup of chowder was served in a twenty-four-ounce mug.

Julie wrote down Steele's order and headed towards the kitchen.

She said, with her back to Steele, "At least Becca will be pleased to learn that you ordered a diet soda."

Steele smiled and shook his head. This was why he loved Barnstable so much: the locals—the people who had lived and worked in the town all of their lives—were good people. And Julie Bennett was one of the best.

"Here you go." Julie Bennett placed John Steele's order on the table in front of him. "Enjoy it." She turned to leave, but stopped when she noticed who was coming through the door. "A friend of yours is here."

Steele lifted his eyes from the mountain of clam strips. Philip Joyce had entered the restaurant. Steele waved his hand in the air to capture Joyce's attention.

The young sheriff nodded and joined Steele. He said to Julie, "I'll have what he's having."

The owner/waitress went to tell the kitchen to put a rush on the sheriff's order.

Joyce said, "Any progress?"

They both knew that the sheriff was talking about the Hannah Burgoff case... what the sheriff euphemistically referred to around the office as "the unfortunate incident at the Windsor compound."

A politician always had his eye on the next election. Elections turned on fund-raising. The Windsors had contributed generously to Joyce's first campaign and he wanted to make sure they did the same during his second.

Steele, of course, realized that. He placed a forkful of clam strips into his mouth. "Some."

"What do you mean by 'some'?"

Steele finished chewing. He took a sip of *Diet Coke*. "That I spent a good two hours looking around Andrew Windsor's studio and another thirty minutes talking to Mr. Windsor himself."

"Did you learn anything?"

Steele was both surprised and impressed that Joyce hadn't snatched a clam strip or two from his plate. Jack Peterson would have bogarted a good dozen by this point. But Philip Joyce had been raised rich. Rich people had good manners. "First and foremost, that Mr. Windsor couldn't have killed Hannah Burgoff."

"Why not?"

Julie Bennett returned with Joyce's order. "Anything else, gentlemen?"

Both Steele and Joyce said no. They watched Julie hustle to another table.

Joyce repeated, "Why not?" He ate a spoonful of clam chowder.

"Because he's too frail. If Hannah Burgoff had been shot, that might not matter. It doesn't take much strength to pull a trigger. But, as you know, Steve Murdoch concluded that she was strangled. It takes strength to strangle someone, even if that someone is a forty year old woman."

Joyce had moved on to his clam strips. Steele had already finished his. "The coroner finally committed to that on the record?"

Steele shook his head. "No. But he said it to me again off the record. I've known Steve Murdoch for ten years. Believe me when I tell you that if he's willing to say that Hannah Burgoff died of strangulation before the final report is in, Hannah Burgoff died of strangulation."

Joyce pushed away his plate. He looked skeptical.

Steele continued, "Don't let looks deceive you, Philip. Steve might not look like much—he might eat at *Flo's* more often than he should—but I've never known him to guess wrong on the cause of death."

CHAPTER 18

The nor'easter that had struck like a punch from Mike Tyson in his prime had moved out to sea. Black-capped chickadees, buff-breasted sandpipers, and gray-cheeked thrushes announced the new morn. Gulls scavenged through the beach for the miscellaneous treats—half-eaten sandwiches, crumbs from potato chip bags, discarded fruit—that the violent winds had scattered from overturned trash receptacles.

Nevin Montgomery slipped on the tee shirt and running shorts that he had purchased before his memorable lunch with Catina Cruz, laced up a new pair of *Nike* cross-trainers that he had brought with him from Boston, and positioned his left leg on top of a bench facing the ocean so that he could stretch his perpetually tight left hamstring. The air smelled fresh and sweet, which was a far cry from the exhaust fumes and stench of rotting garbage that scented the streets of his boyhood neighborhood in Dorchester. Nevin still couldn't believe how far he had come in less than a decade of his work-in-progress of a life.

Nevin made it a point to stay in shape. Jogging was the most efficient way to do that for someone with a schedule as busy as his. He tried to be at his desk by 7:30 a.m., which meant that he would hit the streets of Boston for his morning run no later than 6:00 a.m. It was 6:45 at the moment, but he wasn't in Boston and he didn't have a law firm partner looking over his shoulder and expecting him to be available by 8:00 every morning for whatever last-minute fire the partner might need Nevin to try to put out.

Nevin had never jogged on the beach before and he promptly discovered that his $150 *Nikes* were more of a hindrance than a help. He removed them, tied the laces together, and draped them around his neck. He resumed his run barefooted with much better success. He could see why competitive runners liked to train on the beach: the sand was heavy and it strengthened the legs at the same time that the run itself worked the lungs. The view wasn't shabby either: waves rolling gently to the shore while a burnt orange sun began to rise in the horizon. It beat the heck out of jumping over rats that were digging through garbage in the back streets of Dorchester while an off-key chorus of car horns and random profanity sounded in the air.

Nevin quickened his pace as his legs became acclimated to the sand. He spied a second large compound about a half mile down the beach from that of Andrew Windsor. He surmised that it was the primary residence of U.S. Senator Tommy Kearney. Bart Lodge had mentioned to Nevin that Senator Kearney was Mr. Windsor's closest neighbor, and his closest friend. Senator Kearney's house was older and larger than that of Mr. Windsor. The senator's house had been in the Kearney family for three generations. It was constructed by the senator's grandfather during the Prohibition Era, allegedly with the riches his grandfather had accumulated as a bootlegger. Mr. Windsor's house, in contrast, was built by Mr. Windsor himself about thirty years earlier when his art was at the peak of its commercial appeal. Unfortunately for Mr. Windsor, his art wasn't nearly as popular now as it used to be and the upkeep on his home was beginning to reflect that fact.

A flock of gulls gathered about three hundred yards down the beach. They seemed to be taking turns dive-bombing from the sky. Nevin was curious as to why. He didn't know much about gulls, but in the four days he had spent in Barnstable this was the first time he had witnessed this synchronized behavior. The previous pattern was more random than the current one. When Nevin drew closer, he discovered why: James Windsor was pitching peanuts to the birds in a fashion that encouraged the strangely beautiful precision. It was as if James were training the gulls.

Nevin stopped running. "Hello," he said. He wiped his face with the sleeve of his tee shirt.

James didn't flinch, or acknowledge Nevin's presence.

Perhaps he didn't hear me, Nevin said to himself. He tried again, this time more loudly: "Hello."

"I heard you the first time," James said. His back remained to Nevin, and he continued to pitch peanuts to the gulls.

"They look hungry."

James ignored Nevin this time too.

Nevin repeated himself, again more loudly than the first time. "I said, they look hungry."

James finally turned in Nevin's direction. He had a smirk on his face. "Obviously." Arrogance dripped from his tongue like hot wax from a burning candle.

Nevin drew closer and tried to offer his hand in introduction. "I'm Nevin Montgomery. I'm one of your father's lawyers."

"I know who you are." James didn't bother to shake Nevin's hand. "But why are you still here? And you better not be billing us for your morning jog along the beach."

Nevin smiled and shook his head. "Believe me, I wish I were back in Boston. But as I suspect you know, your father is sick and I had to wait around for a few days before I could speak with him."

"Fuck you," James spat. "Of course I know my father is sick."

"And do you also know that the Sheriff's Office is investigating a possible homicide on your father's property and that we're all supposed to sit tight for the time being?"

"Fuck you, again. Of course I know that. Are you billing for that time too?"

"Yes," Nevin said, without a hint of embarrassment. He wiped his face a second time. "That's how it works: lawyers bill by the hour, and when we're away from the office we bill for every hour we're awake. I'm awake, in case you didn't notice. As I said, I would much rather be back in Boston, but while I'm required to be here, my law firm is going to bill my time for being here. I don't make the rules. I follow them."

"Really? You follow the rules? Does your law firm have a rule about its lawyers trying to date their client's employees?"

"I have no idea what you're talking about."

"'No idea'? Really? You had lunch with Catina because you value her opinion about the Rule against Perpetuities?"

Shit, Nevin said to himself. How does this asshole know about my lunch with Catina? How does he know about the friggin' Rule against Perpetuities? Aloud to James: "I had lunch with her because I ran into her outside of a restaurant on the waterfront and I didn't want to eat alone."

"Bullshit, Mr. Lawyer. I'm not stupid, and I'm certainly not blind. You invited Catina to lunch because she looks like a young Salma Hayek and you want to fuck her." James glanced at the pack of gulls enjoying the peanuts he had tossed to them. Not surprisingly, the largest of the gulls was eating more of the peanuts than the smaller gulls. James's eyes returned to Nevin's. "Let me tell you something else, Mr. Lawyer: Catina's a mighty good fuck. Her pussy tastes like Portuguese sweet bread."

Nevin's brows furrowed. "You're kidding, right? How old are you?"

"Closing in on fifty. But I bang like a teenager in heat, especially when I'm lying on top of a fine piece of ass like hers."

Nevin stood motionless in disbelief. A stiff breeze swept his favorite HARVARD LAW baseball cap from his head. The cap rolled end-over-end down the beach until it disappeared behind a sand dune about a hundred yards away. Nevin was too stunned to try to retrieve it. Was what James Windsor said true? Nevin asked himself. Was Catina—*twenty year old* Catina—having an affair with her fifty-ish year old boss? She didn't seem like the type, whatever "type" that might be. But, then again, Nevin was old enough to know that people often did what they shouldn't do. He was a living testament to that fact: He was raised properly… He knew that drugs were dangerous… But he had nevertheless chosen, of his own free will, to abuse drugs…. To this day, he still had the urge to get high, although he fought it every waking moment of his life.

James smirked again. "I thought lawyers had a quick comeback for everything? I guess I was wrong."

Nevin didn't say anything in reply.

CHAPTER 19

Joshua Jones exited his Beacon Hill townhouse with a copy of the morning's *Boston Globe* tucked under his arm. Most people read the newspaper at their breakfast table with a plate of eggs, a glass of juice, and a pot of coffee. Joshua Jones wasn't most people. He didn't like to waste a minute of the day. Did he read the paper? Absolutely. But he read it while he waited for the crosswalk to switch from red to green.

Jones lived on the Flat of Beacon Hill in a two-bedroom townhouse that overlooked the Charles River. The ivy-covered walls of Harvard University sat majestically on the other side of the water. Jones had spent seven years at Harvard: four in college and three in law school. Most people would have traded their left arm for the opportunity to take classes from eminent professors at the world's top-ranked university. Again, however, Jones wasn't most people. He enrolled in the classes he thought would teach him what he needed to know to get rich—his undergraduate major was finance and he overloaded in law school on courses in corporate law—rather than those that the other students considered interesting. To mention but one example, Jones didn't take a single liberal arts course in his four years as an undergraduate. Every Harvard student was required to take at least two such courses—Introduction to American Literature, Metaphysics, Western Civilization, and so on—but Jones had managed to secure an exemption from that requirement thanks in large part to a telephone call from his grandfather to the Dean of the College of Arts and Sciences. Of course, Jones's grandfather was no ordinary grandfather. He happened to serve on the Harvard Corporation, which was the governing body of the university. The Arts and Sciences dean was, therefore, more than willing to accommodate Jones's grandfather's request.

Jones waited at the crosswalk at the corner of Cedar and Charles Streets. He studied the morning's headlines. The stock market had hit another record high the day before, the lead article trumpeted. That was terrific news for Jones because that meant that both he and most of his clients had made a lot of money yesterday. The next headline wasn't as encouraging: the U.S. Department of Labor's most recent jobs report revealed that the nation's unemployment rate remained at a problematic 8.5%. The *Boston Globe*'s chief economics correspondent likewise pointed out that the unemployment rate in Massachusetts had increased .2% for the quarter to 9.1%. Although the correspondent didn't break down the state statistics by jobs category, the managing partner at Palmer & Lodge had indicated at the most recent partners meeting that the unemployment rate for lawyers in Massachusetts was a staggering 15%.

The light at the crosswalk flashed green. Jones hurried across Charles Street and followed Cedar Street up a steep hill—the precinct was named Beacon Hill for a reason—and through the most expensive neighborhood in the city, Louisburg Square. Quincy Monroe, one of Massachusetts's two U.S. senators, lived in a ten-room townhouse at the head of the square. Bartholomew Lodge lived in an equally glorious residence next door to the senator. Jones glanced briefly through the window that faced the cobblestone street but he couldn't tell whether Lodge had already left for the office. Jones suspected that he hadn't. Jones knew that Lodge was a hard worker, but only a one-dimensional workaholic such as Jones himself would be on his way to the office at 6:30 a.m. Jones glanced at his watch and quickened his pace. He had a lot of work to do before lunch.

Bartholomew Lodge thanked the cook for keeping his eggs warm. Lodge was running late this morning. His eight-year-old granddaughter Alexandra had called from New Hampshire to tell him that she had finished first in an ice skating competition. His daughter-in-law Dina had said that Alexandra had been so excited about her victory that she brought her trophy with her to dinner and slept with it afterwards. Dina had apologized to her father-in-law for calling so early but Alexandra had insisted on sharing the good news with "Grampy." Lodge had said that he wouldn't have wanted it any other way and that it was wonderful to begin the day with such terrific news.

Eduardo Alves, the Lodges' cook, had been with the family for over twenty years. He was what the law referred to as a "lawful resident alien," which meant that he wasn't a U.S. citizen but he did have permission from the federal government to live and work in America. In other words, Eduardo had a green card. He had immigrated to the United States from Portugal in the hopes of securing a job that paid him enough money to support his wife, three children, and elderly parents. He had ended up in Boston because a cousin of his had found work in the city and recommended that he try to do the same. His cousin also had mentioned that New Bedford, which was about a two hour bus ride from Boston, was home to one of the largest Portuguese populations outside of Portugal itself. Eduardo had confirmed that his cousin's representations were correct and set off to find a better life for his family.

Eduardo had started out as a cook in a food truck that specialized in Portuguese cuisine. Fate had led Bartholomew Lodge to purchase a bowl of Caldo Verde from the truck while he was racing to a deposition at a nearby corporation on a particularly frigid New England day. Lodge had never tasted such wonderful soup before; his family was in need of a new cook at the time; and he decided to inquire as to Eduardo's availability. The rest, as the saying went, was history.

"Great eggs, Eddy," Lodge said.

"Obrigado," Eduardo said. "I used the jalapeños I bought at the farmer's market on Saturday."

"They're extra hot, just like I like them."

"Sim, Mr. Bartholomew."

"How's your family doing?"

"Good. My oldest is a mother now."

Eduardo's family had stayed behind in Portugal. He only got to see them for a couple of weeks a year when he returned to Portugal for Christmas. But he sent them money every month like clockwork.

"Izabel's a mom? How old is she now?" Lodge reached for a slice of toasted Portuguese bread and spread a thick sheet of strawberry jam across it.

Eduardo flashed Bartholomew Lodge a grateful smile. Not only did Mr. Bartholomew remember the names of Eduardo's children, but it was he who purchased Eduardo's round-trip airplane ticket to Lisbon every Christmas, where Eduardo's family lived. "She's twenty-eight. I can't believe I'm a grandfather, Mr. Bartholomew."

"Welcome to the club, Eddy. It's the most wonderful club in the world. That was my granddaughter who called earlier."

"Obrigado."

Joshua Jones's administrative assistant rushed to her desk as if she were being chased by a schoolyard bully. In a way, she was. She stretched across her desk to answer her telephone. She knocked to the floor the vase of roses that her husband had given to her for their anniversary in her haste to avoid a second ring of the phone. "Hello," she said.

"I need a copy of the Windsor file ASAP."

No "good morning." No "did you have a nice weekend?" No "is your daughter feeling better?" With Joshua Jones, pleasantries were a waste of time, and wasting time meant wasting money.

"The Windsor file?"

Jones's administrative assistant was perplexed. Why wouldn't she be? The Windsor file wasn't part of Jones's book of business and she had never heard of the Windsor file before.

"Yes, the Windsor file. Ask Bart Lodge's secretary to make you a copy." The politically correct job description was "administrative assistant," but Jones wasn't one for political correctness.

"I'll get it for you right away, Mr. Jones." She stepped over the shattered vase and broken flowers and scurried to the elevator to Mr. Lodge's office.

Bartholomew Lodge was pouring himself a cup of coffee when he saw Joshua Jones's administrative assistant flash by. Lodge added one cream and two sugars to his coffee, stirred it with a plastic spoon he had retrieved from a jar on the counter, and headed back to his office to begin his workday.

Jones's administrative assistant was standing next to Lodge's administrative assistant's desk. Her eyes were as wide as a Wolf Moon over Boston Harbor.

Lodge smiled and said, "Jessie won't be in until about noon today. She had to take her daughter to the doctor." Jessie Young was Lodge's administrative assistant. "Is there anything I can do for you, Cheryl?"

Cheryl Shaw, Jones's administrative assistant, said to herself: Mr. Lodge actually knows my name. She worked fifty hours per week for Joshua Jones, and she often wondered whether Jones remembered it. Jones almost never called her by her name. Aloud to Lodge: "Mr. Jones asked me to get a copy of one of your files."

"Which one?" Lodge took a sip of coffee.

"The Windsor file."

Lodge's face became as tight as the laces on his granddaughter's ice skates. He said, "Did he say why he wanted it?"

"No, sir." Cheryl couldn't help but notice Lodge's sudden mood swing.

Lodge's eyes drifted to the photographs on Jessie Young's desk: her wedding picture from the Catholic Church in Stoneham; her honeymoon on Nantucket; a ski trip to Loon Mountain in New Hampshire; an office party at the *Irish Rose* in Quincy Market (she was chatting with Lodge in that photo); and her holding her daughter in the hospital the day her daughter was born.

Lodge snapped back to the moment with a conciliatory smile. "Let me see if I can find it." He knew it wasn't on his desk because he had delegated the redrafting of Andrew Windsor's testamentary documents to Nevin Montgomery. He opened the ACTIVE FILES cabinet behind Jessie's desk, thumbed through s-t-u-v until he reached w, and removed the file marked ANDREW WINDSOR. He turned to Cheryl. "Can you make a copy and return the original to Jessie's desk?"

"Absolutely. Thank you very much." The look on Cheryl Shaw's face revealed how much she had feared the possibility of returning to Joshua Jones empty handed. The fact that Mr. Lodge had saved her from doing so even though he was clearly uncomfortable giving her the file confirmed all the wonderful things that Jessie Young had said about him.

"Here's the file, Mr. Jones," Cheryl said. She was breathing heavily after running down two flights of stairs from Bartholomew Lodge's office on the 32nd floor to Joshua Jones's office on the 30th floor. Her ankles ached too. Back in the day, Nancy Sinatra might have sung that her boots were made for walking, but Cheryl Shaw was currently learning that four inch stilettos weren't made for running.

Jones said, "Good." He snatched the file from his administrative assistant's hand, which she took as her cue to leave the room and clean up the broken vase and flowers before Jones noticed the mess.

Jones studied the file. Some of what he read was news to him. For example, he hadn't realized that Andrew Windsor had been a client of the firm for more than thirty years. He also hadn't known that Windsor had always been represented by Bart Lodge. That fact would make an already difficult task—wrestling the Windsor account from Lodge—trickier than it already was. But, as the cliché went, where there was a will, there was a way. Jones certainly had the will. What he now needed to figure out was the way.

"Did you find what you were looking for?"

Jones lifted his eyes from the file to find Bartholomew Lodge standing in the threshold with his arms folded across his chest.

Jones said, "I don't know yet."

"If you ask me what you're hoping to find, I can save us both a lot of time and trouble by simply telling you the answer myself."

"Are you sure about that, Bart? I mean, shouldn't I be asking Nevin instead?"

Bartholomew Lodge was an experienced lawyer and he had long ago mastered the maxim, *Don't let 'em see you sweat.* On the inside, he was hopping mad. On the outside, he was having a friendly conversation with a colleague. He said, "I'm sure I can answer it. Now, what's your question?"

"Why is Andrew Windsor so interested in rewriting his testamentary documents?"

Lodge pondered Jones's question. Jones, of course, was one of Lodge's law partners, which meant that Lodge wouldn't be violating the attorney-client privilege if he shared Windsor's confidences with Jones. But Windsor was one of Lodge's oldest clients, and Lodge didn't trust Jones. Lodge decided to say, "That's between Andrew and me." Lodge flashed Jones the sort of mischievous smile that Lodge's granddaughter Alexandra tended to flash after landing a particularly difficult jump. "And between Andrew and Nevin Montgomery as well."

CHAPTER 20

Nevin Montgomery had received word moments earlier that a second meeting he had scheduled with Andrew Windsor for later in the morning had to be postponed to the following afternoon because Mr. Windsor had endured a bad night health wise. "Doctor's orders," Nevin had been told.

Instead of exiting Mr. Windsor's house and returning to the guest cottage at which he was staying, Nevin decided to take a quick tour of the art that decorated Mr. Windsor's residence. Nevin realized he shouldn't be snooping around, but he had spent most of his adolescence doing things he wasn't supposed to be doing.... Old habits were difficult to break.

Nevin had already seen the paintings that hung in the drawing room. His first stop on this impromptu tour was, therefore, the long hallway that led from the front of the house to the back of the house. About half of the paintings were by Andrew Windsor; about a quarter were by James Windsor; and the other quarter were drawings of what eventually became covers for children's books illustrated by Andrew Windsor's father, C. S. Windsor, the most fêted illustrator of children's books in American history. The illustrations were wonderful—farm animals engaged in human activities such as plowing and baling hay; ruby-cheeked children plotting an adventure or playing a game; fields of candy canes and ice cream cones that stretched into the horizon—and it wasn't difficult to tell from whom Andrew Windsor had inherited his talent. James Windsor, on the other hand, was a different story. None of the paintings by him suggested that he was the son and grandson of talented artists... until, that was, Nevin stumbled upon one particular painting in the rear of the house.

The painting was a profile of a young woman in a hurry to get somewhere only she seemed to know existed. Her green-and-black sun-dress fluttered in the breeze. Her long raven hair hung loosely across her thin shoulders, its brown highlights accentuated by the midday light. Her skin was smooth and bronzed by the kiss of summer.

Nevin studied the painting. He couldn't find a flaw in it. The clouds set high against a blue sky... The stand of oak trees in the distance... The field of wild flowers through which the young woman was running... The young woman herself... Everything was perfect, especially the young woman—the centerpiece of the painting and clearly a subject with whom James Windsor was well familiar.

"He painted that last summer," Nevin heard from over his shoulder.

Nevin spun around to find Catina Cruz standing behind him. She was wearing an oversized sweatshirt with BOSTON RED SOX embossed across the chest. Her stonewashed jeans had pre-fabricated holes in the knees and thighs. She was barefooted, with a gold ring on her left index toe. Her face was untouched by cosmetics and her hair was gathered in a loose ponytail that was secured by an inexpensive band probably purchased at the local *Dollar Store*. To Nevin, Catina had never looked more beautiful. He said, "Is that you?"

Catina nodded.

"You model for James Windsor?"

"S—Sometimes. I get paid extra for it, and I need the money." Catina failed to mention what else she did for James.

Nevin returned his attention to the painting. "It's a profile, but now that you mention it, I can tell it's you. You're beautiful. I mean, it's beautiful." Nevin blushed.

Catina smiled and touched Nevin's hand.

A tingle raced through Nevin's body and he forgot where he was for a moment.

Catina said, "Thank you. It's my favorite of the paintings that James has done of me." She examined the painting, as she often did. Her mind traveled back to the weekend that James had painted it. She would never forget that weekend: It was the first time she had slept with him. Aloud to Nevin: "Would you like to see my room? It's around the corner to the right."

Catina led Nevin to her bedroom. She switched on the lights.

Nevin said, pointing to the far wall, "I like that poster. Is that New Bedford?"

"Yes. How did you know?"

"One of my college roommates was from New Bedford. Javier Duarte. Do you know him?"

Catina shook her head and smiled. "No. But you're older than I am."

Nevin returned Catina's smile. "Be careful. I'm not that much older than you."

Catina offered Nevin the lone chair in the room. She turned on the radio and sat on the edge of the bed. She folded into the lotus position. Her legs were lean and freshly shaven. "I love this song." It was Adele's *Rolling in the Deep*.

Nevin said, his eyes drawn to Catina's legs like a moth to a flame, "Me, too. The entire CD is great. It sold, like, ten million copies; or some crazy amount like that."

The chorus sounded:

> *We could have had it all*
> *(You're gonna wish you never had met me)*
> *Rolling in the deep*
> *(Tears are gonna fall, rolling in the deep)*
> *You had my heart inside of your hand*
> *(You're gonna wish you never had met me)*
> *And you played it to the beat*
> *(Tears are gonna fall, rolling in the deep)*

"I wonder if she needs a maid?" Catina was obviously trying to make a joke at her own expense, but it came off as if she were embarrassed by what she did for a living.

Nevin scratched his ear, as he often did when he didn't know what to say. "My grandmother was a housekeeper. I'm proud of how hard she worked and of how she was able to raise my dad and my two uncles as a single mother."

Nevin had managed to say precisely the right thing.

A tear came to Catina's eye. She turned towards the window so that Nevin wouldn't notice. She watched the trees outside her bedroom bend against the breeze. Gulls glided high above, riding the wind and studying the ground below for something to eat. Catina finally said, "Do you party?"

Nevin again didn't know how to respond. He knew he should say no. He knew he should mention that he had kicked the habit several years earlier… before it had killed him. But the question was being posed by the most beautiful woman he had ever seen and they were alone in her bedroom. He answered, "Yes."

"Good." Catina wiped the tear from her eye with a quick flick of her index finger and opened the top drawer to her nightstand. She pushed aside a stack of celebrity magazines—*People, Us, Star*—and removed a small wooden jewelry box that her mother had given to her for her fourteenth birthday. She opened the box and pulled out a small vial of cocaine.

"Is that coke?" Nevin asked.

"Yes," Catina answered.

"How can you afford coke?"

"I can't. It was a gift." Catina didn't bother to mention that it had been given to her by James Windsor for sleeping with him the night before. She unscrewed the vial's cap and dipped a tiny spoon into what appeared to be two grams of cocaine. She offered the first taste to Nevin.

Nevin's face flushed with guilt. Hours and hours of Narcotics Anonymous meetings replayed in his mind. One day at a time, he said to himself. One day at a time. He was almost able to change his mind and say "no thanks." Almost. His eyes met Catina's... coffee-colored invitations to unimaginable pleasures... and he had no choice but to say, "Thanks."

Nevin couldn't remember the rest of the afternoon. All he knew was that he hadn't stopped at one spoonful of cocaine and that he felt both exhilarated and regretful about it. Exhilarated, because that was what good coke did for an addict. Regretful, because Nevin hadn't touched the stuff for about three years.

At least he hadn't slept with Catina after their little drug party.

Nevin walked back to the guest cottage that was fast becoming his second home. His senses were heightened by the cocaine, which meant that the birds sounded prettier, the flowers looked more beautiful, and the ocean breeze smelled fresher. On the downside, he knew what would happen to his career if the partners at Palmer & Lodge found out that he had fallen off the wagon and taken drugs on firm business at the home of a major client: he would be fired on the spot. Not even Bartholomew Lodge would be able to save him. In fact, Nevin suspected that Lodge would be the first partner calling for his ouster. Well, maybe the second... Joshua Jones would make a point to be the first.... "I told you so" would be impossible for Jones to resist.

Nevin opened the cottage's door and noticed a boxed lunch on the table in the cottage's small dining area. Cocaine wasn't marijuana, and Nevin didn't have the munchies, but he was hungry nevertheless. He had a phone call to make before he could eat, however. He had made the call dozens of times over the years, and it had saved his life—literally—each and every time. He pulled his smartphone from his pocket, navigated to the CONTACTS app, and touched the entry for MR. H. The phone rang several times. Nevin said, "Please, Mr. H. Please pick up the phone."

On the fifth ring, he did. "Hello."

"H—Hi, Mr. H. It's me."

"Nevin?"

"Yes, sir."

"Are you OK?"

"No, sir." Nevin could hear the concern rise in Mr. Harrington's voice.

"Did you take a step back?"

What a kind way to put it, Nevin said to himself. *A step back*. Mr. Harrington should have asked whether Nevin had fucked up again, and then surmised as to the reason: because Nevin had been offered drugs by a beautiful woman with whom Nevin wanted to have sex. But instead, Mr. Harrington had simply asked whether Nevin had taken a step back. Aloud to Mr. Harrington: "Yes, sir."

"Where are you?"

"Barnstable."

"Barnstable? What are you doing in Barnstable?"

"I'm meeting with a client."

"A client? Does your client know you've taken a step back? Does your law firm know?" Mr. Harrington had switched to tough love mode.

"No, sir."

Neither man said anything for several minutes. Their silence spoke volumes.

Mr. Harrington finally said, "Can you get to a meeting? I'm sure there are plenty of meetings to be found in a rich community like Barnstable."

"I'm sure you're right."

Nevin managed to locate an evening meeting at St. Peter's Catholic Church in the Barnstable town center. A potpourri of emotions rushed over him as he entered the side door and descended into the basement on his way to the conference room at the end of the hallway: shame, fear, hopelessness. Nevin had felt all of those emotions many times before during his young life.

But then he opened the door to the conference room and was greeted by the empathetic smiles of people he had never met, yet whom he felt he knew better than he knew his own family.

He said, "Hello. My name is Nevin and I'm a drug addict."

CHAPTER 21

Deputy Sheriff John Steele texted Sheriff Philip Joyce that he was on route to the Windsor compound to interview Meredith Adams Windsor about Hannah Burgoff's death. *Texted.* Steele couldn't believe that he and his fellow deputy sheriffs were now required to text their whereabouts to the sheriff. It made Steele feel like a teenaged girl. It made him feel like one of *his* teenaged girls. He and his wife had three of them at home, and they ranged in age from thirteen to fifteen to seventeen. His fifteen year old was texting constantly. His seventeen year old preferred to talk to her friends on the telephone. His thirteen year old had recently received her first smartphone and was still figuring out whether she was a texter or a talker. Steele himself wasn't much of a talker, but he would certainly rather talk than text. But Philip Joyce was a texter; Philip Joyce was the newly elected sheriff of Barnstable County; and, ipso facto, John Steele and the rest of the deputies were now texters too. At least Steele wouldn't have to text while driving. State law forbade it.

Meredith Adams Windsor maneuvered around a misplaced Loo table on her way to the drawing room of her in-laws' house. She made a note to herself to chastise Catina Cruz for leaving the table in such an awkward location. She had scolded Catina on many occasions for failing to remember that her wheelchair required considerably more space than an able-bodied person required. At some point she would need to fire Catina for repeatedly forgetting that basic fact. In the meantime, however, Catina's presence at the compound meant that her husband James wouldn't be spending as much time on Nantucket as he tended to do when pretty young girls weren't around to provide him with a reason to stay in Barnstable.

Meredith reached the spot near the bay window where she liked to read. The sun sat high in the midday sky and warmed the room like a cozy fire on a chilly New England morning. She reached into the pocket of her wheelchair and retrieved the most recent edition of *Sotheby's at Auction*, a leading magazine for collectors and connoisseurs of fine art. The periodical prided itself on its award-winning reporting about artists, private collections, museum exhibitions, and all manner of art world events. Each issue included highlights from every *Sotheby's* sale around the world, featuring the rarest works of art and the most coveted precious objects on the international market.

Meredith always looked forward to perusing the new issue from cover to cover. She was particularly excited when she stumbled across a story about one of the Windsors. Sadly, almost every story about the Windsors was about Andrew Windsor or C. S. Windsor. In fact, in the twenty years that she had been married to James Windsor, only one of the stories had been about him and that story had equated a week-long exhibition of James's work with "an end of the semester display of student art at the Rhode Island School of Design." The current issue was no exception. It contained nothing about James but plenty about Andrew. It listed for auction *Amy's House* and included the following description:

> *Located in Nantucket, Massachusetts in the township of Wauwinet, belonged to a lifelong friend of the artist to whom he gifted the present work. The house and its inhabitants served as subject matter for both Andrew Windsor and his father, C. S., including the former's* Around the Bend, *1999 (Private Collection), and the latter's* Wauwinet, *circa 1935 (Private Collection),* The Calvin House, Wauwinet, *circa 1940 (Farnsworth Art Museum, Maine) and* Dark Harbor Fishermen, *1947 (Portland Museum of Art, Maine).*

Meredith shook her head in disbelief. The magazine had failed to mention that James also had painted the house in question. She heard footsteps in the hallway. She looked up from the magazine to see Deputy Sheriff John Steele entering the drawing room escorted, as always, by the butler. The deputy was on time, which she appreciated. The butler was carrying a silver tray on which sat a sterling silver teapot and two Wedgewood teacups. The butler placed the pot and cups on the Chippendale end table next to Meredith's wheelchair and excused himself from the room.

Meredith asked, "Are you a tea drinker, Deputy Steele?"

Steele answered, "Not really, but I wouldn't say no to a cup. My wife says I need to be more adventurous in my culinary pursuits." *Culinary pursuits?* Steele couldn't recall ever uttering that phrase before. He attributed the remark to the elegant environs in which he currently found himself.

Meredith poured both of them a cup. She tasted the tea. "It's Pekoe Cut Black, my favorite."

Steele tasted it too. "I can't tell one tea from another. I like it, though. Cops tend to drink coffee. The stronger the better. But this is a nice change."

Meredith smiled. "I'm glad you're enjoying it."

Steele glanced at the magazine that was cover-down on Meredith Windsor's lap. A good detective knew that nothing was a coincidence, including the choice of reading material. He pointed to the periodical. "Is that the most recent issue of *Time*? My wife tells me that Clarence Thomas was named Person of the Year."

Clarence Thomas was a U.S. Supreme Court justice who had finally managed to persuade four other members of the nine-person tribunal to rule that the use of racial preferences in college and university admissions programs violated the Equal Protection Clause of the Fourteenth Amendment. *Time* named Justice Thomas person of the year not because the magazine agreed with Thomas's jurisprudence, but rather because of his transformative performance on the nation's highest court.

"I wish," Meredith said. "It's actually the new *Sotheby's at Auction*. I'd much prefer to be reading *Time* or *The New York Review of Books*, but my husband has no head for business so I've got to handle his portfolio for him."

Steele was experienced enough to recognize that Mrs. Windsor actually relished her role as her husband's business manager and that, to quote Shakespeare, "the lady doth protest too much." *He was quoting Shakespeare now?* What he needed to figure out was why she was pretending that she didn't relish it. "How's his portfolio doing?" Yet another phrase that Steele had never uttered before.

Meredith reached for her teacup and took a sip. Her eyes drifted towards the bay window that she loved so much. The sky had changed from blue to gray in the brief time that she had been sitting next to it. She lived in New England, after all. Hail the size of Buffalo nickels began to sound against the roof like a percussionist during a jazz freestyle. She finally said, "Not good."

Scott Douglas Gerber

"How has it done in the past?" Steele had grown up in Barnstable and he knew how successful Andrew Windsor was. But he hadn't known that James Windsor was a painter until he started working on the Hannah Burgoff case. Steele traveled in markedly different circles than the Windsors did.

Meredith hesitated again. Her eyes remained on the weather unfolding through the window. "2009 was a terrific year. That year the Chicago Art Institute featured a number of my husband's paintings in a three-month exhibit about artists who were the children of artists. That led to a spike in interest in James's work. I think we sold five paintings that year, which might not sound like much but really is when you remember how expensive a single painting can be."

"How expensive?" Steele was studying Meredith Windsor's body language as he asked questions. That was another thing that good detectives did.

Meredith smiled. Unless a painting was sold at auction, the price a painting brought was typically kept confidential. She obviously knew that Steele couldn't possibly know that. Besides, she was proud to share the dollar amount. "I think the high was $275,000 for *Great Point Light*, which was James's painting of an eighteenth-century lighthouse located on the northern-most point of Nantucket. The low was about $125,000 for *Range Lights at Brant Point*."

"Isn't Brant Point also on Nantucket?"

"Yes. We own a cottage there."

Steele could sense Meredith Windsor's sudden discomfort, but he couldn't allow that to dissuade him from asking a follow-up question. "Does your husband do much of his painting in Nantucket?"

"He does some of it there."

"How much is 'some'?"

"That's difficult to say. Sometimes he does a lot of it there, and sometimes he does a lot of it here. He's an artist. He's unpredictable."

That wasn't actually true. Meredith could predict where her husband was going to paint on the basis of whether there were any young women around for him to enjoy in Barnstable. If there weren't, he would rush off to Nantucket.

"The big sellers—the ones that sold for a lot of money that you mentioned earlier—were all painted in Nantucket, though. Right?"

"I've never thought about that before. But now that you mention it, you're right. I suspect it's because several of his father's and grandfather's most famous works were painted in Nantucket too. Art collectors are like children: more of the same is always better than something new. They probably think, 'I've got one Windsor painting of the Nantucket shoreline, why not buy another one?'"

"And that bothers you?"

Meredith laughed. "I've never been much of a poker player, obviously. Of course it bothers me. My husband isn't just the son of Andrew Windsor and the grandson of C. S. Windsor. He's a talented artist in his own right. He deserves a lot more respect than he gets. His father could doodle something on a cocktail napkin and the critics would rave about it. But they couldn't care less about James's beautiful paintings. And believe me, he's painted many—dozens—of the most exquisite pictures I've ever seen. I'm biased, though."

Steele felt a vibration against his leg. It took him a moment to realize what it was. He still wasn't used to carrying his smartphone 24/7. "Excuse me," he said to Meredith Windsor. He retrieved his phone from his pocket. A text. He had received another dadgum text. *Dadgum?* He had gone from Shakespeare to Jeff Foxworthy in the matter of minutes.… There was hope for him yet.

Meredith asked, "Is everything OK?"

Steele answered, "I'm not sure. Sheriff Joyce wants me to return to the station ASAP. Can we pick up where we left off at another time?"

"Where'd we leave off?"

"With Hannah Burgoff. I never got to my questions about her."

Steele rushed from the drawing room without looking where he was going. "Sorry," he said, after bumping into a petite young woman. "I didn't hurt you, did I?"

The young woman said, "I'm fine."

She's beautiful, Steele said to himself. He smiled and headed for his squad car.

***

Catina Cruz checked her watch to see if the collision had broken it. It hadn't, which was good. She couldn't afford to replace it. She hadn't purchased it in the first place. It had been a gift from James Windsor, and quite an expensive gift at that: a *Van Cleef & Arpels Ballerine Enchantee*. James rarely gave Catina a gift, and when he did and the gift was something other than drugs he either felt guilty about having an affair with a woman thirty years his junior or he was grateful for a particularly memorable sexual encounter with her.

Catina entered the drawing room. If she had known that Meredith Adams Windsor was using it, she would have found a different room to clean. Catina said, "S—Sorry, Mrs. Windsor. I didn't think anyone was in here."

Meredith Windsor said, "I'm finished with my tea. Take the tray back to the kitchen."

No "please" or "thank you."

Catina gathered the tea set without making eye contact with Mrs. Windsor.

Meredith said, "Is that a new watch?"

Catina said, "Y—Yes."

"Let me see it."

Catina held up her wrist.

Meredith grabbed Catina's arm and studied the watch. "It's lovely. The golden ballerina on the dial is exquisite. It must have cost a fortune, which I know you don't have. Who gave it to you?"

Catina's heart began to race. She knew she shouldn't have worn the watch, but it was too beautiful to leave in a drawer in her bedroom. It was the most beautiful thing that she had ever owned. Besides, she had earned it.

"I said, who gave you the watch?"

Catina tucked a loose strand of hair behind her ear. "I—I don't remember."

"You 'don't remember'?... Bullshit. Of course you remember. Was it my husband? Did James give you that watch?"

Catina's eyes teared.

"I said, did my husband give you the watch?"

Catina began to shake. She nodded.

"I knew it! I knew you were fucking my husband! You're just a worthless slut, aren't you?"

Catina began to cry like the little girl she used to be. Her chest heaved and her breathing became short and erratic.

"I asked whether you were a worthless slut!"

Catina nodded again and raced from the room.

CHAPTER 22

Nevin Montgomery laced his *Nikes* for what he hoped was going to be a relaxing afternoon jog. He knew that the partners at Palmer & Lodge were expecting him to bill other clients while he waited for Andrew Windsor to feel strong enough to review the testamentary documents that Nevin was revising for him but, as his childhood pals used to say about doing things they knew their parents wouldn't like, what they didn't know wouldn't hurt them. Besides, Nevin would never be able to forgive himself if he passed up an opportunity to jog on the beach again. As guilty as he felt about doing drugs with Catina Cruz the previous day, he needed something to make himself feel good. "Exercising usually does that for me," someone at the Narcotics Anonymous meeting had wisely mentioned. "Remember that self-care is an important part of recovery, perhaps the most important part."

Nevin walked to the window of the guest cottage at which he was staying and began to stretch. The afternoon sun hung low on the horizon. It brought to mind a favorite poem by C. P. Cavafy that Mr. Harrington had assigned in AP English during Nevin's senior year at Dorchester's John F. Kennedy High School. Cavafy had been the most original and influential Greek poet of the 20th century. His distaste for the flowery rhetoric common among his contemporaries and his refusal to enter into the marketplace—he never offered a volume of his poems for sale during his lifetime, choosing instead to distribute privately printed pamphlets to relatives and friends—prevented him from realizing all but a few rewards for his genius. *The Afternoon Sun* epitomized Cavafy's unpretentious style. It read:

> *This room, how well I know it.*
> *Now they rent it and the one next door*
> *as commercial offices. The whole house became*
> *offices for agents and merchants and companies.*
> *Ah. this room, how familiar.*
> *The couch was near the door, here;*
> *in front, a Turkish rug;*
> *near the couch, two yellow vases on a shelf.*

On the right, no, across from it, was an armoire with a mirror.
In the middle, the table where he wrote
and three wicker chairs.
Next to the window was the bed
where we made love so many times.
These sad things must still be somewhere.
Next to the window was the bed;
the afternoon sun spread across halfway.
…One afternoon at four o'clock, we separated,
just for a week just for a week…. Alas,
that week became forever.

The poem reminded Nevin of Catina. He had never made love to Catina but, as Mr. Harrington had frequently said, poetry was about dreams.

Recovering addicts were almost always stressed, and Nevin was no exception. Thankfully, the beauty of both Cavafy's poem and the sunset unfolding before him brought temporary respite. Nevin felt the tension release from his body. He felt his mind slow from its frenetic pace. He smiled. He truly smiled. He couldn't remember the last time he had done that.

Nevin started his jog at a brisk pace. The air was cool and sweet. Treetops danced to the ocean breeze. As usual, gulls floated across the sky—their wings extended; their eyes searching for food on the beach below. Nevin decided to make it a long run. In Boston, he tended to limit his runs to two miles: from the Charles Street end of the Charles River to the Mass. Ave. Bridge and back. But in Boston he was pressed for time. In Barnstable, he had come to learn, he was not.

The beach along Barnstable Harbor was deserted. The stretch upon which Nevin was jogging wasn't a public beach, and most of the residents of the expensive homes that he was passing were at work… or on vacation from their lives that were vacations. Nevin enjoyed the quiet. He hadn't felt this relaxed in ages. He rounded the bend that led back to the Windsor compound and spotted someone in the distance.

It was Catina.

"Hi," Nevin said, breathing heavily from the run. He noticed that Catina was upset. "What's wrong?"

Catina was sitting in the sand and staring off into the horizon. Tears streaked her cheeks like rain on smoothed stones. "N—Nothing."

"'Nothing?' You're crying over 'nothing'?... I don't believe you. Come on, Catina. You can tell me." Nevin kneeled on the sand next to her. She looked so sad and alone that he wanted to scoop her up into his arms, kiss her on the forehead, and tell her that everything was going to be OK.

"My mom died last night. I found out this morning."

None of that was true, but Catina was too embarrassed to tell Nevin that Meredith Adams Windsor had called Catina a "worthless slut" and that Catina had agreed with her.

Nevin said, "That's terrible. I'm sorry to hear it. How did it happen?"

In for a penny, in for a pound, as far as Catina was concerned. "She got murdered by a mugger."

Nevin shook his head. "Wow. Who told you?"

"The police. My mom was the only family I had left. Now there's nobody." Catina began to sob uncontrollably. Apparently, she believed her own bullshit.

Nevin moved closer and placed his arm around Catina's slender shoulders. It felt good. It felt right.

Catina buried her face in Nevin's chest to comfort herself. Most of what she was telling Nevin was untrue, but the part about feeling alone couldn't have been truer. She had felt alone for most of her life.

Catina managed to convince Nevin to come to her room for the second time in two days. That took about as much arm twisting as persuading an NFL defensive lineman to eat the last piece of pizza at the end of a training camp two-a-day. Nevin wasn't stupid, though. He knew that he could stay for only a few minutes and he knew that he had to bolt if Catina offered him drugs again. She didn't. This time she offered him herself.

Nevin watched while Catina undressed. She was wearing a faded New England Patriots jersey with TOM BRADY embossed across the back. She might as well have been wearing a Tom Ford evening gown for all Nevin knew. He was more interested in seeing what was underneath her clothes: caramel colored skin that was as smooth as freshly spun silk.

Catina smiled when her eyes met Nevin's, and Nevin almost lost it right then and there. Catina tossed her Patriots jersey onto the chair next to her bed and proceeded to slither out of her jeans like an exotic dancer at a Boston gentlemen's club.

She had done this before, Nevin said to himself. But at this particular moment in time he couldn't care less about whether he was Catina's first guy or her hundred-and-first. He was just glad that she was undressing for him now. He would worry about whether it was right or wrong after he had his fun. That was the way addicts thought about the world. It was about feeling good *now*. Later would come later.

Nevin Montgomery might have been a brilliant young lawyer at a prestigious Boston law firm, but he was also a drug addict. He always would be. No matter how many Narcotics Anonymous meetings he attended, or how many days he remained clean and sober, he would never be able to escape being an addict.

PART III

Oil on Canvas

"There is no blue without yellow and without orange."
    —Vincent Van Gogh

CHAPTER 23

Andrew Windsor slid his legs over the side of the bed and slowly stood to his feet. He waited several beats while he regained his balance. He reached for the stool next to the bed and dragged it closer to the window. He placed a blank canvas on the easel and spread an array of paints across a well-worn palette. He searched for a favorite brush, wiped it clean with a turpentine-soaked rag, and began to paint for the first time in days. His doctor had prescribed bed rest and all manner of medications, but the only thing that ever seemed to make Andrew feel better was painting. It was like air for him. He couldn't live without it. He didn't want to live without it. His father had been the same way.

***

C. S. Windsor bounded through the door, suitcase in hand, and announced to his family that he had returned from New York.

His ten-year-old son raced into the room and tried to wrap his small arms around his father's large waist. "Papa! Papa!"

The father patted the son on the head and mussed the boy's hair. "Hello, son. Were you a good boy while I was away?"

Andrew Windsor said, "Yes, Papa. I finished two paintings while you were gone. Do you want to see them?"

C. S. smiled. He was exhausted from his trip, but he said, "Of course."

Andrew sprinted to his bedroom and returned with two small paintings. One was of the family dog, a chocolate Labrador that almost never sat still. The other was of the family cat, a fifteen-year-old tabby that almost never moved. Andrew held the paintings over his head for his father to inspect. "Do you like them, Papa?"

C. S. examined the paintings and proffered his opinion. "That's fine work, son. But don't you think it's time to paint something other than Hershey and Mittens?" Hershey was the dog. Mittens was the cat. "Artists need to take chances. Artists need to take risks."

Artists? Andrew was still a boy.

"I will, Papa. I promise."

C. S. Windsor had been home for less than an hour and he was already hard at work in his studio. His trip to New York had been a great success. He had been commissioned to illustrate the new children's book by Dorothy Baxter, the author of the recent bestseller *Joey and the Magic Meadow*. Baxter was extremely picky about her illustrators. In fact, even though *Joey and the Magic Meadow* had sold over 50,000 copies she hadn't been satisfied with the illustrations and had refused to work again with the illustrator of that book. That had led to the meeting with C. S. Windsor, whom Baxter had long admired, and a commission for C. S. to illustrate a sequel entitled *Joey and the Mysterious Mountain*. C. S. and his literary agent had celebrated the deal with lunch at *Tavern on the Green*.

C. S. had read Baxter's manuscript twice on the train from New York. He read it for a third time in his studio. He rose from his chair and paced around the room, thinking. He couldn't decide whether to illustrate the book in a cartoon style or with magic realism. Cartooning, a branch of Expressionism, emphasized emotional interpretation of the words, rather than a realistic representation of them. Cartooning was characterized by distortion and exaggeration, and used bright colors. In magic realism the art form was basically realistic, but with a slight intrusion of something unreal—a magical element or overtone that created a supernatural atmosphere. Its images were drawn from dreams and the unconscious, with symbolic allusion and luminous or psychedelic coloration.

C. S. Windsor was famous for his magic realism, but the illustrator of *Joey and the Magic Meadow* had drawn cartoon characters and critics had credited much of the book's success to the illustrations, which was probably why Dorothy Baxter had refused to work with that illustrator again. (Baxter had curtly declined to specify why she was switching illustrators when a reporter for *Publishers Weekly* had asked her about it.) C. S. studied the illustrations that hung on the walls of his studio: the cover art for *Time and Again*; the drawing that framed the epigraph for *Sand and Sea*; the picture that opened the first chapter of *The Neighborhood We Love*; and, of course, several prize-winning pieces from *Pirates Cove*. All were in the style of magic realism, C. S. said to himself. So too would be the illustrations for *Joey and the Mysterious Mountain*.

C. S. reached for his sketch pad. He flipped to a clean page. He began to pencil several possibilities for the cover. A tingle raced through his body. After three decades as a professional illustrator—years after most illustrators had burned out—he remained excited about drawing. Indeed, he remained as excited about it now as he had been when he had first caught the bug as a child. He wondered whether Andrew felt the same way....

Andrew Windsor pushed his paint box and canvas across the field in a rusty wheel barrel that he had retrieved from the barn. He stopped at a shady spot beneath a towering oak. He removed the paint box and canvas, doing his best to hold the wheel barrel steady with his foot as he did. The canvas was bigger than he was. The paint box weighed almost as much. He cleaned his brush and prepared his palette. Both had been gifts from his father.

Andrew couldn't decide what to paint. He remembered what his father had said: paint something other than the family pets. Take a risk.

Like most boys, Andrew worshiped his father. And like most boys, he didn't want to disappoint him.

Andrew sat beneath the tree for over an hour before it occurred to him that what he needed to paint was the very field in which he was sitting. Andrew's father was an encyclopedia of art history and he once had told Andrew that Vincent Van Gogh was renowned for his dozens of paintings of wheat fields and that those paintings were borne out of Van Gogh's religious studies and sermons, connection to nature, appreciation of manual laborers, and desire to provide a means of offering comfort to others. The paintings taken in chronological order demonstrated Van Gogh's progression as an artist from the drab *Wheat Sheaves* of 1885 in the Netherlands to the colorful, dramatic paintings from Arles, Saint-Rémy and Auvers-sur-Oise of rural France.

The field in which Andrew was sitting wasn't wheat, which provided another reason to paint it: Andrew wouldn't be trying to mimic Van Gogh (as if anyone could; a ten year old certainly couldn't). The field was populated by wild flowers, which inspired Andrew to title the series that was unfolding in his young mind *Fields of Wild Flowers*. He mixed orange and yellow to make blue. He began to paint.

C. S. Windsor approached the tall tree under which his son was painting. He said, "Your mother was wondering where you ran off to.

Dinner is ready."

"Look, Papa. I'm painting the field."

C. S. studied his son's work-in-progress. Most children tended towards bright colors and exaggerated depictions—apparently, most children were aspiring Impressionists—but not C. S. Windsor's son. The wild flowers that Andrew had painted were more subdued than the ones he was trying to recreate. The father was overwhelmed by the son's sensibilities at only ten years of age. "This is marvelous, Andrew. I couldn't be more proud of you."

Andrew beamed. His father wasn't one for false praise. He clearly meant what he had said and Andrew would never forget it.

CHAPTER 24

Nevin Montgomery sprinted down the streets of Dorchester like Usain Bolt at the Olympics. Alastair Ainsley, Colin Dunn, and Stewart MacGregor had scattered in three different directions. "They can't catch us all," the childhood friends had declared earlier in the summer when they had devised their escape strategy.

Nevin rounded the corner of First and Carnahan Streets. Sweat streamed across his face and dripped into his eyes. He hurdled over a trash can that had been overturned by the gale force winds that had accompanied the previous evening's thunderstorm. The sirens hadn't faded. He had more running to do. But he was used to it. He and his buddies were frequently fleeing from the police.

Nevin's mother asked, "Where have you been?"
Nevin answered, "Out."
"'Out' where?"
"Shootin' hoops with the fellas."
Nevin's mother knew who the "fellas" were. She also knew they weren't a good influence on her son. But Nevin was her *son* and like every loving mother she gave him the benefit of the doubt. "So that's why you're dripping with sweat?"
"Yes, Ma."
Nevin's mother paused and studied her son's face. He was more pretty than handsome: wavy brown hair; hazel eyes the size of quarters that were framed with lashes as long as a kitten's tail; cheekbones that would have made a fashion model jealous… all capped off with an effervescent smile. She wiped dry her son's face with the rag with which she was about to dust the living room. She kissed him on the cheek like a mother, but only a mother, was allowed to do. "Dinner's in an hour. Your father should be home by six."

Nevin's father arrived home at six on the dot. He was a hard work-er. However, he put his family first and he always tried to be on time for dinner. He usually made it. He stood at the bottom of the stairs of their small house on Bristol Street in the bluest-of-blue-collar neighborhoods of Dorchester, Massachusetts and called out, "Nevin."

Nevin switched off the Red Sox game and hurdled down the stairs. He was already taller than his father, but he still jumped whenever his father summoned him. He said, "Hi, Pop. The Sox are ahead three-to-one in the fourth. Pedroia homered in the first."

Dustin Pedroia was the Red Sox's all-star second baseman. He had a lot of power for such a diminutive athlete.

Nevin's father said, "Good. We need to stay within shouting distance of the Yankees." He silenced his pager. "Dinner's ready. Your mother made pot roast and red potatoes."

"Sounds good to me, Pop."

Nevin's father draped an arm across Nevin's broad shoulders. "And she made strawberry pie for dessert."

Nevin grinned. Strawberry pie was his favorite. His mother didn't make it often, and when she did it was as a reward for something he had done well. He had no idea what that was this time. He hadn't done anything good for a while.

Nevin and his father headed for the kitchen. They took their customary places at the table: Nevin near the door and Nevin's dad at the head. Nevin said, "It smells great, Ma."

Nevin's mother smiled. "Thank you." She dished out generous portions for her husband and son. She handed them their plates. "Help yourself to the salad."

Nevin ate like a starving prisoner of war. He wasn't actually starving, of course. He was a teenaged boy. They all ate like they hadn't eaten in days. He said, mouth full of meat and potatoes, "This is great, Ma."

Nevin's mother smiled again. "Thanks, sweetheart. I'm glad you're enjoying it."

Nevin's father said, "It's wonderful. You've outdone yourself again."

"Thank you."

Nevin said, "Pop said there's strawberry pie for dessert." His mouth was full again.

Nevin's mother said, "There is. It's a special occasion."

Nevin said, "What happened?"

Nevin's mother said, "Mr. Harrington called this afternoon."

"What did he want?" Nevin's voice dripped with concern. Teenagers always got spooked when a teacher called their parents.

"You made the honor roll." Nevin's mother beamed.

Nevin's father said, "That's wonderful, son. Wonderful." He patted

Nevin on the shoulder. "Of course that confirms it: you're going to college."

Nevin sat back in his chair. He wiped his mouth with a paper napkin. "I still haven't decided whether college is for me, Pop."

Nevin's mother was about to say something, but Nevin's father beat her to it. "You're too smart not to go to college, son. Everybody knows it, including your mother and me. Mr. Harrington never lets us forget it." Nevin's father smiled this time. His mother was still smiling. Nevin's father continued, "You're too smart to have to break your back for the rest of your life like I do. Don't get me wrong, son: there's pride in a hard day's work. I'm always exhausted when I get home in the evening, but I'm also proud of what I accomplished that day: keeping the high school clean for you kids, and for the teachers and the staff. But your mother and I want more for you, and for some reason God blessed you with an amazing mind.... Mr. Harrington told your mother that you're the smartest student he's ever taught." Nevin's father turned to Nevin's mother. "Isn't that what he said, hon?"

Nevin's mother said, "He's said that several times in recent months."

Nevin reddened. "Mr. Harrington has called here before?"

"Yes."

"What about?" Nevin fidgeted with his potatoes.

Nevin's mother glanced at Nevin's father, who nodded at his wife. "He's expressed concern that you're fooling around too much and that you're wasting your talent."

Nevin turned to his father. "You work at the school, Pop. You know that's not true."

"I'm the custodian, son. I'm cleaning all day, and fixing broken pipes and the like. It's a big school. I'm just one person. I have no idea what the kids are doing all day, including you." Nevin's father swallowed a mouthful of pot roast. "But what I do know is that Mr. Harrington has been teaching at JFK forever. He's a good man. If he says that you're fooling around too much, I'll take him at his word. He's not trying to get you into trouble, son. He's trying to help you. He's trying to make sure that *we* help you. All your mother and I want is what's best for you."

The telephone rang. Nevin's mother stepped away from the kitchen table to answer it. She said, "Yes, he's here." She cupped her palm over the mouthpiece. "Nevin. Alastair is calling for you."

Nevin glanced sheepishly at his father.

Nevin's father said, "Go ahead."

Nevin rose from the table. "Thanks, Ma." He smiled at his mother. He turned his attention to the telephone. "What's up?" He listened without adding more than a word or two here and there. "I'll ask and call you back." He hung up the phone and returned to the table.

Nevin's mother said, "Is everything OK?"

"It's fine. The guys are going bowling and are wondering if I can come. Can I?"

Nevin's father shook his head. "Did you hear a word of what your mother and I just said to you?"

"I heard, Pop. But it's just bowling."

Nevin's father turned to Nevin's mother.

Nevin's mother said, "Have you finished your homework?"

"Yes, Ma."

"I suppose it's alright then. But bowling and nothing else. And be back by ten."

Nevin smiled and kissed his mother on the forehead. "Thanks, Ma. Thanks, Pop."

The problem was, it wasn't just bowling.

CHAPTER 25

Alastair Ainsley, Colin Dunn, and Stewart MacGregor had already arrived by the time Nevin Montgomery reached the convenience store. Alastair was smoking a cigarette. Colin was drinking a *Mountain Dew*. Stewart was counting a handful of change that he had pulled from his pocket.

Nevin said, "Any problems?"

Alastair said, "My folks were kind of suspicious. I talked my way out of it, though."

Nevin said, "Me, too."

Stewart said, "My folks were still at work when I got home." He finished counting his change. He held up the handful of pennies, nickels, and dimes. "Enough for an *Arizona* iced tea!" He went inside the convenience store to purchase a can.

Colin said, "Iced tea? Come on, boys. We can do better than that."

Nevin smiled.

Alastair did too.

Stewart exited the store, popped opened the iced tea, and noticed the smiles on his friends' faces. "What did I miss?"

Nevin said, "Colin suggests that we find something to drink that has a bit more kick to it than iced tea. You in?"

Stewart said, "Absolutely."

Alastair flicked his cigarette to the pavement and rubbed it out with the bottom of his sneaker. "*Mickey's?*"

Nevin, Colin, and Stewart sang, "*Mickey's!*" The four friends exchanged fist-bumps.

Mickey's was a dive bar in the south end of Dorchester. It was about as far away as Nevin, Stewart, Colin, and Alastair could get from the Savin Hill neighborhood in which they lived without ending up in Quincy. A recent episode on the *Travel* channel described dive bars as "A church for down-and-outers and those who romanticize them, a rare place where high and low rub elbows—bums and poets, thieves and slumming celebrities. It's a place that wears its history proudly."

That was all well and good. However, Nevin, Stewart, Colin, and Alastair frequented *Mickey's* because the longtime proprietor, one Michael "Mickey" Shannon, was willing to serve them alcohol even though he must have known they weren't twenty-one.

Mickey's face brightened when the four young men entered his establishment. "What do you know, boys? What do you say?" He was shouting over the Dropkick Murphys song that was blaring from the jukebox. The band hailed from Quincy and their music was seemingly on continuous loop in every dive bar in the greater Boston metropolitan area. *I'm Shipping Up to Boston* was playing at the moment.

Alastair said, "Four 'Gansett drafts, Mickey. That's what we say."

"Comin' right up." Mickey pulled four frosty mugs from the cooler behind the bar and filled each to the brim with New England's most famous low cost lager. "Isn't this a school night?" he said with a wink.

The four friends laughed. They proceeded to chug their beers and order another round.

Colin said, "No comment." He wiped his mouth with his shirt sleeve.

They all laughed again.

A familiar face at the far end of the bar stubbed out a cigarette and approached the happy group.

Stewart said, "Hey, Dillon. You holdin'?"

Dillon Boyle was the neighborhood drug dealer. He was thirty-two years old, stood six feet four inches tall, and weighed approximately two hundred and fifty pounds. Nobody messed with him, including the local street cops who looked the other way as long as he wasn't peddling hard drugs such as heroin and cocaine. He usually was, but he always told the cops that he wasn't. He nodded in the affirmative to Stewart's question. "How much ya got?"

Stewart counseled with his friends. "Thirty bucks between us."

Dillon walked back to the end of the bar at which he had been sitting and gestured for the four friends to join him. He reached into the inside pocket of his jacket and pulled out a packet of methamphetamine—"speed," "meth," or "chalk" in popular parlance. Other street names included "ice," "crystal," and "crank." It was a white, odorless, bitter-tasting pill that easily dissolved in water or alcohol and was classified as a Schedule II stimulant by the U.S. Drug Enforcement Agency, which meant that it had a high potential for abuse and was available by prescription only. Medically, it was used for the treatment of attention deficit hyperactivity disorder and obesity, but these uses were limited in the U.S. due to the high potential for abuse and diversion. Abusers typically experienced increased activity, wakefulness, talkativeness, and a sense of well-being.

Colin's eyes widened.

Stewart's did too.

Alastair said, "Happy pills."

Dillon said, "I call 'em my Walter White specials."

Walter White was the lead character on the classic TV crime drama *Breaking Bad* who had gotten rich cooking meth. He had also died in the end, but Dillon left that part out.

Nevin didn't say anything for a few moments. His mind was spinning with what his parents had implored him during dinner about not wasting his talent. But he was still a teenager, and he was still joined at the hip with his pals. He said, "I'll take two."

The four friends roughhoused around the back streets of Dorchester. Colin kicked over a trash can. Alastair broke a street light. Stewart slashed a car tire.

Nevin hesitated again. He noticed that his friends noticed.

Alastair said, "What's wrong, Nevin?"

"Nothing."

Colin said, "Bullshit. We know you too well, Nevin. Now what's wrong?"

But before Nevin could answer, five young men approached them from behind. The five were about the same age as Nevin, Alastair, Colin, and Stewart.

One of the five said, "Isn't it past your bedtime boys?"

Another said, "Where are your milk and cookies?"

The other three smirked.

Stewart said, "Let's kick their asses." It was the crank talking.

Alastair started to run towards the five guys.

"Shit," Nevin muttered to himself.

It was on.

The five guys who had appeared out of nowhere were bigger and stronger than Nevin and his friends, but the meth had emboldened the four with a sense of power and invincibility. Alastair, as usual, landed the first punch, a right hook to the jaw of the largest of the five. Stewart wasn't far behind. He delivered a series of body blows that he had learned at the YMCA during his brief flirtation with Golden Gloves boxing. The guy he hit fell to the ground clutching his stomach. Stewart proceeded to kick the guy in the head with the steel re-enforced toe of his work boot. Blood spattered the pavement like leaves shedding from a tree in autumn. Colin wasn't faring as well. Two of the five adversaries were pummeling him with fists to the face, elbows to the chest, and knees to the groin. Nevin grabbed a garbage can lid and whacked his opponent in the mouth with it, which caused the guy to drop to his knees in unfathomable pain and spit out three shattered teeth. Nevin then raced to Colin's assistance and did to the two guys who were beating on Colin what he had just done to the guy whose teeth he had broken.

Police sirens began to blare in the distance. They grew closer with every passing moment.

"The cops!" the guy Alastair was fighting called out. "Run!"

The nine young men stopped the melee as quickly as they had started it. Rule #1 on the street was unambiguous: everything ended when the police showed up.

CHAPTER 26

Hannah Burgoff returned the broom to the closet, emptied the dust pan into the wastebasket, and removed her apron. She studied the clock above the sink. *3:57 p.m.* She had less than five minutes until she was supposed to be there. She hurried out of the house to try to make it in time.

Andrew Windsor glanced at his watch. "You're late."

"Sorry. I lost track of time."

"What I'd like to do today is finish the thing we started yesterday."

"Which 'thing'?" Hannah said, smiling. "The painting or the sex?"

Andrew blushed. "The painting, my dear." He shook his head at the bluntness of Hannah's remark. Her uninhibitedness was one of the qualities he admired most about her.

Hannah removed her coat and draped it over the chair in the corner of the studio. She didn't take off the rest of her clothes, however. Andrew had never painted her nude, even though she had offered to pose naked on a number of occasions. He wasn't that sort of artist. He preferred painting people and places in their everyday state. No one spent a normal day walking around without clothes. Besides, Hannah said to herself as she positioned herself in the same pose that she had held for three hours the previous day, she didn't have the body for it.

Hannah Burgoff wasn't what anyone would call beautiful. She wasn't thin; she wasn't young; and she wasn't tall. She had never been able to figure out why Andrew Windsor—who could have hired any model he wanted—had painted her so often. She also hadn't figured out why the great artist—who could have had any woman he wanted—chose her for a romantic affair. She had once asked him about both issues. He had said, "Because it feels right."

Because it *feels* right? Hannah had no idea what that meant, and Andrew hadn't said anything more about it than that.

"Turn your head a little towards me, please."

Hannah did as she was instructed. Her nose itched. She didn't try to scratch it. Successful models learned never to move. Hannah cleaned houses for a living but she also had been modeling for America's most celebrated living artist for the better part of five years. She must have been doing something right.

Andrew's brush danced across the canvas like a conductor's baton during a symphony. He would glance at Hannah every few moments without breaking the rhythm of his work. Every painter had his or her own style. Some painted slowly and studied each stroke as it was made. Others painted quickly, as if they were in a trance induced by the proverbial muse. Andrew fell somewhere in between: he was confident enough in his talent that he didn't second guess his choices but he was also careful enough to make sure that he was making the proper choices.

"You're doing great, Hannah. Thanks."

Hannah still didn't move. But she was smiling inside.

Four hours later, the painting was completed.

Andrew cleaned his brush and palette. He patted them dry with a chamois. "What do you think?"

Hannah cracked her neck and massaged her shoulders. They often got stiff when she posed. She studied the painting. She said, "I've been posing for you for almost five years now and I'm always overcome with emotion when I see what you've managed to do. It's beautiful."

Andrew beamed and kissed Hannah on the cheek. "It's all about the model, my dear. It's all about the model."

Of course they both knew that wasn't true. It was all about the artist, and Andrew Windsor was a great artist.

Hannah unlocked the door to the modest two-bedroom bungalow she shared with her husband and invited Andrew inside. Her husband was out on the water with his crew. He fished for cod for a living. It was difficult work but, as he always said, it was better than being cooped up in an office all day working for someone who didn't appreciate you. He had tried that life for a while and hadn't liked it.

Hannah said, "Do you want a drink?"

"A cold beer would be great. Thanks."

Hannah went to the kitchen to get the beer.

Andrew made himself comfortable on the couch. He studied the room. Artists were observers by nature. He certainly was. He was always looking for something that would inspire his next painting. He didn't do it consciously; it was how he was wired.

Hannah returned with two bottles of *Narragansett*. They were ice cold.

Andrew smiled. "The champagne of Rhode Island."

Hannah sat down on the couch next to Andrew and clinked her beer bottle against his. "Cheers," she said.

"Cheers." Andrew took a long drink. "That hits the spot." He pointed to a painting above the fireplace. "The piece looks good there."

It was one of Andrew's seascapes.

"It certainly does. My husband asked me why you gave it to us."

Andrew smiled again. "Tell him that it was for all the hard work you've done for us over the years up at the house. I only wish it could've been one of my paintings of you, but you know why it can't be."

Of course Hannah knew why it couldn't be. There were two reasons, actually. First, because it might tip-off her husband about her affair with Andrew. Second, and almost certainly more important for Andrew himself, no one was supposed to know about the series of paintings that he had been doing of Hannah.

***

Lauren Windsor opened the file cabinet in her study and removed the invoices for the paintings that Andrew had sold during the prior calendar year. It was tax season again and everyone had to pay the piper. That included famous artists such as her husband. It had been a good year—a year that almost any other artist would have been delighted about. Andrew was far from the clichéd "starving artist," and Lauren was certainly grateful for that, especially since they had three teenagers to feed. Lauren, however, was focused on the long term. Her husband was fifty years old and sales of his work had been slipping for the last five years or so. It wasn't a large decline, but it was a trend, and Lauren was worried about it. That was why she had advised her husband to begin his "secret" paintings. The theory was that Andrew would build up a large reserve of paintings that no one but Lauren, Andrew, and the model knew about and then leak them to the world years down the road when interest in Andrew's work had ebbed to an unacceptable level. Lauren wasn't certain when that day would be. She had mentioned to her husband that twenty years from now was a best guess, which meant that by the time they really needed a public relations boost Andrew would have compiled quite a cache of "secret" paintings.

Lauren heard on a knock at the door. "Come in," she said.

The butler entered the room. He was accompanied by the youngest of the Windsor children, a sixteen-year-old walking headache that she and Andrew had named after her father.

"What did you do this time, James?" She dismissed the butler with an impersonal thank you.

James Windsor said, "Nothing, Mom. I swear. I didn't do anything."

"Then why did the principal call me an hour ago and tell me to come and get you?"

Lauren herself hadn't retrieved her son. She had dispatched the butler to do it. Rich people rarely did their own dirty work.

"I don't know, Mom. Maybe it's because he's jealous."

"'Jealous'? Jealous of what?"

"Of how famous Dad is, and of how much money we have."

Lauren shook her head. "Listen, James: Almost everyone at that school has a lot of money. It's the most expensive private school in the state. And there are other so-called famous people who send their kids there too. Senator Kearney, for one."

Silence from James. He might have been the son of a famous artist, but that didn't mean he was smart. "I don't know why the principal called you then."

Lauren stood from her desk and approached her son. She brushed the hair from his eyes. As usual, he needed a haircut. "How's this for a reason, James: because you beat up Brandon Kingsley. Does that sound like a possibility?"

More silence from James. He fidgeted with his watch, a *Rolex Sea-Dweller* that used to belong to his grandfather. He finally said something after his mother's disappointed stare had become too much for him to bear. All he could come up with was, "He started it."

Lauren—James's exasperated mother—shook her head again. "Sort of like the way that Peter Wallace 'started it'? or Samuel Smith? or Teddy Brewster?... Do you want me to keep going, James? It's quite a list at this point."

"What do you want me to say, Mom?" James fidgeted again with his watch. He gazed sheepishly at his shoes.

"'I'm sorry' would be a good start. Call Brandon on the telephone right now and tell him that you're sorry. Then you can apologize to the principal. He could have called the police, you know. With your track record, he should have called them. But your father donated money for a new art studio and the principal owed him a favor. Your father is running out of chits, though, James. You better clean up your act. At some point, we won't be able to solve your problems for you."

CHAPTER 27

Meredith Adams shimmied into riding breeches and reached for her favorite pair of *Dublin* turndown boots. She grabbed her soft shell vest and headed to the barn for her afternoon ride. Willie, the family's longtime paddock hand, had promised to have Chestnut, Meredith's favorite horse, saddled and ready to ride.

"Happy birthday, Ms. Meredith," Willie said when the only child of Jefferson and Juliet Adams approached the barn. "I can't believe it's your sweet sixteen already. It seems like it was only yesterday that your mama and daddy were bringing you home from the hospital. You sure were a pretty baby."

Meredith smiled and said, "Thank you, Willie. I can't believe it's my sweet sixteen either.... Is Chestnut ready?"

"Yes, ma'am. He's ready and raring to go. He always loves it when you take him out. But don't be too long now. I promised your mama that you'd be back in time for your party."

A sweet sixteen was a coming of age party celebrating a young woman's sixteenth birthday. The party could be formal, semi-formal, or casual; and it could range from a modest party at home with close family and friends to large affairs with a hired DJ, makeup and hair stylists, yachts, and hotel ballrooms. Jefferson and Juliet Adams were going all out for Meredith's party: they invited more than two hundred guests; they announced the party in the *Boston Globe*; they arranged for a tiara ceremony; and they planned on surprising Meredith with her first car. Meredith's parents knew that Meredith was a huge James Bond fan and the car they bought her was a testament to that fact: a brand-new *Aston Martin DB5*.

Meredith smiled again. "I'll be back in an hour, Willie. I promise." She took a firm grip of the reins, placed her forward foot in the stirrup, grabbed the front of the saddle, and pulled herself up onto the massive horse. She lowered herself slowly into the saddle, adjusted her seat, and tapped Chestnut gently behind his tummy area. He began to move forward, as he had been trained to do.

Meredith and her parents lived on a large estate on the outskirts of Williamstown, Massachusetts in a part of the state known as the

Berkshires. Berkshire County was formed as a governing body in 1761 and it included the western extremity of Massachusetts, with its western boundary bordering New York and its eastern boundary paralleling the watershed divide separating the Connecticut River watershed from the Housatonic River-Hoosic River watersheds. Geologically and physically, the Berkshires were the southern continuation of the Green Mountains of Vermont, distinct from them only by their average lower elevation and the side of the border on which they fell.

Williamstown was home to Williams College, one of the top liberal arts colleges in the United States, and the college at which Meredith's father had been a tenured member of the History Department for nearly thirty years. It was quite a coup for Jefferson Adams to have begun his teaching career at such a prestigious college, but most freshly minted PhDs weren't the great-great-great-great grandson of one of the founders of the United States of America.

John Adams (1735-1826) had been a leader of the American Revolution, an influential diplomat, the vice president of the United States under George Washington, and the successor to Washington as president of the United States. He had been the subject of countless books by historians over the years, including the Pulitzer Prize winning *John Adams* by David McCullough. Adams's eldest son, John Quincy Adams, also had become president of the United States, and every generation of Adams since had spawned men and women who had contributed greatly to American life.

Meredith's father was leaving his legacy in American letters. His first book, an intellectual history of John Adams's stormy relationship with Thomas Jefferson, had received the John Phillip Reid Prize in American History. His second, a discourse on Alexander Hamilton's influence on George Washington, had won the National Book Award. His current project, *The Animating Principles of Early American Law*, was exploring (1) why each of the original thirteen English American colonies had been founded and (2) how a particular colony's laws had effectuated and/or inhibited that particular colony's animating principle. When Meredith's father had mentioned to a colleague what he was working on at the moment, his colleague had laughed and said, "That'll take you twenty years to finish, Jeff. Good thing you've got tenure."

Meredith had been riding horses for as long as she could remember. Her mother had grown up on a horse farm in upstate New York and she had famously conditioned her acceptance of Jefferson Adams's marriage proposal on his promise that they would raise their family on a horse farm too. Jefferson, who had met the former Juliet Roland when they were both undergraduate students at Harvard, was so head over heels in love with Juliet that he would have promised her anything.

And Jefferson had kept his word. As soon as he had joined the History Department at Williams, he took his new bride on a series of house hunting trips throughout Berkshire County. They knew they had found their home the moment they laid eyes on what they eventually named Mountainview Farm. Fifteen years after that, Meredith Roland Adams entered the world.

Meredith tugged lightly on the reins and encouraged Chestnut to switch from a trot to a canter. As usual, Chestnut did as he was instructed. Willie always said that Chestnut brightened every time Meredith was around and that the horse wanted to please her. "Good boy," Meredith said as she patted Chestnut on the neck.

It was a beautiful spring morning. The meadows were exploding with the vibrant colors of blooming wild flowers; the air was fresh and sweet; and the sun reflected off the lake at the bottom of the valley like a new star in a distant galaxy. It was a perfect day for a party, and Meredith was having a difficult time containing her excitement.

"Giddy-up, boy!" she said. She tapped her heels against Chestnut's side to get him to gallop.

And gallop he did. The massive horse accelerated like a race car at the Daytona 500 after a yellow caution flag had been rescinded.

Meredith loved speed, though. She always had. She took after her father in that respect. A large grin captured her pretty face. "Good boy, Chestnut. Good boy." She tapped her heels against the horse's side again to make him go faster.

That was a mistake—the biggest mistake of her young life.

The trail on which she was riding was too narrow to handle the sort of speed that Meredith was demanding of Chestnut. Meredith's mother was constantly reminding her only child to be careful, but Meredith's father had repeatedly encouraged Meredith to take risks. "Successful people take chances, sweetheart," he would say to her. "Look at John Adams and the brave men of his day: they pledged—literally pledged—their 'lives... fortunes... and sacred honor' in the Declaration of Independence so that this country could be free."

Meredith's father was usually correct. Not this time, though...

Chestnut stumbled over a fallen tree and bucked forward. Meredith, who had tremendous balance and coordination, was jarred violently from the saddle. She started to roll down a steep hill to the left of the trail. She reached for something to stop her momentum: tree limbs, bushes—anything she could get her hands on. But nothing worked. She was rolling too fast. She was dizzy and nauseous.

Suddenly, she stopped.

Suddenly, she couldn't feel her legs.

She reached her arms behind her head and felt a large rock.

She started to cry and scream out for help.

She was too far into the countryside for anyone to hear her.

***

Meredith didn't know how much time had passed before Willie found her. Willie said it was only a couple of hours and that it was Meredith's mother who had asked Willie to look for Meredith when Meredith had failed to show for her sweet sixteen.

Willie had saddled another of the Adams's magnificent horses and galloped off in the direction that he had seen Meredith head. His practice had always been to note where she was going when she went for a ride. He had children of his own, and he knew that kids tended to be more reckless than wise and that they frequently made decisions without understanding the consequences. He had known Meredith all of her life and he knew that she was no different. She might have had a famous last name and more money than most, but she was still a kid. Meredith's mother realized that. Willie sometimes wondered whether her father did.

"Don't move," Willie said to a hysterical Meredith. Willie's eyes surveyed the scene. He wasn't a doctor, obviously; but he knew a terrible injury when he saw one. His mind spun like a Ferris wheel as he contemplated what to do. "Don't move," he said again. He reached into his pocket and retrieved his cell phone. He punched the speed dial entry that connected him to the main house.

Juliet Adams answered on the first ring. "Did you find her?" she asked, with a tremble in her voice.

Willie turned away from Meredith and cupped his hand over his mouth so that the injured teenager couldn't hear him. "Yes, ma'am," he whispered into the phone. "We're on Hancock Trail, about a half a mile past Cambridge Lake. Call 911. She's hurt real bad."

CHAPTER 28

Lauren Windsor knocked on the door of her husband's studio. There was no answer. That wasn't unusual. When Andrew Windsor was painting, he was oblivious to the rest of the world. It was as if he were in a trance.

Lauren pushed open the door and stepped into the studio. She felt a cool breeze from a window that was ajar on the east side of the room. The salty air from the ocean mixed with the smells of turpentine and paint. Andrew was sitting on a stool, his back to the door, working on a canvas that Lauren was eager to see. She maneuvered around stacks of supplies: paint cans; turpentine jars; buckets of discarded brushes; canvases, both new and used. She said, "I brought some fresh coffee." She placed a stainless-steel thermos on the small table next to her husband's workstation.

Andrew snapped back to reality, looked at his wife of thirty years, and said, "Thank you, Lauren. I could use a pick-me-up." He noticed that his wife had also brought a tin of *Walker's Shortbread* for him to nibble on.

Lauren finally got to see what Andrew was working on. "That's beautiful…. Is it Hannah?"

Andrew nodded. "We finished it yesterday. I'm touching it up now." He unscrewed the top of the thermos and poured a steaming cup of joe. He dipped a piece of shortbread into the cup and devoured the cookie in two quick bites.

Lauren couldn't take her eyes off the painting, which was always a good sign for any artist. Great art held the viewer hostage. The *Mona Lisa* was the classic example of that fact: it was a simple portrait of a simple woman, but Leonardo Da Vinci had painted it so perfectly that it mesmerized everyone who saw it. Lauren said, "I love it."

Andrew smiled. Thirty years into a sometimes rocky marriage, it still mattered to the great artist what his wife thought of a particular painting. "I'm glad. I like it too."

"I mean, I really love it." Lauren placed her hands on her husband's shoulders and began to massage them.

"That feels great, hon. I haven't taken a break all day."

"I was afraid of that. You shouldn't work so hard, Andrew. It's not good for your shoulder."

Andrew had tripped over a rock earlier in the spring and had torn his right rotator cuff. The doctor had diagnosed a partial tear rather than a full tear, which meant that surgery could be avoided. But the doctor had instructed Andrew to take a fifteen-minute break every hour. The doctor had told Lauren to make sure that Andrew did so.

Andrew said, "I know, Lauren. I guess I got lost in my work and forgot to take a break. Besides, my shoulder has been feeling pretty good lately."

"I'm glad to hear your shoulder is feeling better. That doesn't mean you can stop taking breaks, though. You know what the doctor said."

Andrew nodded. "I know."

Lauren returned her attention to the painting. "I always thought that Hannah was kind of homely. You made her look beautiful, though. I can't believe what I'm seeing."

"It's like the song says, hon: 'Everything is beautiful, in its own way.' Hannah and I were joking about that when I first asked her to pose for me. She said that she thought models had to look like Christie Brinkley. I said she was wrong. I told her that a painter is more interested in inner beauty… in someone's soul. Sort of like what I said to you when we first started dating."

Lauren smiled and slapped her husband on the top of his head. "Ha-ha, funny guy. You're a real David Letterman. You and I both know that you were always interested in my outer beauty."

Andrew chuckled. "You got me there, Lauren. You got me there." He cleaned a smudge from the corner of the painting with the moist rag that he kept draped across the side of the easel.

"Have you thought about doing another one?"

"Of Hannah?"

Lauren nodded. "You could do a series. Monet painted a series of about two hundred and fifty water lilies from his garden in Givery. As you know, they're on display in galleries all over the world: from the Art Institute of Chicago, to the Musée d'Orsay in Paris, to scores of galleries in between. Van Gogh did a famous series of sunflowers. He started with four in Arles and then painted another three. He had originally planned to do a series of twelve, but he got sick. Monet subscribed to Valenciennes's notion that it was good to paint the same object at different times of the day to study the differences that light makes on forms. Sunflowers became a symbol of Van Gogh and also of the way he liked to work. He started painting every morning at dawn because the flowers wilted quickly and he needed to try and finish the paintings in one shot." Lauren paused and looked at her husband. He was as handsome as the day they met.

"Why a series about Hannah, though? A series of seascapes of the Cape I can understand. But Hannah? I don't get it."

Actually, Andrew did get it. However, he wanted Lauren to think it was her idea so she wouldn't start asking other questions about Hannah.

Lauren said, "Because, to the best of my knowledge, no artist has ever painted a series about a person before. That would make your series unique."

Andrew didn't reply to Lauren's most recent point.

"Besides," Lauren continued, "we need to start thinking about the future."

That drew a response from Andrew. "What do you mean?"

"There are a lot of artists out there, Andrew. You know that. None are as talented as you, but the public doesn't always gravitate to talent. A lot of it is marketing. 'Robert Nelson has captured the pulse of a generation.' 'Jorge Batiste is the new Picasso.' Of course their publicists never get any more specific than that, and they certainly never explain what it means to 'capture the pulse of a generation' or to be 'the new Picasso.' But they manage to sell a lot of mediocre art. Your art is far from mediocre, and I want to make sure that the public continues to appreciate it."

Andrew started cleaning his workstation. He dipped his brushes into a jar of turpentine. He reached for a rag to dry them. "OK," he finally said. "I'll see if Hannah is interested."

He already knew that she was.

***

Andrew Windsor and Hannah Burgoff had started sleeping together on the third day that Hannah had posed for the painting that Lauren liked so much. It was Hannah who had initiated the affair. She had worked for the Windsors for more than a decade but posing for Andrew was the first time that she had spent any significant time with him. She had quickly discovered how appealing he was. Sure, he was rich and famous. Hannah didn't care about that, though. She was fascinated by how focused he was about his work, and how good he was at it. Henry Kissinger may have quipped that power was the greatest aphrodisiac, but for Hannah talent—*genius*, in Andrew's case—was what did it for her. Her husband was a wonderful man and a reliable provider. However, he was about as exciting as a meat-loaf dinner. Andrew Windsor was Carne Asada.

CHAPTER 29

Spider webs spiraled throughout the abandoned house like paper snowflakes in an elementary school classroom. Streams of sunlight breached the darkness from the cracks and crevasses that always made the circle of friends wonder how much longer the house would remain standing. Nevin Montgomery, Alastair Ainsley, Colin Dunn, and Stewart MacGregor had been using the house on Essex Street as their makeshift hangout ever since they had become fast friends at Eugene L. McIlroy Middle School. They were now juniors at John F. Kennedy High School. Both schools were public institutions. Private schools were expensive and none of the friends came from wealthy families. Besides, there were no private schools in Dorchester. The benefactors of those elite establishments preferred to locate their schools in suburbs such as Wellesley, Newton, and Lincoln.

Colin asked, "Who's holdin'?"

Alastair answered, "Stewart said he was."

Colin said, "It's time to share the wealth, Stew."

Stewart smiled and reached into his pocket. He pulled out a sandwich bag containing a quarter ounce of marijuana. "Dillon said it's Columbian."

Nevin laughed. "And you believed him? Shit, I bet he grew it in his basement."

Colin said, "But it's better than nothin'. Besides, it'll be like a trip down memory lane. Do you guys remember the first time we got high together?"

***

"Hey. I'm Colin. This here is Alastair, and that mook is Stewart."

"I'm Nevin."

School had ended for the day. The four boys were standing in the circle where the buses waited.

Colin asked, "Are you new?"

Nevin answered, "To Mrs. Flanagan's class? Yeah. To McIlroy? No. I got the boot from Mr. Clarke's class."

"You must've done something pretty rad to get kicked out of Mr. Clarke's class in the middle of the year. My sister had him. She said he's pretty nice. What did you do?"

"Why do you care?"

"Just curious, man. No biggie."

Kids began to board the buses. The cacophony of chatter revealed the innocence of their young lives.

Colin, Alastair, and Stewart were a different story altogether. They began to walk away.

Nevin finally said, "I got in too many fights."

Colin stopped. Alastair and Stewart did likewise.

Stewart said, "Cool."

Alastair said, "How many is 'too many'."

Nevin said, "I lost count."

Colin smiled and said, "You got somewhere you need to be?"

Nevin said, "Why?"

"Because we're headed off to have some fun and I thought you might like to tag along."

Nevin's mother was expecting him at home to mow the lawn. He said, "I'm in."

Colin led the quartet through the back streets of Dorchester. They passed *Southside Pizzeria* on Waterford Street where they usually stopped for a slice after school. This time they kept walking. Stewart peaked into *Foley's Laundromat* to make sure his mom wasn't doing a wash. Alastair ducked into *O'Donnell's Mini-Mart* for a pack of gum and a roll of *Lifesavers*. Colin kept leading the others towards a destination only he seemed to know existed, which forced Alastair to sprint to catch up.

Finally, they arrived at the desired location.

Colin said, "What do you think?"

Alastair said, "About what? About a beat up old house that looks like it's about to crumble to the ground?... What street is this, Essex?"

Stewart starting singing John Cougar Mellencamp's hit, *Crumblin' Down*: "When the walls come tumblin' down. When the walls come crumblin' crumblin'. When the walls come tumblin' tumblin' down. Yeah yeah yeah."

Colin said, "Very funny. But it's not falling down. I've been inside. Come on, I'll show you." He gestured for Stewart, Alastair, and Nevin to follow him into the house.

Stewart said, "Are you sure it's safe?"

Colin said, "I'm sure."

Nevin disagreed, but he kept his lack of confidence to himself. He had just met Colin, Alastair, and Stewart, and he didn't want them to think he wasn't cool.

Alastair said, "How did you find this place?"

Colin said, "I got sticky fingers at *O'Shaunessy's Hardware*, and old man O'Shaunessy wasn't too happy about it."

"Yeah. So?"

"He chased me out of the store, and he kept chasing me. He was carrying a wrench at the time and I ducked into this place to avoid getting whacked upside the head.... That old dude is crazy. My dad says he used to be a Marine."

Stewart said, "What were you doing in his hardware store in the first place?"

"It was my dad's birthday and I needed to get him a gift."

Nevin said, "Now that's a good son: ripping off the neighborhood hardware store for pop's big day. I hope you snagged somethin' better than a bag of nails."

Everybody laughed.

Colin said, "The mummy speaks. I made off with a sweet power drill. My dad loved it. Now let's get stoned." He reached into his pocket and pulled out a joint that would have made Bob Marley proud.

Alastair said, "Rasta mon. Let's fire up that bad boy."

Stewart started singing a Bob Marley song this time. "Get up, stand up: stand up for your rights! Get up, stand up: don't give up the fight!"

"Your wish is my command." Colin struck a match and lit the joint. He took a long drag and held the smoke in his mouth for a good thirty seconds. He finally exhaled.

Stewart said, "Don't bogart that doobie." He started singing a Doobie Brothers song.

Colin passed the joint to Stewart, who took a hit and passed it to Alastair.

Alastair said, "Watch this." He inhaled the marijuana deep into his lungs and held his breath. Ten seconds. Twenty seconds. Thirty seconds. Forty seconds. Fifty seconds. His eyes watered. He finally took a breath. "A new world record." He passed the joint to Nevin.

"Thanks." Nevin studied the marijuana cigarette. "I've never done this before. What's it like?"

Colin said, "It's great, man. Relaxing. It'll make you giggle—"

"—And hungry," Stewart interjected. "Go for it."

Nevin shrugged his shoulders. "What the hell." He brought the joint to his lips, pinched the tip, and inhaled.

Colin said, "Remember to hold it in."

Nevin nodded, and did as Colin instructed. He began to cough and wheeze.

Colin, Stewart, and Alastair laughed.

Alastair said, "Are you OK?"

Nevin hacked out a "Ye—Yeah."

Stewart said, "You don't look OK. My first time was tough too. You'll get used to it, though."

Nevin said "I g—guess," as he continued to cough.

"Here." Colin handed Nevin the can of *Pepsi* that he had been drinking.

Nevin took a sip. "Thanks."

"So? What do you think?" Colin retrieved his *Pepsi* from Nevin's outstretched hand. He wiped the rim clean with his shirt sleeve.

Stewart said, "Give him a minute for it to kick in."

They waited a few moments.

The wind howled through the holes in the dilapidated house. A car horn sounded in the distance. Brakes squealed, but apparently an accident was avoided.

A large grin captured Nevin's handsome face. "I like it," he finally said. "Now who's up for a *Burger King* run?"

CHAPTER 30

Meredith Adams propped herself up on her elbows and swung her legs over the side of her bed. She dreaded this routine, but she had no choice. She had been paralyzed from the waist down ever since she was thrown from her horse two years earlier. She glanced down at her legs, which had atrophied to the point that they now looked more like tree twigs than human appendages. Of course this upset Meredith every time she thought about it. Like most teenaged girls, Meredith cared a lot about her appearance. After all, teenaged girls thought, what mattered most to teenaged boys was what a girl looked like.

Meredith started to cry.

Jefferson Adams entered his daughter's bedroom. "What's wrong, sweetheart?" He rushed to her bedside and wiped her tears with his thumb.

"I—I—I'm ugly, Daddy." Meredith's tears flowed like a river as soon as she said that.

Jefferson Adams felt as if he had been stabbed in the heart. Like any loving parent, he would have switched places with his daughter in an instant. Let her walk, God, he had prayed on more occasions than he could count. Take my legs instead.

But God didn't work like that. As everyone knew, God worked in mysterious ways.

Jefferson's attention promptly returned to his daughter. "Don't be ridiculous. You're beautiful, sweetheart. Lucky for you, you look like your mother and not like me."

Jefferson's self-deprecating remark drew a much appreciated smile from Meredith. She glanced at her father, her eyes still clouded with tears, and said, "I love you, Daddy."

Jefferson's eyes clouded also. "I love you too, sweetheart."

Juliet Adams had just finished preparing breakfast when her husband and daughter entered the kitchen. "Perfect timing," she said with a thousand-watt smile. "Did you finish your term paper, Meredith?"

Meredith maneuvered her wheelchair through the kitchen to her standard place at the table. She locked the brakes. "Yes, thank goodness. I don't see how Daddy does it."

"Does what?" Juliet asked. She poured three glasses of cranberry juice and placed them on the table.

"Write books for a living."

Jefferson Adams smiled this time. His heart sang as it became apparent that Meredith had recovered from her emotional meltdown of a few minutes earlier. He said, "People have different talents, sweetheart. Take your mother, for example. She's a wonderful athlete. She was All-Ivy League in both tennis and squash in college. Me, I'm as uncoordinated as a drunken sailor on shore leave. But I've always been told I'm a good writer. I know that I've always enjoyed writing."

Juliet placed a plate of pancakes in front of Meredith, who had suddenly grown quiet again. Both Juliet and Jefferson knew what this meant: their daughter was trying to figure out her place in the world.

Meredith finally said, "What's my talent, Daddy?"

"Talents, plural, sweetheart. Talents, plural." He leaned down and kissed his daughter on the forehead. "First and foremost, you're incredibly loving and considerate. That's a rare talent in the 'me first' age in which we live. Second, you're extremely bright. Your mother and I are so proud of how well you do in school. Third, you're very creative. Neither your mother nor I can draw a straight line, but your paintings are good enough to hang in galleries. Your art teacher is always raving about them."

Meredith poured maple syrup on her pancakes. "You're saying that because you're my father."

"No I'm not. I'm saying it because it's true. You've known me your entire life, obviously. Have you ever known me to lie?"

Meredith shook her head no.

"I'm telling the truth this time too." Jefferson sat back in his chair. He wiped his mouth with a napkin. "Listen, sweetheart. Your mother and I know that your accident has impacted your life in ways that we can't imagine. But you can't let it make you lose confidence in yourself or cause you to forget how beautiful and talented you are. You're a one-in-a-million young lady, and your mother and I thank God every day that you're our daughter."

"Thank you, Daddy," Meredith whispered as she fought back tears.

James Windsor waited by his locker after school for the cute blonde whose family had moved from San Diego to Barnstable in the middle of the semester. The school's guidance counselor had escorted the young woman to James's homeroom and introduced her to the class. Her name was Melissa Martin. She preferred to be called Missy.

One of James's classmates stopped at his own locker to drop off his math book. He spotted James, and said, "What are you still doing here? You're usually the first one out the door."

Missy Martin came strolling down the corridor. Both young men glanced in her direction.

James's classmate said, "I get it." He placed his math book in his locker and retrieved his history book. "Good luck, Romeo. Let me know how it goes. That's about as good as it gets." He shut his locker and headed for the exit.

Missy Martin was only a few steps away from James's locker.

James sang, "Oh my my, when she walks on by, it's hard not to get lost in the view."

Missy stopped, and said, "Bruce Hornsby & the Range."

"Truer words have never been spoken."

Missy blushed. "Subtle, you're not."

"Life's too short for subtlety."

Missy blushed again. "Don't you think I should know your name first? The guidance counselor already told you mine."

"I'm James. James Windsor." He extended his hand to make Missy's formal introduction. Her hand was soft and warm.

"Nice to meet you, James. How long have you lived around here?"

"Forever, it seems. For three generations, actually. My grandfather bought a bunch of land on the water after he hit it big. We live on the property now."

"You're Andrew Windsor's son, and C. S. Windsor's grandson?"

"Guilty as charged." James finally released Missy's hand.

"Do you paint too?"

"Now that's an interesting question. It depends who you ask. Mr. Miller, the school's art teacher, thinks so. My father doesn't, though.... Dad's a pretty tough audience."

"Do you like to paint?"

"Absolutely. I enjoy transforming what I see to a canvas. Painting is different from photography. Painters aren't trying to reproduce what they see. They're trying to interpret it."

Missy smiled. "That's quite a profound insight for a high school boy."

"Like you said, I'm Andrew Windsor's son and C. S. Windsor's grandson. I've been around painters all my life. Other guys talk about baseball with their dads and grandpas. We talk about painting in my house."

Missy continued smiling.

The world seemed like a better place when she did.

James added, "I usually paint seascapes, but I'd love to paint you. Your smile is spectacular."

So was her body, but James kept that thought to himself.

James and Missy arrived at the Windsor family compound at approximately four p.m. He called for his mother and father, but no one answered. Next he beckoned unsuccessfully for the butler.

James said, "I guess we've got the place to ourselves. Do you want the grand tour?"

Missy said, "Sure."

James described each and every painting that hung on the walls. Most were painted by James's father, with a few of James's grandfather's drawings sprinkled in for variety. None of James's work was displayed.

"They're beautiful," Missy said after they reached the end of the main hallway.

"So are you."

Missy blushed again. "I bet you say that to all the girls."

He did, but he didn't admit it to Missy. "Would you like to see some of my work? Remember, though, it's not as good as my father's or my grandfather's."

"I'll be the judge of that. Let's take a look."

James led Missy up the stairs, and to the back of the house.

"This is my room." James opened the door. "After you, madam."

Missy entered James's bedroom. Unlike the bedrooms of most teenaged boys, there weren't any posters of sports stars or rock bands on the walls. James's room was decorated with James's art. "It's great," Missy said after surveying the paintings.

"Thanks. But those are the best of the lot. I've painted a lot of clunkers as well."

Missy laughed. "I bet your dad could say the same thing."

"Actually, he couldn't. My father could sneeze and it would be declared a triumph in the Arts section of the *New York Times*."

Missy continued studying the paintings. They were all seascapes, just as James had mentioned at school. "Do you still want to paint me?"

"Absolutely. And there's no time like the present. Would you be willing to pose nude?"

CHAPTER 31

"**Y**ou mean with no clothes on?" Missy Martin's blushing had transformed into full-on panic.

James Windsor smiled. "As you'll find out after you've taken Mrs. Jensen for American Lit; yes, nude means that you won't have any clothes on." He stopped smiling. "Seriously, though: I'm an artist. Artists paint portraits of nudes all the time. Of course I'm also a young artist, which means that you'll be my first nude."

Silence filled James's bedroom.

The grandfather clock in the hallway ticked and tocked.

Missy again studied James's paintings. She lingered on each and every one. She finally said, "OK. I'll do it. I guess I should be flattered that I'm your first."

They both laughed at Missy's awkward attempt at a humorous double entendre.

"Great. How about we head down to the beach?"

"Outside? You want me to take off my clothes outside?" Missy wasn't trying to be funny this time.

"No worries. It's a private beach. No one else will be there."

"But *outside*? I'm already nervous enough as it is."

"I can paint you in my room if you want, but indoor nudes are a dime a dozen. I think we'll really have something special with the ocean as the backdrop."

More silence.

Then Missy said, "If you think it best."

"I do." James walked to the corner of his room where he stored his supplies. He grabbed a clean canvas, an easel, and the metal box that contained his paints and brushes. "Ready?"

Missy nodded.

James led Missy through the back part of his parents' house. He opened the door for her. He glanced into the horizon. The sun was beginning to set. Oranges, reds, and yellows glimmered against the blue backdrop of the gloaming.

He said, "This light will be perfect. I bet they don't have sunsets like this in San Diego."

Obviously, that wasn't true. San Diego was famous for its spectacular weather. But James was a Windsor, and as a Windsor he was incapable of imaging a world that he didn't inhabit.

James and Missy arrived at James's favorite spot: an isolated stretch of beach at the east end of his family's compound. A towering red maple provided the extra privacy that Missy obviously wanted, and that James desperately needed.

James positioned his easel on a flat spot of sand. He opened his paint-box and then glanced up at Missy. "I'm ready when you are," he said.

"I'm re—ready." Missy's eyes widened and her hands began to shake. She unbuttoned her blouse, which revealed a black lace bra. Next, she removed her jeans. Her panties matched her bra. She looked at James, who appeared to be observing her in an almost clinical fashion.

James said, "Don't forget the bra and panties."

Missy took a deep breath and complied.

"Thanks." James dipped his brush into the palette that his grandfather had given to him shortly before passing away when James was six. Most artists began a portrait with the model's hair. James was no different. "Hold still, please." He made a series of sweeping yellow strokes that captured the color and texture of Missy's hair.

"S—Sorry." Missy couldn't have sounded more nervous.

James finished painting Missy's hair and face. He moved to her body. Her breasts, while not large, were perfectly shaped and firm. Her legs were long and lean. "Are you a runner?"

"Y—Yes. How did you know?"

"From your legs. They're great, by the way."

By the time James had finished painting Missy's portrait the sun had set and his work was being illuminated by moonlight.

"I'm done," James announced. "Come and see."

Missy had been posing naked for more than four hours. She was lucky it was a warm night. She dressed, and then walked over to examine the painting. "It's great, but my parents are gonna kill me."

"Why?"

"Because I'm naked! My dad is a Navy man, not an artist. All he'll see is a naked picture of his little girl."

"So he'll be mad?"

"'Mad' is an understatement."

"What about your mom?"

"My dad is the mellow one. My mom will want to kill you." Missy laughed at the hyperbole. "I'm kidding, of course. But to be safe, can you not let anyone see it for a while?"

James smirked. "What would I get in return?" He pulled Missy close and tried to kiss her.

"Wh—What are you doing?" She pushed him away, but he was bigger and stronger than she was, and he wouldn't take no for an answer.

***

Missy Martin was awakened by the sunrise. She was in no position to appreciate its majesty, however. She had just experienced the worst night of her life. What had started out as a flattering invitation from a handsome new schoolmate had turned into the sort of sexual assault that so frequently went unreported in the United States. And Missy certainly had no plans to report what had happened to her. After all, she had agreed to take her clothes off. No police officer in the world would believe that she hadn't agreed to the sex that followed. James Windsor certainly hadn't believed that "no" meant *no*.

CHAPTER 32

James Windsor dressed and got ready for school. He was late, as usual. He hurried down the stairs.

His mother said, "What time did you get in last night?"

James said, "About ten."

"That's a bit late for a school night, don't you think?"

"Sorry, Mom. I was painting and lost track of time. I figured that you and dad had gone out for the evening anyway, and that you wouldn't miss me."

"We invited you to come, but you said you had other things to do. At least I know now what you were up to."

The problem was, she didn't.

Missy Martin's father was waiting by the door when his daughter entered the house. "Where have you been, young lady?" His arms were folded tightly across his chest. "Your mother and I have been worried sick."

Missy reddened, but her appearance was otherwise fine: she had shaken the sand from her clothes, tied her hair in a ponytail, and splashed ocean water on her face. Frankly, she looked beautiful. But she always looked beautiful. God had blessed her that way. "I—I fell asleep at a friend's house," she said. "Sorry I didn't call." She maneuvered around one the boxes that had yet to be unpacked from their recent move from San Diego.

Matt Martin studied his daughter's angelic face. He was a tough-as-nails Navy man, but he was a soft touch when it came to disciplining his daughter. He uncrossed his arms and wiped a smudge from Missy's cheek. "Well, as long as you're OK.... I'm glad to know you've made a new friend." He knew how hard it had been on Missy to have been forced to move as often as they did. But that's what Navy families did, and he was glad to hear that Missy had made a friend so quickly. It usually took her quite a while to open up to her new classmates. "You better get ready for school." He checked his watch. "The bus will be here in twenty minutes."

Missy Martin didn't attend school that day. It wasn't because she had missed the bus. In fact, she had exited the house as if she were on her way to the bus stop. But she couldn't bear the thought of seeing James Windsor again, especially so soon after he had raped her.

Missy spent the day wandering around town, trying her best to make it seem like she was simply one of the dozens of tourists who frequented Barnstable each and every day. At precisely three o'clock p.m., she headed for home. Three o'clock was when school adjourned.

James Windsor had spent the day searching for Missy. She wasn't in homeroom. She wasn't in American History. She wasn't in Geography. She wasn't in any of their common classes. He wondered what that meant.

Missy Martin wasn't the first pretty girl who had initially resisted James's charms, and he suspected that she wouldn't be the last. But he had to find her to make sure that she wasn't going to say anything about the previous night.

Missy's mother knocked on her daughter's door. There was no answer. She knocked again and turned the knob. A blood curdling scream filled the house the instant that Missy's mother opened the door and saw her daughter dangling limply from the metal plant hanger that Missy had asked her father to install so that she could decorate her room with a favorite cactus that she had brought from San Diego.

Missy's mother rushed to her daughter and frantically tried to release her only child from the belt that was wrapped tightly around her neck. She managed to do so, and her daughter fell to the floor. Missy's mother cried out, "Missy! Missy!!" She shook her daughter in a desperate attempt to revive her. "*Missy! Missy!!*"

But it was too late. Missy Martin was dead.

***

The squad car was painted a light blue that bespoke the seaside jurisdiction of the Barnstable County Sheriff's Office. A young deputy alighted from the vehicle and made his way to the front of the small house at the end of the short street in one of the few working class neighborhoods in the county. He knocked softly on the door out of respect for the grieving family.

A large man with a wind burned face and a head full of closely cropped blond hair opened the door with what seemed to be his last ounce of energy.

"Mr. Martin?"

The large man nodded.

"I'm Deputy Sheriff John Steele." Steele presented his credentials. "Are you OK to answer a few questions?"

Matt Martin nodded again. He motioned for Deputy Steele to enter the house. He led Steele to the living room. "Please have a seat. I'll get my wife. She's the one who found Missy." Martin took a few steps, spun on his heel, and said, "Would you like something to drink? Coffee or something?"

Steele said, "No thanks. I'm fine."

Martin went to get his wife.

Steele surveyed the room. A flat screen TV hung on the wall farthest from the entrance. A brown corduroy couch adorned with yellow throw pillows was placed on the north side of the room. Family photographs dominated the table tops. Steele's attention was quickly captured by the photograph of Missy Martin posing with her father in front of a Navy ship. Flowing blonde hair; big blue eyes; effervescent smile; long, athletic legs: Missy was the epitome of the sort of California girl that the Beach Boys had made famous. She was certainly the apple of Matt Martin's eye: hardscrabble Navy man or not, it was apparent from the photograph that Missy could do no wrong as far as her father was concerned.

"I took that photograph about a week before Matt got his orders for Sandwich," Molly Martin said. Molly was Missy's mom's name.

Sandwich was where the principal Navy base was located in Massachusetts. Sandwich's other claim to fame was that Bobby Orr, the legendary Hall of Fame defenseman for the Boston Bruins, owned a home in the town.

Steele said, "It's a wonderful photograph, Mrs. Martin." He returned it to the prominent place on the end table. "I'm sorry about your daughter."

Mrs. Martin said, "Thank you." She struggled to hold back tears. Her husband placed a strong arm around her slender shoulders.

"Are you up to answering a couple of questions?"

"Yes."

The Martins sat on the couch. Steele settled into one of the chairs on the other side of the coffee table.

At first, Steele had thought that Missy had favored her father. After all, they both had blond hair and blue eyes—features that dominated their appearances. But Missy actually resembled Mrs. Martin more: the same waves in the hair; the same large mouth; the same small dimple in the chin; the same athletic figure. Steele said, "My sister gave birth to her first child last month… my first niece. I can't imagine how you must be feeling."

Mr. Martin said, "Empty. That's how I'm feeling… And guilty… Guilty as hell."

Steele straightened in his chair. "Guilty about what?"

Mr. Martin leaned forward. His eyes drifted to the same photograph that Steele had been studying before Mr. Martin had returned to the room with his wife. "That I didn't know that something was bothering her. Sure, Molly and I knew that it was difficult for Missy to have to move again, but she was used to it and she always seemed to bounce back after a couple of weeks of being in a new place."

Steele wrote a quick note on his investigations pad. "Do you have any idea what it was that she was upset about?"

Mr. Martin glanced at his wife. They both shook their heads.

Mrs. Martin said, "We've been in Barnstable for less than a week. I wouldn't have thought there was enough time for something bad to happen."

Mr. Martin said, "Besides, Missy told me that she had already met a new friend. She had spent the night at the friend's house the night before she died."

Steele asked, "Do you know the friend's name?"

Mr. Martin answered, "I didn't ask her. She was late for school and I didn't want her to miss the bus."

Steele made another entry in his investigations pad. His attention returned to the photograph of Missy and her dad smiling in front of a Navy ship in San Diego. His thoughts turned to his infant niece and the unbearable pain his family would undoubtedly suffer if anything ever happened to her. He made a solemn commitment to do everything he could to find out why Missy Martin had killed herself.

CHAPTER 33

Nevin Montgomery studied the faces hanging on the wall: William Shakespeare, Charles Dickens, William Faulkner, Jane Austen, Ernest Hemingway, George Eliot, Edgar Allan Poe, Emily Dickinson, Herman Melville, Virginia Wolfe. The ten greatest writers of all time, according to Mr. Harrington. Shakespeare's was the only face Nevin recognized. He had heard of several of the other writers— Faulkner, Austen, Hemingway—but their visages were unfamiliar to him. He had no idea that George Eliot was a woman. Mr. Harrington had said that she had used a male pen name to ensure that her work would be taken seriously in Victorian England. He described her 1872 work *Middlemarch* as the greatest novel in the English language.

Mr. Harrington taught a variety of English courses at John F. Kennedy High School in Dorchester, Massachusetts. Nevin was currently enrolled in his junior level English Literature course. The class had already read a handful of the classics: Dickens's *Great Expectations*, Hemingway's *A Farewell to Arms*, Austen's *Pride and Prejudice*, and Melville's *Billy Budd*. The weekend's homework assignment had been for the students to read a selection of short stories by Edgar Allan Poe and craft one of their own. A parade of Nevin's classmates had crashed and burned by the time Mr. Harrington summoned Nevin to the front of the room.

"Let's hear what ya got!" Colin Dunn shouted from the back row.

Nevin reddened.

Mr. Harrington told Colin to pipe down.

Nevin stood uneasily before his classmates. He glanced over at Mr. Harrington in a silent plea to be allowed to return to his seat.

Mr. Harrington didn't bite. "Whenever you're ready, Nevin."

Nevin reached into his pocket for the three sheets of paper on which he had written his short story. He cleared his throat. "It's called 'Alone.'" He began to read his story aloud to his teacher and classmates:

You wouldn't know by looking at him. He was bright, handsome, and witty. Women loved his eyes: big, brown, and rich with character. Men enjoyed his company, especially his encyclopedic knowledge of sports and pop culture. Yes, he was quiet; some called him shy. He wasn't socially awkward, though. But he was almost always alone.

He first realized how often he was alone during his junior year abroad at the London School of Economics. That was almost twenty years ago, yet he remembered it as if it were yesterday. It was Christmas Eve. It was cold, gray, and snowy. He was attending Mass at St. Paul's Cathedral. He had been alone before. Everyone had. But he hadn't realized it. He hadn't felt it. It hadn't washed over him like a chill wind through an ill-fitting door. What he felt that Christmas Eve made him realize how much he had been alone throughout his entire life.

His junior year abroad had been everything he hoped for, and more. It was his father's idea that he spend a year away. "It'll be good for you," his father had said. "You'll learn a lot." His family had lived in the Caribbean for a short time when he was little, but he didn't remember anything about it. Other than that, he had never traveled outside the continental United States. He fell in love with London the moment he stepped foot off the airplane: the accents; the history; the culture—surprisingly, even the food. His roommate was also a Yank and they bonded immediately. They would go to the theater together in the West End. Shakespeare performed by the Royal Shakespeare Company was as good as it could possibly get. They would sightsee. They participated in more than their fair share of pub crawls. He also began dating a British girl within a month of arriving.

Her name was Simone. She lived in the apartment next to his, although he didn't know that at first. She knocked on his door, introduced herself, and asked if he was going to the "pahty" at Pete's flat. He had never heard of Pete before and he certainly didn't know anything about a party. But he was in. Simone was beautiful, and he was a nineteen year old guy. It was no more complicated than that. The fact that she was British sealed the deal. He melted every time she said his name.

They slept together the night of the party, and almost every night thereafter for the next several months. They fought like cats and dogs. Her tag line was always that he was a "typical American," and his was "what does that mean?" (To this day, he doesn't know what it means.) They never stayed mad long: she, because she loved his eyes, wit, and intelligence; he, because she was beautiful and British. Eventually, though, she strayed. Eventually, they broke up. But that wasn't what made him feel alone. He had had other relationships end. Everyone had. It was part of growing up. It was part of the search for "the one." It was part of life.

He wasn't sure what about the Christmas Eve Mass had made him feel alone. St. Paul's was the most famous Anglican church in the world, and it was the seat of the Bishop of London. The building itself dated from the seventeenth century and was almost universally regarded as Sir Christopher Wren's architectural masterpiece. People and events of singular importance in British history had been celebrated, mourned, and commemorated there ever since, and had ranged from the funerals of Lord Nelson and Winston Churchill, to Jubilee celebrations for Queens Victoria and Elizabeth II, to memorial services for the victims of the September 11, 2001, terrorist attacks.

It was all of that which had led him to St. Paul's for Midnight Mass and carol service. Readings and hymns told the story of Joseph and his journey from Nazareth to Bethlehem for the first registration while Quirinius was governor of Syria, the birth of Jesus by Mary in a manger because there was no room for them at the inn, and the angel's revelation to the shepherds that a savior had been born. The cathedral's great dome filled with the glorious sound of the Cathedral Choir singing songs of praise. Individual voices summoned angels during solos, and the accompanying organ music blended perfectly. The Anglican priest, the Right Reverend and Right Honorable David Michael Hope, had done a fine job officiating and offered a poignant reminder of the spiritual message of Christmas.

But from that evening forward he felt alone. From that evening forward he was consumed by his isolation. Time marched forward, inevitably and invariably forward. He grew older, as everyone did. He spent his days as most people did, working and trying to keep a roof over his head. He spent his evenings reading the books that he had always wanted to read when he was younger but for which he had never found the time. He reached for one, cracked the spine, and began. Alone.

Nevin glanced up from the final sheet of paper and into the sea of desks and chairs that filled the classroom. Every eye was fixed on him. Every faced sported a look of astonishment. Where had this come from?, was the sense of the room. This wasn't the Nevin they had come to know.

The bell sounded.

No one seemed to hear it.

Mr. Harrington traced his hands through his thinning hair. "That was beautiful, Nevin. Beautiful. That's all I can think of to say."

CHAPTER 34

Alastair asked, "What was up with that poem, Shakespeare?"

Nevin answered, "It was a short story, not a poem. No wonder you're flunking Mr. Harrington's class."

"Whatever. But how did you come up with that stuff?"

"I made it up. That's what Mr. H asked us to do."

"I know he asked us to write something. But yours was pretty thick on the tugging-at-the-heartstrings crap."

Nevin sighed and shook his head. "What did you write about?"

"That B & E we did last week."

"We weren't supposed to write about real events. I've never been to London, obviously. And I've certainly never attended the London School of Economics."

"I added some stuff to mine that didn't happen."

Stewart chimed in, "Like the fact that we got something worth something out of the deal?"

Alastair chuckled. "Yeah. Like that."

Colin said, "We can always try again. Like now, for instance. A new family has moved into that triplex on Hanson. Maybe they've got something we can sell. My pockets are empty. I could use the coin."

Colin led the friends to the multi-family residence on the corner of Hanson and Murray Streets.

Nevin said, "Is this it?"

"Yeah. I watched them unload the moving van. They've got some pretty nice stuff." Colin spit the gum he had been chewing to the pavement.

Stewart started walking towards the house. "Who's comin'?"

They all went.

They climbed the freshly painted steps to the third floor.

Colin removed a credit card from his pocket and slid it through the lock. "It's one of my mom's expired cards but it still works great for some things." The lock clicked open. He turned the knob and pushed open the door. "After you, gentlemen."

Alastair said, "You continue to amaze, Colin. Where did you learn to do that?"

"On the internet. You can learn how to do almost anything with a quick *Google* search. Shit, after we're finished here I can show you how to build a nuclear bomb if you want."

Alastair, Stewart, and Nevin laughed.

Nevin was the first one through the door. "Nice place."

The four scattered to different rooms.

"Five minutes," Colin said. "In and out. Nothing too big for your pockets."

Stewart said, "I found a watch. Looks like a *Rolex*." He stuffed it into his pocket.

Alastair said, "Add a cool necklace to the list."

Colin said, "Bingo! A wad of cash in the bureau.... Anything, Nevin?"

"Not yet. I'll try the room at the end of the hall. It might be a home office."

Alastair cried out, "Paul Pierce! Paul Pierce!"

Paul Pierce was the Boston Celtics' first round draft pick out of the University of Kansas in 1998. He had been an All American in college and was Larry Bird's successor at small forward. He was also Alastair, Colin, Stewart, and Nevin's May Day signal for when someone was coming.

Alastair, Colin, and Stewart were close enough to the back door to make a quick exit down the fire escape.

Nevin wasn't so fortunate. Two Dorchester beat cops caught him red handed.

The larger of the two cops said, "Put down the candlestick and face the wall with your hands behind your back."

Nevin did as he was told. His heart was racing.

The smaller of the two cops cuffed Nevin and patted Nevin down. He said, "What's your name, kid?"

Nevin had seen dozens of cop shows on TV and he knew he was supposed to clam up. He was nervous, though. "Ne—Nevin."

"'Nevin' what?"

"Mont—Montgomery."

"Well, Nevin Montgomery, I'm sorry to say that we've got to take a trip to the station."

Nevin had never been inside the Dorchester Police Station before. He quickly discovered that he hadn't been missing anything.

Scott Douglas Gerber

Trash spilled from overflowing wastebaskets. A stray dog with filthy fur sniffed every pair of legs that entered the building. Ten-dollar hookers and *Boone's Farm* drunks muttered profanities in the holding cells. Lawyers who advertised in local bars and on neighborhood billboards loitered for clients. Repeated requests from a multitude of police officers for "some goddam quiet" went unheeded.

The larger of the two cops who had arrested Nevin brought Nevin to the Duty Sergeant's Desk and asked, "Where should we put this one?"

Nevin sported the look of the proverbial deer in the headlights.

The Duty Sergeant answered, "Three is open. Take the kid in there and find out why he's adding to my stack of paperwork."

Nevin was led down a dingy corridor to a small room with a rusting metal table and four matching chairs in various states of disrepair.

"Sit," the smaller of the cops said.

Nevin did as he was told.

The larger of the cops grabbed one of the empty chairs, flipped it backwards, and sat across the table from Nevin. "You don't look like a dumb kid, but you sure did a dumb thing. Why did you break into that house?"

Nevin stammered, "D—Don't I get a lawyer?"

The large cop chuckled. "If you want one you do. But I was hoping we could handle this without the fuss. Lawyers are assholes."

Nevin didn't say anything for several minutes. Then, "Like you said, I did a stupid thing. I was bored, I guess."

The small cop said, "Have you ever heard of organized sports, or the YMCA? Those are much better outlets for bored kids, obviously. Or, you could join the pep band if you're not athletically inclined."

"I know. Like I said, I made a stupid mistake."

The large cop pulled on the sleeves of his uniform in a futile effort to find more fabric. "Was anyone with you?"

Nevin shook his head. "Absolutely not. It was just me. Hand to God."

Of course Nevin was lying.

CHAPTER 35

Daniel Harrington was the first to arrive at the faculty meeting. He dreaded faculty meetings and had somehow managed to convince himself that if he arrived early the meeting would end early. It never worked out that way.

Harrington's colleagues filed into the conference room, cups of coffee firmly in hand, and offered one another the sorts of perfunctory greetings that beleaguered co-workers often exchanged.

The principal was the final person to enter the room. He took the seat at the head of the table and said, "Before we get to this week's agenda items, I need to mention that I received a call last night from Nevin Montgomery's mother. Apparently, Nevin got himself arrested yesterday afternoon." The principal didn't sound surprised. Although this might have been the first time that Nevin Montgomery had been arrested, some JFK High student or other was always getting into trouble with the police for something. In fact, the principal had received three such telephone calls the previous week.

Daniel Harrington was surprised, however. "What did Nevin do? Where is he?" Harrington was a tea drinker and he almost knocked his cup to the floor from the shock.

The principal said, "His mom said that he was arrested for breaking and entering. As far as where he is, I'm not sure about that one. He was at the police station when his mom called, but she said Ronan was on his way to bail him out."

Everyone at the meeting knew who Ronan was. He was Nevin's father. He had worked as a custodian at JFK High for almost thirty years. He was a nose-to-the-grindstone employee who never asked for a favor and never caused any trouble. In short, he was every principal's dream.

One of the senior teachers said, "We should make sure that Ronan and Maeve are OK too. They love that kid, and this can't be easy on either of them. Ronan in particular must be mortified."

Maeve was Nevin's mother.

The principal said, "Good idea. I'll follow-up with Ronan right after the meeting." The principal proceeded to the week's agenda. As usual, the budget crunch was at the top of the list and dominated the discussion.

Daniel Harrington hurried back to his classroom. Unlike college professors, high school teachers didn't have private offices. They had a desk in the front of the classroom, several file cabinets in which to store their supplies, and most important of all as far as Harrington was concerned at the moment, a telephone. He had fifteen minutes before his first class of the day began. He looked up the number for the Suffolk County District Attorney's Office, picked up the phone, and dialed.

The receptionist answered on the second ring. "District Attorney's Office. How may I direct your call?"

Harrington said, "Derek Nettles, please."

The receptionist transferred the call.

"This is Derek Nettles."

"Derek. It's Daniel Harrington. How are you?"

"Mr. H! Great to hear from you. How long has it been?"

"About ten years, I think. Your five year reunion was the last time I saw you. So, how are you?"

"Busy. The D.A. isn't much on prosecutorial discretion. If there's an arrest and the cops think they can make it stick, he prosecutes.... How are you doing?"

"Busy, like you. The students certainly keep me on my toes. That's why I'm calling, actually. Do you have a minute?"

"For you, absolutely. What's up?"

"I don't quite know how to put it."

Nettles chuckled. "'Short and sweet,' as you always used to say in class."

"Touché." Harrington cleared his throat. He took a sip of tea, which had grown cold by this point. "One of my students was arrested last night."

"For what?"

"Breaking and entering. He's a great kid. Smart as a whip. But he runs with the wrong crowd."

"Hmm." Nettles chuckled again. "Where have I heard that before? Oh, yeah. I remember: that's what you used to say about me."

"Which is why I'm calling. Once you started down the straight and narrow, there's been no stopping you. We're very proud of you here at JFK."

"Thanks, Mr. H. I owe it all to you. If it hadn't been for you, God knows where I'd be right now. Probably dead.... What's the student's name?"

"Nevin Montgomery. Anything you could do to help would be appreciated. His dad works at JFK."

"Ronan? Ronan Montgomery is Nevin's father?"

"Yes."

"I remember Ronan. He's a great guy. Hardworking. No b.s. He also saved my behind once when I was getting the heck beat out of me in the locker room by Hank Laughlin."

"He hasn't changed a bit. He tried to hide it when he called me last night, but I could tell how worried he is about Nevin. This could keep Nevin out of college. What a waste of talent that would be."

"I'll talk to the D.A. and try to convince him that sometimes prosecutorial discretion is a good thing. I think I can get him to tell the troops down in Dorchester to let this one slide. He owes me one, and they owe him several."

***

Ronan Montgomery put down his rag and bottle of *Windex* and held the door for Daniel Harrington.

Harrington said, "Good morning, Ronan."

"Good morning. I got a call last night from a Mr. Derek Nettles. He said the D.A. doesn't plan to prosecute Nevin. He also said you went to bat for Nevin and that's why they aren't prosecuting him." Ronan's voice caught. "Th—Thank you, Mr. Harrington." He reached into his lunch pail and removed a *Tupperware* container filled with chocolate chip/peanut butter cookies. "My wife baked these for you after I told her what you did. It's not much, but she makes great cookies. Chocolate chip and peanut butter are her specialty. They last about five minutes in our house, especially when Nevin's around."

Harrington patted his stomach. He was a good twenty pounds overweight. "My doctor keeps telling me to shed a few pounds, but I think he would make an exception for these." He popped the top off the *Tupperware* and took a bite of one of the cookies. "Tell Maeve thank you, and tell her how great these taste. As for Nevin, I was happy to do it. He made a stupid mistake, that's all. He's young. He'll grow out of it. He's too smart not to."

Nevin Montgomery arrived forty-five minutes late. Alastair Ainsley, Colin Dunn, and Stewart MacGregor were already high by the time he got there.

Colin said, "Where have you been? We looked all over for you."

Nevin said, "Mr. Harrington wanted to see me."

Alastair said, "About what?"

Nevin shook his head. "The arrest, obviously. Geez, how high are you Alastair?"

Alastair smiled. "Pretty freakin' high. Colin brought some new candy for us to try. In the immortal words of Tony the Tiger, 'It's grrrreat!'"

Colin held up the small clear pipe they were using to smoke crack cocaine. The rod was about half an inch in diameter and two to three inches long. The bowl was the size of a gumball, hollow, and had a small hole on top. An off-white nugget with jagged edges—the "rock"—sat inside the bottom of the bowl. Colin struck a match and proceeded to heat the bottom of the bowl. The rock melted. He said, "Round two." He placed the pipe in his mouth and inhaled. He tried to hand the pipe to Nevin. "Your turn."

Nevin shook his head again. "No thanks."

Colin coughed. "What?"

"I said, no thanks."

"Why?"

Stewart shot up from the garbage can on which he had been sitting. A large rat scurried from underneath it. "I'll take Nevin's turn!" He scratched his arm. "Maybe it'll kill these bugs crawling under my skin."

There weren't any bugs. Stewart was experiencing one of the more typical psychological reactions to smoking crack: formication. In the vernacular, coke bugs. He had scratched his arm so much that it was bleeding.

"Stop scratching," Alastair said to him. "You're grossing me out." Alastair's pupils were dilated and his heart was racing. He started shouting and punching the walls of the abandoned building that they had selected for this particular evening's drug party.

Nevin said, "Calm down, Alastair. What's gotten in to you?"

The crack... The crack had gotten in to Alastair, just like it had gotten in to Stewart. Colin seemed to be doing OK.

Alastair said, "Fuck you, Nevin."

Nevin was taken aback. Alastair was by far the mellowest of the group. Nevin had never seen him so agitated.

Colin didn't seem concerned. He said to Nevin, "Do you want your turn or not?"

"No thanks."

"Why not?"

Stewart interjected, "Maybe it's because he's an undercover cop. Have you been pulling a 21 Jump Street on us this whole time?" He looked suspiciously at Nevin. Paranoia was another common psychological side effect of crack cocaine, and Stewart was currently experiencing it in spades.

Nevin said, "Don't be an idiot, Stewart. I just got out of jail, remember."

"But you weren't there long. Were they debriefing you about us? You know, to build a case against us." Stewart started pacing around the abandoned house like a caged animal.

Nevin was about to issue another firm denial to Stewart's ridiculous accusation until he noticed Alastair out of the corner of his eye. "Alastair! Something's wrong with Alastair!"

Everybody looked at Alastair, who was in the process of vomiting. His muscles began to twitch. He appeared to be having a seizure.

Colin said, "He's OD-ing! We need to get him to the hospital! We need to call an ambulance!" Colin was obviously concerned now.

Alastair suddenly stopped convulsing.

Nevin said, "Alastair?"

Alastair didn't say a word.

Colin said, "Alastair?!"

Still no response.

Nevin rushed to Alastair's side. "*Alastair!*" He shook their friend.

Still nothing.

Nevin kept shaking him.

But it was too late. Alastair Ainsley was dead of a drug overdose at sixteen years of age.

CHAPTER 36

Meredith Adams wheeled herself up the handicapped ramp and through the main entrance to Boston's Museum of Fine Arts. The MFA, as it was typically known, opened on the nation's centennial, July 4, 1876. Originally located on Copley Square, it moved to its present home on Huntington Avenue in 1909. The MFA was one of the most comprehensive art museums in the world, and the collection encompassed nearly four hundred and fifty thousand works of art. According to its mission statement, the MFA's "ultimate aim is to encourage inquiry and to heighten public understanding and appreciation of the visual world." In order to accomplish this, the MFA sponsored exhibitions, programs, research, and publications.

Meredith had come for the debut exhibition of a young painter with a famous pedigree: James Windsor, son of Andrew Windsor and grandson of C. S. Windsor. This was Meredith's first visit to an art museum without her parents. Although she was eighteen years old and technically an adult, her parents were extremely protective of her. Meredith understood why: she was only two years removed from the tragic horse riding accident that had left her a paraplegic. Her parents initially had objected to her decision to attend the exhibition alone, but she had reminded them that she would be leaving for college at the conclusion of the summer and they certainly couldn't accompany her to Harvard. "You wanna bet?" her father had said at the time. But they all knew he was joking, and they agreed that a "trial run" at the MFA would probably be a good thing. Meredith's mother nevertheless had convinced Meredith to let them drive her to Boston if they promised to remain behind at the hotel.

Meredith looked lovely for the exhibition. She was wearing a new *Ann Taylor* textured sheath-dress that she had purchased earlier in the day at the Newbury Street store. It was sleeveless, with a scoop neck, and was a sizzling shade of coral. Shine-worthy accessories and nude strappy heels balanced the sporty summer look. Her mother had mentioned how perfectly the dress fit Meredith. Her father had said that his little girl was all grown up.

Meredith grabbed a glass of sparkling water from one of the waiters circling the room and began to study James Windsor's paintings. The program listed his age as twenty-three. She could see from the biographical photograph on the front of the program that he enjoyed the outdoors and that he was handsome. Young, talented, good-looking, and the child of privilege: some people had all the luck.

"Isn't he dreamy," a beautiful young woman said over Meredith's shoulder. "I'm just dying to meet him." She was wearing a tight dress with a plunging neckline.

And to seduce him, Meredith suspected the beautiful woman also wanted to say. Meredith's parents might have been overly protective of her, but she had read enough Jane Austen novels and watched enough Oprah Winfrey shows to know how the female mind worked.

Meredith spent a lot of time reading—time that two years earlier she had devoted to riding—and she particularly enjoyed books about art history. She could tell from the very first painting of James Windsor's on display that he was a painter whose work drew upon his own distinguished artistic heritage as well as from the long tradition of American realist painting and its contemporary revival. *Portrait of Duke*, which James had painted when he was Meredith's age, was a bravura picture of a local lobsterman. Duke was a man who had lived in Barnstable since before James was born and who spoke only to other lobstermen and, inexplicably, to James himself. The composition of an unkempt Duke against an elegant wing chair was what made the painting so unexpected.

Meredith wheeled herself to the next painting. This one was entitled *Portrait of a Goat* and, not surprisingly, it was James's painting of a goat that lived on the Windsors' Barnstable compound. The placard describing the picture indicated that when painting animals James would change the textures of the paint to reflect fur, wool, or feathers. The next two paintings were also of animals. Meredith thought they were all wonderful and reflected a kinship with animals. But it was the subsequent painting that Meredith found inarguably great. *Portrait of Andrew Windsor* depicted James's famous father with a serious expression: determined and focused eyes; ruddy face; dressed in a naval coat with large buttons; arriving home from a brisk walk by the sea. Meredith studied the portrait for a solid fifteen minutes.

"What do you think?"

Meredith turned to find the young artist himself. He was dressed in black jeans, a green *Ralph Lauren* polo shirt, and a pair of *Church's* English loafers. He had a glass of champagne in his hand. Far from a starving artist, Meredith said to herself. Aloud to James: "I love it. It's as if his eyes were a window into his soul."

James bowed like an actor on a Broadway stage during a curtain call. "Thank you, madam. That's precisely what I was aiming for. The critics had no clue. They thought I made dad look like the captain of a lobster boat." James laughed. He extended his hand. "I'm James Windsor."

Meredith shook James's hand. She blushed like the schoolgirl she was. "I know."

James smiled. "And you are…?"

"Meredith. Meredith Adams."

"Nice to meet you, Meredith. Are you from Boston?"

"No. I'm from Williamstown. My dad teaches at Williams."

"Are you in college?"

"I start in the fall."

"Where?"

"Harvard. I'll be studying art history, which is why I'm here this evening."

"So it's not because you had heard that the artist looked like Brad Pitt's handsomer brother…. Is 'handsomer' a word?"

Meredith blushed again. "I don't know. My dad teaches history, not English."

James glanced at the drink in Meredith's hand. "Do you need a refill?"

Meredith shook her head. "I'm fine. Besides, aren't you supposed to be mingling with the art dealers so you can charm them into buying your work?"

"Probably," James said. He reached again for Meredith's hand. "But I'd much prefer to get to know you better."

***

When Meredith arrived for freshman orientation at Harvard, her new classmates didn't seem to know how to relate to her. They were certainly kind to her; perhaps too kind. Clearly, most of them had never spent much time around someone in a wheelchair and the upper-class sensibilities with which they had been imbued caused them to handle her like a china doll rather than as an equal who was trying to make her way in the world after suffering a devastating injury. Her roommate was especially prone to being overprotective.

A gorgeous young woman from Philadelphia, Sophia Scialo was from a large Italian family. Her father had graduated from both Harvard College and Harvard Medical School, and he was now one of the leading heart surgeons on the east coast. He recently had performed a quadruple bypass on the Vice President of the United States, and the Chairman of the Harvard Corporation considered him a friend. Known officially as "President and Fellows of Harvard College," the Harvard Corporation was the oldest corporation in the Western Hemisphere and it met periodically to consult with Harvard's president, who was the day-to-day head of the university. The Harvard Corporation was self-perpetuating: it appointed new members to fill its own vacancies as they arose. Only the elite of the elite—this was Harvard after all—were appointed to it, and Sophia's mother had mentioned shortly before driving Sophia to Cambridge that Sophia's father would likely be tapped to fill the next vacancy.

Sophia asked Meredith, "What's your first class this morning?" She checked her lipstick in the mirror, and then turned her full attention to her roommate.

Meredith answered, "Re-imagining an Introduction to the History of American Art."

"Re-examining what?"

Meredith smiled. "Re-*imagining*, not re-examining."

Sophia returned Meredith's smile. "'Re-imagining' what?"

"... an Introduction to the History of American Art."

"What's that class about?"

Meredith reached for the backpack strapped to her wheelchair and retrieved the syllabus that she had printed from the internet. "Here's the course description: *Since its beginnings, the history of art has been conceived of as a teleological process defined largely in terms of progress, culminating in the triumph of modernism. As a counter-heuristic, we will teach the history of art from the present and looking back to the past. After a historiographical introduction, focused on Vasari, Winckelmann, Hegel and historicism, also in reverse, each section will consist of a critical chain of appropriations made by modern artists who constructed their own understanding of tradition, ending in*

Antiquity. Each section will focus on a major artist."

Sophia said, "I heard what you said, but I didn't understand a word of it."

Meredith said, "Welcome to Harvard."

CHAPTER 37

That first semester of classes went well. Meredith's professors were nice—or, more precisely, the graduate students who taught the courses so that her professors could concentrate on research were nice—the campus was abuzz with extracurricular activities in which to participate, and the girls in her dorm were a lot of fun. Her dorm-mates made her forget about her disability most of the time, which was in stark contrast to how they had treated her when she had arrived on campus five months earlier.

Meredith wasn't certain what explained the different treatment, but she was fairly confident it traced to the fact that her dorm-mates knew she was dating James Windsor. At first, they were shocked when they discovered it. Not only was James handsome enough to be a model himself, he was the son of the most famous living artist in America. Meredith didn't brag about either of those things. Indeed, she had tried to keep her relationship with James on the down-low. Initially, only Sophia knew, and Sophia knew only because James would sometimes call when Meredith was out and Sophia would take a message. The rest of the dorm had learned about the relationship when James showed up on campus the day before fall break to drive Meredith to Barnstable for the holiday. Meredith's stock had skyrocketed after that.

Sophia said, "Did you have a nice Christmas? How are your folks? How is James?"

Meredith closed the suitcase she was unpacking, placed several tops and pairs of jeans in the bureau next to her bed, and spun her wheelchair to face Sophia. "My folks are fine. Thanks for asking. They still wish I had enrolled at Williams, where my dad teaches, or at Smith or Mt. Holyoke, which are both much closer to our house than Harvard is. They're getting used to the idea, though."

"And James?"

"He's fine too. He came out for New Year's Eve to meet my parents. He charmed them, of course. He brought my mom a painting that he had done of me during fall break, and he spent New Year's Day watching football with my dad."

Sophia smiled. "I'm not surprised. He's smooth, that's for sure."

Meredith said, "How was your break?"

"Good. I got to satisfy my Philly Cheese Steak fixation. It wasn't good for my figure, but the six I ate Christmas week tasted as wonderful as ever. We've got *Pat's* on speed dial at the house."

Pat's King of Steaks was the originator and inventor of steak and cheese sandwiches. It was still owned and operated by the Olivieri family and was open twenty-four hours a day, seven days a week.

Meredith said, "You look fantastic. If anything, it looks like you lost a couple of pounds."

"I *gained* five. I appreciate the effort, though."

"Did you meet any cute guys during break?"

Sophia shook her head. "Not really. I went on a couple of dates with one of my brother's fraternity brothers, but they were pretty uneventful."

***

James Windsor knocked on the door of Meredith's dorm room. He was armed with a box of chocolates and a dozen roses.

Sophia answered the door. "You shouldn't have."

"You must be Sophia."

"Guilty as charged. And you're definitely James. I recognize you from the photos on Meredith's desk. She's not here, by the way. Was she expecting you? She didn't mention you were coming."

"I wanted to surprise her. You know, for Valentine's Day. When will she be back?"

"Tomorrow. She went on a field trip to New York with her art history class. They're going to the Met and the Guggenheim. And to the Museum of Modern Art, I think.… I'm surprised she didn't tell you."

James reddened. "She did. I forgot. For the past week or so I've been working day and night at my dad's fishing cabin in Maine. I'm trying to finish a painting. Meredith's NYC trip slipped my mind. I guess I'll turn around and head back to the cabin. I'm not done with the painting anyway."

Sophia did the little flip-of-the-hair move that beautiful women sometimes did. She didn't appear to know she was doing it.

But James knew.

Sophia said, "Don't be silly. It's at least a four-hour drive back to Maine. You're welcome to spend the night in Meredith's bed. She'll be back by lunch tomorrow."

James paused to make it seem as if he was indifferent to the proposition. And make no mistake about it, James viewed it as a proposition.... He said, "OK. Thanks. But let me buy you dinner for your troubles. I know a great place down the street."

"Sounds like a plan!" Sophia flipped her hair again.

James and Sophia dined at *Toscano*. The Harvard Square location had opened about six months earlier, but James had been to the original Beacon Hill location with his parents on several occasions in the past. The restaurant specialized in Tuscan cuisine: starting with flavorful olive oil—the base of most Tuscan meals—their dishes incorporated handmade pastas, fine local and imported cheeses, house-made sausages, wild mushrooms, and fresh vine-ripened tomatoes. Pizzas were crisped in a stone oven, and game and fish cooked alla griglia were enhanced with oak, hickory, and maple. Tuscan tradition was likewise expressed in *Toscano*'s wines. The Sangiovese grape's vino rosso, suffused with the flavors of its surrounds, colored the palate of many celebrated names: Brunello di Montellocino, Chianti, and Chianti Reserva. *Toscano*'s temperature-controlled wine room, holding up to a thousand bottles, featured these and others among the hundred Tuscan labels.

Sophia started with the Rucola E Pomodoro salad: baby arugula, tomato, shaved Parmigiano, and balsamic dressing. She had Ravioli Anatra for her entree: a delicious concoction of handmade spinach ricotta ravioli and ground duck sauce fiorentina. James began with Minestrone Di Verdura, which was a Tuscan-style vegetable soup, and for the main course he ordered the Speck pizza, which was topped with fresh prosciutto, tomato, fresh mozzarella, and arugula. Meredith and James split an antipasto and several bottles of wine.

James asked, "Would you care for anything else? Dessert, perhaps?"

Sophia answered, "I couldn't possibly eat another bite. It was all wonderful. Thank you for bringing me here. My Italian father was threatening to disown me if I didn't try it."

James smiled. "It was my pleasure. Shall we head back? I'm exhausted from the drive."

"Follow me!"

Scott Douglas Gerber

James decided to stop and buy a bottle of wine on the walk back to Sophia and Meredith's dorm room. He made his move after one more glass. Sophia was well past being able to think rationally, which went a long way towards explaining her actions. She prided herself on being a good person, but she was about to do the worst possible thing that one friend could do to another: have sex with her friend's significant other.

CHAPTER 38

Catina Cruz retrieved the laundry from the clothes line in the tiny back yard of the New Bedford triplex in which she lived with her mother. She had no idea who her father was. She had never met him, and her mother refused to tell her anything about the man.

Catina folded the clothes and put them away. She re-checked the To Do List taped to the refrigerator. Homework was underlined. Catina's grades weren't great, and her mother wasn't happy about it. No TV was also underlined. Catina got the message. She needed to eat first, though. As usual, she hadn't had enough money for lunch at the school cafeteria and she went without. It was now seven o'clock in the evening. Her mom was working third shift at the *Holiday Inn* and wouldn't be home until after midnight. Catina opened the door to the refrigerator in the vain hope that her mom had prepared something for her before going to work. She hadn't. She almost never did. The only exception was when her mom brought home a doggy bag after one of her many dates with one of her many suitors. Catina was allowed to reheat those leftovers. Unfortunately, her mom hadn't been on a date in a couple of days.

The refrigerator wasn't completely barren, however. Catina found enough of what she needed to make Batatas Madierense: hard boiled eggs, milk, butter, onion, Azorean cheese, and parsley. She fetched several potatoes and salt from the cupboard. She peeled the potatoes, cut them in pieces, and cooked them in a pot of boiling water. She transferred the potatoes to a large bowl, added two hard-boiled egg yolks and a small amount of milk, and mashed it all together. She then mixed in more milk, added a tablespoon of butter and 1/4 cup of onion, and salted to taste. Next, she transferred the ingredients to an oven-safe dish, sprinkled the top with grated cheese, and baked it all in the oven at 350 degrees until the top was golden brown. She garnished the dish with chopped parsley and chopped egg white.

Not bad for a fifteen-year-old girl. She'd had plenty of practice. Her mom meant well, but she wasn't around much. She worked a lot and dated even more. When Catina pressed her on each, her mom would say that she was doing it for Catina: working paid the bills and dating might mean a stepfather for Catina who could make their lives more comfortable than the virtual poverty in which they presently lived. Chambermaids at the local hotel chain earned minimum wage.

The doorbell rang.

Catina turned down the oven and went to answer the door.

It was one of her mother's many boyfriends, Javier DeBrito. He was short, pudgy, and balding. He was in his late-fifties. Catina's mother was thirty-two.

When Catina had asked her mother why she dated Javier, her mother had said it was because he owned his own business, the *Midas* muffler shop on Central Avenue. "Looks aren't everything," she had reminded her daughter. "Besides, I'm not getting any younger."

Thirty-two was apparently old for a woman trading on her looks.

Catina said, "Oi, Javier."

Javier said, "Oi. Como està? Is your mother home?"

Catina shook her head. "She's at work. Was she expecting you?"

"Não. I thought I'd stop by to see if she wanted to have dinner.... Speaking of dinner, whatever you're cooking smells wonderful. Apparently, you take after your mother in that regard."

"Obrigada." Catina didn't know what to say next. She knew how badly her mother wanted things to keep progressing with Javier, but she had never spent any time with Javier by herself. She finally said, "Would you like some? I made plen—"

Javier was through the door before Catina had finished the invitation. Culinary skills weren't the only thing that Catina had inherited from her mother: She was blessed with her mother's beautiful looks.... She was a younger version to boot.

Catina set the table with a dinner set that her mother had purchased from a local yard sale. "What would you like to drink?"

Javier said, "Is there any beer?"

Catina checked the refrigerator. "Sim. There's a six pack of *Sagres*."

"Great. That's my favorite."

Sagres was a Portuguese beer. It was a pale lager made of 100% natural product and brewed according to traditional methods with water, malt, cereals that hadn't been malted, and a rigorous selection of the finest hops. No additives or preservatives were used in its brewing. It had a dry and pleasantly bitter taste.

Catina already knew that Javier liked *Sagres*. Her mother bought it to have around for when he dropped by. Catina brought a bottle of the lager to him.

Javier said, "Obrigado. Grab one for yourself. I won't tell your mother. I promise."

Catina smiled. She returned to the refrigerator. She opened a bottle of *Sagres* and took a sip. "Esteva delicioso, although it's a bit bitter. I'm used to drinking *Sumol.* Pineapple is my favorite."

Sumol was a Portuguese soda.

Catina removed the Batatas Madierense from the oven and dished out a generous helping for Javier and a smaller portion for herself.

Javier said, "That's all you're having?"

"A girl's gotta watch her figure." Catina didn't mean anything by it. It was a common response to a question women sometimes got when they didn't appear to eat much.

Javier read plenty into Catina's remark, though. He didn't say anything out loud, but his eyes danced over Catina's nubile body as she was enjoying her food.

It took Javier a good hour to finish his food. Who could blame him? Catina was a beautiful young woman and almost any heterosexual male in America would want to be around her for as long as he could. So, Javier dragged out the meal. He asked for seconds more than once.

He continued with the plan: "Café?"

Catina said that she would make some.

Javier adjourned to the living room, which was a few short steps from the kitchen where they had been eating. Like most working-class triplexes in New Bedford, Massachusetts, the apartment in which Catina lived with her mother was far from spacious.

Catina joined Javier a few minutes later with two cups of coffee, a tiny pitcher of milk, and a sugar bowl. She handed Javier his coffee and asked, "Leite? Açúcar?"

"Não. Obrigado." Javier patted the place on the couch next to him to invite Catina to take a seat.

The only other chair in the living room was piled high with her mother's celebrity magazines. Apparently, Miley Cyrus was in trouble again.

Catina sat next to Javier.

Javier said, "I forgot. What time did you say your mother will be coming home?"

"About midnight or so."

Javier tried his best to suppress a smile. He had been hoping to get Catina alone since the first time he saw her. He remembered that day as if it were yesterday. He had taken Catina's mother on several dates around town and she had insisted on cooking him an authentic Portuguese supper of fish stew and sweet bread. He had gladly accepted. Twenty minutes after he had arrived, Catina had emerged from the bathroom wearing nothing but a towel and a look of embarrassment. "You're early," was all she had said as she rushed to her room to dress.

The seductive image of Catina in a towel, her young skin fresh and tan, was forever etched in Javier's mind like an engraver's stenciling on a championship trophy.

Javier reached into his pocket and pulled out an oblong, olive green tablet. He made sure that Catina didn't see it. He waited until her head was turned and dropped the pill into her coffee. It dissolved quickly. Fifteen minutes later, Catina's inhibitions were gone.

The roofy had done its job.

Rohypnol, as it was called in the trade, was a drug that acted as a sedative, muscle relaxant, hypnotic, and antidepressant. As a prescription medication, Rohypnol was used as a pre-anesthetic and as a short-term treatment for insomnia. As a recreational drug, Rohypnol was often seen at nightclubs, parties, and raves. It was sometimes employed in connection with rape, and was known as the date-rape drug because it could incapacitate the victim and prevent her from recalling the crime.

Javier was counting on precisely that.

Rohypnol was illegal to manufacture, sell, or use in the United States because taking it could produce physiological and psychological dependence and benzodiazepine withdrawal syndrome. It was legal in other countries and was smuggled into the U.S. through the mail or other delivery services. Javier had purchased his from one of his mechanics at the muffler shop. He didn't need it for seducing a woman in her thirties like Catina's mom. He knew he was considered quite a catch to women of that age. But he would have had no chance with a teenaged beauty like Catina without the assistance of his little green friend.

The roofy made Catina remarkably free with her body. And what a body it was. Her skin didn't have a blemish and she didn't carry an ounce of fat. Her black hair shone like a new star against the night sky. Her breasts were small, but perfectly portioned for her petite frame. Her eyes, albeit glassy from the drug, were the color of dark chocolate.

Javier thought he was going to have a heart attack when he first placed himself inside of Catina. But what a way to go, he said to himself against the sounds of Catina's moans and rhythmic movements. He could tell she didn't have much experience in matters of sex. He was pleased he was contributing to her education on the subject.

CHAPTER 39

For the next several months Javier DeBrito made a habit out of dropping by at least once a week. It was always when Catina's mother wasn't around. After the second or third visit, Javier didn't need the roofies anymore: Catina began submitting voluntarily to his sexual advances. Perhaps it had something to do with the gifts he would bring her: chocolates, perfumes, jewelry, and the like. Apparently, everyone had a price, and Catina's appeared to be anything that wasn't purchased from the *Dollar Store* that she and her mom were forced to frequent.

But Javier had stopped dropping by shortly after Thanksgiving. Winter came early that year. Snow was piled high on the curbs. Ice coated the sidewalks. Plows piloted by sleep-deprived city workers gulping thermoses of *Cumberland Farms* coffee scraped against the New Bedford streets like children scratching their fingernails across a middle school chalkboard.

Catina pulled open the curtains to confirm the radio report that it was going to be a snow day at school. She asked her mom, "Is Javier OK? I haven't seen him around for a while."

Of course Catina's mother had no idea that Catina was sleeping with Javier—or at least she didn't let on that she knew.

Catina's mom unzipped her parka. She had returned home from work moments earlier. "He's fine, I think."

"Then where's he been?" Catina wadded her hair into a ponytail, which made her look like she was twelve rather than fifteen.

Catina's mother hung her parka in the hall closet. "I have no idea. I haven't seen him for a couple of weeks. He broke it off."

"Why?"

"I guess I wasn't young enough for him."

***

It didn't take long for Catina's mother to find another suitor. She might no longer have been blessed with the dewy complexion of a teenaged girl, but Catina's mom was still an attractive woman. Her thick black hair framed a heart-shaped face. Her dark eyes were large and expressive. Her smile lit a room. Her arms and legs were strong and trim from cleaning hotel rooms for the past ten years.

Catina's mother's new boyfriend knocked on the door.

Catina answered it. "Olá, Andrés. My mom isn't here."

Andrés Clemente was the same age as Catina's mother: thirty-two. He was a bartender at the *United Fisherman's Club*, the neighborhood bar at which Catina's mom occasionally partied on a rare evening off. He wasn't nearly as successful as Javier DeBrito. He was a lot better looking, though. In fact, he was so handsome that Catina didn't need pharmacological encouragement to agree to sleep with him.

The multiple times that Catina had slept with Javier had made her a much more confident lover than when she and Javier had first started having sex. Indeed, Andrés had commended Catina on several occasions about her skills in the bedroom. Well, they weren't always employed in the bedroom. Andrés lived with a couple of roommates in a small house near the water, and neither of his roommates were the type of person who would have been willing to look the other way about Catina's age. Catina lived at home, and she couldn't very well have sex in her mother's house with her mother's boyfriend... or at least not as frequently as they wished. As a result, Andrés and Catina tended to hookup on the fly: a bathroom stall here, a park bench there, and an occasional quickie in the store room at the *United Fisherman's Club*.

Tonight, though, they would be able to use Catina's bed. Catina's mom had telephoned to inform her daughter that she would be tied up at the *Holiday Inn* for another three hours. *Amway* had booked the hotel for its annual New England sales convention and there were a lot of rooms to clean.

Catina's mother stopped seeing Andrés after dating him for a little more than two months. Catina once again inquired as to the reason. This time, her mom knew why: Andrés didn't make enough money for it to be worth the trouble. "Good looks alone don't pay the bills," she had told her daughter. "At my age, I don't have time to waste on a pretty boy."

Catina was sorry to hear it. She'd had fun with Andrés, and he certainly was a "pretty boy." But, like most teenaged girls, Catina had heard what her mother had said and she decided to stop seeing Andrés too. Shortly thereafter, her mom resumed shepherding one prospective husband after another through the house, and Catina ended up sleeping with seventy-five percent of them. As far as the other twenty-five percent were concerned, not every man in America was without boundaries. No matter how beautiful Catina was, and no matter how unambiguously Catina would signal her receptiveness to any "romantic" overtures they would care to offer, there were lines that some men were unwilling to cross. Sleeping with the under-aged daughter of the woman they were dating was one of those lines.

Eventually, Catina's luck ran out. It was bound to have happened. Her mother was supposed to be at work. The boyfriend of the moment, a thirty-five-year-old Boston lawyer named Joshua Jones who had met Catina's mom while he was staying at the New Bedford *Holiday Inn* the night before a deposition, had driven an hour and fifteen minutes from Boston to New Bedford because, like Javier DeBrito before him, he had caught a glimpse of Catina in nothing but a towel and had hoped he could get a glimpse of what was underneath. When Jones arrived to find Catina home alone, he made his case to the beautiful young woman like the silver-tongued litigator he was.

"You've got beautiful eyes," Jones said to Catina as they made themselves comfortable on the couch in the small home's cluttered living room.

Catina said, "Thank you." She knew that Jones wasn't Portuguese and wouldn't have understood what "obrigado" meant.

"And your skin is so smooth and soft." Jones caressed Catina's cheek.

Catina didn't resist, which meant that Jones could go farther. He unbuttoned her shirt. She helped him remove her jeans. Jones almost popped in his haste to take off his own pants.

They were ten minutes into the best sex that Jones had ever experienced when they heard the front door open.

It was Catina's mother. She had left work early with a fever.

"Catina! Joshua! H—How dare you disrespect me like this! In—In my own house!"

Catina and Jones fumbled for their clothes.

Catina's mom reached for a ceramic flower pot that she had purchased at the *Walmart* next to the *Holiday Inn*. She hurled it at Jones's head. She missed, but not by much.

Jones said, "Are you crazy? You could've killed me!"

"Better luck next time." Catina's mother reached for another object to pitch at Jones's head. This time it was a framed photograph of

Catina. "Here's a picture of your favorite slut. Take it home and whack off to it."

The frame hit Jones in the forehead and made a gash. Blood seeped onto his tailored shirt. "Shit, woman. That hurt." He turned to Catina. "Good luck, kiddo. I'm outta here."

Catina's eyes widened. With Joshua Jones out the door, she was left to face her mother by herself. Catina feared the worst, but she didn't get it. Instead, her mother collapsed onto the floor and started to sob.

"How—How could you?" her mother asked between convulsions. "You're my daughter. You're all I have in this world."

Catina had no acceptable answer. She wished that her mother had thrown something at her too. It wouldn't have hurt as much. "I'm sorry," was all Catina could think of to say.

Catina Cruz went to her bedroom early that night. She couldn't sleep, though. She studied the posters hanging on the walls. Jesse McCartney. Justin Timberlake. Robert Pattinson. Schoolgirl crushes all. But Catina wasn't a schoolgirl anymore, or at least she wasn't acting like one.

She got out of bed and put on the shirt and jeans that Joshua Jones had so hurriedly removed. She placed her ear against the door to ascertain whether her mother was awake. She wasn't.

Catina tiptoed down the hallway and quietly exited the house. She had no idea where she was going. She started walking, hoping that she would figure it out along the way.

PART IV

The Masterpiece

"The painter has the Universe in his mind and hands."
—Leonardo da Vinci

CHAPTER 40

An army of wait staff circled the room with sterling silver serving trays packed with exotic hors d'oeuvres. A-list guests snacked on Smoked Bluefish Pate on Crisp Endive, Melted Gorgonzola & Parmesan over Fresh sliced Peach on Toasted Crostini, Lollipop Lamb Chops, and Chatham Sea Scallops Wrapped in Prosciutto. There was a Raw Bar in the corner featuring Wellfleet and Dennis oysters, little necks, medium shrimp, cocktail sauce, lemons, ice, and seaweed and garnish with edible flowers. An assortment of wines from *Truro Vineyards*, the only vinifera growing vineyard on Cape Cod, flowed freely. The Cape's sandy soil, warm ocean breezes, and temperate climate combined to produce grapes with intense flavor and lush varietal character. *Truro* specialized in Chardonnay, Cabernet Franc, and Merlot, all of which were handpicked by the winery at harvest time. James Windsor was friends with the owner and had somehow managed to convince his friend to provide the wine gratis. James had promised a good time in exchange, which they both had understood as involving beautiful young women.

James grabbed a glass of Triumph Meritage from one of the waiters. He took a sip. It was a well-balanced blend of Cabernet Sauvignon, Merlot, and Cabernet Franc that exhibited a nice, firm tannic structure plus plenty of dry, inviting oak. He smiled at the great success his first party of the season obviously was. Ric Ocasek, the lead singer of The Cars, was standing near the window chatting with Michelle Kwan, the former champion ice skater and now wife of a Rhode Island politician. Matt Damon and his wife were sampling the options at the Raw Bar. Stephen King was waxing poetic to James Taylor about the most recent Red Sox game he had attended as a longtime season ticket holder.

U.S. Senator Tommy Kearney caught James's eye from across the crowded room. He walked in James's direction to say hello. He stopped a dozen times along the way to shake hands, inquire about family members, and otherwise engage in the schmoozing required of an elected official. When the senator finally reached the host of the party, his first question was: "How's your dad?"

Tommy Kearney and Andrew Windsor had been best friends for nearly sixty years. They had met during freshman year at Phillips Academy Andover, the most prestigious prep school in the United States. Andover, as it was commonly known, was established in 1778 by Samuel Phillips Jr. as a boys-only private preparatory school. Paul Revere had designed the school's great seal, and John Hancock had signed its articles of incorporation. George Washington had spoken at Andover during its inaugural year and had been so impressed with the school that he recommended that his nephews enroll. The vast majority of Andover's graduates matriculated to Harvard, Yale, and Princeton. Notable alumni included U.S. presidents George H. W. Bush and George W. Bush, NFL head coach Bill Belichick, *Law & Order* creator Dick Wolf, Lyman Spitzer (namesake of NASA's Spitzer Space Telescope), six Medal of Honor recipients, inventor Samuel Morse, and author Oliver Wendell Holmes, Sr. (father of the legendary Supreme Court justice).

Writer William S. Dietrich II had famously described Andover and other elite prep schools as being part of a "WASP ascendancy," while the J. D. Salinger classic *The Catcher in the Rye* included a scene in which Sally Hayes introduced Holden Caulfield to a boy who attended Andover. Holden wasn't impressed:

> *You'd have thought they'd taken baths in the same bathtub or something when they were little kids. Old buddyroos. It was nauseating. The funny part was, they probably met each other just once, at some phony party. Finally, when they were all done slobbering around, old Sally introduced us. His name was George something—I don't even remember—and he went to Andover. Big, big deal.*

Tommy Kearney and Andrew Windsor had met more than once at "some phony party." They had competed for playing time on the Andover squash team, pulled pranks together on schoolmates, and were frequent rivals for the affections of the comely lasses at Abbot Academy. In short, they were, some used to say, joined at the hip. But once Kearney had gotten elected to the Senate, most of his time had been spent in Washington.

James Windsor said, "Dad's being a real trooper and he's hangin' in as best as can be expected under the circumstances. I'll pass along your best wishes."

Senator Kearney said, "Please do. I've tried to set up a time to see him during the couple of days I'll be home, but your mom said he's not well enough for visitors at the moment."

James smiled and shook his head. "Mom's always been overly protective of Dad. You know that."

"Indeed I do. She's like the doorman in *The Wizard of Oz*: 'Nobody gets in to see the wizard. Not nobody.'"

They both laughed.

Senator Kearney accepted a glass of wine from one of the waiters circling the room. He took a sip. "Has your dad been able to paint since he got sick?"

"A bit. Frankly, probably more than he should."

Senator Kearney took another sip of wine. "Glad to hear it. I can't imagine your father without a paintbrush or a sketchbook in his hand. Gosh, he was obsessed with it way back in the day at Andover."

"That's what Grandpa used to say too. And that's why Grandpa said Dad would become a great artist, not merely a good one: Because he never wanted to do anything else."

"Chasing skirts aside," Senator Kearney said with a wink and a smile. "Your dad always did like the ladies.... Like father, like son, as the saying goes."

James lifted his glass to acknowledge the accuracy of the senator's observation.

A waitress carrying a tray of Chatham Sea Scallops Wrapped in Prosciutto entered James's line of sight. He gestured for her to bring the tray to him and the senator. But it wasn't because either of them wanted something to eat.

James said, "Are you doing OK? This is your first time helping out the wait staff, correct?"

"Yes," Catina Cruz said, in barely more than a whisper.

Senator Kearney couldn't help but notice how beautiful this particular server was. However, knowing the Windsor men as well as he did, he couldn't possibly have been surprised.

"'Yes' to which?" Senator Kearney interjected. "That you're doing OK, or that this is the first time you've helped out the wait staff?" He reached for an hors d'oeuvre and ate it. "You're doing marvelously as a server," he added.

Catina reddened. "Thank you."

James grabbed an hors d'oeuvre too. "Say hello to Mr. Kearney, Catina. He's our U.S. Senator."

Catina said, "Hello."

Senator Kearney chuckled. "It doesn't appear that she knows who I am, which suggests she didn't vote for me. Say it ain't so, young lady."

"I'm not old enough to vote."

"You're not eighteen?"

Catina shook her head.

Senator Kearney glanced over at James and smiled.

James knew what that meant. They had played this game before. When the senator was in town, James would throw a party and introduce the senator to the beautiful young woman of the moment. Andrew Windsor had long ago apprized his son of the senator's fondness for young women, and he had encouraged his son to accommodate the senator whenever possible.

James had outdone himself this time, Senator Kearney appeared to be saying to himself. Catina was flawless.

James said, "Catina, why don't you give the senator a tour of the house?"

Catina understood what she was being directed to do. Senator Kearney wasn't the first older man to whom James had introduced her. He was, however, the oldest so far. She said, "Follow me, please, Senator."

Sixteen-year-old Catina Cruz and seventy-six-year-old Thomas Kearney disappeared into the back of the house.

***

Deputy Sheriff John Steele was at his desk by seven a.m. every morning. This particular morning was no exception. He found the quiet conducive to the paperwork that every cop detested but couldn't avoid. As usual, he had a mug of *Dunkin' Donuts* coffee and a bran muffin next to his computer. He was preparing his daily update on the Hannah Burgoff case for Sheriff Joyce. It had been two weeks since her death and the investigation was progressing at a snail's pace. He had interviewed Andrew Windsor, albeit briefly, as well as Andrew's wife Lauren and daughter-in-law Meredith. James Windsor had been out of town. Steele also had spoken with several members of the Windsors' staff and, of course, with Nevin Montgomery, the young Boston lawyer who had stated the night of Hannah's death that he thought he had heard something strange.

Jack Peterson entered the room with his own cup of coffee firmly in hand. His deputy sheriff's uniform was freshly creased, as it usually was. "Did you hear about the party?"

Steele said, "What party?" He leaned back in his chair.

"The one at James Windsor's house."

Steele seemed stunned by the news.

Peterson continued, "I thought you'd like that one. As my grandfather used to say, 'Money can't buy common sense.' It goes to show that what I said before is true: The Windsors are living in their own little world."

"A world in which they think the rules don't apply to them?"

"Yes."

"A world in which it's OK to kill the help?"

Peterson blew on his coffee to cool it. "Could be. But I'll leave that bit to you. It's your investigation."

Peterson exited the room.

Steele added a new paragraph to his report for Sheriff Joyce summarizing what Jack Peterson had just told him about the party hosted by James Windsor. Steele mentioned that, obviously, James Windsor was back in town and that he was planning to interview him ASAP.

CHAPTER 41

Deputy Steele's interview with James Windsor would have to wait. Ninety minutes after being informed by Jack Peterson about James's curiously-timed party, the news broke that Andrew Windsor had passed away. Sheriff Joyce had told Steele about it. Joyce had received a *Google* alert that linked him to a breaking news story at *Boston.com*, the *Boston Globe*'s website.

Steele had more than his fair share of things he didn't like about Philip Joyce—Joyce's youth and inexperience topped the list—but Steele was in awe of how Joyce used modern technology to make the Sheriff's Office more efficient. Steele had resisted the change at first, and Tom Watkins had retired early because of it. Steele had come to appreciate it, though; and he had tried to incorporate at least some technological innovations into his own investigations.

Steeled clicked on the link that Joyce had forwarded to him via email. The *Boston.com* story read:

> *Andrew Windsor, one of the most popular painters in the history of American art and the reclusive linchpin of a family dynasty of artists, died early this morning at his Barnstable home. He was seventy-seven.*
>
> *Windsor portrayed a prim and flinty view of New England through parched gray and brown pictures of dilapidated farmhouses, desiccated fields, deserted beaches, circling buzzards, and craggy-faced locals. His art existed within a diverse American context that encompassed illustrators like his father, C. S. Windsor, and Norman Rockwell, as well as landscape painters such as John Marin, Winslow Homer, Albert Bierstadt, and Fitz Hugh Lane.*
>
> *Windsor is survived by Lauren, his wife of fifty-six years; daughter Amanda and son James. The family has yet to release details of the funeral.*

***

The historic streets of Boston were alive with the sounds of twenty-first century commerce: taxi drivers honked horns so that they could squeeze in an extra fare or two per hour; sidewalk vendors trumpeted the virtues of all manner of goods that were available for purchase at discount prices; men and women in business attire charged through a sea of kindred spirits in their haste to get to the office to commence yet another fourteen-hour day.

Boston was a far cry from the rural environs of Barnstable and, as strange as it seemed, Nevin Montgomery already missed the latter. Of course, it wasn't merely the ocean breezes and the fragrant scents of wildflowers that Nevin missed. He also missed Catina Cruz. In fact, he couldn't stop thinking about the night they had slept together.

But Nevin was glad to be back in Boston, at least temporarily. Deputy Sheriff John Steele had granted Nevin permission to leave the Windsor compound to return to the city to discuss what the death of Andrew Windsor meant for Nevin's work on the Windsor estate.

Nevin picked up his pace. He had a ten a.m. meeting scheduled with Bartholomew Lodge and he didn't want to be late. He crossed Tremont Street and continued several more blocks on Beacon Street until he reached Federal Street. He turned right, walked about two hundred yards, and entered the building at 100 Federal Street.

The security guard at the desk said, "Long time, no see, kid. Did you watch the game last night?"

Nevin smiled and shook his head. "Nice to see you, Jimmy. No, I didn't get to see it. You can fill me in on how it went later. But right now, Mr. Lodge is waiting for me."

Nevin hurried to the bank of elevators in the center of the lobby. He punched the UP button, and then hit the button for the 32nd floor once an elevator arrived. The elevator stopped on several floors before finally arriving at the 32nd.

Nevin nodded hello to a couple of colleagues he passed in the corridor. When he reached Bartholomew Lodge's office, he said, "Good morning, Jessie. Is Bart available?"

Jessie Young was Bartholomew Lodge's longtime secretary. She said, "Good morning, Nevin. It's nice to see you. You can go right in. Mr. Lodge is expecting you."

Nevin knocked on Lodge's door.

"Come in."

Nevin entered Lodge's spacious office. A walnut conference table was situated to Nevin's left and a brown leather couch to his right.

Framed photographs of historic Boston sporting events—Bobby Orr's championship-winning goal in the 1970 Stanley Cup, Larry Bird's last second steal in the 1987 NBA eastern conference finals, Johnny Damon's lead-off homerun in game 4 of the 2004 World Series, Tom Brady's miraculous drive in the 2017 Super Bowl—adorned the walls. Nevin said, "Good morning, Bart."

Lodge closed the computer screen he was perusing at his desk and directed his attention to his most talented associate. "Good morning. It's good to see you in the flesh. What's it been, two weeks?"

Nevin nodded in the affirmative.

"How did it go?" Lodge gestured for Nevin to take a seat in one of the captain's chairs that faced his desk.

"Surreal." Nevin sat. "As you know, my first night at the Windsor compound was interrupted by a murder. The cops aren't calling it murder, but it's pretty clear that it was."

"That's what this morning's *Globe* said too." Lodge slid a copy of the *Boston Globe* across his desk for Nevin to read. "Front page, lower right."

Nevin studied the article. When he had finished, he said, "I didn't know about the party at James Windsor's house. I left the compound at about five to drive back to Boston. It seems odd that James would be hosting a party when there was a police investigation underway. It fits, though."

Lodge reached for his coffee cup. "What do you mean?"

"He's an asshole, if you'll pardon my French. I ran into him one morning when I was jogging on the beach. He was about as friendly as a porcupine startled by a coyote."

"Were you able to meet with Andrew before he died? You had mentioned when we spoke on the phone about ten days ago that Lauren was making it difficult for you to meet with him."

"She was. But I finally managed to get a few minutes alone with him. I made the changes he requested."

"You helped him write his wife and kids out of the will?"

"Yes."

"Did you satisfy the formalities?"

"Yes." Nevin offered a wry smile. He had heard Lodge wax poetic on many occasions about the importance of testamentary formalities. Moreover, Lodge had given all the associates a copy of the letter he had written to Yale Law School Professor John Langbein—the original of which hung framed on the back of Lodge's door—criticizing the celebrated professor for leading the reform movement that had liberalized the requirements for testamentary documents.

"Andrew signed at the end of the will?"

"Yes."

"In the presence of the requisite number of witnesses?"

"Yes."

"And you included an attestation clause?"

"Yes."

"Good."

Nevin adjusted his tie. "Now what?"

"You probate the will."

Probate was the process by which a court validated a will. In Andrew Windsor's case, it meant that Nevin had to contact the executor of Mr. Windsor's will, Senator Thomas Kearney; file the will in the Barnstable County Probate Court; and provide due notice to all of Mr. Windsor's heirs. The latter would be the tricky part, insofar as Mr. Windsor had cut his wife and kids out of his will. In short, a will contest was about as close to an absolute certainty as anything in the law could possibly be.

A will could be contested on any number of grounds, including lack of capacity by the testator, undue influence over the testator, fraud, or lack of proper execution. Lodge's insistence that the common law formalities be followed when redrafting Andrew Windsor's testamentary documents meant that lack of proper execution wouldn't be an issue. The other three grounds were in play, however; and with millions of dollars at stake, Nevin Montgomery and Bartholomew Lodge both knew that Lauren and James Windsor would plead all three.

CHAPTER 42

U.S. Senator Thomas Kearney was in the middle of a Foreign Affairs Committee hearing about the latest crisis in the Middle East when he received a text from his secretary that read: *Andrew Windsor died this morning.*

Senator Kearney leaned back in his seat and closed his eyes.

The chair of the Foreign Affairs Committee, a five-term Republican from Indiana, glanced over at his colleague from Massachusetts, who was next in line to question the afternoon's witness. The chair asked, "Are you OK, Senator Kearney?"

Kearney answered, "No, I'm not OK. I just received a text that Andrew Windsor passed away this morning. We've been best friends since Andover."

The chair did what any decent human being would do. He sounded his gavel and called for a ninety-minute recess so that Senator Kearney could tend to a sensitive personal matter.

Kearney opted for the stairs rather than the elevator. He might have been seventy-six years old, but he remained in fine shape and the gaggle of reporters in front of the private elevator that senators usually used was more than he could stomach at the moment. He wanted to reach his office as quickly as he could so that he could gather as much information as possible about the devastating news.

When he arrived at his office, his secretary said, "I'm sorry about Mr. Windsor."

"Thank you. How did you learn he died?"

"His lawyer called. He needs for you to call him right away." Kearney's secretary handed Kearney a slip of paper with Andrew Windsor's lawyer's telephone number written on it.

Kearney studied it. It was a Boston telephone number, which made sense, given how much money was at stake. Barnstable lawyers tended to specialize in boating accidents, DUIs, and the like.

Unlike the vast majority of U.S. senators, Tommy Kearney wasn't a lawyer. However, Andrew Windsor had asked Kearney years earlier whether Kearney would be willing to serve as the executor of Andrew's will. Kearney wasn't sure what that would entail, but Andrew almost never asked for favors and Kearney couldn't imagine saying no to a favor as serious as that involving his best friend's will. Consequently, Kearney had said yes.

Kearney placed his Foreign Affairs Committee materials on his desk, reached for his telephone, and dialed the number that his secretary had provided.

Nevin Montgomery answered on the second ring.

"This is Tommy Kearney. My secretary said you needed to speak with me."

"Yes I do, Senator. Thanks for returning my call so promptly. I know you're a very busy man."

"Indeed I am. I was in the middle of a Foreign Affairs Committee meeting when I received word of Andrew's death. The chairman kindly called a brief recess so I can process the terrible news."

"You have my condolences. I didn't know Mr. Windsor well, but he was very kind to me when we spoke about his testamentary documents."

"His what?"

"His will and trust, which brings me to the purpose of my call."

"I'm the executor of his will, right? That's why you're calling?"

"Correct."

"I figured as much. Of course, I have no idea what an executor is supposed to do. I would be grateful to know."

"No problem, Senator," Nevin said. "In a nutshell, you're the person Mr. Windsor designated to carry out the wishes he expressed in his will. Technically, the court must appoint you before you can act, but that's merely a formality that's quickly addressed during probate."

"During what?"

"Probate. That's when the court validates or invalidates the will. Usually, it's a painless process. I don't think it will be in Mr. Windsor's case, however."

Silence dominated Kearney's end of the line. He was obviously paying close attention to what Nevin was saying. Finally, the senator said, "So you're saying that someone's going to challenge Andrew's will? Who on earth would do such a thing?"

"Lauren and James Windsor. As you'll see when I email you a PDF of the will, Mr. Windsor cut them out."

"Why would he do that?" Kearney had a will of his own. It had never occurred to him to cut his wife and kids out of it.

"I'm afraid I'm not allowed to say."

"Attorney-client privilege?"

"Yes."

"But Andrew is dead."

"The privilege survives the client's death."

"Do Lauren and James know?"

"No."

"Who's going to tell them?"

"You are. You're the executor."

"Have you ever met Lauren and James?"

"Yes."

"Then you know this is going to go over about as well as locker room humor at a NOW convention."

NOW was the acronym for the National Organization of Women.

"I agree. It won't be fun to tell them, to put it mildly."

More silence from Kearney's end of the line. Then, "Am I allowed to resign as executor?"

"Yes. Is that what I should tell the court: that you decline to serve as executor of Mr. Windsor's will?"

"No. I couldn't do that to Andrew. I promised him that I would make sure his estate was handled properly and, despite the fact that I'm a politician, a promise is a promise."

"Thank you, Senator. Please let me know how Lauren and James react to the news."

"Do you have any doubt about how they'll react?"

"No. But I still need to know so that we can prepare for a will contest, if it comes to that."

***

Less than an hour after Lauren and James Windsor had received a call from Tommy Kearney informing them that Andrew had cut them out of his will, they had scheduled an appointment with a lawyer to discuss their options. Three hours after that, they were meeting with Joshua Jones of Palmer & Lodge in a secluded conference room at Boston's historic *Parker House* hotel.

The *Parker House* opened in 1855 and was now a member of the National Historic Preservation's Historic Hotels of America program.

It perfected the state dessert of Massachusetts, Boston cream pie; invented the *Parker House* roll; and coined the term "scrod." Charles Dickens had lived at the *Parker House* for two years and had first recited *A Christmas Carol* at the hotel to a group of fellow writers known as the Saturday Club that included Henry Wadsworth Longfellow, Ralph Waldo Emerson, and Oliver Wendell Holmes, Sr. The hotel's close proximity to the Massachusetts state capitol had long made it a rendezvous for elected officials.

Joshua Jones asked, "Where did you get my name?"

James Windsor answered, "From a lawyer friend of mine. She said you were smart as a whip and tough as nails."

Jones smiled and reached for the pitcher of ice water in the middle of the table. "Who was that?" He poured three glasses of water and distributed them proportionally.

"Cindy Wilson."

Jones smiled again. "I know Cindy well. We went to law school together. She's an excellent lawyer. Why didn't you hire her?"

"Because she said she's not a trial lawyer. She said you are."

"I am. But if this is about what I think it's about, I've got a conflict of interest."

Lauren Windsor joined the conversation. "What do you mean?"

"The Massachusetts Rules of Professional Conduct forbid a lawyer from representing a client whose interests are adverse to another client represented by the firm. As you know, Palmer & Lodge represents Andrew Windsor."

Lauren said, "But he's dead."

Jones took a sip of water. He reached for a hard candy in the crystal bowl in the center of the conference table. "That doesn't matter. The prohibition survives his death because the firm would be defending his will against any contest that you and James would be filing."

"Are there any exceptions?"

"Of course. But unless Mr. Windsor's side of the dispute agrees to waive the conflict rules, none apply."

"Can you ask? Who would you ask?"

"Sure, I can ask. Senator Kearney is the executor of the will, so technically he's the person I would ask. In reality, though, I need to go through my partner Bart Lodge. Your husband was his client."

James interjected, "You ask Lodge. I'll talk to Kearney. He owes me a favor, and this is it."

Only James knew what that favor was. Her name was Catina Cruz.

CHAPTER 43

Bartholomew Lodge placed his favorite album into the CD player behind his desk and hit the PLAY button. Norah Jones's sultry voice and virtuoso piano groves filled Lodge's capacious office on the 32nd floor of 100 Federal Street in Boston's financial district. Jessie Young entered her boss's office with a pot of coffee and a plate of blueberry muffins. She smiled when she heard Jones's most famous song, *Don't Know Why*, sounding in the background.

Jessie said, "She's made more than one CD, you know."

Lodge lifted his eyes from the Windsor file. "I know. But her first is my favorite. Besides, I'm forced to use it as white noise these days." He motioned to the large window to the left of his desk. Cranes were maneuvering towards the scaffolding surrounding the skyscraper across the street. "Did you ever find out how much longer the construction is going to last?"

"About a month, they said. Sorry."

Lodge grimaced. "It's not your fault." He reached for a muffin and took a bite. Next, he poured himself a cup of coffee.

Jessie turned to leave. "Don't forget you're meeting your wife at noon for lunch at the *Union Oyster House*. She texted me this morning to ask me to remind you."

"I won't forget. How could I?" Lodge said with a smile. "She's reminded me every day this week."

"She thinks you're working too hard, which you are. There's no crime in taking a long lunch with your wife."

Jessie Young checked her watch. It read 11:55 a.m. The *Union Oyster House* was a ten-minute walk from the office. Bart must be buried in that darn Windsor file again and lost track of time, she said to herself. She knew he was almost always on time, especially where his family was concerned. One reason she liked working for Lodge so much was because he was such a conscientious family man. She stood from her chair, walked to his door, and knocked. She said, "Bart. It's almost noon. You're going to be late for lunch with Leslie."

Leslie was Mrs. Lodge's first name.

Lodge issued no reply.

Jessie knocked again. This time, she pushed open the door. "Oh, God!" she screamed. "Help! I need help!" She rushed to the center of the room where Bartholomew Lodge lay motionless on the floor.

Paramedics arrived in less than fifteen minutes. Ten minutes after that, Bartholomew Lodge was in the ER at *Massachusetts General Hospital*. The attending physician remarked how lucky Lodge had been to have suffered cardiac arrest in Boston, a city that hosted more hospitals per capita than any but New York. Lodge was likewise fortunate that the paramedics had transported him to *Mass General* itself, which recently had surpassed *Johns Hopkins Hospital* as the top-rated hospital in the United States. It also didn't hurt that *Mass General* was particularly well known for treating patients who had been poisoned.

The attending physician specialized in it. A serious man in his mid-fifties of Asian descent, Dr. Chen Tsai was studying the preliminary lab results so that he could determine as quickly as possible what treatment to prescribe. He announced to his team, "We've got a good old-fashioned case of cyanide poisoning on our hands, ladies and gentlemen. I haven't seen one of these in years."

When cyanide was ingested at sufficiently high doses, it was capable of causing a coma with seizures, apnea, and cardiac arrest, with death following in a matter of seconds. Fortunately for Bartholomew Lodge, the dosage he had ingested was less than the fatal level.

The team's head nurse retrieved the cyanide antidote kit from the cabinet in the east corner of the room and handed it to Dr. Tsai.

Dr. Tsai placed an oxygen mask over Lodge's face and piped a small dose of amyl nitrite through it. He instructed the head nurse to administer an intravenous regime of sodium nitrite and sodium thiosulfate. He said, "I'll be back in thirty minutes to check on the patient's progress. Page me if there are any developments before then."

***

News of Bartholomew Lodge's sudden illness swept through the ornate offices of Palmer & Lodge like a brush fire through the Berkshires. Nobody knew what had actually transpired. Some people thought that Lodge had suffered a stroke. Others speculated that he had tripped and hit his head. A handful suspected that he had collapsed from exhaustion. The latter theory was being promoted by Joshua Jones, who reminded anyone who would listen that Lodge was no spring chicken and that his time would be better spent relaxing on his sailboat and playing with his grandchildren.

Nevin Montgomery was bound and determined to find out for himself what had really happened. He jumped on the *T* and traveled two quick stops on the red line to *Mass General.*

A white-haired volunteer greeted Nevin with a grandmotherly smile. "May I help you?" she said.

Nevin returned her smile. "Yes, ma'am. Can you tell me what room Bartholomew Lodge is in? He was admitted about three hours ago, I think."

The elderly candy striper swiveled in her chair and searched the patients list on the hospital computer. Her eyes strained to locate the requested information. She finally did. "The computer says he's still in the ICU. That's on the sixth floor. The elevators are around the corner to the left."

Nevin said, "Thank you."

Hospital elevators were notoriously slow. Nevin wondered whether this particular elevator was moving at all. On the plus side, he was sharing his slow ride with a cute nurse. As tempting as it was to try to flirt with her, Nevin knew that this was neither the time nor the place.

Nevin finally arrived at his desired destination. On this occasion, he was greeted by a full-time hospital employee. Chronologically, she was about half-way between the octogenarian who greeted him at the hospital's main entrance and the nurse with whom he had shared an elevator ride.

Nevin repeated his request for Lodge's location.

The ICU receptionist checked the spreadsheet on her computer. She said, "He's in number seven."

Nevin started to walk in that direction. He got about five steps.

"Excuse me, please," the receptionist said. "The ICU is a restricted visitors unit. Are you a family member of Mr. Lodge's?"

"No, ma'am. I work for him."

"Then I'm afraid you're not allowed to see him until he's released from the ICU. It's a critical period in his recovery. I hope you understand that it's for his own good."

Nevin didn't know what to say. But he was certain that he needed to see Bart Lodge right away. He decided to do what he used to do when he was a teenager and his parents wouldn't let him go out with his buddies on a school night: He waited for the receptionist to turn her back so he could sneak past her.

Thirty seconds later, Nevin was standing in Room 7 of the Intensive Care Unit at *Mass General Hospital*. He couldn't help but notice that Lodge looked as if he had gone ten rounds with an MMA fighter. Frankly, Nevin wasn't sure whether Lodge was alive.

"Bart," Nevin whispered. "Can you hear me?... Bart?"

No response.

Nevin walked closer to Lodge's bedside. "Bart?... Can you hear me?"

An eyelid... Nevin thought he saw an eyelid flutter.

"Bart?"

Ne—Nevin? Is—Is that you?"

"Yes, Bart. It's me."

"Wh—Where am I?"

"You're in the hospital."

"The hospital? Why?"

"You passed out. I'm not sure why you passed out, but you passed out. Jessie found you collapsed on the floor in your office."

Lodge glanced to his right and noticed a saline bag hanging from a metal pole next to his bed. He looked at his arm and saw the tube and needle to which it was attached. "I guess I owe Jessie lunch at *City Landing*."

Nevin smiled. "I guess you do."

City Landing was a popular restaurant on Boston's waterfront. It incorporated local ingredients into specialty dishes such as Cape Clams and Day Boat Scallops. Lodge took Jessie Young to *City Landing* every year on Administrative Assistants Day. It was her favorite place to eat.

"Does my wife know? Is she here? I was supposed to meet her for lunch at the *Union Oyster House*."

"I think I saw her smoking a cigarette near the front entrance."

Lodge's brow furrowed. "Smoking? Are you sure it was her? She said she had stopped that nasty habit five years ago. I'd been asking her to stop since the day I met her some forty years ago now."

"Maybe it wasn't her. I think it was, though. I'm sure she's quite stressed out at the moment. She probably fell off the wagon for a day or so. With all due respect, Bart: I'd cut her some slack if I were you."

Lodge glanced again at the tube and needle attached to his arm. "Fair enough."

Nevin scratched his ear. "Can I ask you something about the Windsor case? I mean, are you strong enough to talk shop for a minute?"

"Ask away. Please. It'll take my mind off my current state of affairs."

"Joshua Jones told me a couple of hours ago that Lauren and James Windsor have asked him to represent them in their challenge to Andrew Windsor's will. He said he told them he'd like to help but that he needs Senator Kearney to waive the conflict of interest objection first. What should we do?"

A mischievous smile that would have made Jack Nicholson proud crossed Bartholomew Lodge's distinguished face. "It might be the pain medicine talking, but I think we should waive the conflict. I also think you should be first chair on the will contest. If you win, you'll finally be able to shut Joshua up. Besides, I doubt I'll be strong enough to do it myself."

If I win, Nevin said to himself. That's a big *if.*

CHAPTER 44

Nevin grabbed an empty table in an isolated corner on the basement level of *Anna's Taqueria* on Cambridge Street, which two days earlier had received the "best burrito" award for the third consecutive year from *Boston Magazine*. A twelve-inch "super burrito" stuffed to the breaking point with grilled chicken, brown rice, black beans, sour cream, shredded cheddar, lettuce, tomato, onions, and a green salsa hot enough to start a forest fire sat invitingly on a plate in front of him. He had added, as he often did, a side of rice and beans. He was washing it all down with a bottle of Mexican orange soda. Besides the fact that Nevin loved burritos, he knew that Joshua Jones wouldn't be caught dead in a no-frills restaurant like *Anna's*, which meant that Nevin could review the Windsor file in peace.

Nevin didn't want to spill food on a case file. He therefore decided to get caught up on what was known in the legal profession as continuing legal education reading before turning to the Windsor file. He sorted through his stack of mail and started with the monthly newsletter from the estate planning section of the Massachusetts Bar Association. This year's section chair was a senior partner at Ropes & Gray who represented many of the old money family trusts of southern New England. Nevin perused the chair's introductory column. He almost choked on a spoonful of rice and beans when he read the news that the governor had recently signed Bill No. 361 into law, the general assembly's legislation making the Uniform Probate Code the law of the Commonwealth of Massachusetts. More to the point, that meant that for a will to be valid in the state, it had to be witnessed by three people instead of two. In short, the one proposal that Yale Law Professor John Langbein had proffered that didn't liberalize the common law testamentary formalities appeared to have bitten Nevin in the butt.

Nevin pushed aside his plate and rushed to the bathroom to throw up.

***

Nevin checked into *The Lamb and the Lion Inn* at 2504 Bay Street in West Barnstable. He had asked his secretary to find him a place to stay for a couple of days in the area so that he could do a bit more legwork on the Windsor file. Moreover, he had promised the Barnstable County Sheriff's Office that he would return. His most significant motivation was, however, that he wanted to see Catina Cruz, especially after he had discovered that he had screwed up the testamentary formalities on Andrew Windsor's will. It would have been more convenient for Nevin to stay in one of the guest cottages on the Windsor compound again, but with Mr. Windsor dead and Lauren and James Windsor preparing to challenge his will in court, Nevin knew that was never going to happen.

Nevin asked the innkeeper whether his room had WiFi access.

She told the Jack Russell terrier that was yapping at her heels to hush, and then answered, "Absolutely."

Nevin was relieved to hear it. He needed to consult *Westlaw*, a leading legal research computer database, to try to figure out some way to wiggle out of the mistake he had made on Mr. Windsor's will. Nevin's favorite law professor at Harvard used to remind students all the time that a good lawyer could find a case to support any proposition, and Nevin desperately needed to find one that said two witnesses to a will were as good as three. Good luck with that, he said to himself as he followed the innkeeper to his room, a spacious suite called *Innkeeper's Pride* that was equipped with a wood-burning fireplace, a living room area, a private deck overlooking the bay, a Jacuzzi, and a kitchenette.

The innkeeper said, "This is my favorite room in the hotel. I hope you enjoy it."

Nevin surveyed the room. "It's beautiful."

The innkeeper beckoned for the Jack Russell terrier to follow her back to the lobby as she said goodbye to her handsome young guest.

Nevin sent a quick text to his secretary to let her know that he had arrived and to thank her for finding such a nice room for him on short notice. He alerted her that he would be difficult to reach for a while as he immersed himself in the Windsor file. He didn't tell her about the mistake he had made.

Next, Nevin switched on his laptop and navigated to the *Westlaw* homepage. I can't do this right now, he said to himself as the database's logo greeted him in blue and gray swatches. He grabbed his windbreaker and headed for Barnstable's town center to purchase flowers and chocolate for Catina.

Deputy Sheriff John Steele was on a routine patrol through Barnstable when he spotted Nevin Montgomery entering *Sandra's Flower Shop* at the corner of Main and Shriver Streets. He maneuvered his squad car into a parking space across from a fire hydrant, exited his car, and entered the shop.

Nevin noticed Steele immediately. "Good afternoon, Deputy Steele."

Steele removed his hat. "Good afternoon, Mr. Montgomery. Thanks for coming back."

Nevin said, "You're welcome. I learned a long time ago that it makes sense to do what the police tell you to do. You were kind enough to let me return to Boston for a few days and I promised to come back. A promise is a promise."

Steele nodded. "I appreciate that. But if you don't mind me asking, why are you shopping at *Sandra's*?"

The proprietor, a middle-aged woman with a mischievous twinkle in her eye, said, "Now, John: don't you be trying to run off my customers."

Steele smiled. "I wouldn't dream of it, Sandra. I'm curious, is all. You know I give you plenty of business."

The proprietor returned Steele's smile. "Well, now that you mention it, we've got some lovely tulip baskets on special this week. I suspect Becca would appreciate one."

Becca was Steele's wife.

"You're shameless, Sandra, you know that. But I suspect you're correct. Box one up for me, if you would."

The proprietor headed to the back of the store to do precisely that.

Nevin asked, "Any progress on the investigation?"

Steele answered, "I'm not allowed to comment. Suffice it to say that we're aggressively working several promising leads."

Nevin had no idea what that meant. He strongly suspected that Steele hadn't made much headway on the case, but he was smart enough not to let Steele know he thought that. After all, Steele hadn't cleared anyone who was at the Windsor compound on the night of Hannah Burgoff's death, including Nevin.

Nevin said, "Do you need to ask me anything else?"

Steele shook his head. "Not at the moment, no. But I might in a couple of days. Can you stick around for a bit longer? I apologize for the inconvenience, but Mr. Windsor's death has thrown a bit of a monkey wrench into the works."

"I know what you mean, Deputy Steele. Remember that my law firm is representing his estate. Needless to say, his death has made things a whole lot more complicated.

***

Nevin walked the quaint streets of Barnstable with two things on his mind: (1) remedying the mistake he had made on Mr. Windsor's will and (2) trying to find Catina. Nevin knew that, as a lawyer, the first was far more significant than the second but, as a twenty-something-year-old single guy, the second was what Nevin was most interested in accomplishing at the moment. He realized, given the current adversarial nature of his relationship with Lauren and James Windsor, it would be next to impossible to try to find Catina at the Windsor compound, even though that was where she was most likely to be. He didn't know where else to look, however. He spotted a pub across the street from where he was standing and decided to ponder his options over a beer.

Nevin was three-quarters of the way through his second beer when his problem was solved: Catina Cruz came strolling through the door of *The Anchor Pub* on Main Street. She was even more beautiful than Nevin remembered: her thick black hair was tied into a ponytail, which accentuated her high cheekbones; her full lips were glossed as red as a fresh strawberry; her bronze skin glistened against the light shining through the large windows overlooking the bay; and her tight sweater and jeans made seemingly every head in the bar follow her every move.

Unfortunately for Nevin, Catina walked past his table without appearing to notice him. Before Nevin could try to get her attention, she had said hello to a group of men in the back of the bar and disappeared with them into a room marked PRIVATE.

CHAPTER 45

Nevin was deep into his fifth beer of the night when he felt a tap on his shoulder.

It was Catina. Her ponytail was disheveled, her lipstick smudged, and her eyes betrayed a weariness far beyond her years. She asked, "May I join you?"

Nevin answered, "Of course. Would you like something to drink?"

"Yes, please."

Nevin signaled for the waitress.

Catina ordered a rum and cola.

"What were you doing back there?" Nevin gestured to the private room in the rear of the bar. "Are you OK?"

Catina blushed. "I'm fine. I was talking to some guys I know."

Nevin wanted to believe her, but he didn't. "About what?"

The waitress brought Catina's drink and then hurried to another table to check on some of her other customers.

Catina grew quiet. She traced a finger across the top of her glass. She took a sip, and she took another. She finally said, "Nothing important." She changed the subject. "What are you doing back in Barnstable?"

Nevin took a swig of beer. "I promised the Sheriff's Office that I would come back. You know, because of the murder investigation involving Hannah Burgoff."

Catina flinched a bit when Nevin mentioned Hannah Burgoff. She didn't say anything, though. Instead, she made the necessary adjustments to her disheveled ponytail. "It's too bad about Mr. Windsor. He was always nice to me. Mrs. Windsor, on the other hand, has never liked having me around and now that Mr. Windsor is dead I suspect that my days in Barnstable are numbered."

"I thought you worked for James and Meredith?"

"Technically, I do. Meredith was the one who hired me, but I've always done things for the senior Windsors too, and James and Meredith tend to defer to what Mrs. Windsor wants. Mr. Windsor pretty much stayed out of it."

"Why would Mrs. Windsor want you gone?"

Catina grew quiet again. Her eyes met Nevin's. She didn't seem to know what he wanted from her, other than the obvious physical pleasures that most men enjoyed. Her eyes shifted to the door marked PRIVATE in the back of the bar. "I think she thinks I'm too much of a distraction for her son."

"Distraction?"

"Temptation is probably a better word for it." She blushed again.

"OK. I get it. But do you want to keep working for the Windsors?"

"What choice do I have? You went to law school. I didn't finish high school. I suppose I could follow in my mom's footsteps and clean rooms at the New Bedford *Holiday Inn*."

"As I've said before, there's no shame in manual labor. My dad's the janitor at my old high school, and there's not a person in the world I admire more than him. I suspect your mom is doing the best she can. I know you are."

Catina's eyes began to water. She reached across the table and placed her hand on Nevin's. "Do you wanna get out of here? We could go for a walk. It's nice outside."

"Sure," Nevin said. He finished his beer and followed Catina out of the bar.

Several drunken locals patted Nevin on the back in admiration of his apparent success with the most beautiful woman in the place.

Nevin didn't respond to them. He was focusing his full attention on Catina.

A brisk breeze tussled Nevin's and Catina's hair. Wind chimes hanging from front porches along cobble-stone streets serenaded the night. Nevin glanced at Catina. The moonlight framed her face like a halo on a sacred statue. Nothing could have been more misleading….

Catina asked, "Where do you wanna go?"

Nevin answered, "I don't care. You know the town a lot better than I do."

Catina reached for Nevin's hand. "How about my room?"

Nevin registered no objection. No straight man would.

Catina's room was precisely as Nevin had remembered it: small, but neat. A bouquet of wildflowers in a glass vase sat on the nightstand next to her bed. A poster of a whale watching expedition hung above the headboard, and another poster—this one of Robert Pattinson—was displayed near the door.

Nevin pointed to the poster of Robert Pattinson. "I see you've still got a thing for that *Twilight* guy. Should I be jealous?"

Catina smiled slyly and reached for the zipper on Nevin's pants. "You tell me."

Forty-five minutes later—forty-five minutes after the best sex of Nevin's life—Nevin said, "Apparently not." He kissed Catina on the cheek and rolled onto his side. "Now what?"

Catina's eyes searched the room. She spent a lot of time in her room and she knew every square inch of it. "What do you mean?"

"What are we doing? I mean, is this a fling, or is it something more serious? It's certainly not a one-night stand. After all, this was our second time together."

"Are you complaining?" Catina reached her hand under the sheets and placed it between Nevin's legs. His erection returned in less than five seconds. "I didn't think so."

They made love again. At least that's what Nevin thought they were doing. He had no idea what Catina considered it. Nevin always had a difficult time trying to figure out what was going on inside a woman's head, but trying to read Catina was like trying to understand the tax code. In short, he had no idea what she was thinking.

Catina said, "You need to leave."

"Why? Did I do something wrong?"

"No. But I'm not allowed to have boys in my room."

Boys? Nevin said to himself. Aloud to Catina: "Why not?"

"Because the Windsors said so." Catina got out of bed, retrieved Nevin's clothes, and tossed them to him. She was naked.

Her body was flawless: Carmel and unblemished and with curves in all the right places. Nevin could only imagine why she was meeting with those men in the bar. It made him sick to think about it. "Can I see you tomorrow? Can I buy you dinner? I'd like to take you on a proper date."

Catina blushed. She couldn't recall ever going on a "proper date" with any of the many men with whom she'd had sex. "You don't need to do that. You already got what you wanted."

Nevin shot to his feet. "Don't say that. *You're* what I want, and it's pretty obvious that I don't have you yet.... I barely know anything about you."

"OK, Nevin. You win. What do you wanna know?"

Catina had told Nevin the first time they had spent time together that she was from New Bedford and how she had come to work for the Windsors. This time, she mentioned that she was Portuguese-American, that her mother was an undocumented immigrant, and that she didn't know anything about her father. She said that "Catina" meant "pure" in English, and she indicated that she was far from pure. Most important of all, she confessed that she had been modeling secretly for James Windsor like Hannah Burgoff had done for Andrew Windsor and that she had been having an affair with James from almost the first day she had arrived at the compound. She then said, "So, am I still the one you want?"

Nevin looked as if he had seen a ghost.

"I didn't think so." Catina grabbed her robe and sat back on the bed. She stared at the wall in the opposite direction from where Nevin was situated.

Nevin finally said, "Yes, you're still the one I want. But why are you sleeping with James Windsor? He's old enough to be your father? Did your mother know?"

Nevin was using the past tense when referring to Catina's mother because Catina had previously told him that her mother had died.

"Of course she knew. She wouldn't admit it, but she knew."

"Then why didn't she bring you home?"

"Because she thought I was better off with the Windsors. She thought more doors would open for me here than in low-income housing in New Bedford. I guess she felt that sleeping with James was the price I had to pay for a better future.... She said God made me, quote, 'beautiful' for a reason."

CHAPTER 46

The smart thing for Nevin to have done would have been to kiss Catina on the forehead and leave. But most men weren't smart where a beautiful woman was concerned and, as Catina had mentioned moments earlier, God had certainly made her beautiful. So, instead of heading back to *The Lamb and the Lion Inn* to try to figure out a solution to the problem he had recently discovered with the formalities of Andrew Windsor's will, Nevin let Catina talk him into snorting bath salts.

Just like old times, Nevin said to himself as the effects of the bath salts began to kick in. Alastair, Colin, and Stewart had been big fans of the so-called working man's cocaine, a drug that Dillon Boyle, the neighborhood dealer, had introduced them to the summer before their junior year at John F. Kennedy High School.

Nevin glanced over at Catina. The room was spinning like a merry go 'round at a South Shore fare but he couldn't help but notice that she was pulling on her hair and scratching her arms. "Don't do that," Nevin said to her. "You'll hurt yourself."

"Don't do what?" Catina continued doing what she was doing, apparently oblivious to the fact that she was doing it.

"Scratch yourself and pull your hair."

"But I've got bugs on me."

Nevin examined Catina's scalp and arms. "No, you don't. It's the salts talking. Believe me, I should know."

***

The bell rang. The room full of students snapped shut their books, grabbed their belongings, and slid their chairs under their desks. They raced for the door as if the classroom were on fire.

Mr. Harrington said, "No running, please. And remember to read chapters 4 and 5 of *Snow Falling on Cedars* for tomorrow." He began to erase the chalkboard. "Mr. O'Connor: may I speak to you for a moment, please."

Seamus O'Connor stopped in his tracks. He directed his eyes to the front of the classroom. "Yes, sir."

Mr. Harrington finished erasing the chalkboard. He handed the erasers to Seamus. "Can you clap these clean for me?"

"Yes, sir." Seamus sounded as if he had dodged a bullet. "I'll do it right now."

But Seamus was incorrect.

"Thank you. You can do it in a few minutes, though. I want to talk to you first."

"A—About what?"

"You know what. You're high again, aren't you?"

Seamus nodded. "I'm sorry, Mr. Harrington. I'm trying. I really am. But I screwed up again. Are you gonna tell my parents?"

"That depends."

"On what?"

"On whether you promise to go to a meeting." Mr. Harrington checked the clock above the chalkboard. "There's a 3:30 meeting at St. Luke's."

"I'll be there. I promise."

Mr. Harrington's smartphone vibrated while he was watching Seamus exit the classroom. He reached into his pocket to answer it. The caller was saved on his contacts list. "Nevin? Are you OK?"

"To borrow a famous line from Bill Clinton, that depends on what the definition of 'OK' is. But seriously: no, I'm sorry to say I'm not OK."

"Another slip?"

"Yes. I'm sorry, Mr. H. I'm trying, but it's hard. I mean, it's really, really hard."

"Of course it's hard. You're an addict. You've got an addiction. By definition, it's going to be hard. How did it happen this time? What did you take?"

"I was with a girl. She wanted to party. I should've said no, but I didn't."

"Of course you should've said no. You can't risk your sobriety for a girl. I don't care how pretty she is.… You didn't say what you took. What was it?"

"Bath salts."

"Jesus, Mary, and Joseph. Are you crazy? That stuff will kill you." Mr. Harrington taught in a poorly funded high school in a lower-class neighborhood in a major metropolitan area. He knew perfectly well what bath salts were. Moments earlier he had finished chastising Seamus O'Connor for getting high on the very same thing.

"I know. I'm sorry. Like I said, I slipped up."

"You know what you've got to do: get to a meeting and stay away from that girl. I just finished telling a bright young man who reminds me a lot of you the same thing."

"I'm back in Barnstable. I'll check the web to see when the next meeting is."

Nevin thanked Mr. Harrington for always being there for him. He didn't make any promises about Catina, though. He knew that would be a promise he couldn't keep.

***

Nevin Montgomery hurdled down the stairs at Our Lady of Lourdes Catholic Church. The church's website said that the Narcotics Anonymous meeting started at 5:00 p.m. and he didn't want to be late. The group leader was pouring a cup of coffee from an industrial size thermos and arranging the Twelve Step literature on the card table that he had borrowed from the rectory when Nevin entered the room at the south end of the corridor of the church's basement.

The group leader said, "Good to see you again. Nevin, isn't it?"

"Yes. It's good to see you again too. How's the coffee today?"

The group leader blew on his cup to cool it. He took a sip. "Strong: just like addicts like it."

Nevin and the group leader shared a laugh. In any other venue the group leader's comment would have been regarded as politically incorrect at best. But this was a Narcotics Anonymous meeting and recovering addicts needed to confront their demons head on and an occasional joke at their own expense helped keep them sane.

Nevin grabbed a Styrofoam cup from the stack next to the thermos and filled it with coffee that was as black as a judge's robe. He added two *Mini Moos* and a packet of sugar to cut the edge off the java. "Where is everybody?"

"We changed the starting time to 5:15 last week. Folks were coming straight from work and the group thought we should give people a chance to get here on time. It was distracting to have so many people walking in late because they couldn't leave the office until 5:00."

"Sounds reasonable." Nevin scanned the room. About two dozen folding chairs were arranged in a circle to encourage the honest conversation—"sharing," it was called—that was at the heart of all Twelve Step programs.

A Twelve Step program was a set of guiding principles articulating a course of action for recovery from addiction. It originated in 1938 with Alcoholics Anonymous, but the method had been adapted to address other addictions too, including to narcotics. Twelve Step programs involved the following: (1) admitting that one couldn't control one's addiction; (2) recognizing a higher power that could give strength; (3) examining prior mistakes with the help of an experienced member; (4) making amends for those mistakes; (5) learning to live a new life with a new code of behavior; and (6) helping others who suffered from the same addiction.

The group leader called the meeting to order. He then said, "We'll now go around the room and read the steps. Please introduce yourself by your first name only and please read a couple of steps." He handed the list to the woman to his left.

The woman said, "Hi, my name is Penny."

The others in attendance said in unison, "Hi, Penny."

Penny read the first three steps. "One. 'We admitted that we were powerless over our addictions; that our lives had become unmanageable.' Two. 'Came to believe that a power greater than ourselves could restore us to sanity.' Three. 'Made a decision to turn our will and our lives over to the care of God as we understood Him.'" She handed the list to Nevin.

Nevin cleared his throat and said, "I'm Nevin."

The others in attendance said, "Hi, Nevin."

Nevin read the next three steps. "Four. 'Made a searching and fearless moral inventory of ourselves.' Five. 'Admitted to God, to ourselves, and to another human being the exact nature of our wrongs.' Six. 'Were entirely ready to have God remove all these defects of character.'" Nevin handed the list to a young woman to his left.

The young woman said, "Hello. I'm Arlene."

"Hi, Arlene."

Arlene read steps seven though nine. "Seven. 'Humbly asked Him to remove our shortcomings.' Eight. 'Made a list of all persons we had harmed, and became willing to make amends to them all.' Nine. 'Made direct amends to such people wherever possible, except when to do so would injure them or others.'"

A barrel-chested man in his mid-fifties entered the room and sat in the empty chair next to Arlene, who immediately handed him the list, adding with a smile, "Good timing."

The barrel-chested man returned Arlene's smile. "I'm John."

It was Deputy Sheriff John Steele.

CHAPTER 47

S teele noticed Nevin and nodded in the quick and authoritative manner that tough guys tended to do. Steele said to everyone else, "Ten. 'Continued to take personal inventory, and when we were wrong, promptly admitted it.' Eleven. 'Sought through prayer and meditation to improve our conscious contact with God as we understood Him, praying only for knowledge of His will for us and the power to carry that out.' Twelve. 'Having had a spiritual awakening as the result of these steps, we tried to carry this message to others, and to practice these principles in all our affairs.'" Steele passed the list of the Twelve Steps back to the group leader.

The group leader thanked those who had read the steps and asked the remaining members to introduce themselves by first name only, which they promptly did. The group leader then said, "Thank you, everyone. The floor is now open for anyone who wishes to share."

As usual, a few awkward moments of silence filled the room before someone was ready to speak.

That someone was Nevin, who cleared his throat again and said, "I guess I'll go first. My name is Nevin."

The group said, "Hi, Nevin."

"This is my second time at this particular meeting." Nevin's eyes drifted to his shoes. "I'm from out of town. I attend meetings back home when I can, although probably not as much as I should. I'm in Barnstable on business for a few days—like I was a couple of weeks ago the other time I attended this meeting. I didn't speak last time. I should have, though. I came this time for the same reason that I came last time: I've stumbled in my sobriety." Nevin lifted his eyes from his shoes and saw empathy etched on the faces of each and every member of the Barnstable Narcotics Anonymous group. This was truly a fellowship, he said to himself. Aloud to the group, with a cracking voice: "Last time it was coke. This time it was bath salts."

The group issued the customary "Thanks for sharing" when it became clear that Nevin had finished speaking.

A few moments of silent reflection swept over the meeting, as it usually did when someone admitted to relapsing.

A petite young woman sitting across the circle of trust from where Nevin was sitting broke the silence. "I'm Gale."

The group said, "Hi, Gale."

"Hi." Gale directed her bright green eyes to Nevin. "Thanks for the share, Nevin. I'm in the same boat as you. I've stumbled in my sobriety recently too. In fact, I got high three times this week." She struggled to fight back tears. "It—It's tough. I'm—I'm trying to stay on program. But it's really tough."

The group member sitting next to the young woman reached for the box of tissues on the literature table and handed it to the young woman with a fatherly smile.

The young woman thanked the kind gentleman and began to cry a cry that shook the group to its core.

No one said anything else for the remainder of the meeting.

John Steele was standing on the sidewalk in front of Our Lady of Lourdes clutching a cup of coffee when Nevin Montgomery emerged from the church.

Steele said, "Good meeting, huh?"

Nevin issued a knowing smile. "If by 'good' you mean 'emotionally draining,' then yes it was a good meeting."

"That's exactly what I mean. The program works only if we work it." Steele was quoting one of the program's better-known slogans.

"It's working great, because I'm spent."

"Been there, done that." Steele reached into his pocket for a pack of chewing gum. He offered Nevin a stick. "I was surprised to see you in there."

"Same here." Nevin unwrapped the stick of gum and popped it into his mouth. "If you don't mind me asking, what was your drug of choice?"

Conversations between Twelve Step participants were confidential to encourage candor during recovery.

Steele said, "Painkillers. Demerol was what got me hooked, but I didn't discriminate. Vicodin was a favorite too."

"Why did you start taking them?… Work injury?"

"Yeah. I got shot chasing a robbery suspect about ten years ago. The bullet wedged into my shoulder. It hurt like a motherfucker. I started taking Demerol for the pain, and before I knew it I was hooked."

"Demerol, huh? I know it well."

"Was that your drug of choice too?"

Nevin chuckled. "I wish. But I'd take anything. I only had one rule as far as drugs were concerned: it had to get me high. If it did, it was for me."

"I guess that explains the bath salts."

"Absolutely. I mean, how much more pathetic can someone possibly be? Snorting bath salts? It's embarrassing."

"Not to mention dangerous. I've seen a lot of kids messed up on that stuff in my line of work. As they saying goes, 'It ain't pretty.'"

"I know," Nevin whispered. He bent down and picked up a stone. He tossed the stone at the telephone pole to his left. "A buddy of mine OD-ed in high school."

"And you still can't kick the stuff? Man, that shows its power."

"We're called 'addicts' for a reason."

Steele rubbed his hands across his closely cropped hair. "You got that right. I don't know about you, but every day's a struggle for me."

The two men grew quiet. They were lost in a complex mix of emotions: sadness, embarrassment, anger. It was difficult to tell which feeling was dominant. Truth be told, trying to stay sober was a roller-coaster ride for almost every addict.

Nevin Montgomery and John Steele weren't exceptions to the rule.

Nevin finally said, "At the risk of making us both even more bummed out than we already are, what's the status of the Hannah Burgoff investigation?"

Steele popped another stick of gum into his mouth. "We still don't have any suspects, I'm sorry to say. And with Andrew Windsor's passing, my job just got a lot more difficult."

"Nothing? No leads at all?"

"I didn't say 'nothing,' or at least that's not what I meant. I meant 'suspect' in the literal sense of the word: a person believed to have committed the crime. We've identified a number of persons of interest, including you, I might add. But we don't have any suspects."

Nevin said, "Gee. Thanks. The distinction makes me feel about as safe as John Farrell after the Sox finished dead last in the standings."

John Farrell was the highly unpopular manager of the Boston Red Sox who had gotten fired a few years back.

Steele said, "Don't sweat it. That only means we want to talk to you about the night Hannah Burgoff died.... Got a minute?"

CHAPTER 48

Deputy Sheriff John Steele had been satisfied with Nevin Montgomery's answers about the night that Hannah Burgoff was killed and he had allowed Nevin to return to Boston to defend Andrew Windsor's will against the contest filed by Joshua Jones on behalf of Lauren and James Windsor. Steele had been persuaded by the facts that (1) at the request of Bartholomew Lodge of the Boston-based law firm of Palmer & Lodge, Nevin had arrived at the Windsor compound earlier on the same day that Hannah was killed; (2) Nevin had never before met any of the Windsors; and (3) all that Nevin knew about what had happened on the night in question was that he had been awakened by the flickering lights of an ambulance—flickering lights that Nevin had initally attributed to a drug flashback. Steele couldn't help but smile at the latter proposition. "I've had many a night like that," Steele had told Nevin during their frank conversation after the Narcotics Anonymous meeting.

Nevin glanced at his watch. It was 9:50 a.m. In ten minutes he was scheduled to meet with The Honorable Francis M. Doyle of the Suffolk County Probate and Family Court of the Commonwealth of Massachusetts for a case management conference about the contest involving Andrew Windsor's will. Joshua Jones also would be in attendance.

The probate and family court had jurisdiction over issues such as divorce, paternity, child support, custody, visitation, adoption, termination of parental rights, abuse prevention, wills, estates, trusts, guardianships, conservatorships, and name changes. A probate and family court judge—technically referred to as a "justice" in Massachusetts—was a fairly low-ranking judicial officer, but he wielded a lot of power over matters that impacted the heart of family life in the state. Judge Doyle knew that and he was widely known to be aggressive in exercising his judicial discretion. And given that his was primarily a court of equity rather than a court of law, he possessed *a lot* of judicial discretion.

Judge Doyle hailed from a blue-collar background in Medford. He had worked his way through college at the University of Massachusetts at Lowell by serving as a night watchman for a local textile factory, and he had graduated from the evening division at Suffolk University Law School while trying to put food on the table for his wife and twin daughters by delivering packages for *UPS* during the day. He got appointed to the bench because of family connections: his wife's cousin was chief of staff to the Mayor of Boston. As both Nevin and Jones were about to find out, Judge Doyle wasn't particularly fond of Ivy League lawyers from silk stocking law firms.

The door to Judge Doyle's chambers swung open. The judge himself stepped into the corridor. "Are you Mr. Montgomery or Mr. Jones?"

Nevin stood to his feet. "I'm Nevin Montgomery, Your Honor."

"Where's Mr. Jones?"

Jones came barreling around the corner. "Right here, Judge." Jones's heavy breath revealed a want of physical fitness.

"Fine. But don't be late next time."

It was 9:57 a.m. To a hard-ass judge such as Francis Doyle, three minutes early was late.

Prior to a case management conference, the attorneys and/or parties were encouraged to confer for the purpose of agreeing on a proposed schedule of deadlines and dates through trial. Nevin and Jones had tried to do that but failed to accomplish much.

Judge Doyle wasn't pleased to hear it. "You're both highly skilled lawyers at a leading downtown law firm. In fact, you work at the same firm, if I'm reading the docket sheet correctly."

Jones, who always tried to take control of every meeting he attended, said, "That's correct, Your Honor. Mr. Montgomery has waived any objection on behalf of the respondent to the potential conflict of interest."

Respondent was a fancy legal term. In the present matter, the respondent was Andrew Windsor's estate. The petitioners—the persons who had filed the lawsuit—were Lauren and James Windsor.

Judge Doyle fiddled with a paperclip. "It's more than a 'potential' conflict of interest, Mr. Jones. It's an *actual* conflict of interest: lawyers from the same law firm are representing opposing sides in a will contest. That's about as blatant a conflict as there can be. Rule 1.7 speaks unambiguously to that effect."

Rule 1.7 was the conflict of interest provision of the Massachusetts lawyers' ethics rules.

The judge reached for his coffee cup and took a sip. He continued, "And you're OK with that, Mr. Montgomery? More to the point, Bart Lodge is OK with it? How is Bart, by the way?"

"Mr. Lodge is a bit under the weather, Your Honor, which is why I'm defending the will. Rest assured, though: he authorized me to waive the conflict. We've got full confidence in the validity of Mr. Windsor's will and we have no objection to Mr. Jones representing Lauren and James Windsor in this matter."

Judge Doyle memorialized that important point on his iPad. He then said, "Andrew Windsor lived and died in Barnstable, correct?"

Nevin said, "Yes."

"And Lauren and James Windsor also live in Barnstable, correct?"

Jones said, "Correct."

"Then why did you file this case in Suffolk County?" Judge Doyle was looking directly at Jones as he posed this question.

"Because venue isn't jurisdictional, Your Honor. I discussed the venue issue with Mr. Montgomery before I filed the case and we agreed that, in light of the Windsors' celebrity status, it would be better to try the case in Boston rather than Barnstable." Jones adjusted his tie.

"Is that true, Mr. Montgomery?" Judge Doyle asked.

"Yes," Nevin answered. "Mr. Jones and I agreed that trying the case in Barnstable would prove unworkable."

Judge Doyle memorialized this point on his iPad too. He then asked, "Have you discussed the possibility of settlement?"

Judges were always interested in settling cases. Their dockets were crowded and anything that would help ease that burden was a plus.

Nevin said, "We talked about it briefly, Your Honor. But my client had expressed his wishes to me shortly before he died and they were unambiguous: he wanted the entirety of his estate to go to the Cape Cod Preservation Society."

Judge Doyle took another sip of coffee. He directed his gaze squarely on Nevin this time. The judge's penetrating brown eyes were framed by deep crow's-feet that testified to his many years on the bench. "Andrew Windsor was a very successful artist, obviously. Even a lowbrow Medford guy like me has heard of him. His estate must be worth a pretty penny. You can't set aside a small portion of that for his wife and kids?"

Nevin shifted in his seat. "I'm sorry to say I can't, Your Honor. Mr. Windsor was unambiguous about that also."

"Can you tell me why?"

"With all due respect, Your Honor, that'll become clear at trial."

Nevin *hoped* it would, at any rate. This was the first trial he would be handling by himself.

The judge typed feverishly on his iPad. He was filling in the blanks on a form he had retrieved from the case management meta-folder. He had done it hundreds of times before. He printed four copies of the completed document: one for the official file in the Clerk's Office, one for the file he kept for himself in chambers, and one each for Nevin and Jones. The document read:

1. The case management conference was conducted on September 23.

2. After consultation with counsel, the Court determined that this case will proceed on the standard track.

3. Deadline for amending pleadings and adding parties: December 1.

4. Discovery:

    a. Rule 26(a) disclosures: October 17

    b. Fact Discovery: June 30

    c. Petitioners' disclosure report(s): February 1

    d. Respondent's disclosure report(s): March 15

    e. Expert depositions: May 1.

5. Telephone status hearing (Court will initiate the call): February 3 at 10:30 AM.

6. Discovery disputes:

    a. No motion relating to discovery may be filed unless the parties, as required by Local Rule 37.1, have undertaken in good faith to resolve discovery disputes, and, if unable to do so, have contacted the Court with a request for judicial resolution. Counsel may notify the Court of a request to resolve a discovery dispute by telephone, e-mail, fax or other informal means.

7. Inadvertent Disclosure:

    a. Pursuant to Evidence Rule 502(d), an inadvertent disclosure of a communication or information covered by the attorney-client privilege or work-product protection made in connection with this litigation shall not constitute a waiver of that privilege or protection in this or any other federal or state proceeding.

8. *Without leave of Court, no discovery material shall be filed, except as necessary to support dispositive motions.*
9. *Dispositive motions:*
    a. *Motion(s) to be filed by July 31*
    b. *Opposition to be filed by August 21*
    c. *Reply to be filed by September 4.*

It is So Ordered.

/s/ Francis M. Doyle
Associate Justice, Probate and Family Court

***

Catina Cruz returned the vacuum cleaner to the closet and proceeded to dust the living room with a rag she had retrieved from a drawer in the laundry room. This was the first time she had cleaned the main house since Andrew Windsor's death. Dust and dirt mourned for no one, and three weeks of inattention had made her task a lot harder than it was when she was on her normal every-other-day cleaning cycle.

"What are you doing?" Meredith Adams Windsor snapped when she saw Catina inching towards one of her father-in-law's magnificent seascapes. She invoked one of her favorite put-downs: "That painting is worth more than you'll make in your entire life."

Catina said, "Mrs. Windsor asked me to clean. I was going to dust the frame, is all. I'm supposed to dust it."

"Well, make sure you don't damage it.... Have you seen my husband?"

"No, ma'am."

"Are you sure? I thought you two were joined at the hip. Or, should I say 'at the crotch'?"

Catina had been ridiculed almost nonstop ever since Meredith had started suspecting that Catina and James were having an affair. She chose to respond to the most recent invective in the same manner that she had responded to all the others: by ignoring it.

Meredith wheeled herself out of Catina's sight, as she typically did when she was met with silence from Catina.

Catina disliked most aspects of the cleaning process: it was difficult, demeaning and, by definition, dirty. But she enjoyed the peace and quiet that accompanied it. The main house at the Windsor compound was massive, and there were plenty of rooms in which Catina would be left alone to dust, vacuum, scrub, and mop. Unfortunately, James Windsor frequently managed to find her and, when he did, he almost always wanted her to take a break and attend to his needs.

This day was no different.

James sauntered into the guest room Catina was sweeping. "I heard my wife was giving you a hard time a little while ago. Was she?"

Catina tried to handle James the same way she had handled Meredith. But, unlike his wife, James wouldn't accept silence for an answer.

"I asked you a question," he said, raising his voice.

Catina said, "Yes, she gave me a hard time a few minutes ago. But for the reasons that you know well, I'm used to it by now."

James reached into his jacket and pulled out a vial of cocaine. "This is for your troubles." He tossed the vial to Catina.

Catina caught the vial, examined it, and placed it in the front pocket of her jeans. She rested the broom she was using against the wall and walked towards James.

She was all too familiar with what he expected as payment for the drugs.

PART V

Art

"Art is not what you see, but what you make others see."
—Edgar Degas

CHAPTER 49

Movies and television did a poor job of depicting how legal disputes actually got resolved. On TV and in the movies, litigation was almost always portrayed as a speedy process. A heroic lawyer—typically, one who resembled a fashion model—filed a groundbreaking lawsuit and, ninety minutes later, the jury was selected, the media gathered, and the "trial of the century" began. In the real world, the average lawsuit took eighteen months to get to trial because (1) courts were overburdened and understaffed and (2) there was a standard process that civil lawsuits generally followed. Both factors were playing out in the contest involving Andrew Windsor's will: Judge Doyle's docket was bursting with disputes and his case management order mandated the full array of discovery and motion practice. But the case management steps the judge had enumerated the previous September were now completed, and the Windsor matter was scheduled for trial at the end of the week.

Nevin Montgomery was holed up in the law library at the lavish offices of Palmer & Lodge in Boston's financial district. Several stacks of *Massachusetts Reports*, the commonwealth's official compendium of judicial decisions, were piled high around him. His laptop was opened to a law journal article about testamentary formalities written by *the* John Langbein, the said same Yale Law School professor who effected the change in the required number of witnesses to the signing of a will that was causing Nevin many sleepless nights. Nevin spotted Joshua Jones out of the corner of his eye. He snapped shut his laptop so that Jones couldn't see what he was reading. Subtle, Nevin wasn't.

"Don't worry, I won't ask what you're working on," Jones said with a wink. "But I think I can guess." Jones retrieved a book from a shelf near where Nevin was sitting. "I'm looking forward to finally getting a chance to see for myself how you handle yourself in a courtroom. Bart certainly speaks highly of you. As you know, I have my doubts."

Doubts was an understatement, to put it mildly. Nevin knew all too well that Jones didn't think Nevin was a good lawyer. How could he not? Jones always appended a separate statement to Nevin's performance review that was filled with nothing but criticism. Nevin also knew, however, that Bart Lodge had instructed Nevin to waive the conflict of interest concern about Jones representing Lauren and James Windsor in the dispute over Andrew Windsor's will in large part so that Nevin could prove Jones wrong. "Success is the ultimate vindication," Lodge had said to his young charge at the time. "Beat him in court and he'll have to get off your back. Even Joshua knows that."

Judge Doyle had scheduled opening statements for the day after Halloween, which meant that the Windsor matter had come to trial a bit faster than the norm: fourteen months after the case was filed rather than eighteen. Discovery—the exchanging of documents, the answering of interrogatories, the taking of depositions—had gone surprisingly smooth. No dispositive motions had been filed either, which was likewise unusual. Nevin figured that Jones was planning on taking full advantage of the high-profile nature of the case and wanted most of the drama to play out in open court so that the media could report it. The case had already been the subject of a handful of front page stories in the *Boston Globe* and Jones had been interviewed on several occasions on the local television news. Nevin, in contrast, had politely declined multiple requests to speak to the press. As Lodge had frequently reminded Nevin, "A true lawyer tries his cases in the courtroom rather than in the newspapers or on TV."

***

Nevin nibbled on a piece of leftover Halloween candy as he hurdled up the marble stairs of the Suffolk County Courthouse. The previous evening had been Nevin's first Halloween on Beacon Hill and he had overestimated by a considerable margin how many trick-or-treaters would be knocking on his door. He had purchased *Reese's Peanut Butter Cups*, his favorite junk food, to distribute to the children so at least he would enjoy finishing the extras.

The Suffolk County Courthouse, also known as the John Adams Courthouse, was a historic building on Pemberton Square in Boston. It was home to the Massachusetts Supreme Judicial Court, the Massachusetts Appeals Court, and the state law library. It was also serving as the temporary site of the Massachusetts Family and Probate Court while that court's permanent quarters in the Edward W. Brooke Courthouse near the Boston Garden were undergoing renovations. The six-story granite Suffolk County Courthouse was built in 1893, and stylistically the building was described at the time as German Renaissance, although now it was viewed as a transitional design between the monumental Second Empire style of Boston's Old City Hall and the Classical Revival. The building was added to the National Register of Historic Places in 1974.

What have I gotten myself into? Nevin said to himself as Judge Francis M. Doyle gaveled the proceedings to order. *Litigation stresses me out, and stress and I don't get along too well.* He tried to force the idea of getting high from his mind.

Probate courts, being courts of equity, sat without a jury, which meant that Judge Doyle, rather than twelve ordinary citizens of Suffolk County, would be deciding whether Andrew Windsor had been of sound mind when instructing Nevin to cut his wife and children out of his will.

Equity had developed in England several hundred years after the formation of the common law system to address disputes in which money damages were inadequate and to introduce fairness into the legal process. Litigants could appeal directly to the Crown who, as sovereign, was seen as the fount of justice. Eventually, the Crown began to delegate the resolution of the petitions to the Chancellor, who was an important member of the Crown's Council, and the Chancery eventually began to resemble a judicial body that became known as the Court of Chancery. The English American Colonies, of which Massachusetts had been a preeminent member in the seventeenth- and eighteenth-centuries, had adopted the distinction between law and equity from the beginning.

Nevin sat alone at the respondent's table: no co-counsel, no paralegal and, of course, no Andrew Windsor. Joshua Jones, by contrast, was accompanied at the petitioners' table by both Lauren Windsor and James Windsor.

Judge Doyle said, "Good morning, counselors. Good morning, ladies and gentlemen."

The latter salutation was directed to the packed house of reporters and other interested persons in attendance. Usually, nobody outside of family members with a financial stake in a specific will or trust attended a probate court hearing. But this was an unusual case: the widow and son of the most famous American artist of the last fifty years were contesting his competency to make the testamentary choice to leave them nothing.

Judge Doyle continued, "This morning we will hear the opening statement on behalf of Petitioners Lauren and James Windsor in their challenge to the validity of the late Andrew Windsor's will, which respondent would like to probate. Obviously, given the decedent's stature in the history of American art, this is a matter that has generated a lot more interest than a typical will contest. But let me be clear: I intend to handle this matter with the same dignity and respect to which every matter that comes before this court is entitled."

The dozens of reporters who were seated in the courtroom were taking notes as quickly as they could.

Judge Doyle next said, "You may proceed, Mr. Jones."

Joshua Jones stood to his feet and walked to the lectern from which he would be addressing the Court. "May it please the Court," he said, voice dripping with formality. "My name is Joshua Jones and I have the privilege of representing the petitioners in this case." He turned and nodded at Lauren and James Windsor. "Petitioners are well aware that a testator enjoys considerable autonomy when deciding to whom he will be bequeathing his property upon death. But that autonomy is not absolute: choices as significant as whom to name as a beneficiary of his estate, as well as whom to exclude, must be made while the testator is in full control of his mental faculties. We believe that the evidence will show that Andrew Windsor was not of sound mind when he directed Mr. Montgomery to cut his beloved wife of fifty-plus years and his talented son out of his will. Thank you, Your Honor."

Jones returned to his seat. He obviously knew that most judges in a bench trial preferred opening statements that were short and sweet: elaborate monologues were reserved for jury trials.

Judge Doyle was about to learn whether Nevin Montgomery had learned that lesson too.

CHAPTER 50

Nevin Montgomery stood to his feet and flushed the toilet. He watched his vomit disappear into the recesses of the courthouse's sewage system. He washed his hands and splashed cold water onto his face. He couldn't remember the last time he had been this nervous. He also couldn't remember the last time he had craved a joint this much. Pot had always relaxed him in the past, and he certainly needed to relax in the present.

Five minutes later, Judge Doyle said, "Are you OK, Mr. Montgomery? The color's disappeared from your face." The judge leaned forward in his chair. "There's fresh water in the pitcher on your table."

Nevin said, "I'm fine, Your Honor. A bit nervous, is all."

A confident smile captured Joshua Jones's face. This will be even easier than I thought, he seemed to be saying to himself.

Nevin clutched the podium for support. "May it please the Court: My name is Nevin Montgomery and I represent the estate of Andrew Windsor in this matter." Nevin poured himself a glass of water from the pitcher that Judge Doyle had mentioned. He returned to the podium. "As the Court knows, Bartholomew Lodge of the law firm of Palmer & Lodge sent me to Barnstable about a year ago to re-draft Mr. Windsor's testamentary documents at Mr. Windsor's request. As the Court also knows, Mr. Windsor was one of the most famous artists in the world, as well as one of Palmer & Lodge's most significant clients. The fact that Mr. Lodge sent me, a second-year associate, to re-draft Mr. Windsor's testamentary documents speaks volumes about the uncontroversial nature of Mr. Windsor's assignment for our law firm. Put directly, Your Honor, people re-write their wills and trusts all the time, and just because they do doesn't mean they're of unsound mind." Nevin let go of the podium. His nervousness was gone: dissipated by his straightforward appeal to common sense.

Nevin closed his brief opening statement with yet another appeal to common sense: "I certainly understand why the petitioners would be upset by Mr. Windsor's decision to bequeath his assets to the Cape Cod Preservation Society rather than to them. But they, better than anyone, should understand why he did it: because the majesty that is the land and sea of Cape Cod made Mr. Windsor's life possible as an artist. Mr. Windsor's daughter certainly understood that, which is why she isn't a party to this litigation. Seemingly everyone else who knew anything about Mr. Windsor understands it, too. If I may, Your Honor, I'd like to quote Mr. Windsor's obituary from the *Boston Globe*."

Judge Doyle said, "You may."

Nevin retrieved the article from a manila folder in his trial bag. "Mr. Windsor was a celebrity, and his obituary is long. But here's the operative portion: 'An Andrew Windsor painting was a hymn to the beauty of the natural world. For Mr. Windsor, that world was Cape Cod, the place where he was born, grew up, lived, and died. It is not an overstatement to say that no person in the history of American art was more closely tied to a particular region than Andrew Windsor was to Cape Cod. Without Cape Cod, there would have been no Andrew Windsor. And without Andrew Windsor and the paintings he has left behind for generations to enjoy, Cape Cod—Massachusetts, America, the world—would be a less beautiful place.'"

After a brief ten-minute recess, Judge Doyle instructed Joshua Jones to call his first witness.

"The petitioners call Lauren Windsor, Your Honor," Jones said.

Lauren Windsor strode to the witness stand. Attired in an ivory-colored *Stella McCartney* pants suit that she had purchased at a chic Newbury Street boutique earlier in the week, Mrs. Windsor commanded the courtroom like she did every room in which she was present.

Judge Doyle administered the oath to her.

She swore to tell the truth, the whole truth, and nothing but the truth.

Jones began his direct examination of his most important witness. "Good morning, Mrs. Windsor."

"Good morning."

"Please state your name and current address for the record."

"Lauren Taylor Windsor. One Bay Road, Barnstable, Massachusetts."

"Did you know the decedent?"

"I did. I was married to him for fifty-six years."

"For fifty-six years?" Jones repeated for emphasis. "Is it fair to say that you knew him well?"

"Of course. I knew him better than anyone else did." Mrs. Windsor offered a sheepish smile. "You might say that I knew him better than he knew himself."

"Objection," Nevin said, standing to his feet.

"Sustained," Judge Doyle ruled. "Please limit your answer to the question you're being asked, Mrs. Windsor."

Lauren Windsor nodded her assent.

Jones tried to repair the damage. "I apologize in advance, Mrs. Windsor, for the next few questions that I'm going to ask. But I've got to ask them."

"Go ahead. I know this isn't afternoon tea at *The Four Seasons*."

"Did you notice any change in your husband's behavior towards the end of his life?"

"I'm sorry to say that I did. People probably think that my husband was always a famous artist and that I married him because of that. But he was young and unaccomplished when we met, and I had no idea how successful he would become." Lauren Windsor swept a loose strand of gray-blonde hair from her perfectly-presented face. She continued, "What attracted me to him, and what kept me married to him for more than five decades, was how smart and caring he was. Obviously, I knew that his father was a famous illustrator, but that didn't mean that Andrew would become a famous artist. Frankly, the odds against Andrew replicating—let alone surpassing—his father's success were enormous.… Sort of like Frank Sinatra's kids trying to out sing Ol' Blue Eyes when Andrew and I first met: I didn't think it was possible." She smiled again, this time with pride. "He did it, though. He became the most celebrated artist of the century."

"How did he change? You mentioned that his intelligence and compassion were what attracted you to him. What do you mean by that, Mrs. Windsor?"

"Well, Andrew was smarter than anyone I had ever met. I later learned about the connection between intelligence and creativity, but when we first met I just thought he was really, really bright. As far as compassion is concerned, he was also the kindest person I had ever met. He was nice to everyone he encountered: from the grounds crew who cut our grass at the compound to the President of the United States… and to everyone in between."

"How about you and your kids? Did he show you compassion? Them?"

Lauren Windsor's eyes welled with tears. She dabbed them dry with a tissue she retrieved from her purse. "Absolutely." Her voice caught. "He never forgot a birthday, and he never denied us anything, no matter how extravagant our requests might have been. And believe me, our kids used to make some pretty extravagant requests when they were little. That's what convinced me that he couldn't possibly have been of sound mind when he cut us out of his will."

"Objection," Nevin said.

"Sustained," Judge Doyle ruled. "Mr. Jones's question calls for an expert opinion that a lay witness such as Mrs. Windsor is not qualified to give. She is permitted to testify to her observations about the changes in her husband's behavior, as she has been doing, but she can't offer an opinion about the ultimate issue in the case."

In a trial, to appropriately gather evidence and relevant opinions, both fact witnesses and expert witnesses were frequently called to testify. There were fundamental differences between the two types of witnesses. An expert witness was someone who testified according to his or her knowledge of a subject that pertained to the evidence given. The witness's expertise was needed to identify, test, and explain the evidence and how it was useful in providing information for either the innocence or guilt of a suspect in a criminal case or, in a civil matter such as that involving Andrew Windsor's testamentary documents, to establish one or more elements of the claim. A lay witness, on the other hand, was a person who provided testimony based on direct knowledge of the person or crime.

Jones said, "I understand completely, Your Honor. I'll call my next witness then."

James Windsor was almost fifty years old. He looked thirty, which explained why so many young women were attracted to him… that and the fact that they thought he was rich and famous. He was wearing a navy *Brooks Brothers* suit and a freshly pressed white shirt of the same high-end brand. He sported no tie, which everyone else in the courtroom probably took as a sign of his artistic independence.

Judge Doyle administered the oath to the witness.

Jones got James to state his name and current address for the record. His address was the same as that of his mother, although he testified that he lived in a separate house on the compound. He also testified that he spent a lot of time at the family getaway in Popham Beach, Maine.

Jones said, "May I call you James?"

"Of course."

"Thank you." Jones turned to the page of his legal pad that contained the questions he planned to ask James. "Let me begin by saying, as I should've said to your mother, how sorry I am for your loss. Andrew Windsor was a larger than life figure in the art world, and I suspect he was a larger than life figure at home."

"He was," James said. "And that's what's made what he did on his deathbed so difficult to accept."

Jones said, "I can only imagine."

"It's been tough enough on me," James continued, "but the person I'm really fighting for is my mom. As she mentioned a few minutes ago, she and my dad were married for more than fifty years. And he left her with nothing but the roof over her head and the clothes on her back." James grew visibly agitated. Unlike his mother, however, he didn't cry. Apparently, he didn't care enough about his father to shed a tear for the man... even a crocodile tear that would help his legal case. He turned and faced the judge. "Obviously I'm not a lawyer, Your Honor, and I heard what you said about what I think you called 'expert' testimony. But how could someone in his right mind treat his wife of fifty-plus years like that? I mean, it makes no sense."

Nevin stood to his feet again. "Objection."

"Sustained," Judge Doyle ruled again. "As I mentioned to your mother, Mr. Windsor, please try not to offer an opinion about the ultimate issue in the case."

"I apologize, Judge. This is all very upsetting."

Jones continued: "What, if anything, do you know about your dad's association with the Cape Cod Preservation Society?"

"I didn't know he had one. Frankly, I was shocked to learn that he left his money to them."

"What do you mean?"

"That I've lived with or near my parents for each of the nearly fifty years I've been on this earth. I knew what was important to my father, and who he associated with. I never once heard him mention the Cape Cod Preservation Society, and I never saw anyone from that organization step foot on our property. Why in the world would he leave his money to them? I mean, come on. I don't believe it for a second."

Nevin jotted a note on his legal pad and underlined it: <u>undue influence?</u>

Undue influence over a decedent's testamentary decisions involved disrupting the decedent's natural impulse to provide for family members and convincing him or her to bequeath his or her assets to the person exerting the influence. Undue influence was a close cousin in the law to challenging testamentary decisions on the ground that the decedent was not of sound mind when he or she made them, but the elements of the claim were slightly different. To prove undue influence the challenger was required to demonstrate: (1) the will left property in an unexpected fashion (e.g., close family members were left out in favor of others, without an obvious explanation); (2) the decedent was particularly dependent on the person or group who exerted influence; (3) illness or frailty made the decedent susceptible to undue influence; and (4) the influencer took advantage of the decedent and benefitted from the will by substituting his or her own wishes for those of the decedent.

Nevin now knew that he would need to nail down Andrew Windsor's commitment to the mission of the Cape Cod Preservation Society. Unfortunately, he had no idea how he was going to do it, especially during the middle of a trial.

CHAPTER 51

"The petitioners call Meredith Adams Windsor to the stand."

Joshua Jones had alerted the Court that James Windsor's wife was confined to a wheelchair. The wooden seat that accompanied the witness stand had been removed so that she could testify comfortably. Jones also had mentioned that Meredith was a lineal descendent of the man after whom the courthouse was named, John Adams—an intellectual leader of the American Founding and the second President of the United States.

Judge Doyle watched Meredith position herself in the witness box. He asked, "Do you have everything you need, Mrs. Windsor?"

Meredith answered, "Yes, Your Honor." She activated the wheel-lock on her wheelchair. She was wearing a yellow *Calvin Klein* color-blocked fit and flare dress that was as bright as the summer sun.

"Good. Feel free to let me know if you need anything."

"Thank you, Your Honor."

The judge administered the oath to the witness. Next, he directed his attention to Jones and said, "You may proceed when you're ready."

That was judicial shorthand for, Ask your first question *now*, counselor.

Jones had remained standing while Meredith was getting acclimated to the witness stand. He said, "Please state your name for the record."

"Meredith Adams Windsor."

"'Adams': as in John Adams?"

"Yes."

No harm in reminding the judge of Meredith's pedigree, Jones had apparently decided. Then he asked a relevant question: "Did you know the decedent?"

"Yes. He was my father-in-law."

"You're married to James Windsor?" Jones gestured in the direction of the younger of his two clients.

"I am. We've been married for about twenty years."

"Where did you meet your husband?" Jones checked off each question after he had asked it. He was reading from a sheet of paper that listed the questions he considered important.

"At the Museum of Fine Arts here in Boston. It was during my senior year of high school. I was planning on majoring in Art History at Harvard, and James was a rising star of American art at the time."

"Did you end up majoring in Art History?"

"I did."

"Was your father-in-law's work ever discussed in class?"

"It was." Meredith adjusted the hem of her dress. "He was a significant figure in the history of American art. Harvard offered a special course on his work, which I took."

"You mentioned that your husband James is an artist too, correct?"

"Yes. He's a very good one."

"Was James proud of his father? Was he close to him?"

"Yes to both. James was in awe of his father's talent. James also was the only son, and was arguably closer to his father than his sisters were for that reason. Note, for example, that his sister Amanda isn't here today."

Judge Doyle interjected: "Sara is deceased, I'm told. Do you know why Amanda isn't here, Mrs. Windsor? Mr. Montgomery had mentioned that also."

A judge is permitted to ask a witness a question. However, he needs to tread lightly so as to avoid coming across as an advocate for one party or the other.

"I don't, Your Honor. I'm sorry."

Jones continued with his line of questions. "Were you close to Andrew Windsor?"

"Absolutely. Pop—that's what I called him—always doted on me. Because of my disability, I'm sure, although he never said why. He would always make sure I was comfortable—like the judge did a few minutes ago. He also had his housekeeper, a young woman named Catina, clean our house too."

Nevin couldn't help but notice the insincerity in Meredith's voice when she had mentioned Catina's name.... He wondered whether the judge noticed it too. He made a note to himself to try to find out why Meredith had implied that she wasn't the one who had hired Catina.

"Was Andrew proud of James?"

Meredith hesitated. She obviously didn't want to hurt James's case, but she had taken an oath to tell the truth. She finally said, "I'm sorry to say that I don't think he was."

"Why was that?" Jones asked as calmly as he could. He certainly knew that he had to be careful with Meredith, given what he knew about James's wandering eye and James's resentment of his father.

"Pop didn't think James was a good artist. I strongly disagree with that conclusion, but I know Pop felt that way."

"How do you know it?"

"Because Pop would tell me. Pop knew I had majored in Art History and we would talk about that topic from time to time. Pop was very aware of his standing in the history of American art. James's name would sometimes come up in that context."

"How so?" Jones was no longer running down a checklist of questions.

Trial testimony ebbed and flowed, and a good trial lawyer needed to be capable of adjusting to it. Jones was a jerk, but he was also a good trial lawyer. Even Bartholomew Lodge would have acknowledged that much.

"Pop wondered whether James's work would adversely impact Pop's legacy and the legacy of Pop's dad as well. Pop's father, C. S. Windsor, was a famous artist too." Meredith adjusted her hem again. "C. S. was an illustrator of children's books, but that's art also, at least if it's done well. C. S. did it very well."

Nevin glanced over at James Windsor. James didn't seem pleased with his wife's testimony, to put it mildly.

Jones prepared to ask the million-dollar question or, more precisely, the seventy-five million dollar question, which was the reputed value of Andrew Windsor's estate. He took a sip of water. "Do you think that would cause the decedent to cut James and Lauren out of his will?"

"Just the opposite, actually. Pop might not have respected James as an artist, but he loved him very much. James was his son, for gosh sake. He worried about him, and he wanted to make sure that he and Lauren were taken care of. Pop was less worried about James's sisters. They had married well—to a doctor and to an investment banker, respectively— and they were more than secure financially. That's why it makes no sense that Pop disinherited James and Lauren."

Jones said, "I have no further questions, Your Honor." He collected his notes and returned to his seat.

Judge Doyle said, "Mr. Montgomery: any cross-examination?"

Nevin stood. "Yes, Your Honor. And then I'll call James and Lauren Windsor as hostile witnesses during my case-in-chief."

Judge Doyle studied his watch. "It's almost five. I'd prefer to adjourn for the day and start back up tomorrow at nine a.m. sharp. But I don't want to inconvenience Mrs. Windsor."

The judge was talking about Meredith, not Lauren. Judges didn't mind inconveniencing parties. Witnesses were another story, though; especially a witness in a wheelchair.

Meredith said, "I'm fine, Your Honor. I'm spending the night in the city anyway. Don't worry. I won't break."

The judge smiled. "Nine a.m. tomorrow it is, then." The judge stood this time.

Everyone in the courtroom who could stand also stood.

Nevin Montgomery gathered his materials and stuffed them into his trial bag. As he was exiting the courtroom he noticed an older man in a khaki suit shooting daggers with his eyes at James Windsor.

CHAPTER 52

Pemberton Square, where the John Adams Courthouse was located, was a stone's throw from the North End, the famed Italian section of Boston. Nevin hadn't been to *Giacomo's Civita Farnese* in at least a month, it was dinnertime, and he was starving. It was a no-brainer where he would be heading now that court had adjourned for the day.

Giacomo's was a no-reservations restaurant in a congested space that was the quintessential North End experience. Chalkboard menus hung in a tiny brick dining room and offered every kind of meat/sauce/pasta combination a person could imagine. Nevin ordered his usual: veal parmigiana. The fresh-made bread that accompanied it was perfect for mopping up a tomato sauce that would have made Giada De Laurentiis proud, and the antipasto that would be preceding it was a perfect blend of cured meats, olives, pepperoncini, mushrooms, anchovies, provolone, and vegetables in virgin olive oil.

Nevin devoured his meal in about fifteen minutes. It was both a blessing and a curse that the wait-staff dropped more than a few not-so-subtle hints for a patron to exit the moment he or she had ingested the last bite of Tiramisu. The blessing for Nevin was that he had to get back to work on the Windsor case. The curse was the same: that he had to get back to work on the Windsor case.

Nevin paid the check in cash—*Giacomo's*, like most North End eateries, operated on a cash-only basis—and squeezed past the long line of people waiting for their turn in heaven, crossed the street, and walked a short block to *Mike's Pastry* for a cannoli. Nevin was stuffed, and he hadn't skipped the Tiramisu at *Giacomo's*, but he couldn't be this close to *Mike's* without buying at least one of the legendary ricotta-filled tubes of fried dough. However, as he was about to enter the bakery he noticed the same older man in a khaki suit who had seemed so displeased with James Windsor in the courtroom. The man was sipping a cappuccino at *Café Victoria*, another North End landmark that happened to be next door to *Mike's Pastry*.

"Pardon me, sir," Nevin said. "I don't mean to interrupt, but weren't you watching the trial today about Andrew Windsor's will?"

The older man said, "Yes." He looked to be in his early-seventies.

"Can you tell me why? Are you a journalist or something?"

The older man shook his head. "No, I'm not a journalist. I've been following the case in the *Globe*, I'm retired, and I wanted to see for myself what was really going on."

"What do you think so far?" Nevin gestured to an empty seat at the small table where the older man was sitting. "Do you mind?"

The older man said, "Be my guest."

Nevin signaled to a waitress. "An espresso, please. And another cappuccino for my friend." Nevin returned his attention to the older man. "I'm Nevin Montgomery."

"Matt Martin."

The two men shook hands.

The waitress brought their coffee drinks.

Nevin thanked her and watched her move to another table. He repeated his question to Mr. Martin about how Mr. Martin thought the trial was unfolding.

"I'm certainly no lawyer, Nevin; but I think you're winning."

"Why do you think that? I haven't presented any evidence yet."

"I know you haven't. But it's clear to me that Mr. Windsor's wife, son, and daughter-in-law are lying.…. That all they care about is getting their hands on Mr. Windsor's money."

Nevin took a sip of his espresso. It was strong enough to melt metal.

Martin continued, "Besides, I know James Windsor. He's one of the most despicable people I've ever met."

Nevin almost dropped his cup after hearing Mr. Martin's pronouncements. "H—How do you know James Windsor? Wh—Why do you say he's despicable?"

"Because he raped my daughter when they were teenagers."

"What?!"

"And the bastard got away with it because of who he was… or, more precisely, because of whose son he was. But he did it, and my daughter, God rest her soul, committed suicide because of him."

***

Nevin Montgomery sat at the respondent's table staring into space as he struggled to process what Matt Martin had told him the prior evening in the North End: James Windsor had raped Mr. Martin's daughter and had gotten away with it. That made Nevin even more determined than he already was to win the case. After all, James was on the other side of it.

"All rise!" the court clerk called out.

Everybody did.

Judge Doyle entered the courtroom and took his seat on the bench. His morning coffee accompanied him. "Good morning," the judge said to the capacity crowd. "Are you ready, Mr. Montgomery?"

"I am, Your Honor." Nevin didn't feel ready, though. "The respondent calls Lauren Windsor to the stand."

Andrew Windsor's widow was attired in yet another expensive pants suit. This time the designer was Michael Kors. The soft brown fabric highlighted Mrs. Windsor's mournful eyes.

"Good morning, Mrs. Windsor."

"Good morning, Mr. Montgomery. Nice to see you again."

Nevin knew that Mrs. Windsor wasn't actually pleased to see him again—she wasn't happy to see him when he was staying at the compound so he could revise her husband's testamentary documents, either—but she played the part of the well-mannered wealthy woman like the award-winning actress she had once aspired to be. Besides, she'd had lots of practice in the role. If she had learned anything during her decades in high society, it was the outward appearance of good manners.

Nevin said, "Nice to see you again, too. I know this must be stressful for you, so I'll get right to it: why were the Hannah paintings kept secret for so long?"

Joshua Jones shot to his feet. "Objection, Your Honor! This is a will contest, not an interview for *People* magazine."

Judge Doyle leaned forward in his chair. "Relevance, Mr. Montgomery?"

"Well, as you might suspect, Your Honor, respondent's position is that this will contest is about nothing more than the petitioners' desire for money, plain and simple. I've come to learn during my time working on this case that keeping the Hannah paintings secret was about money too. I need to get that information into the record, and Mrs. Windsor is the witness who can accomplish that for me... assuming, of course, she testifies honestly."

Mrs. Windsor interrupted: "I always testify honestly."

Judge Doyle said, "I'll allow the question. But I'm only willing to give you so much running room on this, Mr. Montgomery."

"Understood. Thank you, Your Honor. Should I repeat the question, Mrs. Windsor?"

"Yes."

"Why were the Hannah paintings kept secret for so long?"

Trial lawyers were taught never to ask *why* questions on cross-examination. Why? Because they were considered too open-ended. Exceptions existed, however: by definition, a witness subjected to cross-examination wasn't what the law referred to as "friendly" and the cross-examiner hadn't had an opportunity to prep the witness, which meant there was always a chance the witness would say something other than what the lawyer had expected. And, sometimes, that provided an opening for the lawyer to dig deeper and work to undermine the witness's credibility. Although Nevin had never tried a case before, he was a bright person with surprisingly good courtroom instincts.

Mrs. Windsor fidgeted with a button on her pants suit. "Because we—Andrew and me—thought it might be fun."

"'Fun'?"

"Exciting is perhaps a better word for it. We were both big fans of mystery novels and we were trying to write one of our own, you might say."

"*You* 'might say' it. *I* never would…. You said you were going to tell the truth. No offense, Mrs. Windsor, but that doesn't sound like the truth to me."

Jones jumped to his feet again. "Objection!"

"Sustained," Judge Doyle ruled. "Please refrain from offering testimony of your own, Mr. Montgomery. You're a lawyer, not a witness."

Nevin apologized to the Court, but his point had been made. He turned from the podium as if he were finished questioning Mrs. Windsor. He stopped when he reached his chair at the respondent's table. He asked, as he began to sit, "Was your husband having an affair with Hannah Burgoff, Mrs. Windsor?"

"Objection!" Jones shouted. He knocked his legal pad to the floor in his haste to stand to his feet.

"Overruled," Judge Doyle said. "You may answer the question, Mrs. Windsor."

Lauren Windsor glared at Nevin Montgomery. No amount of high society parties could have prepared her for this particular public humiliation. But she wasn't about to let a young lawyer who had grown up on the streets of Dorchester get the better of her. She straightened in the witness stand. "Not to my knowledge," she said, employing the standard dodge that witnesses employed when they didn't want to answer truthfully.

Nevin next called Meredith Adams Windsor. He originally had planned to question Meredith before Lauren, but his gut had told him to call Lauren first. Unfortunately, Lauren's answer to Nevin's final query had left Nevin questioning his instincts again. However, now he needed to focus on Meredith.

Court personnel removed the wooden chair from the witness stand for a second time so that Meredith could navigate her wheelchair into position.

Judge Doyle said, "Please remember that you're still under oath, Mrs. Windsor."

"I will." Meredith activated the wheel-lock.

"Are you comfortable?" Judge Doyle flashed a warm smile.

"I'm fine. Thank you, Your Honor."

The judge returned his attention to Nevin. "You may proceed."

Nevin thanked the judge, and then said, "What do you know about the Hannah paintings, Mrs. Windsor?"

"I know they exist."

"Anything else?"

"That Lauren and Pop were doing what you suggest: keeping the paintings secret and then letting it leak out that they exist to try to push up the price."

"Whose idea was that?"

"Lauren's, probably. She handled the business end of things. All Pop wanted to do was paint. He couldn't have cared less about money."

"How about Lauren and James? Do they care about money?"

Meredith pursed her lips. "Don't we all?"

Nevin was supposed to ask questions, not answer them, but he couldn't resist answering Meredith's. "You just said that Andrew Windsor didn't care about money. So, no, we don't all care about money." Nevin remembered what Catina had told him about James's own secret paintings. "Do you, Mrs. Windsor? Do you care about money?"

"Of course. Everybody needs money to live. We—James and I— are no different from anybody else on that score."

"Did you try to make money by copying what your father-in-law did with Hannah Burgoff?"

Meredith whitened. She obviously didn't want to answer the question but she knew she was under oath and she hadn't been prepped by Joshua Jones in the art of the dodge like her mother-in-law had been. "Yes," she whispered.

"Did Mr. Windsor know about it?"

"You mean Pop?"

Nevin nodded in the affirmative.

"I—I think he did. Yes."

"Did your husband know that his father knew that you and your husband were trying to do what his father and your mother-in-law were trying to do?"

"Yes. I'm pretty sure he did.... Yes."

Joshua Jones scribbled notes onto his legal pad. He tried to appear unfazed by the points Nevin was scoring but only a fool would think he wasn't nervous about this turn of events.

Judge Doyle was certainly no fool.

Nevin ran his hands through his hair. He needed a haircut. This was hardly the time or the place to notice that particular grooming detail but Nevin, like everybody else, couldn't control the random thoughts that fluttered in and out of his subconscious every minute of the day. Aloud to Meredith Windsor: "Hannah Burgoff was your father-in-law's secret model. Who was your husband's?"

"Objection," Jones said. "This is totally irrelevant."

"Overruled," Judge Doyle said. "Please answer the question, Mrs. Windsor."

Meredith Adams Windsor looked more uncomfortable now than she did moments earlier when Nevin had asked her a general question about whether James had secret paintings too, and that was saying something.

Nevin knew why she looked uncomfortable. He repeated the question so that the judge would also know why: "Who was your husband's secret model, Mrs. Windsor?"

"Th—The housekeeper."

"Her name?"

"Catina Cruz."

CHAPTER 53

Nevin Montgomery rushed through a laundry list of questions for James Windsor. He was lucky he had written them down because all he could think about was Catina Cruz.

James Windsor admitted under oath that he had grown to dislike his father. A hero who could do no wrong when James was young, James testified that his father had constantly belittled his art once he had declared that he too wanted to paint for a living. "Buy a pair of overalls, join a paint crew, and work on houses, then," the father was reported to have told the son. "Because the only thing you've got going for you as far as art is concerned is the family name."

But James denied filing the will contest to get even with his dad. "As I mentioned when Mr. Jones was questioning me," James had said in reply to one of Nevin's questions, "I did it to protect my mother."

Of course Nevin had wanted to ask James about what Matt Martin had told Nevin the evening before. Nevin knew better than to do so, however. If Nevin had asked James about Missy Martin, Judge Doyle would have barred James from answering on the grounds of relevancy—this was a will contest, not a criminal trial—and read Nevin the riot act.

Instead, Nevin called his final witness to the stand. Joshua Jones had objected—like most litigators, Jones seemed to think that only his evidence was admissible—but the judge ruled that he was allowing it because of the similarity between the secret Hannah paintings by Andrew Windsor and James Windsor's current project.

"Please state your name and address for the record," Nevin said. His heart was racing.

"Catina Cruz." Her voiced cracked. She was wearing an age appropriate knit shift dress that was almost certainly her fanciest attire. Her hair fell loosely across her shoulders. "One Bay Road, Barnstable, Massachusetts."

"Is that the same address as the Windsors'?"

"Yes. I stay in a room in the main house."

"How long have you worked for the Windsors?"

"About two years."

"And how well did you know the decedent?"

"The what?" Catina fidgeted in her chair.

"The decedent." Nevin flashed the witness a reassuring smile. "Sorry for the legalese, Ms. Cruz. I meant how well did you know Andrew Windsor?"

Ms. Cruz? Nevin said to himself. Who was he kidding? He had slept with the woman.

Catina said, "He was a very important man, and a very busy man—what with his painting and all. I tried not to bother him. But, to answer your question, of course I knew him. I worked for him, and I lived in his house."

Technically, Catina hadn't answered Nevin's question because she didn't say how *well* she knew Andrew Windsor.

Nevin asked a related question next: "Did you like him?"

"Yes. He was always kind to me. He would always say hello and he would always make sure that I had everything I needed to do my job and live my life."

"Did you attend his funeral?"

"I went to part of it. Mrs. Windsor didn't invite me to the actual funeral but I went to the public memorial at St. Mary's."

"By 'Mrs. Windsor,' do you mean Lauren Windsor?"

"Yes."

"How do you feel about her?"

"Objection," Jones said.

Judge Doyle said, "I'll allow it."

Catina fidgeted again in her seat. "Honestly?" she said, with hesitation in her voice.

Nevin said, "Honestly. You're under oath, as you know."

"She isn't nice to me like Mr. Windsor was. I'm sorry to say that I don't like her much."

There went Catina's job, everybody must have realized.

Catina quickly added, "To be fair, she does let me use the computer occasionally to download songs to my iPod."

"How about Meredith Adams Windsor? Is she nice to you?"

"Hardly." Catina's hesitation was gone.

"What does that mean?"

Nevin knew what it meant, but the judge didn't and the judge was the person who mattered most at the moment.

"It means that she thought I was sleeping with her husband and that she was mad at me for it."

"Were you?"

"Sleeping with her husband?"

Nevin nodded.

"Yes. I regret it. But, yes I was."

"How do you feel about James Windsor?"

Catina's jaw clenched and her eyes began to well with tears. "Not good," she finally said.

Nevin noticed a box of tissues on the courtroom deputy's desk. "May I?" he asked.

The courtroom deputy handed the box to Nevin, who then handed it to Catina.

Catina wiped her eyes and blew her nose. "Thank you."

"Are you OK to continue?"

Catina nodded in the affirmative.

"Could you expand on why you feel negatively about James Windsor?"

"Well, for one thing he took advantage of me sexually. For another, he plied me with drugs to do so."

Jones rocketed to his feet. "Objection!"

The journalists in the gallery were typing feverishly on their tablets and smartphones. The headline wrote itself: **Renowned Artist's Son Drugged Young Woman for Sex**.

Unfortunately for the media, however, Judge Doyle wasn't having any of it. "Sustained," he ruled. "This is a will contest, Mr. Montgomery, not an episode of *The Rich Kids of Cape Cod*."

"I understand, Your Honor. But it's relevant to the case."

"I've made my ruling, Mr. Montgomery," the judge said, with a sudden edge to his voice. "You can take it up on appeal if an appeal becomes necessary."

Nevin got the message. He asked a different question: "Did you model for James Windsor?"

"Yes."

"Did anyone know?"

"Yes."

"Who?"

"His wife." Catina took a sip of water. She wiped her mouth with the tissue that Nevin had provided. "I think his mother knew too, but

Scott Douglas Gerber

I'm not certain of that."

"Do you know why James was doing a secret line of paintings?"

"He never told me why. But I'm pretty sure it was because he wanted to make money on them like his father was trying to do."

"James cared about money?"

"Yes."

"Do you know why he selected you to model for him?"

Catina had yet to make eye contact with James. She finally did. "Because he wanted to fuck me."

The judge blanched at Catina's word choice. He didn't say anything about it, though.

"How old are you?"

Nevin knew the answer but, again, the judge didn't.

"Eighteen."

"And how old is James Windsor?"

"In his forties, I think. But I'm not sure exactly."

Precision didn't matter when the age discrepancy was that great.

"For how long were you sleeping with him?" Nevin glanced over at a visibly uncomfortable James Windsor.

"About two years."

"So you were sixteen when it started?"

Catina nodded yes. She was apparently too embarrassed to audibilize her answer. She also failed to mention that she was still sleeping with James.

Nevin rubbed a hand across the lectern and began to return to his seat at the respondent's table. "I've got nothing further for Ms. Cruz, Your Honor." He quickly did an about-face. "On second thought, I've got one more subject to touch upon with this witness."

"Fine, but make it snappy, please."

"I will, Your Honor." Nevin looked Catina directly in the eyes, which were as wide as a half dollar and as brown as Columbian coffee. She was so beautiful that he lost his train of thought for a moment. Then, "Have you ever heard of the Cape Cod Preservation Society?"

"Yes."

"How so?"

"I was responsible for getting and sorting the mail every day. They used to write letters to Mr. Windsor."

"Do you know what those letters were about?"

"No. But they must have been important."

"Why do you say that?"

"Because the men who ran the group came to see Mr. Windsor."

"How do you know that?"

"Because I was the one who answered the door the day they came and they told me who they were so that I could let Mr. Windsor know they had arrived for their meeting."

"Do you remember when they came?"

Catina tucked a loose strand of hair behind her ear. "Yes. It was a couple of weeks before you came to see him."

A slight smile captured Nevin's handsome face. "Nothing further, Your Honor."

Judge Doyle said, "Your witness, Mr. Jones."

Joshua Jones approached the lectern. He was usually brimming with confidence, but not this time. Fear was the emotion that best described his deportment at the moment. He didn't say anything for a while.

"We're ready when you are," the judge said. "Are you OK, Mr. Jones?"

Jones wasn't OK, but he told the judge that he was. He turned to Catina. "We know each other, don't we?"

Nevin straightened in his chair. How could Joshua possibly know Catina? he said to himself. He took a sip of water.

"Yes."

"In what capacity?" Judge Doyle asked the witness. Apparently, even the judge was caught off-guard by the strange turn of events.

"Mr. Jones used to date my mother." Catina left out the part about sleeping with Jones herself.

Obviously, Jones was grateful that she had. Statutory rape was not something the authorities tended to let slide.

Jones next asked, "You testified that James Windsor 'forced' you to model for him, or words to that effect, correct?"

"Yes."

"Did you ever complain to anyone about it?"

"No."

"Not even to your mother?"

"Right."

"As you mentioned, I dated your mom for a short while. Isn't it fair to say that if she thought someone was mistreating you that she would have done everything in her power to put a stop to it?"

"That's the point, Mr. Jones. I knew that my mother didn't have any power, and I also knew that the Windsors have a lot of it." Catina glanced into the gallery. "Just look at how many people are watching the trial. They're not here because of my family. My mother was a housekeeper at a local hotel who raised me without a husband. I'm a maid for a famous artist and his family. I know I'm only eighteen, but I've been around long enough to learn who wins those battles."

"Maybe so, Catina. But have you also been around long enough to learn how unpleasant a middling life can be, especially when, as you imply, you're at the mercy of your social betters?"

"Absolutely."

"So why have you continued to work for the Windsors? I mean, there must be other housekeeping jobs you could find."

"Probably."

"So why have you stayed? For the drugs?"

"Objection!" Nevin said. "I thought the drug question was off the table?"

Judge Doyle said, "It is, and I'll sustain your objection, Mr. Montgomery." The judge directed his attention to Jones. "Anything else for this witness?"

"Only one more thing, Your Honor." Jones began to collect his notes. He said, almost in passing, "Ms. Cruz: Have you ever seen yourself decades down the line as Hannah Burgoff?"

"Yes."

"How do you feel about that?"

"Not good." Catina's eyes welled with tears.

CHAPTER 54

Nevin Montgomery pulled into the parking lot of *Flo's Clam Shack* in Barnstable. Both he and Joshua Jones had made their closing arguments, and the fate of Andrew Windsor's testamentary wishes was now in the hands of the Court. Judge Doyle had said that he should be able to render a decision in about two weeks. The lead story in the morning's *Boston Globe* was littered with quotations from so-called legal analysts—local lawyers who didn't have enough clients to keep them busy, if they were being honest about it—offering confident-sounding predictions about which side would win the case. About half of them said that Lauren and James Windsor would win, and about half said that Nevin's client—Andrew Windsor's estate—would win. In short, it was anybody's guess.

Deputy Sheriff John Steele entered the restaurant. He said hello to some of the locals as he did. He scanned the room and spotted his lunch companion. "I've gotta say that the suspense is killing me," he said as he took a seat in the booth in the back where Nevin was sitting. "You said on the phone that it was important." He reached across the table and shook Nevin's hand.

"It is. Let's order first, though. I'm starving and *Yelp* raves about this place."

Julie Bennett, Flo's granddaughter and the current proprietor of the popular seafood joint, hurried over with a welcoming smile. "Long time no see, John.... Oops. I forgot. You were here yesterday, weren't you? Who's this handsome young man?"

Steele said, "Nevin Montgomery. He drove in from Boston. And, yes, I was here yesterday. But Nevin wasn't."

Nevin and Julie smiled at each other the way that strangers who were introduced by a mutual acquaintance typically did: awkwardly but with warmth and good intentions.

Julie said, "The usual, John?"

"Yes. But don't tell my wife I have a usual. My cholesterol was a bit elevated during my last check-up."

Julie pulled a pencil from behind her ear and wrote down Steele's usual on her order pad: clam strips, clam chowder, and a *Diet Coke.*

"And for you, my Boston friend?"

"A lobster roll and fries would be great. Limeade to drink, please. Thanks."

"You got it. Great choice." Julie wrote down Nevin's order, and then rushed off to inform the cook.

Steele asked, "Well, what's so important?"

Nevin answered, "Have you been following the trial?"

"Off and on in the *Globe* when I can. Why?"

"Because some of the testimony seems relevant for your investigation into Hannah Burgoff's death."

Steele's eyes widened. "How so?"

"I'll start with Mrs. Windsor."

"Lauren? Andrew's wife?"

"Yeah. Sorry. I forgot there are two Mrs. Windsors.... But how's this for a motive: Lauren killed Hannah because Hannah was sleeping with Andrew?"

"Is that true? I've never been able to confirm it. Did Lauren admit that Mr. Windsor was sleeping with Hannah?"

"Not really."

"What do you mean, 'Not really'?"

"She testified that she had, quote, 'no knowledge' of any such affair."

"Then it's not much of a motive, at least at the moment it's not."

"How about James Windsor? He admitted there was no love lost between him and his father, especially because of the way his father would always trivialize his work."

Steele scratched an itch on his forearm. "Damn mosquitos. They're as big as horseflies this year. But about James Windsor; shoot, everyone in town knows that James resented his dad. I'm not sure that gets me anywhere, though. Hannah's the one who got killed. Andrew died of old age and poor health. What does one have to do with the other?"

"Fair enough," Nevin said. "I never said I was Sherlock Holmes. But what about James's wife, Meredith?"

"The other Mrs. Windsor? The lady in the wheelchair? What about her?"

"It came out in court that, although Mr. Windsor was always kind to Meredith, Meredith resented the fact that he had such a low opinion of her husband's skills as an artist."

Julie returned with their lunches. Both platters were overflowing with wonderful smelling seafood. "Can I get you boys anything else?"

Steele checked with Nevin.

Nevin shook his head no.

Steele said to Julie, "I think we're all set for now, thanks."

"Enjoy." Julie left the two men to continue their conversation.

Steele said, "Like I said before, Hannah's the one who got killed, not Mr. Windsor."

Nevin poured ketchup over his French fries and salted them. He popped one into his mouth. "Did you know that James had a series of secret paintings of his own underway and that Meredith had encouraged it?"

Steele said, "No."

Nevin ate another French fry. He reached for his lobster roll. "How's this for a motive: killing Hannah would have kept the Hannah paintings secret and thereby increased the significance of the secret paintings James was doing? James needed money and that would have been an easy way to get some."

Steele stabbed several clam strips with his fork. "Now you might be onto something, Nevin. Let me do some more digging. As I said, I didn't know that James had secret paintings too." Steele swallowed the clam strips. "Do you happen to know the name of the model James was using?"

***

Nevin parked his car on the side of the road about a half mile from the Windsor compound. He knew he was no longer welcome there and he didn't want to draw attention to himself. He grabbed the takeout bag from the passenger's seat, locked his car, and headed to the compound anyway.

The first person Nevin saw was James Windsor, who was exiting his studio. Luckily for Nevin, James didn't appear to have seen him. Nevin ducked behind a tree and waited for James to get into his car and drive away. A few moments later, Catina Cruz exited from the same studio.

Nevin's heart skipped a beat. He surveyed the area. He didn't see anyone else. He stepped out from behind the tree and said, "Catina."

She jumped. She relaxed when she saw who it was. She said, "What are you doing here?"

"I had a meeting with Deputy Steele at *Flo's* about Hannah Burgoff's death. I thought you might like a lobster roll." Nevin handed Catina the takeout bag. "There are fries too."

Catina peeked into the bag. "Thank you. I'm the only one here at the moment. Do you wanna go to my room and chat?"

Nevin hoped that "chat" didn't mean talk.

It didn't. They had barely crossed the threshold of Catina's room before Catina started to kiss and undress Nevin.

"Don't smush the lobster roll," Nevin said. "It cost me fifteen bucks."

Catina laughed. "Fifteen dollars is all I'm worth to you?" She unbuckled Nevin's pants and pushed him onto the bed.

CHAPTER 55

Two hours later, Nevin said, "Sorry I was a bit brusque in court. I had to be." He traced his fingers across the small of Catina's back.

Catina rolled onto her side. Her eyes met Nevin's. She brushed a loose strand of hair from Nevin's face. "Why? So nobody would know we're sleeping together?"

Nevin nodded in the affirmative.

"I thought so." Catina gave Nevin a peck on the cheek and hopped out of bed. "Where did you put that lobster roll? I'm starving."

Nevin pointed to the top of Catina's bureau. He smiled. "They say that good sex will make someone hungry. I must be good then, huh?"

"I've had better." Catina retrieved the lobster roll and ate it in four bites. "That was good. So were you, by the way. I was kidding a minute ago."

"I know you were. The ladies call me the Larry Bird of the boudoir. You know, because I'm a legend in the sack. But how are you going to repay me: great sex *and* a lobster roll!"

"I said you were good. I didn't say you were great."

Nevin knew that Catina was still kidding…. He thought she was going to repay him with another roll in the hay.

Instead, she opened the top drawer to her nightstand, pushed aside a stack of celebrity magazines, and removed a small wooden jewelry box.

Nevin knew where this was going. Catina had gone through the same routine the first time they had slept together. He said, "I can't, or at least I shouldn't."

"I shouldn't do a lot of things I do," Catina teased. "Life is short. Live a little. Gosh, you've certainly earned it after all the hard work you put in on the court case."

The addict's hiss, Nevin said to himself. *I earned it.* Rationalization. Sweet, wonderful rationalization… Rationalization almost never ended well for addicts: addicts were addicts because they were weak when it came to the subject matter of their particular addiction (alcohol, gambling, sex, food, drugs, and the like). Nevin was no different. He may have been blessed with tremendous intelligence, but intelligence didn't stand a chance against physiological urges. History was littered with bright and talented people whose lives had ended badly because of an inability to triumph over addiction.

Catina dipped a small spoon into the vial that she retrieved from the wooden jewelry box and snorted some grade A cocaine. Her eyes rolled into the back of her head. "Your turn," she said, eyes closed.

Nevin hesitated, but not for long. He snatched the vial from Catina's outstretched hand. He dipped the spoon into the vial with the precision of the addict that he was and inhaled its contents. He repeated the task. He should have felt guilty but the drug induced euphoria he was experiencing at the moment banished that sentiment from his consciousness.

Catina rejoined Nevin on the bed. "You know what they say," she said as she placed a warm hand on Nevin's thigh.

"What's that?"

"Nothing beats sex when you're high."

Nevin heard a car pull into the driveway. He jumped out of bed and raced to the window. "Uh-oh," he said.

Catina sat up to find out what Nevin was worried about. "What's wrong?"

"James just got home and he's headed this way."

Catina scrambled for Nevin's clothes and threw them at him. "You've gotta go, Nevin. You've got to."

Nevin already knew that. He hustled into his clothes like a philanderer in an old Matthew McConaughey rom-com. But Nevin wasn't fast enough, and this wasn't a comedy.

James Windsor gave Catina's door one quick rap and tried to open it.

Catina had foolishly failed to lock it. She said, "Wait!" She pushed against the door to try to prevent James from entering.

"For what?" James said, overwhelming Catina's resistance with ease. He spotted Nevin standing in a disheveled state near the window. "What the hell are you doing here?"

"I came to see Catina. It's a free country."

"Free, my ass. This is private property, pal. And the last time I checked, your invitation got revoked when my old man died."

"Catina's not allowed visitors?"

Catina cowered in the corner.

"Not without asking, she's not. She knows the rules." James could see that Catina's clothes were in a state of disrepair equal to Nevin's. "You were screwing, weren't you?"

Catina said, "That's none of your business."

James reddened with rage. He lunged at Catina and struck her on the face with the back of his hand. "The hell it's not."

Catina collapsed in pain.

Nevin hurried to her defense. He pushed James against the wall. A painting that James had made and given to Catina as a gift after a particularly enjoyable afternoon of sex crashed to the floor.

Nevin said, "Touch her again and I'll kill you."

Nevin had been in a lot of street fights in his teenage years in Dorchester, but he had never before threatened to kill someone.

"Fuck you," James said. He picked up the painting from the ground and broke it across Nevin's head.

Blood spewed from a gash.

Nevin countered with a right cross to James's jaw.

"Ow!" James screamed. He obviously didn't think a lawyer could pack such a wallop.

Nevin doubled-down with a left hook to the other side of James's face.

"Ow!" James said again. He reached for the lamp on Catina's night-stand and prepared to hit Nevin with it.

Nevin didn't see what was about to happen, but Catina did.

"Duck!" Catina said.

Nevin did.

"Stop it!" Catina shouted. "Enough! Enough!"

***

Deputy Sheriff John Steele slid a crisp dollar bill into the vending machine and pressed the *Mtn Dew* button. He headed to the inter-rogation room and handed the soft drink to the suspect he was inter-rogating.

"Thank you," Nevin Montgomery said. He held the cold can against his swollen eye.

Steele chuckled. "I thought you said you were thirsty?"

"I am. But I also need to bring down the swelling. It's called mul-titasking."

Steele chuckled again. He left the room for a second time and returned with a bag of ice. "Try this instead."

Nevin replaced the soda can with the bag of ice that Steele handed to him. He popped open the soda and took a long drink. "Both hit the spot."

"Speaking of hitting the spot," Steele said, taking the seat across from Nevin. "What the hell were you thinking back there?"

"That's just it: I wasn't thinking. I was reacting. He hit Catina. I was trying to protect her."

"Fair enough, I suppose. But what were you doing with Ms. Cruz in the first place? I hope it wasn't what I think it was. She's only seventeen, you know."

Seventeen! Nevin said to himself. She testified in court that she was eighteen! And she had told me she was twenty!

Nevin had learned the age of consent for the bar exam but he couldn't remember what it was. Different states set different ages. He had never imagined that he would need to know what Massachusetts' was after he had finished the attorney licensing test.

Nevin didn't answer Steele's question about what Nevin was doing with Catina, and Steele didn't press him on it. Steele either understood that Nevin had a Fifth Amendment right not to incriminate himself, or he had come to like the young lawyer and couldn't blame him for succumbing to the temptations of such a beautiful girl.

Nevin broke the silence. "Do I need a lawyer for getting into a fight with James Windsor?"

Steele said, "I don't know yet. I'll let the sheriff know that you were trying to protect Ms. Cruz, but I'll need to interview her and Mr. Windsor before we can make a final determination." Steele tossed Nevin's empty soda can into the wastebasket in the corner of the room. "Is your contact information the same as before?"

"Yes. Am I free to return to Boston?"

"I don't see why not. Nobody got killed this time. People get in fights a lot around here. Try not to worry about it too much. I'll give you a call one way or the other in a couple of weeks."

CHAPTER 56

A different call came.

A call from the courthouse had come at 10:45 a.m. on an otherwise routine Wednesday morning. The clerk had said that Judge Doyle would be issuing his decision in the Andrew Windsor case at 3:00 p.m. and that because of the intense public interest in the litigation, the judge would be summarizing it in open court at that same hour.

The law offices of Palmer & Lodge were only a few blocks from the courthouse and neither Nevin Montgomery nor Joshua Jones had any difficulty getting to the courthouse on time. They traveled separately. Lauren Windsor happened to be in Boston on a shopping spree and she managed to make it too. James Windsor had informed the clerk that he probably couldn't arrive in time from Barnstable, and he decided not to try. The media had no trouble getting there, however: the courtroom was filled to capacity and at least three-quarters of those present were journalists. Matt Martin was a notable exception. Nevin had apprized Mr. Martin about the judge's plan via a quick text and Martin had driven all the way from the Cape for the event.

"All rise!" the courtroom deputy called out.

Judge Francis M. Doyle took his seat on the bench. "Good afternoon, ladies and gentlemen. Please be seated." The judge placed the folder containing his decision on the desk in front of him. "My typical practice is to release my decisions in writing. However, this is not a typical case. As the size of the crowd in the gallery makes clear, there's substantial public interest in the disposition of Andrew Windsor's estate. Courts are public institutions, and I've decided to summarize my decision orally from the bench because of the public's interest in the matter and also because of the technical nature of what probate courts do. The clerk's office will be distributing written copies of the full decision after I've finished summarizing it."

The media were memorializing the judge's comments in a variety of ways: on tablets, on smartphones, on laptops… a few reporters were still using pen and paper.

Nevin and Jones were listening attentively. Lauren Windsor was too.

Judge Doyle continued: "When I first learned that two lawyers from the same law firm would be working on opposite sides of this case I was concerned, to put it mildly, as both Mr. Jones and Mr. Montgomery can attest. I'm pleased to say that my concerns were misplaced. Both lawyers did a fine job, and I'd like to commend them publicly for it."

Nevin and Jones briefly made eye contact. Nevin could tell that it pained Jones to hear Nevin commended for anything, let alone for something Nevin had done as a lawyer. As everyone at Palmer & Lodge seemed to know, Jones had long ago decided that Nevin wasn't Palmer & Lodge material and nothing—including compliments from a judge—was going to change his mind on the subject.

Jones said, "Thank you, Your Honor."

Nevin echoed Jones's remarks.

Judge Doyle acknowledged the lawyers' expressions of gratitude and then opened the folder that contained his decision. "Massachusetts, like most states, requires the testator—Andrew Windsor, in the case at bar—to be of 'sound mind,'" the judge said, commencing the substance of his remarks. "That phrase—'sound mind'—is not defined by statute. It is, however, defined by case law. To be of 'sound mind' the testator must (1) know the nature and extent of his or her property, (2) know the people who are the 'natural objects' of his or her bounty, and (3) understand the disposition his or her will makes of his or her property."

The judge turned to page two of his decision. "Mental incapacity can occur for a variety of reasons: it can be congenital; it can be caused by disease; or it can be brought on by old age. Medical evidence is typically used to determine mental incapacity, although it's not always necessary for the petitioner to rely upon expert testimony. Lauren and James Windsor did not employ expert testimony in the present contest; instead, they relied upon their own personal observations of the decedent. In effect, they seem to be invoking the ancient maxim about the 'unnaturalness' of Mr. Windsor's will, or what is sometimes called the 'lack of family feeling' it evidences."

So far, Nevin was impressed with Judge Doyle's opinion: the judge was explaining esoteric legal concepts in understandable language, for instance. But Nevin was reserving final judgment until after the judge explained who won the case.

"As Mr. Jones accurately pointed out," the judge said next, "it's highly unusual for a testator to disinherit his wife and children, given that they are the 'natural objects' of his bounty. But what Mr. Montgomery said was also correct: a will that seems unnatural on its face may be upheld when a rational explanation for the dispositions is made known."

The judge took a sip of water from the BOSTON BRUINS mug that revealed what a true-blue New Englander he was. He turned to the third page of his decision. "The issue of 'undue influence' also was raised by the petitioners. To prevail on this ground, they were required to prove that (1) Mr. Windsor was susceptible to undue influence, (2) the alleged influencer—in this case, the Cape Cod Preservation Society—had an opportunity to exercise undue influence over Mr. Windsor, (3) the Cape Cod Preservation Society had a disposition to influence unduly in order to obtain an inappropriate favor, and (4) the will reflects a disposition clearly appearing to be the product of the undue influence. As this case illustrates, because of the susceptibility requirement, it is not uncommon for wills challenged on mental incapacity grounds to be challenged on undue influence grounds too. Indeed, the same evidence is usually relevant to both issues. As in claims of incapacity, the naturalness or unnaturalness of the dispositions at issue is significant. There's one notable difference between the two claims, however: in undue influence cases, the impropriety, or lack thereof, of the influencer's conduct is a point of focus."

Yet another person tried to squeeze into the courtroom. The security officer monitoring the crowd made it known to that person with a shake of his head that there were no empty seats available. The person got the message and left.

Judge Doyle quickly added, "I should have mentioned a technical point at the outset: the Commonwealth recently amended the probate code to require three witnesses to the signing of a will. Mr. Windsor's signature was witnessed by two people only, Messrs. Michael Kinstler and William Morrone. But, as Mr. Jones graciously conceded, that amendment to the statute doesn't take effect until next year and it has no bearing on this case."

Joshua "graciously" conceded the point? Nevin said to himself. Hardly. Joshua caved only after a forty-five-minute conference in chambers with Judge Doyle and Nevin. More importantly, Nevin knew, Nevin—and Mr. Windsor's will—had been saved by a technicality in how the amendment to testamentary formalities had been drafted by the Massachusetts legislature.

Judge Doyle glanced up from the printout from which he was reading and smiled. "Now to the part for which you've all been waiting: This Court finds that Andrew Windsor was of sound mind when he rewrote his testamentary documents and that he was not subjected to undue influence when he did so."

Audible gasps saturated the courtroom.

The judge gaveled everyone to order. "Order!" he said. "Order in the court!"

The spectators complied.

The judge carried on. "To be blunt, it was a close call. Obviously, it concerns the Court greatly that Mr. Windsor rewrote his will near the end of his life to disinherit his wife and children. But the evidence was overwhelming that he understood what he was doing and that there was an explanation for why he did it: because the beauty of Cape Cod was at the heart and soul of his art and he wanted to preserve that beauty for others to enjoy in the future. Hence, he decided to leave his money to the Cape Cod Preservation Society. And with respect to the Cape Cod Preservation Society itself, there is nothing in the record to indicate that that charitable organization attempted to exercise, or in fact did exercise, any undue influence over Mr. Windsor. It's not uncommon for wealthy people to leave their money to charity. Look at what Bill Gates and Warren Buffet plan to do, for example. Mr. Windsor was entitled to do it too. For the foregoing reasons, the petitioners' challenge to the respondent's will is dismissed."

The judge stood.

"All rise!" the courtroom deputy called out.

Everybody did.

The judge returned to his chambers.

The courtroom then erupted into the chaos that frequently followed the announcement of a controversial decision.

"Are you available for a quick interview?" the legal affairs reporter for WBZ-TV asked.

"Me?" Nevin answered.

Nevin's only prior television appearance had been captured on cell phone when he and his neighborhood pals were fleeing from the police after a fight during his senior year in high school. Lucky for Nevin, the back of his head was all that had made the news that time.

The reporter said, "Yes, please. I'll meet you outside on the steps."

"This is Stephanie Swanson reporting live from the John Adams Courthouse in downtown Boston. Less than five minutes ago the probate court upheld the last will and testament of Andrew Windsor, one of the great artists in American history. I'm joined by Nevin Montgomery, who represented Mr. Windsor's estate in this matter."

The camera panned from the attractive young reporter to the attractive young lawyer.

The reporter asked, "Were you surprised by the judge's decision?"

Nevin answered, "Not at all. The law and the facts were on our side."

"Why did the judge take so long to issue a decision then?"

"He didn't take long, actually. He's got other cases. He decided this one pretty quickly."

"Can the public draw any lessons from the case?"

Nevin paused for a couple of seconds, which on live TV seemed like an eternity. He said, "The big lesson, at least to me, is that each of us is free to decide to whom we wish to leave our assets when we die. The Court understood that, and protected Mr. Windsor's right to decide for himself what to do with his money."

"Thank you for speaking with us, Mr. Montgomery." The camera panned back to the reporter. Her bright blue eyes sparkled with the exuberance of youth. "This is Stephanie Swanson reporting live from the John Adams Courthouse."

The reporter thanked Nevin and hurried on her way.

Nevin began to descend the courthouse steps to head back to the offices of Palmer & Lodge.

Lauren Windsor confronted Nevin before Nevin had traveled more than three or four steps. She said, "You're milking this for all it's worth, aren't you, Mr. Big Shot?"

"Hardly," Nevin said. "Post-trial interviews aren't uncommon."

The Andrew Windsor matter was Nevin's first trial and he had no idea about whether what he had said to Mrs. Windsor was accurate. His goal was to try to defuse an awkward situation.

It didn't work.

Mrs. Windsor said, "You're young and you've already sold out. How can you possibly believe that it was appropriate for my husband to disinherit my children and me, especially after I looked the other way for years about his sleeping with that slut Hannah Burgoff? She wasn't just his model, you know."

I knew that Mrs. Windsor wasn't testifying truthfully when she stated in court that she had "no knowledge" of her husband's affair with Hannah Burgoff, Nevin said to himself. Aloud to Mrs. Windsor: "With all due respect, ma'am, it doesn't matter what I think. It's what the Court thinks that matters, and the Court has ruled that Mr. Windsor was entitled to bequeath his assets to the Cape Cod Preservation Society. Now if you'll excuse me, I need to get back to the office."

"We're going to appeal the decision!" Mrs. Windsor shouted to the back of Nevin's disappearing head. "We're going to appeal it!"

***

James Windsor's smartphone rang. It was Joshua Jones calling to relay the unfortunate news that the Court had rejected the challenge that he and his mother had filed against his father's testamentary documents. James accused Jones of being an "incompetent moron" and then hurled his smartphone against the wall. His mind raced. He didn't know what to do next... until, that was, he spotted Catina Cruz heading towards her bedroom.

"Get out!" Catina shouted when James burst through her bedroom door.

"Why? I don't see your boyfriend around. Someone's gotta fuck you. It might as well be me."

James pushed Catina onto the bed. Catina tried to resist, but James was too strong for her. He hit her across the face with the back of his hand, as he had done a few weeks earlier when he had caught Nevin Montgomery in Catina's room.

Catina quickly realized that it would be foolish to resist. Nevin had texted her about the Court's decision and she knew all too well how upset James got when he received news he didn't like.

CHAPTER 57

The nurse said that Mr. Lodge was recovering well and that it was fine for Nevin to visit him, albeit briefly. "Keep it light," she added. "We need to keep his stress down."

Nevin assured the nurse that he would comply with her instructions. He walked down the corridor to room 743 in the cardiac unit of *Massachusetts General Hospital* and knocked on the door.

"Just a second," Bartholomew Lodge said. "OK."

Nevin opened the door and entered the room.

Lodge sat up in his bed and beamed at his young charge. "The office already let me know. I also saw the Channel 4 interview. Great job, Nevin. Congratulations. You deserve it."

"Thanks, Bart. How are you feeling?" Nevin placed a couple of magazines that he had brought for Lodge on the nightstand.

"Better with your news, obviously. I should be back in the office by the end of the week." Lodge thumbed through the magazines and thanked Nevin for them. He placed *The Economist* on the top of the stack to peruse first.

"You're welcome," Nevin said. "But did the doctor say you can come back to work that soon? Coming back early didn't work out too well last time."

"Not in so many words, he didn't. I can read between the lines, though."

"With all due respect, Bart, I think you should wait until the doctor actually says it's OK to come back."

"My wife keeps telling me the same thing." Lodge grinned. He retrieved a case file from underneath his pillow. "I thought you were her when I heard the knock on the door. That's why I asked you to wait a minute." He opened the file. "Can I ask you a few questions about the Windsor case?"

Nevin's brows furrowed. "Are you sure it's OK?"

"Absolutely."

Nevin remained skeptical, but he knew Lodge wouldn't take no for an answer. "Fire away."

Lodge did. He started with, "How did Joshua do?"

Nevin was the one who grinned this time. "He was fine. As you like to say, good law and good facts usually lead to a good result. The law and the facts were on our side. Frankly, Joshua made it a lot closer than it should have been."

"Did he congratulate you?"

Nevin shook his head. "No. But I didn't expect him to."

Lodge's lips pursed and his eyes narrowed. "I do. He's a partner in the firm. He knows he's supposed to be encouraging to the associates when they've earned it."

Nevin didn't say anything else about Joshua Jones. He seriously doubted that Joshua would commend him, even if Bart Lodge told him to do so.

Lodge next asked, "Any word about an appeal?"

"Yeah. Mrs. Windsor confronted me outside the courthouse and told me she was planning on it."

"We'll cross that bridge when we come to it. To be honest, I don't see how she can afford an appeal. Obviously, we're not going to pay for it out of the estate."

Lodge's comment made Nevin realize for the first time since the trial had ended that the Court's ruling upholding Andrew Windsor's testamentary choices wasn't some sort of law school hypothetical. It had real world implications for Mrs. Windsor. Nevin didn't feel particularly good about that state of affairs. But there was nothing he could do about it. He pointed to the photograph on the nightstand next to Lodge's hospital bed. "Who's that?" he asked.

Lodge reached for the photograph and studied it like he often did. "It's Jeremy, my son," he whispered. "He died from a drug overdose about twenty years ago."

"Sorry," was all Nevin could think of to say.

Nevin had long wondered why the senior partner of a prestigious Boston law firm was so protective of the firm's most junior associate. Now he finally knew the reason.

***

Nevin hiked up Anderson Street to the last brownstone on the left. His heart rate had increased about threefold by the time he arrived at the top of the hill. He inserted his key into the lock, scaled four flights of stairs, and entered his apartment. He grabbed a bottle of water from the refrigerator, turned on the Red Sox game with a punch of the remote, and proceeded to flip through the stack of mail that had accumulated during the trial. Bills and takeout coupons were about all that were in the stack. Then, his smartphone alerted him that he had received a new email. It read:

Dear Nevin:

Thanks for stopping James the last time I saw you. He thinks I'm his and he's obviously jealous of you. Be careful. He's got a volcanic temper. Believe me, I know.

Love,
Catina

Love? Nevin said to himself. A huge smile captured his cleanly shaven face. He turned down the volume on the baseball game and tried to figure out whether Catina meant it. Frankly, he wasn't sure whether she knew what love was. Unlike Nevin—whose parents, friends, and teachers had showered him with more love than he deserved—Catina didn't seem to have ever experienced love. Lust, yes. Men certainly wanted her.

But love?

CHAPTER 58

Nevin decided to find out for himself whether Catina knew what love was. He once again parked his car down the road from the Windsor compound and snuck onto the property. An ocean breeze rustled the trees that shielded him from sight. He hopped over a felled limb and scurried to Catina's window. He tapped lightly on the glass.

That was all it took. Catina dropped the magazine she was reading, glided to the window, and slid the window open. "What are you doing here?" she asked, with a smile that could light the night.

Nevin pulled himself through the window, brushed the dirt from his clothes, and answered, "I got your email. I came to see what it meant."

But before Catina could respond, Nevin noticed bruises on Catina's face and arms.

"What happened?" he said. "Did James do this to you?"

"Y—Yes." The smile vanished from Catina's face. "I finally said no to him, and he didn't like it."

Nevin's jaw became as taut as a bowline on a jib sheet. His fist clenched. "Where is he?"

"Let it go," Catina pleaded. "It looks worse than it is. I'm fine. Really, I am."

"Where is he?" Nevin said again.

The door to Catina's bedroom burst open. "I'm right here, you son of a bitch. What the fuck are you gonna do about it?"

"This!" Nevin thundered. He struck James Windsor with a right cross that would have made Floyd Mayweather proud.

"Shit!" James howled.

Round 2 had begun.

James grabbed his jaw to check whether it was broken. He shook the cobwebs from his head and rushed full bore towards Nevin. He placed Nevin into a headlock and began to punch him in the face like Nolan Ryan had done to Robin Ventura years earlier in that famous baseball brawl that *ESPN* looped on the opening credits to *Sports Center*.

Nevin was younger and stronger than James, but James was enraged and that increased his strength exponentially. Adrenalin was a curious thing.

"Stop it!" Catina screamed. "Stop!"

James wouldn't stop, though. In fact, Catina's pleas for mercy added fuel to James's fire. James spotted the table lamp on Catina's nightstand. He pushed Nevin aside for a moment, snatched the lamp, and broke the lamp across Nevin's face.

Nevin hadn't been able to duck this time. He crumbled to the floor. Blood spotted Catina's throw rug like confetti at a victory parade.

Jones began kicking Nevin in the head.

"Please, James!" Catina said. "No more! I'll do whatever you want! You're killing him! Stop it! Please, stop it!"

***

Thirty minutes later, Nevin Montgomery and James Windsor were sitting in separate rooms in the Barnstable County Sheriff's Office.

Nevin was lucky that Deputy Steele had returned to the Windsor compound to conduct follow-up interviews for the Hannah Burgoff investigation at the very moment that James was in the process of beating Nevin to a pulp. Otherwise, Nevin might not have survived the attack.

Steele had arrested James on the spot for assault and battery. He also had delivered the shocking news that James was likewise under arrest for the murder of Hannah Burgoff. Nevin couldn't believe his ears when Steele had made the latter pronouncement.

As far as Nevin was concerned, Steele had chewed out the young lawyer for showing up at the Windsor compound again. He also told him to stop thinking with the lower half of his body. After Steele had regained his composure, he asked Nevin to provide a full written statement about the assault and battery. Nevin was happy to oblige. Nevin couldn't stand James Windsor. More to the point, Nevin wanted to keep James away from Catina and helping Steele put James behind bars seemed like a good way to do it.

Nevin watched attentively while two of Deputy Steele's colleagues escorted James Windsor to lockup.

Steele returned from the break room and tossed Nevin a bag of ice that he had retrieved from the freezer. Steele said, "Haven't I seen this movie before?"

Nevin said, "Yeah. Sorry about that. I guess not all sequels are worth the price of admission."

Steele smiled and shook his head. He had been young once. He remembered how difficult it was to break it off with a beautiful woman. Only later, after Steele's wife had given birth to their first child, had Steele realized what was truly important between a man and a woman. He was confident that Nevin would eventually realize it too.

Steele snapped back to the moment. He said, "Are you sure you don't want me to call a doctor to check you out? I probably should. It's standard procedure around here in assault cases."

Nevin pressed the ice bag to the side of his face. "Let me try the ice first. I'm pretty sure I'm OK. The bleeding stopped before we left the Windsors'…. Thanks for showing up when you did, by the way. That's twice I owe you."

Steele smiled again at his young Twelve Step friend. "I was in the right place at the right time, is all… *Again*… But you need to be more careful. You're not a cat. You don't have nine lives." Steele scribbled a note on his charge-pad that Nevin had declined medical attention. He lifted his eyes to Nevin. "I don't want to know what you were doing in Catina Cruz's room. I already told you she's only seventeen."

Nevin started to say something about Catina but Steele held up a hand to signal for Nevin to keep it to himself.

Steele said, "Like I said, I don't wanna know."

Nevin knew why Steele didn't want to know: because of their Narc-Anon connection. Recovering substance abusers had a special bond, and Nevin and Steele's bond was more special than most.

Steele shouldn't have let their Twelve Step connection influence him, but he was human, Nevin was young, and Steele wanted Nevin to make it in life. Frankly, Steele was in awe of how far Nevin had already come given what Nevin had relayed to Steele about his past.

Nevin adjusted the ice bag. "Can I ask you something, John?"

"You may. I might choose not to answer, but you're free to ask."

"I obviously understand why you arrested James Windsor for assault and battery. My face is all the proof you need on that score. But what proof do you have that he's the one who killed Hannah Burgoff?"

Steele leaned back in his chair. He traced a hand across his fresh buzz cut. He studied Nevin's eyes for a long moment. He finally said, "Normally, that's the type of question I wouldn't answer because I haven't discussed why I did what I did with the D.A. yet. But given all that I've put you through over the course of the investigation, I think you've earned an answer."

"Thanks." Nevin adjusted the ice bag again.

Steele took a quick sip of coffee. "There are basically two reasons why I charged James Windsor with the murder of Hannah Burgoff. First, because the other suspects have airtight alibis. Like James, there was a motive for each of them to want Hannah dead, but they weren't present at the scene when Ms. Burgoff was killed. Mr. Windsor's wife—Andrew's wife—Lauren was meeting with their staff at the time of the incident putting the finishing touches on a party she and her husband were planning to host. I was getting final confirmation of that this evening, in fact, which is why I was at the compound when James assaulted you."

Nevin interjected, "What about Meredith Windsor? As I mentioned at *Flo's*, it came out in court how much she resented Mr. Windsor for belittling James's talent."

"Meredith certainly had motive. But, as I said, all of the suspects had motive. Lauren Windsor's motive was obvious: Hannah Burgoff had been engaged in a decades-long affair with her husband. I managed to confirm that after you and I had spoken about it after the trial. I agree that Meredith had a motive too, and I agree it's the motive you identified in court. She was out for the evening, though. She was at a play in Boston with friends. Her friends vouched for her. The theater itself confirmed she was there because they remembered the wheelchair."

Nevin said, "You said there were two reasons that you concluded that James was the killer. His motive is obvious, I assume. James hated his father for the same reason that Meredith hated him: because he thought James was a lousy artist and said so seemingly every chance he got."

Steele nodded in agreement. "And he had no alibi. Most important of all, though, at the crime scene we found a high thread count handkerchief with the initials *JW* embroidered on it. James's fingerprints were on it. That, Nevin, is the second reason. And that, Nevin, is why James Windsor will be convicted of murder."

CHAPTER 59

Matt Martin sat in his living room watching the local PBS roundtable *This Week on Cape Cod*. The show was dedicated to discussing the major happenings on the Cape during the previous week. This week's program was devoted entirely to the recent events involving the Windsor family.

When *This Week on Cape Cod* first aired more than three decades earlier, Molly Martin, Matt Martin's wife, enjoyed watching the show with her husband and a nice bottle of wine. But Matt had been relegated to viewing the program alone ever since their daughter Missy had committed suicide after being raped by James Windsor when she was a teenager. In fact, the heartbreak of losing Missy was what had led to Molly's own death shortly thereafter.

Julian Dell, the longtime host of *This Week on Cape Cod*, said, "It's been quite a week for the Windsors, wouldn't you agree, Diane Wallace?"

Diane Wallace was the legal affairs reporter for the *Boston Globe*. She had been in the courtroom for the contest involving Andrew Windsor's will and she also had broken the story that James Windsor had been charged with the murder of Hannah Burgoff. She said, "I agree one hundred percent, Julian. I can't imagine how it could have been any worse, especially for James Windsor, obviously. I know John Steele pretty well and he wouldn't have arrested James for Hannah Burgoff's death unless he had overwhelming evidence to prove it."

Nate Blackburn of WBZ-TV in Boston chimed in: "Diane's right, Julian. Deputy Steele is an experienced law enforcement officer. He does everything by the book and he doesn't play games." Blackburn glanced at the camera, his eyes slitting with solemnity. "It'll only get worse for James. He'll need a lawyer—a damn good lawyer—but now he'll have to come up with the money himself to pay for it after the judge upheld Andrew Windsor's decision to cut James and his mother out of his will."

Given the focus of this week's program, Julian Dell had invited Anastasia Trilling, the *Boston Herald*'s society-page columnist, to join the panel for the hour. Dell asked, "What's your take on all of this Anastasia?... Welcome to the program, by the way."

Trilling was dressed as if she were covering Boston Fashion Week at the Hynes Convention Center. Her strawberry blonde hair was tied in an Audrey Hepburn-style top knot, her *Chanel* pants suit probably cost more than the other panelists' monthly mortgage payments, and her jewelry was a strong candidate for transportation in a *Brink's* armored car. She said, "I'm delighted to be here, Julian. I appreciate the invitation. I'm a big fan of the show.... With respect to your question, I strongly believe that the Windsors are finished in high society on Cape Cod. Lauren Windsor came off as a greedy widow and James is both greedy and accused of murder. Claus Von Bulow never regained his social standing after he was accused of trying to kill his wife in Newport many years ago and the Windsors—particularly James—will never recover theirs, either. Don't forget that Von Bulow was eventually cleared of any wrongdoing. The evidence against James, in contrast, seems pretty overwhelming."

The panelists continued to banter back and forth for the remainder of the show. The clear consensus was that Lauren and James Windsor were unlikely to prevail on appeal and that James was at great risk for being convicted of murder. "The monogrammed handkerchief that John Steele had discovered at the scene of the crime will doom James with the jury," Diane Wallace had said.

Matt Martin switched off the television and took a sip of iced tea. He sneezed, and sneezed again. It was the height of pollen season on Cape Cod and Martin was allergic to pollen. He reached into his pocket and pulled out a handkerchief with *JW* monogrammed on it. He wiped his nose, and then tossed the handkerchief into the fire and watched it burn.

***

Nevin Montgomery steered his *Subaru Impreza* into a parking spot in the visitors' lot. It was the first new car he had ever owned and he loved it. He grabbed his sports coat from the back seat, snapped shut the door, and activated his car alarm with the quick press of a button on his key. This was Dorchester, after all. Cars were stolen in broad daylight at an astonishing rate.

Nevin surveyed the area. *This place hasn't changed a bit,* he said to himself. He noticed broken chain-link fences, athletic fields overgrown with weeds, and pavement with holes the size of craters.

A bell rang. Nevin checked his watch. It read 3:15 p.m. Classes were adjourned for the day. An avalanche of teenagers burst through the exits at John F. Kennedy High School. Man, they look young, Nevin thought.

Memories washed over Nevin like waves over rocks as he navigated the familiar corridors of his former high school. Nevin's dad had retired from the custodial staff two years earlier, and Nevin hadn't returned since. But he still remembered every faded wall and each yellowed floor tile as if it were yesterday.

Nevin bounded up two flights of stairs to the third floor. He walked to the end of the hallway. He peeked through the window of classroom 326 and knocked gently on the door.

"Come in," the voice from inside called out.

Nevin pushed open the door and said, "Hi, Mr. H. Is now a good time?"

Daniel Harrington's wrinkled face broke into a wide smile. "Now is the perfect time, Nevin. I penciled you in to my calendar after you called last night. It's great to see you."

"It's great to see you too." Nevin took a seat in a wooden desk at the front of the classroom. "I'm not used to the view from the box seats.... I like that Boston snow globe on your desk: 'The Cradle of Liberty.' I never noticed it before." Nevin was pointing at the snow globe.

Mr. Harrington was seated at his desk, still smiling. He reached for the snow globe. "It's been in the same spot for thirty years. But you were a backbencher, weren't you? I guess it was difficult to see it from Nantucket."

Nevin smiled, and nodded in the affirmative.

Mr. Harrington continued: "I saw that interview you did on Channel 4. You handled yourself very well. Congratulations on the case, by the way. Was that your first trial?"

"Yeah."

"'Yes,' Nevin. Not 'yeah,'" the longtime English teacher said.

Nevin blushed. "Sorry about that."

Mr. Harrington accepted Nevin's apology with a gap-toothed smile and wave of the hand. Then he said: "Are you staying on the straight and narrow? I must say that I was concerned when you called me last month and mentioned that you had relapsed. Is that why you needed to see me today? Are you going to your meetings? You've got to go to your meetings, Nevin. You know that. 'It works if you work it so work it because you're worth it,' as the saying goes."

"Amen to that, Mr. H." Nevin bowed his head and stared at a floor desperately in need of waxing. "But you guessed right. I had another relapse recently. Several, in fact... I can't beat it, Mr. H. I can't beat it."

Mr. Harrington returned the snow globe to its privileged spot on his desk. He leaned forward in his seat. "You sound like Casey Affleck's character in *Manchester by the Sea*. But you *can* beat it, Nevin. People beat drug addictions all the time. It takes work, but you've always been willing to put in the work. It wasn't just natural talent—a lot of brain cells—that got you out of Dorchester. You worked at it. And look how far you've come. Unlike me, you're still a young man. The sky's the limit for you. It won't be easy, but you can beat it. I know you can."

Nevin's eyes welled with tears.

The two men sat in silence for a full ten minutes.

Nevin stood to his feet, shook Mr. Harrington's weakening hand, and exited the classroom that had turned his life around a decade earlier.

ACKNOWLEDGMENTS

I thank Stanford Gerber, Sandra McDonald, and Wes Tugia for reading the entire manuscript; and Dina Egge, Margot Gerber, Margaret McDonald, and Ron Mollick for reading portions of it. I also thank the University of Akron Law School and the Ada Chats program for inviting me to workshop it. I am likewise grateful for the generous "blurbs" I received for *The Art of the Law* from Ron Barak, David Crump, and Adam Mitzner.

ABOUT THE AUTHOR

Scott Douglas Gerber is a law professor at Ohio Northern University and an associated scholar at Brown University's Political Theory Project. His eight previous books include, most recently, *Mr. Justice: A Novel.*

CPSIA information can be obtained
at www.ICGtesting.com
Printed in the USA
FFOW02n1231160718
47404524-50561FF